THE GRIZZLY WAS AS BIG
AS A BULL STANDING
ON TWO LEGS

The bear hung over him, huge furry arms ready to cuff
and strike. Hugh jerked up his rifle, but it was upon
him before he got his gun halfway up. It struck. The
right paw cuffed him on the side of the head, across
the ear and along the jaw. Its claws ripped open his
scalp. Hugh screamed, drew his knife and stabbed
wildly and frantically. Then the bear's head dug down
into him. He felt its dogteeth crunch into his skull.

Hugh sank away, half-conscious. . . .

"Man . . .   to
hurricanes, deluges, volcanic eruptions, and
the ponderous formation of continents."—
Wallace Stegner

FREDERICK MANFRED is a unique figure in con-
temporary American writing. Born on a farm in
northwestern Iowa, he writes with fervor of the
plains region where he now resides, and which he
refers to as Siouxland. His is a stirring vision of the
men and women who forged the American dream
and put roots down in the untamed West.

LORD GRIZZLY

Frederick Manfred

A SIGNET BOOK

SIGNET
Published by the Penguin Group
Penguin Books USA Inc., 375 Hudson Street,
New York, New York 10014, U.S.A.
Penguin Books Ltd, 27 Wrights Lane,
London W8 5TZ, England
Penguin Books Australia Ltd, Ringwood,
Victoria, Australia
Penguin Books Canada Ltd, 10 Alcorn Avenue,
Toronto, Ontario, Canada M4V 3B2
Penguin Books (N.Z.) Ltd, 182–190 Wairau Road,
Auckland 10, New Zealand

Penguin Books Ltd, Registered Offices:
Harmondsworth, Middlesex, England

Published by Signet, an imprint of Dutton Signet,
a division of Penguin Books USA Inc.

First Signet Printing, March, 1964
21 20 19 18 17 16 15 14 13

 REGISTERED TRADEMARK—MARCA REGISTRADA

Printed in the United States of America

For
Mother Mary Shorba
and
My Wife Maryanna
who once again pitched in

Preface

Although Hugh Glass was a real person whose most notable adventures occurred between 1822 and 1833, this book is a novel—not a history.

The very first time I ran into the Hugh Glass legend I knew that someday I would have to do something about it. Hugh's great wrestle with the grizzly, his desertion by friends, his fabulous crawl, his vengeful chase after the deserters, and its outcome—all these things seized hold of my imagination. I saw Hugh and his agony. I saw his matted grizzled beard, his flashing grieving eyes, his torn bleeding body, his godlike stubborn manner. I saw all this not with the eye of an historian but with the eye of a novelist.

For the last ten years, when I found the time, I sought out all the available accounts and legends of Hugh and the grizzly. Finally last year, a plot, a way of going for Hugh, came to me that seemed to be true to the spirit of this vision I had of him.

In a few instances I did not follow what some claim as fact or the most plausible legend. (There are many versions which conflict in part, though almost all versions agree on the three basic elements: the wrestle, the desertion and the crawl, and the showdown.)

But nowhere, so far as I know, did I go against the vision.

Frederick F. Manfred

Contents

Then went Samson down . . . and came to the vine-yards of Timnath: and, behold, a young lion roared against him.

And the Spirit of the Lord came mightily upon him, and he rent him as he would have rent a kid, and he had nothing in his hand: but he told not his father and his mother what he had done.

And he went down, and talked with the woman; and she pleased Samson well.

And after a time he returned to take her, and he turned aside to see the carcase of the lion: and, behold, there was a swarm of bees and honey in the carcase of the lion.

And he took thereof in his hands, and went on eating, and came to his father and mother, and he gave them, and they did eat: but he told not them that he had taken the honey out of the carcase of the lion . . .

Out of the eater came forth meat, and out of the strong came forth sweetness. . . . —Judges 14:5–14

For the animals and savages are isolate, each one in its own pristine self. The animal lifts its head, sniffs, and knows within the dark, passionate belly. It knows at once, in dark mindlessness. And at once it flees in immediate recoil; or it crouches predatory, in the mysterious storm of exultant anticipation of seizing a victim; or it lowers its head in blank indifference again; or it advances in the insatiable wild curiosity, insatiable passion to approach that which is unspeakably strange and incalculable; or it draws near in the slow trust of wild, sensual love.
—D. H. LAWRENCE,
Studies in Classic American Literature

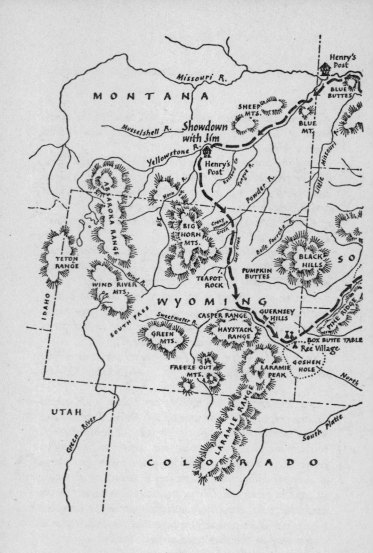

Part I

The Wrestle

Chapter 1

It all began the second day of the Moon of Fattening, June 2, 1823. In the pre-dawn dark the Missouri River bluffs lay like sleeping mountain lions. There was for once no wind. A heavy dew mizzled down on the horseshoe-shaped sand bar, beading the hair of the sleeping men and the fur of the restless mustangs and the tips of the riverbank willows and the faintly cliddering leaves of the cottonwoods.

The mosquitoes near the river swarmed thick. Men to either side of Old Hugh Glass slapped softly at them in their sleep. Old Hugh couldn't see the men in the dark on the sand bar but he could hear them. The men were dead-tired from all the poling up the wild Missouri and their day-long orgy with the pennyskinned Arikaree maidens, and might have slept on had bees been working them over.

For early June the night was quite hot, and the ground under the men was at last warm enough for comfortable sleeping. From now until late in October the men could rest any place at all on the Old Bed. Except where the madding red ants bristled. Or where the prickly-pear cactus flourished. Or where diamondback rattlers liked to nest.

Old Hugh was on watch duty and was lying flat on his belly on the sand bar. He was anxiously awaiting the return of the lads Jim Anderson and Augie Neill who still were out sparking the Arikaree maidens. The spot Hugh's company was in, below and between the two Ree villages, and the stealthy sibilant silence, and the occasional rustling behind the Ree picket fence ahead was not at all to Hugh's liking.

Hugh peered past the jagged edge of the driftwood behind which he'd forted up, a cottonwood butt that had washed up on shore, and tried to catch movement on the sand bar. But narrow his gray eyes as he might he couldn't make out a thing. It was still too dark out. He scrounged around in the grit sand until his buckskin-clad body found a comfortable lay. With a deft touch of his weather-cracked fingers he made sure of his flint, made sure Old Bullthrower his rifle was cocked.

A pony snorted behind him, snorted again, and stamped on the giving sand, and flailed the night air with a whistling tail, trying to get rid of the mosquitoes. Immediately all the other Indian ponies joined in, some twenty of them, stamping, snorting, pounding the sliding dry sand with hard crisp hooves. Sometimes in their desperation they whinnied under their breath.

"Give us just two more hours," Hugh muttered, pulling wolfskin cap down over his ears and forehead and wriggling bone-bulky shoulders inside his buckskin shirt, "give us just two more hours and we'll be up and away with our hair still in place. Whaugh! This child'll be mighty glad to be on the move at last."

Glancing back over his shoulder Hugh could just make out, across a long narrow island in the river, a faint lessening of the nightdark all along the tumbled eastern horizon. The ripples and the floating bonebare tree skeletons in the main channel of the swift rousting Missouri, which ran on the west side of the island, had begun to gleam a little. And looking sharper, Hugh could just make out the low whorled silhouettes of the fur company's keelboats, *Rocky Mountains* and *Yellowstone Packet*. The keelboats rode at anchor between the sand bar and the cottonwood-covered island, slowly dipping and rising some ninety feet from shore, each at a right angle to the horseshoe-shaped sandy beach.

It was good to know the boats were there. Hugh felt sure of the forty or so men sleeping beside and behind him, always with loaded flintlock rifle in hand. They could probably hold off a small nation, if need be, but those fifty extra armed men on board the two keelboats, plus the two swivel guns and sure-handed General Ashley in command, were a comfort.

Imperceptibly the darkness lessened. Imperceptibly. Looking ahead Hugh at last could begin to make out the toothlike ten-foot-high picket fence at the head of the sand bar behind which he was sure the Rees had been crawling all night. He was sure they were waiting for dawn, their usual hour of attack. The picket fence had been made of barked cottonwood set in a ridge of sand. A deep dry moat ran all around the fence on the outside, with inside still another trench, not so deep, through which the Ree braves could slither in and out without being seen from the sand bar even in daylight.

"Doggone my skin, this old hoss sure wishes the lads would show up. They've already been with them Ree squaws long enough to sprout a half-dozen family trees. Let alone pushin' their luck." Hugh grumbled to himself. "Rollin' helps clear the mind all right. But too much'll take away what little a man has to begin with." Hugh tried to make out the opening in the picket fence off to the right where the lads and all the others in the company had passed in and out during the previous day when it looked like the Rees were going to behave peacefully. "I don't like it. I don't like it at all. The lads should've been back long ago."

Not a half hour before, right after he'd taken his turn at watch, he'd heard a short quick yell, the sort of yelp a man might make surprised in the act of love. It was so short a yelp, in fact, it sounded cut off.

Hugh nodded. It could easily have been one of the lads caught in the arms of one of the Ree maidens. One of the braves might have at last had enough of renting out his woman for what little fofurraw he got for it: mirrors, ribbons, vermilion, and such.

"Yesterday wasn't enough for the lads," Hugh grumbled on. "Oh, no. They had to go back and push their luck some more."

Hugh remembered the trouble General Ashley had keeping even a small watch on board. All the way up the Missouri the lads had heard how easy the pennyskinned Ree squaws were, so that when they at last got to the villages they were primed for a wild spree. From early in the forenoon on, the cherry-eyed chattering Ree women had entertained the boys in the tall bluejoint grass to either side of the villages and in the jungle growth of riverbank willows along the rolling Missouri.

Some of the boys hadn't even bothered to seek cover with their pennyskinned quick loves, had womaned where they found it, in the roundhouses with the husband brave standing guard in the doorway for them or in the shadow of the picket fence with Ree policemen trying to keep giggling chokecherry-eyed little girls and little boys from watching from behind the midden piles. Even more scandalous had been the behavior of the Ree women when they spotted Willis the Nigger. They'd fought for a touch and a chance at that black oak, like he might have been big medicine itself.

Hugh had sensed animosity in the villages while the desperate coupling went on. With a surly Ree brave named Stabbed, he'd been assigned policeman for the day and so couldn't participate himself. And as watchdog policeman with Stabbed, and looking with a different pair of eyes, Hugh had caught an undercurrent in the villages that meant danger to the mountain men.

On the surface the Rees seemed willing enough to trade some twenty Indian-trained mustangs for powder and guns and vermilion, and they might palaver civilly enough about a treaty General Ashley wished to bring about between the Sioux and the Rees and between the

Mandans up the river and the Rees, but underneath they were thinking secret council. For Hugh, the ripe-cherry eyes of both Stabbed and other Ree chiefs glittered a little too fiercely out of their oldpenny faces. The Rees weren't holding out the open hand so fully and so far as they might. Any time an Indian refused liquor, even watered-down whisky, as both Stabbed and the Ree chiefs had done, it was sign, and time to keep one's eyes peeled.

Thinking about all this, Hugh cautiously reached down to rub his right thigh and knee. Then he exercised his right calf a little, the buckskin legging making a soft tussing sound on the grit sand. "Doggone that leg. Gettin' stiffer by the day." Hugh kneaded it with powerful stub fingers, all the while warily watching the picket fence ahead for the least movement of stealth. "Well, it was kill or cure then," Hugh muttered under his breath, thinking of the time he had jumped off Pirate Lafitte's good ship *The Pride* and escaped to the coasts of Texas and in so doing had severely wrenched and strained his right leg. "Kill or cure then, and dog me if it don't look like we're in for the same peedoodles again."

By mountain-man standards Hugh Glass was an old man—in his late fifties. Most of the recruits in General Ashley's fur company were men in the bloom of life, ranging in age from the boy Jim Bridger's seventeen to General Ashley's own forty-five, with most of the men running middle twenties, fellows like Jim Clyman, Tom Fitzpatrick, Johnnie Gardner, John S. Fitzgerald, and Willis the Nigger.

Yet Hugh was a well-preserved man. He couldn't run as far or as fast as, say, Johnnie Gardner or the boy Jim Bridger maybe, but he was stronger, tougher, wiser. And around women he was still as much a green buck as any of the lads. If Bending Reed, who'd once been his young sweet squaw, could see him today, she'd see he was still some. Some, and shining with the best. He might have the miseries in his right leg now and again, yes, but his thoughts were young willow and his narrowed gray eyes could still spark like a hungry wolf's with down buffalo calf in sight.

Hugh was about six feet two in height, which, not counting the boat crews of pork-eating neds or the half-breed voyageurs, was about the average of Ashley's company. Hugh was bulky in the shoulders, round and slim as a young cottonwood bole through the middle, with ash limbs for arms and young forked oak for legs. For all his six two he didn't look tall until someone of average height stood up to him, and then he not only towered but loomed.

His hair was gray and thick. Even the hair over his arms and his brushlike brows and the matt over his chest and back was thick and gray. He didn't shave like the other mountain men did, something both General Ashley and Major Henry requested of all their men. Major Henry had been in the mountains many years as an explorer and a leader of trappers, and it was his opinion that shaven palefaces got along better with the beardless Indians. Instead, Hugh clipped his beard, or rather sawed it off with his skinning knife, when it got more than a couple inches long. Hugh said he liked the comfort of the gray bush in winter blizzards and the shade of it in the summer. Major Henry also wanted his men shaved as a way of keeping the graybacks—the lice—under control, but Hugh said he wasn't bothered much with graybacks, probably because there was bitter alkali in his sweat which gave them the spits.

Since the days of his captivity with the Pawnees along the Platte River, Hugh had worn hide instead of cloth for clothes: a wolfskin cap, a fringed elkskin hunting shirt that came almost down to his knees, a soft clay-worked doeskin undershirt, soft doeskin breeches, tough buckskin leggings stagged at the knees, and double-soled moccasins fashioned out of the neck leather of tough old buffalo bull. His leathers were dark with sweat and dirt and the fat of many a feast of buffalo meat, and they smelled a little like an open crock of old rancid lard. He wore a powder horn and bullet pouch slung over his left shoulder and under his right arm. In the pouch he carried such other possibles as flint and steel for fire-making and a small whetstone.

He wore a belt around his middle with a long sheathed butcher or skinning knife stuck in it along with a loaded horse pistol. Hugh's set of possibles, the knife, the gun, the flint, the steel, were prime. He knew the value of being prepared for the worst with the best. His rifle, which he affectionately called Old Bullthrower, and which he kept at his side night and day, was a Henry, made in Lancaster, Pennsylvania, a flintlock of a simple though sturdy make with a thirty-six-inch barrel and a .59 bore and a full stock of hard maple. With it Hugh had made many a spectacular shot, plumb center, well-aimed or snap shot.

Unlike most mountain men, Hugh was not much for trapping. He didn't like the bone-chilling icy water that a man had to wade in before dawn to set the beaver traps and again after dusk to pick up the beaver. Such cold doings were not for his game leg. From a long life with the Pawnees he had picked up the Indian brave's scorn for trapping. That was squaw work, not work for braves. He liked hunting and scouting better, alone, at which he was the company's acknowledged master. Making meat and scalping red devils was an honorable profession for a brave.

Hugh didn't take easily to other men, nor they to him. He had a look about him that kept others from confiding in him. His brushy brows shadowed haunted gray eyes, eyes that one moment could be fierce with battle, the next closed over with inward reverie. He had killed often, and well, and there was an air about him that suggested he could easily kill again, at any moment if there was need.

There was about him too the lonesome aggrieved

mien of the touchy old grizzly bear, the grizzly who would probably leave you alone if you left him alone, but if you didn't—whaugh! mind your topknot. Even General Ashley was afraid of Old Hugh and had trouble controlling him. Hugh hated taking orders, and, taking them, acted as if maybe in youth he'd gotten his crop full of taking too many and still felt rebellious about it.

But if Old Hugh once set his cap for an adventure, if he once agreed to undertake an order, nothing could deter him. Under fire he was a bold, daring man of great ingenuity. When the action became furious, he had a way of shouting as if he were taking part in a revolution.

Every man flashes a little flag when aroused. With some it's a widening or a whitening of the nostrils, with others it's a narrowing or darkening of the eye. With Hugh it was little arteries that ran down either side of his nose, one on each side, a rivulet of red that vanished into the brush of his gray beard. When he got mad, or showed passion, or became involved in the action of battle, a pulse could be seen beating in the little red rivulets, a pulse so clear it was as if blood were trickling in spurts out of a wound.

The old wind came up then, stirring the chiddering cottonwood leaves overhead, and the fluttering heart-shaped willow leaves down river. The dew quit and the air dried, though in the rising soughing wind there was the fine sweet smell of rain far off.

The wind slipped in under Hugh's buckskin hunting shirt and brushed the gray hairs over his back and gave him a sudden rash of itching goose-pimples. "This child don't feel easy," he muttered to himself. Looking up at the sky, he was surprised to see that the stars were gone, and that in the renewed darkness, a darkness even deeper than before, the trees and the Ree picket fence had disappeared. "In this country, if it ain't mosquitoes it's goose-pimples."

Even as he spoke a notched spear of blue flaming lightning stroked out of the southwest sky high up and near. The lightning stabbed into the close tumbled hills, then flat-handed them with a loud quick spank of thunder.

"Storm," Hugh said. "Now what?"

The wind relieved the ponies of the terrible mosquitoes, only to fill them with fear of an onrushing storm. The ponies neighed shrilly, and stomped in the plaffing sand, and drew back tight on their tie-ropes, and tried to gallop about despite tight rawhide hobbles. In the pitch dark only the spotted ponies could be made out, though sometimes Hugh wasn't sure whether it was ponies or spots before his eyes.

Hugh reached back a hand and touched the shoulder of his companyero sleeping near, the lad Johnnie Gardner. Johnnie's buckskin shirt was soft with sleep's sweat and buffalo grease. "Johnnie. Wake up, lad. Johnnie."

"Huh?" Johnnie rose out of his rest with his flintlock already in hand, finger crooked around the trigger. "What? Where's the varmints?"

"Down, you wild rabbit you. You want a second part through your topknot?"

"Oh. What's up, Hugh, old hoss?"

"Storm comin' up. Slide along low now and wake up Dave Howard and George Flager and Wes Piper. And a couple more of the boys, Jim Clyman and Reed Gibson maybe, and make fast the ponies. They'll sceer if it blows dust-devils. Or rains too much lightnin'. And stay down."

Johnnie was awake at last. "Boys back yet?"

"No, consarn it. But I heard a bad yell about an hour ago. I'm feared they had trouble."

"Not gone under?" It was too dark to make out Johnnie's lean face, dusky with its day-old beard, but the whites of his eyes almost glowed the way they owled up at Hugh.

There was another jab of lightning; then a quick low blat of thunder.

The wild ponies squealed.

"I dunno." Hugh motioned impatiently in the dark. "Get, now, and slide along like a good snake and get them ponies in hand. March!"

Johnnie crawled away on hands and knees. Hugh could hear his young companyero gliding along quietly, could hear him gently waking the boys. Some of the boys woke with a start like Johnnie's, sure the red devils were upon them at last and they about to go under.

Two huge drops of rain the size of well-chewed wads of tobacco plakked onto Hugh, one hitting the buckskin over his back and the other on his game leg. Then huge drops by the hundreds, by the thousands, pelted down. And the pushing wind became loud and bold, and it whined in the cottonwoods overhead and then in among the men, blowing pluming veils of fine grit sand over them, blinding, and at last waking them all, lashing them up into quick hands-over-the-face protective gestures. Some jerked down old wool hats and wolfskin caps, some lifted up hunting shirts over neck and head.

"Storm is right," Hugh said, ducking flintlock and horse pistol and powder pouch around under his body.

Wham! A great ball of eerie whiteblue fire slammed into the sand bars immediately in front of Hugh, igniting the sand into a momentary molten glow of redgold.

In the thundering welter, in the intermittent lightning, Hugh's quick eye caught sight of two forms sliding over the sand bar, coming across the gap between the Ree barricade and his cottonwood butt, coming directly toward him, crawling right over where the lightning had just hit. Indians? Red devils? Sneaking up under the cover of all the heavenly shooting? Quick as the thought itself, Hugh trained his flintlock on them, left hand capped protectively over flint and the powder in the frizen.

He got ready to pull the hair trigger, when an urgent

voice whuskered hoarsely across to him. "Hugh! Hugh! Don't shoot! It's us."

" 'Us' who? Or sure's you're born you're headed for wolfmeat."

"Hugh! it's us! Jim and Augie! Companyeros!"

"Whaugh! Climb in. And don't be slow about it. And lucky you are too. Because I took as fine a bead on your noddle as I ever took on a squirrel's eye."

Jim Anderson and August Neill hunched toward him, bumping Hugh with their elbows and rifle butts as they slithered past him on their bellies and forted up with him behind the cottonwood butt. They were puffing. Their eyes were wide with fright, so wide Hugh could make them out in the dark without the aid of lightning. There was an oily herb-aromatic boary smell about the slim wiry lads, a smell they'd no doubt picked up while womaning with the Ree maidens.

Hugh asked, "Well, had enough of squaw meat now?"

"Hugh," Jim Anderson said.

"You dumb nuts, stickin' behind so long. If a blackbird had your brains he'd fly backwards."

"Hugh," Jim said.

"Yeh?" Hugh grunted. "By the bye, where's Aaron Stephens?"

"That's what I was tryin' to tell you. Aaron's gone under."

"What? Lost his hair?"

"Stabbed in a lodge and skulped."

In a flash of lightning Hugh got a quick look at Jim Anderson's drawn haggard face. Jim looked puke-sick. "Then I did hear that yelp then."

Augie Neill said, "They were like to get us too, only we saw them runnin' the kids and the old women and the dogs to the far side of the villages. And the braves were puttin' on red warpaint. Old Chief Grey Eyes too."

"So that's why we ain't heard the dogs all night.

27

There's trouble ahead all right. They mean war, or this child don't know sign."

"That's what we was thinkin'," Augie said, his face showing that he too was shaken to the roots by what he had seen—a pounce and then a death. "So we pulled stakes pronto."

Old Hugh thought a moment. "We better let the general know about Aaron. And that the red devils mean trouble soon's it's light. Lead and arrers will be as thick as a blizzard afore long." Hugh kept squinting past the cottonwood butt, shivering under the hitting rain. Hugh could feel water trickling along the skin under his beard. It made him think of biting graybacks. "Augie, while all this commotion is goin' on, I want you to swim out to the gen'ral's boat and warn him. Tell him I think we ought to get up all the men and pull out with the ponies to high ground. That's my advice."

"Now?" Augie asked. "Swim over in the cold and dark now?"

"We ain't got a skiff here. So you'll have to swim."

"Why not Jim here?"

"What? Ye turned squaw now?" Hugh barked.

Augie hated to go. "Can't it wait awhile?"

"By the beard of bull barley, lad, ye're the ones as saw the kids and squaws and dogs hid. And saw the chiefs puttin' on red clay, didn't ye?"

"True enough," Augie said reluctantly. "All right. I'll go. Shall I tell him Aaron's dead then?"

"What else? Unless the Resurrection has commenced in the meantime."

Shortly after Augie Neill left, the storm quit, the sky became silent, the cottonwood leaves fell to whispering, and the restless mustangs took to flailing their whistling tails at the mosquitoes again. Hugh slapped at mosquito bites on his neck and under his chin and over the backs of his hands. He hit the back of his right hand so hard he almost pulled the trigger.

A quick series of yipping animal sounds, then of bird calls, came to them from the Ree picket fence.

"Listen," Hugh said, cocking his grizzled head.

Jim listened; said after a moment, "Signals, them is. They're callin' to each other."

Hugh put his ear to the ground. "They're movin' their horses too," he grunted. "Just what I was afraid of. Well, it's the butcher shop for sure now at dawn."

Jim shivered and his eyes half-closed over.

"Jim," Hugh snapped, "Jim, I want you to make sure all the men're awake, every dag one of them, and tell 'em to dry their flint and frizen and make sure of their charge."

Jim said, "Maybe we should let the ponies go and get the devil aboard the boats again."

"What, show tail to the red devils? Not in this country we don't, not if we want to live in it. If we do, every red nigger up the river, the Blackfeet and the Minnetaree, even our friends the Mandans, will know about it and then we'll really be in a fix."

The quick thunderhead moved north. Stars came out. Then the delayed dawn opened up the east at last, and light came up all around them like a lamp turned up rapidly in a dark room. The cottonwood butt, the sand ahead, the picket fence curving around and slightly above them, and then the live cottonwoods beyond showed up clear and true in the crisp pink light.

The moiling Missouri came up clear too, below the island, spreading wide and immense to where its shoal waters lapped a cutbank a half-mile away. The tan river was almost wide and mighty enough to suggest a little of the earth's curvature. Ripples raced, eddies curled and uncurled, and tiny foaming whirlpools appeared and disappeared and reappeared. Floating uprooted trees and caught snags and riding sawyers sloshed about like old skeletons in a half-submerged dinosaur boneyard. A low roushing sound rose from the wrestling waters. Far over, on a sand bar in a farther shoal, the body of a blue heron hovered above the water, its stick legs lost in the distant perspective. The sharp cutbank of the far shore lifted abruptly into sleek-grassed tufted tumuli. And above them rose the rolling bluffs of the endless Dakota prairie lands.

Hugh saw Jim crawling in among the men, saw the men give one wild look around and then recharge their priming pans. There weren't enough cottonwood butts and other driftwood boles to go around; so some of the men barehanded began to scoop out low trenches in the sand bar. The men with the wild Indian ponies carefully kept horseflesh between themselves and the bristling Ree picket fence. The oncoming red dawn deepened the colors of the ponies, making gray a gun-barrel blue, and white a flashing silver, and chestnut a vivid maroon. The manes and tails of the ponies glowed like fox brush in firelight. Most of the ponies were broomtail hammerheads, though a few of the stallions were handsome. All were grassers and all were as mean as Satan.

Augie came back, dripping from his swim in the swift Missouri. He slid along the grit sand, the sand sticking in patches to his wet buckskins. "The general says not to worry, Hugh."

Hugh glared at Augie. "Not to worry? Can't he read sign?"

Augie's young freckled face was mottled blue with river cold. Before Old Hugh's fierce whiskered glare, Augie's brown eyes slid off to one side. He shrugged. "Well, the gen'ral says he's goin' to take Grey Eyes' word for it that the Rees mean to keep peace with the Great White Chief. He thinks Grey Eyes'll honor his pledge."

"Pledge! Might as well take the pledge of a snake. What a curious fix we're in now. The gen'ral's green as grass and the Rees have put on warpaint as red as buffalo blood and—"

A rifle popped from behind the Ree barricade. There

was a quick whistling sound and then a groan behind Hugh. Hugh whirled around just in time to see Johnnie Gardner stagger against a sorrel pony. Johnnie's eyes rolled and he grabbed at his belly. The sorrel pony snorted; tried to rear away from Johnnie. But Johnnie grabbed the yellow mane and hung on. Men all around on the ground instinctively cowered in their shallow trenches.

"Johnnie!" Hugh yelled. "Johnnie lad! Down with ye. Down you darn fool. I told ye ... oh! the boy's been hit mortal."

A whole series of shots rang out then, one after the other, irregularly, the balls whistling by overhead. More groans escaped Johnnie and he pitched ahead in two little forward motions. Feathered arrows sailed in, whistling; hit the sorrel pony with dull punking sounds.

"Them red devils got my Johnnie lad!" Hugh groaned. He blinked his eyes. "Poor devil. Hit by so many balls he's been made a riddle of."

There were more erratic shots, this time coming from all points along the circling Ree barricade. A deadly crossfire poured in among the exposed mountain men. Puffs of smoke rose in the wet air and slowly floated northward across the picket fence and above the breast-shaped dirt-covered lodges behind the fence.

The mountain men dodged and cursed. They began to return irregular fire. They reloaded methodically, swiftly, pouring in powder, driving home the patched ball with hickory wiping stick.

Another mountain man finally got hit. His slow writhing on the sand set off a howl of triumph from behind the Ree picket fence. When still another mountain man was hit, the Ree warwhoops rose to a shrill earsplitting crescendo.

"Listen to that horrible hubbub," Jim Anderson said, shivering. "It's enough to curdle your blood into fly pepper."

Hugh said, "Fust time ye heard it, is it, lad? Wait'll

ye hear the Ree death cry. Right after he's skulped ye with a whole pack of cheerin' squaws lookin' on."

The ponies smelled blood; began to whistle shrilly. They plunged from one end of their rawhide tethers to the other and in desperate terror shat quick mounds of steaming droppings and pawed at the moon.

"Rise and shine, boys!" Hugh yelled. "It's hard doin's now."

Carefully studying the puffs of smoke and flashes of fire coming out of the Ree cottonwood pickets, Hugh thought he saw a movement at the foot of a particularly large upright barked pole. After a second he saw a red-streaked oldpenny face peer out at him. The dark cherry eyes danced wildly; the sensitive mobile mouth was drawn up into a ferocious pout. It was a Ree and he wore a warrior's headdress—the thighbone of a hawk caught in braids over the temple and standing up on each side of the head like horse ears. Hugh aimed Old Bullthrower carefully; fired. The red-streaked wild-eyed face vanished.

Arrows and balls continued to thud into the cluster of mountain men and dancing mustangs on the sand bar. The ponies shrieked like ravaged mothers; reared up at the skies, fear-crazed eyeballs flashing; fell mortally wounded. One blue stallion, hit in the rear quarters, whistled shrilly as it dragged itself around with frantically chopping forefeet. Blood poured down its rain-soaked hide and spilled on the sand.

Jim Clyman, Reed Gibson, Jack Larrison, Dave Howard, Prayin' Diah Smith, George Flager, Wes Piper, and others lay forted up behind the fallen ponies. Clyman took dead-aim at a Ree only to have his flesh fort give one last convulsive heave and throw his aim off just as he pulled the trigger. The ball whacked into a picket instead.

As the light increased, the crossfire from the roaring Ree barricade became murderous. Men to either side of Hugh got hit by arrows and balls. Mathews, Collins,

Sneed, Penn, Ogle. They rolled over; groaned. They looked inward, then outward at the red dawn and their comrades, then inward again, and died. The dead men continued to get hit, and the dead men grunted, and shook a little each time. The dead men soon ran watery blood from their new wounds.

Through it and over it all the mosquitoes kept working. Flies too came out of the riverbank willows and buzzed wildly and thickly around the rich feast of flowing blood.

There was sudden activity on the gray keelboats anchored out on the Missouri River. Men boiled on the bow of General Ashley's gray keelboat, *Rocky Mountains*, with the general, a slim figure in Missouri state militia blue, waving commands. The general tried to get the voyageurs to move the keelboat closer to shore in order to take on men. But the pork-eating neds were panicstricken and they refused and ducked down out of sight in the hold. The general then called for volunteers, and finally a dozen men climbed down into a white skiff below the keelboat on the water. Oars flashed out; began to clobber the tan and turbulent Missouri. The white skiff started to move toward the sand bar. Another gang of men on the stern of the general's boat boiled around the swivel-gun.

Arrows and balls streaked across the water. The rowers hesitated. The general's mouth opened into a little black working hole, and he waved his arm commandingly once more and the white skiff moved again.

The white skiff came on, the buckskin-clad men in it huddled low, firing at the Rees from over one another's shoulders. The rowers pulled like madmen, ducking shot and arrow as best they could.

The white skiff came on slowly, bucking the tan tossing Missouri, working like a frantic centipede trying to swim water.

At last the white skiff touched the ensanguined sandy shore and the riflemen piled out and, like hurrying lizards, slithered up behind the fallen ponies. The rowers, still in the skiff, ducked down and hid behind the gunwales.

The riflemen first picked up Johnnie Gardner—he was still miraculously alive—and lifted him aboard the skiff. Then they loaded other wounded men aboard the skiff. Full up, the skiff pulled back to the *Rocky Mountains;* unloaded; came back for more.

All the ponies but one had fallen. The one left was a black stallion, fifteen hands high with a windcombed purple mane and huge flowing purple tail. By dint of massive muscle-coagulated leaps the black stallion managed to break its leather hobbles and rip loose its tether. The black stallion had swallowed its head and was running madly about inside the circle of fallen horses and men. The black stallion screamed; whistled a great cry. Its nostrils fluttered like rags in a violent wind. The black stallion's great opal eyeballs rolled and glistened. Then a dozen Ree balls hit the big black boy, and with a final whistling shriek, more hellish than human, the stallion pitched forward head first, hit the ground, collapsed, rolled over, four legs stiff and upright like a roast pig on its back in a platter.

Suddenly Rose the horse-faced interpreter was puffing at Hugh's side behind the cottonwood butt. Rose was a halfbreed: part Indian, part Negro, part white. "The gen'ral says to get the devil out of here!" Rose shouted between breaths. Rose's blue-red face was drawn up into a half-snarl half-smile. His redblack cherry eyes rolled. His buckskins were blotted with dark sweat rings. Rose puffed. "Get back on the boat, the gen'ral says!" Rose knew he wasn't very well liked, and he couldn't quite look Hugh in the eye.

"Why didn't he follow my advice in the first place?" Hugh raged. The red rivulets down either side of his big Scotch nose began to pulse a little. "Should have let some of the men pull out with the ponies before it got light, and let the rest of us aboard."

"I know, I know," Rose shouted over the uproar. "I know. I told him that too. But it's too late now." Rose puffed and he spoke in surges, like an Indian. He had a heavy guttural voice. "The gen'ral trusted Grey Eyes when he shouldn't've."

Hugh gave it all a quick once-over. More than half the men were already gone under, and all the ponies were dead or dying, and the Ree fire was getting to be more accurate by the minute. "I hate to leave the gone-under lads behind to be skulped. Them red devils'll mangle them something awful. Specially if their wild squaws get hold of 'em. You won't know 'em from slaughterhouse waste after. They deserve a decent burial at least."

"I know." Rose puffed. His redblack cherry eyes flicked from side to side, from Hugh's grizzled dark tan face to the Rees ahead and back again.

Hugh said, "Damme if I'll retreat, now that the ponies is all dead. Might as well fort up behind them here on the bar and hang on. The Rees won't dare rush us, and if the gen'ral'll start using them swivel-guns on them we'll make out yet."

Rose muttered under his breath. It was plain he thought Hugh's idea crazy. "The gen'ral says to pull out pronto."

"Well, damme, pull out then, if you've got squaw blood. Me, I'm stayin'."

Rose gave Hugh an evasive, almost pouting look and then crept back to join the men still alive behind the fallen ponies. Rose told the men what the general had to say. The men listened with open slack mouths—then suddenly rushed the white skiff, almost swamping it. The overloaded white skiff turned slowly in the current, shipping water. Those in the rear who had been hidden behind the men up front found themselves suddenly exposed to the fire, and they promptly crowded toward the other end, once again almost swamping it. Two rowers were hit; slid wounded to the bottom of the skiff; were trampled underfoot.

Then the sun broke over the horizon, limning the white skiff sharply in streaming saffron light. Ree cross-fire increased still more, some eight hundred howling whooping braves firing with everything they had, London fusils, double-curved bone bows, single-curved wood bows. The coffee waters churned around the skiff as much from shot and arrow as from the frantic oars. Slowly the heavy skiff made for the *Rocky Mountains*.

The general waved frantically from his keelboat and his mouth worked little and black and soundless, and presently a second white skiff came out hesitantly from the other keelboat, *Yellowstone Packet*. When it was nearly ashore a second rush of men nearly swamped it too as they all, wounded as well as hale, tried to climb aboard at once.

The swivel-guns aboard both keelboats began to pitch in then. The heavy shot whacked into the toothlike cottonwood pickets.

Finally stubborn Hugh saw too that he was doomed if he stayed up front behind his cottonwood fort. Waving to Augie Neill to follow him, he slithered behind the bloodied dead mustangs. He and Augie found only Jim Clyman and Jim Anderson left alive and behind on the shore.

Hugh caught Jim Clyman's grim look. "Well, Jim, what do you say?"

"Dummed red devils. But I guess we better swim for it." Jim Clyman was a strapping young fellow, well over six feet tall with a big bulging forehead and sharp small blue eyes and dark brown hair hanging in ringlets to his shoulders. Like all mountain men he was dressed in buckskin.

Hugh looked out toward the keelboats, saw that the skiffs were safe enough under their bows. Hugh cursed. "Them cowardly neds." He waved an arm at the blue-

clad general for him to order one of the white skiffs
back to shore.

The general caught Hugh's signal. Immediately the
general leaned over the railing on the bow and,
exposing himself recklessly to the flying shot, made
angry commanding gestures at the rowers in the white
skiff.

The white skiff hesitated; went out a way on the
rousting coffee waters; then went back despite the general's fierce working mouth and waving blue arms. The
rowers aboard the skiff surged up the sides of the keelboat instead, in their haste letting the skiff drift away
with some of the riflemen still aboard. The white skiff
drifted down river toward the shore. In an instant a
dozen pennynaked high-shouldered Rees, clad only in
breechcloth and hawkbone headdress, darted from behind their barricade and, whooping and waving knives
and tomahawks, ran splashing out into the tan water;
and before the white skiff even touched shore, they cat-
apulted into the water and began tomahawking and
slashing at the riflemen. Almost immediately three
braves leaped up out of the melee of legs and arms and
butts and triumphantly proclaimed coups by waving
aloft dripping paleface scalps. A savage roar of triumph
burst up from behind the pickets.

A particularly daring brave came out on all fours
through the opening in the barricade through which
the men had passed in and out the day previous. The
high-shouldered brave was dressed like the others, but
with a single golden eagle feather in back, and a necklace of grizzly claws. The single eagle feather rode in a
socket made of hawk thighbone and it tossed back and
forth in the light wind. Mimicking a grizzly, the brave
carried what was left of Aaron Stephen's body, shagging
it along in his teeth. The body would have been unrec-
ognizable except for what was left of Aaron's golden
hair. He'd been scalped; his nose had been cut off; his
feet and hands were gone; he'd been gutted and cas-

trated; his nipples had been torn off; and even part of his right thigh was gone. The pennyskinned Ree dropped his griesly burden and pretended to tear out lumps of flesh with his teeth, growling, pawing, tearing, in perfect mimicry of a raging grizzly.

Hugh recognized the brave as Bear Mouth, a brother of Stabbed, the Ree policeman. Hugh bellied up behind a dead bay mustang; leveled Old Bullthrower on Bear Mouth; shot him.

The white skiff at the foot of the other keelboat, *Yellowstone Packet*, started to come out then. It came out a dozen yards and then everybody in it ducked down and the skiff began to drift downstream toward the shore too. Again some high-shoulder pennyskinned braves rushed out, waiting for it to hit shore. But one of the riflemen, a grizzly mountain man, stood over the men and, using his flintlock for a club, drove the pork-eaters back to their oars. They rowed away; then buckled completely. It was all the mountain man could do to get the skiff back to the *Yellowstone Packet*'s side again by himself.

Hugh gave the other three still with him on shore a quick flicking look. "Well, lads, Clyman here is right. There's nothin' left but to swim for it."

Jim Clyman's blue eyes flashed as he looked over his shoulder at the fallen mustangs and mute mountain men, out to where the bear-mimicking brave lay over what was left of Aaron Stephens. "Them red devils. We'll be back someday to collect damages for this."

Jim Clyman led the way, with Augie Neill and Jim Anderson close behind, and Old Hugh coming along last and doing well for all his fifty-odd years.

The moment they leaped into view, howls of rage rose from the Rees behind the picket fence. Some ran out into the open on the sand bar and, kneeling, with bows and guns let fly at the running men. Arrows sleeted and balls streaked around the running men.

One shot caught Hugh, stung him in the thigh of his

already game leg. It went in deep. His whole leg went numb. It threw him into a crablike unwieldy run. A yowl of triumph rose from the Arikarees.

Jim Clyman looked back. "Hugh?"

"Run, lad, save your hair. Don't wait for me." Hugh held his hand over the wound. Blood squirted between his fingers.

"You're hit, Hugh, old hoss!"

"Just a nick, lad. Run! Don't pay me no mind. Dive in!"

They ran up the sandy shore until they were well beyond the *Rocky Mountains* and then turned and ran into the water, splashing, hoping to make the boat despite the strong current.

Just before he went in over the hips, Hugh reached up and, barrel first, shoved his flintlock down inside his shirt along his backbone, thrust it down until it was well caught between his belt and body. Then he let himself down into the rushing tan water and swam out.

His numb leg dragged. He rode the water deep. His buckskin clothing bellied full of water after a while, and it dragged him down too. He had to work like fury to keep his nose above water. He puffed. His gray hair lay sleek over his head and neck. He nosed along like an old gray-whiskered muskrat.

Augie Neill and Jim Anderson, swimming like slim channel catfish, made it. Each caught hold of a rung on the near side of the *Rocky Mountains* and clambered aboard helped by the eager hands above.

Despite a numb leg and waterlogged buckskins, Hugh turned in the water to see what had happened to Jim Clyman. He couldn't find him at first. On his third heave up out of the water he saw Jim. The lad was downstream from him and was having trouble staying afloat. His heels were out of the water; his head under. Hit in the head? Hugh lunged up in the water for a better look and at last saw what the trouble was. Jim Clyman had tried to slip his flintlock down inside his

39

shirt along his backbone too. But something had gone wrong. Hugh watched him go somersaulting with the rushing current, heels, head, back, then heels again, all the while trying to get rid of the gun. Then finally Jim Clyman got rid of it and came up for air and started swimming along. Jim was too far along to catch on with the *Rocky Mountains* so he turned and headed for the *Yellowstone Packet* down river. Hugh waited until he was sure the lad would make it.

By that time Hugh himself was in danger of missing the *Rocky Mountains*. He'd waited just long enough for the coffee waters to push him toward the stern of the boat. Hugh let out a mighty bellow. "Throw out a rope, lads. Here I come!"

Augie Neill, leaning over the railing with a dozen other feartight faces, and still gasping from his swim and dripping wet, saw him. "Hugh!"

Hugh volved past, grizzly face and nose and stroking arms awash in the chasing tan surface.

Quickly Augie caught hold of a punting pole and, leaning, reached out as far as he could.

Hugh lunged for the end of the pole; missed it; went under. And going under, felt his rifle slide down his back and into the legging of his one good leg, making both his legs useless.

Hugh gave it one more try. He dug his way to the surface. He clubbed the water with powerful arms. Arrows and balls pelted the water all around him; hit the gray sides of the keelboat above him.

Augie ran down the polers' walk and, once again, from the extreme stern of the boat, reached out the punting pole as far as he could.

This time Hugh made it. He managed to get a good grip on the end of it and hung on with a bulldog's grimness. Slowly Augie pulled him over to the rungs and then helped him climb up, helped him up over the top into the hold.

"Thankee, lad," Hugh grunted, as he slid down under

the polers' walk and out of reach of arrow and shot, "thankee, lad. I was almost fishmeat that time, I was. Ye saved me me life. And at a risk too."

" 'Twas nothin', Hugh."

"Ae, but this old hoss wouldn't have made it to the other boat. Too old. I won't forget, lad."

"Ye all right, Hugh?"

"Tolerable. Just ham-shot a little. By a small ball." Hugh ganted for breath. "The worst was that swim. For an old man it was some, it was."

"Ye'd best rest now, Hugh."

Hugh nodded. His tangled gray hair and matted gray beard dripped water. Drops ran down his neck. His floppy buckskins were sopping wet and as viscous as chewed-over fatback. "I'll rest me a little after we've dug out the ball, lad." Hugh breathed. "Lad, sharpen up me butcher knife on the hone, will you, and we'll get at it presently." Gritting his teeth against pain and a faint coming on, Hugh slid down until his head rested on a smelly bundle of beaver plew.

"I'd best get the doc, Hugh," Augie said. "I wouldn't trust myself with a butcher knife."

"Who said ye was to do it? It's me that will, lad. As soon as I've had me that rest."

"I'd best get the doc, old hoss," Augie said.

"Aw, let the doc help them that needs it. I ain't hit bad."

Hugh looked around after a while. To either side of him, propped up against barrels of gunpowder and stores of food and supplies, sat others who'd been wounded. They were bleeding; they were soaked through and through with dirty Missouri water; and they looked out at the world with bleary fatigue-gray eyes. There was mountain man David McClane, and Willis the Nigger, and pork-eater August Dufrain and ned-hearted Joseph Monso. They lay staring vacantly at the golden morning sky arching high above them.

Hugh asked suddenly, "Where's Johnnie?"

"Johnnie who?"

"Johnnie Gardner."

"He's dead," Augie said. "Prayin' Diah Smith prayed powerful over him, but the Lord took him just the same."

"I feel mighty queersome," Hugh murmured. "Is my topknot gone, lad?" And then Hugh slipped away into a faint.

The anchor had been cut and the keelboat *Rocky Mountains* was drifting downstream past the point of the island, with the *Yellowstone Packet* just ahead. General Ashley had ordered a regrouping of forces below the mouth of the Grand River.

Old Hugh sat amidships, ball removed and bandaged leg propped up on a pack of prime beaver. A hot sun shone on him. In places his buckskins already felt dry enough to be shingles, had shrunk enough to pinch him over the back and along the thigh of his good leg.

Slow talk rose and fell around him. One of the nearby wounded groaned and moved a trifle and groaned some more.

Presently Hugh heard General Ashley talking to Rose the half-breed interpreter.

The two of them were standing near the mast, with General Ashley a good head shorter than ugly horse-faced Rose. Pain and shock crimped the general's blue eyes. The general waved quick hands as his thin trembling lips mouthed the words. "I don't understand it. I don't understand it. Grey Eyes specifically promised me yesterday that there'd be peace between us, that he'd forget they'd lost a couple of their men at Fort Kiowa. That extra gunpowder I gave him was supposed to make up for that loss. Even though it was the rival fur company that did the shooting."

"It did," Rose grunted, looking at the wounded men. Rose's dark skin glowed bluish red in the sun.

"What?" General Ashley snapped. "Oh. Yes." Gen-

eral Ashley's eyes flicked toward the wounded too.
"Yes." General Ashley looked at the golden sky overhead. "And anyway, what were they doing attacking
Fort Kiowa, the fools? What did they expect, the
other cheek?"

Rose's heavy guttural voice came in surges. "Never
believe an Indian chief right after he's just lost some of
his men. It's a disgrace for a chief to lose men, and he's
going to be an ornery cuss until he's had himself some
revenge." Rose coughed up some Missouri water; spat
over the side. "And he's going to be specially ornery
when he loses 'em over a slave squaw."

"A what?" General Ashley's voice rose a little.

"A Sioux squaw. She was a slave of one of his men
and she got away."

"Oho! So that was why they dared tackle Fort
Kiowa then."

"That was why," Rose grunted, thick lips drawn up
in his usual habitual sneer.

"Good Lord."

"Grey Eyes said they didn't mean to shoot at the
white men at Fort Kiowa. They only wanted the slave
squaw back." Rose's eyes were evasive. He couldn't
quite look the general in the eye.

"All that fuss over a squaw. A slave squaw at that."
General Ashley stamped around in blue indignity, gold
epaulets glistening in the morning sun. General Ashley
looked with grief at the wounded men underfoot. "And
we had to get the hell shot out of us because of another
Sabine woman raped and ravaged. Damn."

"Grey Eyes said she was a good squaw. Grey Eyes
said his brave was very sad he'd lost her, that he had
to have her back in his roundhouse to cook and sew
for him. He said the white man was wrong to hold her.
Bending Reed belonged to him."

Old Hugh jerked up. What? Bending Reed.

Old Hugh called out. "Gen'ral, did Rose there say
her name was Bending Reed?"

General Ashley gave Rose a look. "Was it?"

"Bending Reed," Rose said, sullen redblack cherry eyes holding Hugh's for a moment and then sliding off.

Hugh's gray eyes lighted up with joy. "You say she's at Fort Kiowa now?"

"That's what Grey Eyes said."

"Whaugh! So!" Hugh's old eyes rolled. "But how in tarnation did she get in with them Rees? When I last saw her she was down on the Platte with the Pawnees. Well I never. That's some, that is." Hugh shook his head in amazement. "Well, well. This child is going to be mighty glad to see her again."

"You know her?" General Ashley asked, inclining his head in friendly manner.

"Know her? By the bull barley, man, yessiree! I womaned up with her for three years when I was a half-slave myself on the Platte. She's my wife. And there never was a better, white included. She cooked and made clothes for me with never a complaint or a sigh. Whaugh! Well I know how that Ree brave felt losin' her. She was some, she was. Graybacks or no."

Chapter 2

It was the Moon of Cherries Blackening, July. The minute Hugh stepped into her tepee within the gates of Ft. Kiowa, he knew it wasn't the same Bending Reed. She was a changed squaw somehow.

For one thing, when she first spotted him, she didn't quick put a hand over her mouth and look at him for a while in dead silence, something the Indians usually did to show they'd been surprised. For another, after a quick flash of blackcherry slant eyes at his bleeding game leg, she refrained from looking at it again, which was most unusual, since always in the past she'd been very attentive to his aches and pains. In the old days let him but scratch a callus and she was not only johnny-on-the-spot with her bag of herb medicines but also with whatever hocuspocus chanting medicine men that were handy. Nor had she spread out the welcome mat, her best buffalo robe, for him to sit on when he came in.

Carrying his rifle, Hugh crab-walked past the small fire of pyramided sticks burning in the center of the tepee and selected a woven-willow lazy-back and threw a musty brown buffalo robe over it and leaned back easy. It was a cool day and the robe felt good.

He tried to sit crosslegged but couldn't. The bullet-torn thigh still hurt too much.

He got out his pipe, and with careful tamping forefinger filled up and then lit up with a burning fagot from the twig fire.

"Ahhh," he breathed, puffing deeply on his old com-

45

rade pipe, stroking his grizzly beard, "ahh, doggone my skin if this ain't livin' again." He patted Old Bullthrower, his flintlock, at his side and looked across at Bending Reed. "Good 'bacca and a man's two best friends right handy."

He savored the smoke puff by puff, all the while taking in the effects of the tepee with roving musing eyes. Clerk Bonner in the fort had told him how she'd begged him for the tepee. It was an old leather one that her band had once given in trade for gunpowder and it was almost in shreds. But she had taken it and patched it up with a couple of freshly worked buffalo-bull hides and had cut some straight willows for its upright poles. From the dump near the river she'd dug up a couple of old pots and pans. Next she'd made a broom with some bulrushes bound around a stout ash stick. Then she'd gone out and gathered up some herbs and trapped some beaver in Medicine Creek behind Red Butte. Somehow, perhaps by stealing, she'd managed to get her hands on a bladder of pemmican and a bag of dried fruit and a leather sack of dried berries. And last, she piled up some surplus wealth by selling dressed moccasins to the men in the fort.

The tepee was spic-span clean. Not a mouseball in sight—when mice were one of the plagues of the plains. Everything was in its place and everything had its function. A medicine bundle hung over the doorflap, from which came protection against evil spirits. The door itself faced east, from whence came the power of the sun. The base of the tepee made a perfect circle, from which came life magic.

The food and the supplies had their appointed place too. Two jerks of buffalo-cow meat hung from an upright in the rising gray smoke of the fire. Buffalo-bull hide for making moccasin soles also hung toughening in the smoke. The rawhide case of dried fruit and the skin sack of dried berries stood neatly beside a huge shiny iron firepot. A set of old beaver traps well-smeared with beargrease hung from another upright nearby. Four packs of beaver plew stood square against the leather wall of the tepee deep in the back. Farther still in the back, the place of honor in the tepee, spread a bed of aromatic dried sweetgrass covered with a buffalo robe.

All the while that he carefully surveyed the tepee, Old Hugh felt Bending Reed busy trying to ignore him. Her slant eyes glittered in the half-dusk of the tepee. Her redstone face she held impassive.

He wondered what had happened to make her so indifferent to him. Maybe she had changed her mind about the Ree brave and was sorry she'd left him. Or maybe Clerk Bonner had claim to her charms in exchange for the old tepee. Hugh remembered that Clerk Bonner had given him a pair of fish eyes while they talked about her. Or maybe she'd turned against her Old Hugh—White Grizzly, as she'd once called him— just on general female principles, like some women did after a lengthy separation. Some women made a man fight his way back all over again. Or maybe she was mad he'd left her in the soup when he escaped the Pawnees. Well, now, for that she had no right to blame him. Not at all.

"Let's see, how many years is it since I seen ee, Reed?" Hugh ciphered it off on his fingers. Last year he'd joined General Ashley. The year before he'd keelboated the Mississippi from St. Louis to New Orleans. The year before that he'd hunted for a party out on the Arkansas River. And the year before that he'd escaped the Pawnees. "Four years. Four years."

Bending Reed moved to the front of the tepee. Afternoon sunlight coming in through the open flap silhouetted her legs and lower body, while light coming from the fire and from the leather smoke-smudged chimney overhead illuminated her bosom and face. Hugh, looking her over with critical eyes, thought her as handsome as ever. She was a little fatter under the chucklychin perhaps. And the pout of her lips had deepened some. And her Siberian-slanted blackcherry eyes seemed set a bit deeper in the redstone flesh over her high cheeks maybe. And her hair sleeked-down with beargrease and hanging in two long braids was not quite so glossy blueblack as in the old days. And her bosom under the white doeskin dress wasn't quite so bunnyround as before. And her hands had broadened some, and maybe had picked up an extra callus or two. But otherwise she was as good as ever.

And like always, she had on good leathers. The best. Her dress was a tunic of deerskin which came well down below her knees, almost to her ankles. It had been worked soft with mashed deer brains and had been made white with a special kind of prairie clay. She'd ornamented it with gay figures done in blue and red and white porcupine quills. Long fringes dangled from the seams and hem. Fancy quill work also decked her ankle-high elkskin moccasins. White conch-shell pendants tinkled from her ears. A necklace of soft stones circled her neck.

Hugh nodded. Yessiree, the best, the best.

Bending Reed picked up her round broom of rushes and began sweeping up the dust and grass his dragging leg had shagged in. When she finished, the dirt floor was so clean it looked like flagging made of pale brown stone.

"Reed-that-bends," Hugh said suddenly in a rough voice meant to be pleasantly gruff, "Reed-that-bends, sit at my feet. Your man, White Grizzly, wishes to have good words with you. Sit."

Instead, Bending Reed darted for the door. The seashells at the ends of her heavy black braids clinked and bangled.

Hugh blinked. "Ho-ah! What's got into you, Reed? Why so contrary all of a sudden?"

Bending Reed stared dully at his feet, blackcherry eyes blinking uneasily.

48

Hugh said, "I suppose if I told ye to run away ye'd sit down instead. Like most contrary squaws. Red or white."

And amazingly she did sit down. Folding her legs to the right under her dress. At his feet. Head bowed demurely. Bowed so far over he could see in the smoky light how well and how thoroughly she'd rubbed vermilion all along the parting of her black horsetaillike hair.

"By the beard of bull barley, ye are the contrary one today, ain't ye?"

She shook her head. Her heavy braids rustled on her shoulders.

"Oh, then you're of a mind to be agreeable maybe?"

Again she shook her head.

"Reed, cut out the peedoodles. I'm back. It's too bad I was gone so long, yes. But that I couldn't help. I'm back. That's it. Talk up like ye used to."

She said nothing.

Hugh clapped out his pipe in a gnarled palm, dropped the crisp ball of burnt tobacco into the fire. The ball of tobacco wasn't altogether burnt up, and when it landed in the hottest part of the tuffing fire, it shot out one last quick spit of blue flame.

"Well then, shut up, if it pleases ee," Hugh said.

Bending Reed immediately broke into a hurrying rattling chattering talk. It went on and on. Her pout lips and thick tongue couldn't fashion the words fast enough. She spoke in Sioux.

Hugh sat back astounded, huge brows lifted, gray eyes for once wide open and showing rings of fine-veined white.

The swift words didn't make sense to him at first. It had been some time since he'd heard her particular dialect of Sioux. And it had also been some time since he'd heard her peculiar kind of sentence-making. Had the young squaw bitten the bitter loco weed? Had herself one bite of the herb too many?

But then, listening intently, he got it. She was telling him everything that had happened to her since she'd last seen him.

Shortly after he had made good his escape from the Pawnees on the Platte River, a band of Arikaree braves came down from the north to visit their tribal cousins the Pawnees. The Rees needed horses, they said, and gunpowder, and they were willing to trade some of their new wonder seedcorn to get both. The Rees, already famous on the plains for having developed a new kind of green watermelon and a white squash and a yellow pumpkin, the Rees had worked up a great medicine for the growing of this corn. The medicine made the corn ripen early with the ears fully as fat and fully as mature as later corn.

While the friendly bartering was going on, one of the Ree braves spotted Bending Reed at work dressing some moccasins, a work for which she'd become well known among the Pawnees. The Ree brave took a shine to her; wanted her after he tried on one of her moccasins. The Pawnees were willing to sell her in exchange for some of the new corn with the great medicine in it. They were short of horses and were loath to get rid of the few they had. Also Bending Reed had caused them much trouble because lately she'd developed a balky streak. Her heart was sad that her brave, White Grizzly, had deserted her.

Bending Reed took one quick robin-shy look at the Ree brave, and instantly disliked him. The Ree brave had the soft hands of a dressmaker. And he gestured like a girlman. A soft-handed brave for her after having lived with her great bull of a White Grizzly? She wanted children. If White Grizzly couldn't father them on her, how could this girlman Ree? So she said, "I'll marry you when the pine leaves turn yellow."

But the Ree brave especially wanted her, and she had to go. And shortly, along with a few mustangs, she went north with her new husband Can't Father.

Hugh broke into Bending Reed's telling. "What? Can't who?"

Bending Reed shut up on the instant.

"Who did you say, Reed?"

She looked down, tongue contrary again. Her darting blackcherry eyes flickered. She worked to bite back the words.

Old Hugh snorted. Then he laughed. "I forgot, Reed. Now shut up, will ee?"

Immediately she rattled on. Yes, her husband was a brave named Can't Father.

Once more Old Hugh couldn't help but break in. "You mean, Can't Fornicate, don't you?"

This time Bending Reed momentarily forgot her contrary set. "No, Can't Father. It is not the same."

"How's that, Reed?"

She remembered, then, and fell silent.

Old Hugh let out a merry bellow. "Reed, if that's the way your stick floats, all right, shut up."

Once again she chattered away. Except she didn't go on to explain just what the difference was between a brave who couldn't fornicate and a brave who couldn't father.

She said Can't Father was kind to her. He treated her well. Gave her the best of everything: mirrors, awls, ribbons, red silk from the Great White Father in Britain, porcupine quills, necklaces, woolen blankets from the English mills, all such fine things. Nor could she complain that he wasn't a brave man in battle. He counted many a coup, brought home many an enemy scalp.

"Not a coward then."

She shut up.

Hugh laughed. "Shut up, Reed."

"He was a brave man full of wise council. His tongue was short, his arm was long. But he was not a father."

Then Bending Reed told Hugh something that made his jaw drop.

One day Can't Father came home from a hunt and fell upon her and almost beat her to death. When she'd recovered enough to crawl around again, Can't Father made her cut off some of her beautiful blueblack hair, shorten it until his own hair was at least two hands longer. A couple days later Bending Reed found out what it was all about. On the hunting party Can't Father and his friends had run into a small party of hostile Sioux braves. The Sioux braves were from her band and they, knowing her to have long braids, and seeing his were short, taunted him with not having as much medicine in his hair as Bending Reed had in hers. And if there was one thing Can't Father was touchy about, aside from his fatherlessness, it was his pride and glory, his glossy black braids of hair. When he wasn't hunting he was always busy preening his raven horsetail hair with a rough-cut ivory comb he'd gotten in trade with the English in Canada.

Of course a squaw prided herself on her hair too. And Bending Reed promptly fell into a pet. For dim in her memory and out of her tribal pantheon came a god called Heyoka and he took possession of her. The god Heyoka was a little old man with a short body and very long legs who went naked in the winter suffering intensely from the heat and who went about warmly clad in the summer suffering intensely from the cold. Suddenly after Heyoka the contrary god had taken possession of her, Bending Reed felt full of power and purpose. She could do anything. Defy Can't Father even if he beat her. Defy even the chief of the Arikaree tribes, Grey Eyes. Defy all of the Rees in fact. She had great medicine. The Rees were astounded by her conversion to a life of going about butt-first. But because they respected superstitions they respected her curious new religion. All day long the old squaws thought of things for her to do just to see her do the opposite. Many times too they had her do something they wanted her to do by telling her its contrary.

Strangely enough, shortly after the god Heyoka had taken possession of her, Can't Father changed subtly, both in person and manner. He could once more satisfactorily perform the role of the male. He was no longer Can't Father but Man-Who-Wants-Many-Sons.

Listening, Hugh hunkered down over the fire. First his eyes opened a little; then they closed. He nodded sagely. He understood it. He had heard of such things happening. He knew of a case where two men went into the mountains together to trap beaver, one of them having a bad case of the rheumatiz and the other not—and lo and behold, the one who'd always complained of the rheumatiz came back out of the mountains completely cured while the healthy one came back a cripple. The rheumatiz spirit or devil, or whatever rheumatiz was, had jumped across to the other.

It was as a result of the Rees respecting her contrary religion that Bending Reed got away. One day her husband, being of an amorous frame of mind, and she not, told her to come in under the bull buffalo robe with him. She refused; did the opposite. She ran out of the breast-shaped dirt-covered lodge. Then Man-Who-Wants-Many-Sons in his male frustration and rage leaped up and ran after her, yelling, "You she-dog, you she-wolf, you she-coyote, you mouse of a squaw, come back to my lodge and woman with me or I'll lodgepole you!" His yelling, his scolding, only made her run the faster. By the time she reached the edge of the village, all the Ree braves and squaws and children were out of their dirt-mound lodges listening and laughing, the squaws especially delighting in the show. When Bending Reed vanished beyond the picket barricade, out past the guards, out over the last hill and finally out of sight, they suddenly understood, too late, that she'd played a ruse on them. And had escaped.

Old Hugh had to laugh. "That was some, Reed, that was. As good a peedoodle as any I ever heard of. But how come ye're still playin' this contrary fiddle, Reed?

Now that Heyoka has helped ee get away, can't ee lay him to one side, Reed?"

Reed shut up.

Old Hugh laughed aloud. "Ho-ah! I see. It's a habit that's took hold, has it? Well, well. That's some, that is."

Abruptly Bending Reed seemed to remember something. She bustled around in the tepee like one possessed. She grabbed up a fire-blacked pot and filled it with water from a leather bag and set it on the cookstone at the edge of the twig fire. She pushed the twig ends up into the pyramid fire all around and added a few small logs. She grabbed up a stone club, and a piece of savory meat, and rushed out through the doorflap. She whistled up the fort dogs. A moment later there was a short yelp and the punking sound of stone hitting skull. Then she came back in dragging a dead yellow-haired puppy. She gutted it and prepared it and dropped it into the pot. Next she got out the skin of pemmican and with an old worndown butcher knife cut off a few slices and laid them on some fresh green cottonwood leaves at Hugh's feet. She made some gruel out of hump fat and ground corn and berry pits. She dug out some buffalo marrow for butter.

Slowly the water warmed; became uneasy with heat; began to boil.

While the meat cooked, she slipped down the legging on Hugh's bad leg. She shook her head when she saw how red and angry the bullet wound was. It had begun to look like a big red boil. She put a hand over open mouth a moment and her paired blackcherry eyes rolled big and shiny. Then she pitched in. She made a fine paste out of powdered cedar-tree needles and rattlesnake oil. She rubbed the fragrant ointment gently but firmly into his leg around and over the touchy wound. And last she got out a bag of grizzly-bear grease and gave his entire body a rubdown with it. The grizzly grease gave her brave husband great power.

Old Hugh sighed. He lay back on the musky robe and enjoyed it all. It had been many a moon since he'd had a warm even urgent rubdown. He groaned both in pleasure and pain.

Presently the puppy meat was ready and she motioned for him to dip in.

And Hugh did. The meat was very tender. It fell off the bones at the least touch of his butcher knife. The pemmican, made of pounded buffalo-cow meat and tallow, was as sweet as fresh cheese. And the corn gruel went down like heated honey. It was a feast fit for the Great White Father himself.

Finished, Hugh jabbed his knife in the ground a few times and then wiped it clean on his leather sleeve. He lay back on the buffalo robe. He groaned with both pleasure and pain again. It was a great life.

He lit his pipe.

He watched Bending Reed take her turn at the pot and the pemmican. She ate demurely, even delicately, like a bunny nibbling grasstips. Hugh had always liked the way she ate. She was a bunny one, she was. Ae. She didn't chew with her mouth open like some squaws did.

After a while, thoroughly relaxed, and moved by a need to talk to someone, he began to gossip a little about the old days.

He told her a little of his adventures since he'd escaped from the Pawnees. She listened while she began to work on a new leather hunting shirt for him. Every now and then her wondering blackcherry eyes studied his old gray eyes and grizzled leathery face.

On his second pipe, Hugh went back a little further, before the time of his capture by the Pawnees, before he had met her while with them. He told of how as a young man he'd run away from home in Pennsylvania, from the very Lancaster County where his gun, Old Bullthrower, had been made; told how he had gone to sea on a ship out of Philadelphia, how he had sailed before the mast over most of the globe, to the East

Indies, to China, to the great Northwest south of Alaska, to the Scandinavian countries, even to Scotland the land of his fathers, and to such ports as Antwerp, London, Amsterdam, Marseilles, New Orleans, Boston.

One day out on the seas of the Gulf of Mexico his ship was attacked and captured by the famous pirate Lafitte. He and his mates fought like men, but the pirates proved too much for them. Finally when only a half-dozen men were left, with the captain and first mate dead, Hugh and his comrades surrendered.

Lafitte was quick in his justice. Either join up as pirates or walk the plank. Hugh and a man named Clint decided to join up. The rest walked the plank into a watery blue death. Hugh and Clint had to swear a horrible oath of allegiance to pirate Lafitte. From then on Hugh's life was uncertain and bloody at most. Lafitte worked out of the Baratarian Coast south of New Orleans, and as a buccaneer Hugh had to help prey on Spanish shipping, had to help sell stolen goods through merchant contacts in New Orleans.

Hugh shivered as he remembered some of it: poor food, long hours, devilishly brutal and lawless companions, scurvy, cholera, cruel bloodlettings. For two years Hugh suffered it.

One day he had enough of it and refused to shoot down a captive. His companyero Clint refused too. Both were thrown in irons; were told that the next day it would be their turn to walk the plank.

During the night, however, the two of them managed to slip out of their chains, escape the ship, and swim to shore.

The land they found themselves in was the far free wild. They wandered through it, heading north, later northeast, hoping to come onto St. Louis. They lived off tree buds, green grass, mice, berries. Sometimes they even ate partly smoked snakemeat. And once they ate of flesh unmentionable.

They managed to get safely through the land of the

fierce Comanches. Then their luck ran out. A raiding party of Pawnees caught them around a fire in a gully. The Pawnees took them back to the tribal headquarters on the Platte River. The chief of the Pawnees questioned them at length; condemned them to be burnt at the stake.

Tied to a tree, Hugh and Clint watched the preparations. A stake was driven into the earth; fagots were arranged around it; ceremonies were enacted; dances were danced.

Clint was the first. He was led to the stake and tied securely. The chief pierced Clint with the first pitchpine splinter, then backed off to let his sadistic braves finish the job. Accompanied by Clint's cries of pain and their own howls of triumph, the braves stuck Clint's skin so full of splinters he looked like a shaggy badger. The fagots at Clint's feet were lit and the final agony began. It didn't last long. Flames swept up over Clint's besplintered body, and with an awful scream in the midnight blackness, companyero Clint passed away into tomorrow.

Hugh's turn came then. Two scalplocked braves untied him from the tree; led him to the chief.

Just as the chief got ready to stick Hugh with the first splinter of pitchpine, Hugh, desperate, bethought himself of something. Hugh reached inside his buckskin shirt; pulled out a thin package. He handed it over to the proud and haughty chief with an air of affection and respect. There was not a trace of fear in Hugh's demeanor. Then he bowed a final farewell to life.

The chief opened the package, found it to be vermilion, an article the Pawnees, as well as all plains' savages, valued above all price. The chief started. He looked Hugh over carefully. Then, majestically, he stepped up to Hugh and embraced him. And with paternal regard and affection, and smiling, the chief declared Hugh free, out of respect for his great bravery and his gift, and led him to his lodge as his guest.

Old Hugh served the Pawnees well. They considered him a very brave warrior. They respected his strategies of battle. His feats of strength and his terrible rage in battle earned him the name of White Grizzly.

He lived like a king. And like a king, he was under constant watch, so that he often lamented that while he had women and food and gunpowder and horse galore, he actually was worse off than a slave.

Some months after his capture he met Bending Reed, just captured by a raiding party into Siouxland. Old Hugh and Bending Reed took to each other on the instant. Both were strangers amongst the Pawnees and both privately hated them and both longed for the day of their escape. They were married with the chief's blessing.

All the while that Hugh ruminated about the old days with the Pawnees, Bending Reed kept on working on her new elkskin hunting shirt. As he talked along, Hugh noted out of the corner of his eye that Reed was using an odd new stitch. It bent back on itself. Heyoka had apparently reversed her stitching style too.

Bending Reed asked suddenly, "My husband says he ran away from his father's tepee when he was a boy. Why did my husband run away?" Her paired black-cherry eyes were bright on him for a moment; then shied off.

Hugh started. His gray eyes clouded over.

Ae, why indeed?

Hugh shook his head. That was something he couldn't talk about. That belonged to a long and terrible time ago. And it was better left untold.

Hugh finally managed a laugh. "Wimmen! they always know how to ask you that one perticular question that brings blood on the run. Reed, red or no, ye're no better than the rest."

Bending Reed laid aside her needlework and nestled against him and cast him sly slant eyes.

There was the smell of a clean washed mink about

her. Hugh knew of her habit of taking a daily bath in the Missouri, summer or winter, a habit that not even the most elegant white woman practiced back in the settlements during the summer. The white women sometimes stank awful, Hugh remembered, especially the free and easy ones, while the most one could say against an Indian woman was that she sometimes was a little strong with prairie-root ointments and a little slippery from excessive use of wildrose-scented beargrease.

Hugh took a deep breath. He thought her animal smell peculiarly rich and stirring. He thought it a good thing that from birth on Indian women were taught to serve their lord and master. They knew exactly how to arouse the man in him. They knew how to keep a brave man brave.

Bending Reed said, "My husband is not afraid to tell of that time, is he?"

Hugh chuckled in his grizzled beard. He tugged at his beard a little. "Reed, an' now I suppose ye'll be holdin' me off until I tell ee?"

But Reed surprised him. Heyoka was still in her and she pressed him back on the musty brown buffalo-bull robe and became his wife again.

Afterward she lay smiling and contented beside him. Playfully she matched the redstone skin of her plump arm against the white of his lean biceps.

Hugh smiled. "Can't Father or no, my little squaw is still young and gentle and in first-rate order, I see." Hugh nodded. "Yessiree, ye suit me longways and sideways both."

Bending Reed laughed and rolled shy blackcherry eyes at him.

But their contentment was short-lived.

There was an etching sound behind them. She heard it after a while and sat up.

It came again, *etch-itch*, *etch-itch*.

"Mouse!" she exclaimed and in a bound was up and after it with a broom. She was once again at war with the furtive pest of the prairies.

Chapter 3

General Ashley left word there would be a meeting before sundown. It would be held outside the fort on the banks of the Missouri out of earshot of the opposition's commander and under a huge cottonwood to which two keelboats were moored. The general and his mountain men had to decide whether to go on into the northwest or to go back to St. Louis.

Hugh had his afternoon nap and then got up from his warm buffalo robe and slipped on his moccasins and hobbled out through the flap of his tepee.

He stood stretching in the hot August sun. Shadows were tight and black along the foot of the south stockade wall. The dazzling summer sun on the bare white cottonwood boles in the north wall made them hard to look at. Even the gray beaten ground underfoot was hard on the eyes.

Hugh stood blinking. Out of the corner of his eye he could see buckskin-clad sentinels armed with Hawken rifles slowly pacing back and forth on the riflewalk along the top and inside the stockade wall. The riflewalk was some fifteen feet off the ground, just high enough to permit the sentinels to shoot over the twenty-foot wall. The cross-braced cottonwood palings shone like old dull teeth in a weathered jawbone. Behind him in the carpenter's shop someone was nailing together a wooden coffin, another in the meathouse was sawing up buffalo bones, and still another in the blacksmith shop was pounding out some crude horseshoes. The boss's house was silent, but from the men's quarters came the sound of trappers playing cards, with now and then a loud coarse voice saying, "By the eternal, this is one hand I'll put my pile on." In the entrance to the warehouse Sioux squaws from tepees outside the fort were protesting shrilly to frail Clerk Bonner that he'd cheated them out of some fofurraw.

Hugh noticed that both blockhouses, the one on the northwest corner as well as the one on the southwest corner, rumbled as if men were rolling cannon balls in them. The blockhouses had been built at opposite corners of the stockade so that in case of sudden Indian attack the cannon in them could sweep all four walls of the fort with deadly grapeshot at the same time.

Hugh limped out through the wicket in the main gate, waving a gruff hello to bent Old Childress the gatekeeper. Outside the fort two drunken Sioux braves lay asleep in the shadow of the wall, mouths open and slack and crawling with flies. A few Sioux tepees, with skin pennants and bushy animal tails dangling in a slow breeze, stood well back west of the fort. The cone tepees made a sawtooth pattern against the horizon. Beyond the smoke-tipped tepees lifted lofty tan bluffs, rising up like massive shouldering waves of earth held back as if by the command of some Moses. A few stunted plum trees clung to the crests of the bluffs. Far to the north two hunters picked their way warily up a ravine, intent on a half-dozen white-tailed antelope. The land was dry on the tumbled bluffs, and the dead bunch grass glowed like mounds of rusted iron.

The footpath from Ft. Kiowa to the landing site at the base of the huge cottonwood was worn and deep. Gray dust in it ran like barley flour. Hugh walked to one side of it, but even on the untrodden ground his moccasins raised quick puffs of gray. Hugh coughed a couple of times.

The single cottonwood towered over them like a great dreamland mushroom. Below, the two gray keelboats rode easy and free in the wide rolling tan Missouri. The far east cutbank knifed up sharp and gray from the waterline. A small grove of oak and ash and cottonwood crested the cutbank. Behind it some wild rose and gooseberry and wolfberry brush spread all the way back to where the land sloped up onto the plateau of far prairies.

The meeting had already begun by the time Hugh got to the rendezvous. General Ashley, still wearing the blue uniform of the Missouri state militia, was haranguing the men from behind a storebox while Major Andrew Henry sat on a stump behind another box.

The sight of Major Henry made Hugh haul up short. Ae, then Prayin' Diah Smith had made it safe, after all, across wild Indian land to bring Major Henry down on the run from his post on the mouth of the Yellowstone. Good boy, Jedediah. Brave lad. Hugh swept the crowd of seated mountain men with a quick narrowed look and immediately recognized Diah. Prayin' Diah sat alone off to one side. He sat calm and reserved. Not a face muscle moved. Only Diah's grave gray eyes showed that he was holding himself in.

Looking around further Hugh spotted other newcomers: cautious book-learned John S. Fitzgerald, gaunt Allen, proud George Yount, and even the boy, slim redhaired Jim Bridger. Ho-ah. The major had taken along some of his best shots to help fight the Rees. No wonder everybody was mad that General Leavenworth had funked his attack on the villages. Hugh shook his head. Ae, a lot had happened since he'd taken to bed in Bending Reed's tepee.

Hugh sat on the grass well to the rear. Like all mountain men he sat crosslegged, knees out, feet folded inward. Sitting at the rear of the crowd he could watch the men to see what their mind might be before he himself made up his mind.

Some of the mountain men were smoking their pipes. Others sat with averted eyes. Still others, like Diah, sat with backbone erect and eyes flashing. Some of the boatmen were present too, and they lolled easy on their sides. There were some fifty men present, and all were armed with rifles and knives, and almost all, except the boatmen, wore skin suits. Some of the skin suits were so greased and weathered brown it took a close look to see what they were made of.

General Ashley was speaking. He had a high pleasant voice when aroused, and his little mouth worked furiously and eloquently. He sweat as he talked and sometimes he stopped to wipe his redblond brow and occasionally he swapped a light hand around at a passing fly. The general's light tenor voice was in sharp contrast to the rousting Missouri awash below the bank.

General Ashley said, yes, it was true that General Leavenworth had failed them all when he refused to press home his advantage after having successfully surrounded the Ree villages above the Grand River and after having killed Chief Grey Eyes on the very first cannon shot. Yes, it was true that the Rees had escaped in the night and that they now were all over the prairies like angry wild bees chased out of their hives and ready to sting anything that moved. Yes, it was true that the Rees' escape had encouraged even the friendly Mandans to go on the warpath against the whites. Yes, it was true that until the Rees had been taught a lesson the savages all up and down the Missouri would be twice, perhaps a hundred times, as treacherous as before.

But, General Ashley said, but, he was still of a mind to go on with the trapping expedition into the Rocky Mountains.

General Ashley pounded the storebox with a small hard fist, hit it so hard he made even the surly grumblers shut up.

General Ashley had a new plan. He was asking for two sets of volunteers. One set would return with Major Henry to the post on the Yellowstone and the Missouri, the other set under Diah would start directly west for the Black Hills and beyond, with the two companies trapping beaver all through the fall and eventually meeting somewhere near the Big Horn Mountains by the time the winter snows set in.

"Where'll we get the ponies, Gen'ral?" Jack Larrison called out. Jack Larrison could hardly be blamed for being cautious. During the slaughter on the sand bar before the Ree villages he had somehow become wedged between two dead mustangs and thus had been overlooked by the Rees when they came down to count coup on the dead after the battle. Despite a bad wound Jack didn't dare move until after dark. A ball had passed through one thigh and had lodged in the other. He bled badly. When darkness at last set in, Jack pried himself out from between the dead mustangs. He found the boats gone. They'd retreated far down the river. Jack saw no other chance of escape but to swim the river. He stripped himself of his clothes in the dark and bound up his wounds and took to water. Some Ree women spotted him just as he entered the river and they called out an alarm. Quickly some Ree warriors came out and fired at his bobbing head. But Jack got away. Four days later Jack appeared at the fort as naked as the day he was born. His skin was peeling off him in black strips.

"What was that?" General Ashley said, inclining his head in friendly manner.

"Where do we get the ponies?" Jack Larrison repeated. Jack's face was still haggard from the experience.

"From our friends the Sioux. They've agreed to bring me forty mounts. The horses'll be here by tomorrow morning. Fresh and frisky."

"Indian promises," crippled Joseph Monso grumbled. Ned-hearted Joe sat at Jack Larrison's left. Both were dead-set against any further adventures into the wild.

"They'll be here," General Ashley said, "if I have to get them myself. That's the least of my worries."

"What if some of us don't want to go nohow?" another voice called out from the other side of the crowd.

"I'm not holding any man here against his will. We're starting from scratch right here and now. What's happened so far is gone and done. You're free to return to St. Lou if that's your mind. One of the keelboats leaves tomorrow with some of Leavenworth's men, and you can ride down with them. And in another month I myself will take the second keelboat down to Fort Atkinson, and you can come along with me then if you can't make up your mind today."

"Suppose we did quit now?" Jack Larrison asked. "Do we still get paid?"

General Ashley's mild blue eyes flashed. His face shone red in the mellow shade of the cottonwood. "Well . . . yes, I guess so. Though you actually agreed otherwise."

Silence. Below the bank the Missouri washed rough and rolling. The lone cottonwood's glossy green leaves cliddered overhead. A single oriole darted silent and golden through the high branches. The sun shone dazzling and white on the dead yellow grass outside the cottonwood's wide round shadow. The cottonwood and the single bird in it and the men under it held against the sizzing vast wilderness.

Hugh sized up the men. Of the hundred or so who had started out from St. Louis earlier in the year, only fifty were left. The other fifty were either dead, or wounded, or had deserted. Luckily Major Henry's brigade of fifteen tough hand-picked men with their bark still on were around to buck up what was left.

Hugh saw Jim Clyman near him and his eyes lighted. Hugh was glad to see Clyman had got through alive.

Hugh slid along the dry grass over to Clyman's side. "Well, lad, I see ye made it to the *Packet* after all."

"I did." Clyman gave a short snort and tossed his dark big head. "But not the way you think."

"Ae? How's that?"

"I made it to the *Packet* the long way home, you might say. I missed the boat. And worse yet, got Gibson killed for tryin' to save me."

"No! Tough, that is."

Clyman told a little about it, small mouth grim, dark blue eyes looking right through Old Hugh. "Gibson jumped in to help me climb aboard a skiff the men had let go. I was still havin' trouble with my possibles and couldn't keep afloat. Gibson got me into the skiff all right but got shot doin' it. We got across the river, too, only to find four Ree braves swimmin' after us. So I had to leave him wounded in the skiff."

"What happened then?"

"I started runnin' with three of the four Rees after me, one t'either side and one behind. Pretty soon I seen I wasn't goin' to make it, so when I spotted a little washout in some tall grass just as I come over the top of a hill, I rolled in it. They ran by. I hid out all that night. The next day I went back to the river, and some men aboard the *Packet* spotted me in the brush."

"And Gibson?"

"Skulped by the other Ree."

Hugh shook his head. "Another gone under."

Clyman said, "Ye goin' to join up again, Hugh?"

"I might. I'm thinkin' on it."

Clyman looked at the dark disgruntled faces around him, at the pork-eating boatmen and the grumbling river roughnecks, and then growled in Hugh's ear, "The gen'ral ought a take a club to 'em. They'd soon come to their milk then."

Old Hugh said slowly, "Wal, Jim, I'll allow to bein' a little offish myself since that fix."

Clyman gave Hugh a disbelieving look.

"Oh, I'll join the lads all right when the lads need joinin'," Hugh said quietly. "But I allow myself the right to set on it a night or so."

General Ashley finished his spieling, and then it was Major Henry's turn. General Ashley was glad to rest a few minutes. He sat down on his storebox and wiped his sweating face carefully and thoroughly. There were black patches of sweat under the armpits of his blue uniform.

Major Henry was tall, slender, slightly bent in the shoulders. He had a slow calm manner and a commanding presence. His hair was dark and his light eyes were inclined to blue. When he talked, his slightly buckset upper teeth flashed white. Except for his blue army cap, he wore buckskins like the rest of his men. Major Henry was a man of exceeding honesty. Some years back, some of his friends in St. Louis, for whom he had become surety, defaulted on their debts, and he lost a great sum of money. Advised beforehand to put his property in his wife's name, Major Henry angrily refused; said he preferred living like a poor man if it meant he couldn't live honest as a rich man. All the mountain men had heard the story and they respected him for it. Some of the men told too how they'd once heard Major Henry play the violin. He hadn't played it like a fiddle at a shindig either, but like it might be a voice. They told how it sang clear like a mourning dove.

Major Henry said, "While we're at it, I suppose I should tell you the latest news I've just got by runner from the post. All right, General?"

General Ashley nodded.

Major Henry went on. He had a baritone voice that went well with the rushing basso of the Missouri. His upper teeth flashed clean in the shadow of the cottonwood. "First off, I suppose I'd best give you men some of the worst news first. We've just got word that Jones and Immel and a small company of men from the opposition, the Missouri Fur Company, were caught in a ravine by Blackfeet. Twenty-nine whites against some four hundred red devils. Jones and Immel and all but five men were killed. The Blackfeet captured twenty-five packs of beaver, got all the horses and mules and all the traps. Bill Gordon and four others managed to get away and they made it through open country, some six hundred miles, back to the forks of the Yellowstone and Missouri."

At the mention of the Blackfeet, an involuntary sigh rose from the men. Here and there a mouth hung open a second; then snapped shut. Heads rode forward on the neck a little.

"I told ee," Jack Larrison said, "fightin' them red devils and gettin' out alive is unpossible."

Major Henry went on, baritone voice clear, slow, emphatic. "We think the British are behind it. They've had it all their own way up to now. They've made many a fortune out of the Blackfoot country, up there high on the Missouri, and of course they don't want us to cut in on it."

"I've heard enough," Joseph Monso said, and he got up and stepped quickly to the edge of the Missouri and climbed down out of sight.

All eyes watched Joe go. A few trappers stirred. But the hard eyes of Diah Smith and Jim Clyman and General Ashley and Major Henry stared them down.

"Yes," Major Henry continued, upper teeth flashing in a neat white row, "yes, the British don't want us to cut in. And I'll tell you why. Bill Gordon said he never saw such beaver in all his life. Around the Big Horns and up the far Missouri. Why! Gordon said the beaver was thicker'n lice on a fat dog. There were so many beaver, Gordon said, it was like in a dream. They were there for the taking. Fat and tame. The fur thick and the tail sweet. A man could catch as many as he could set traps for. A hundred a day if he wanted to. A power of beaver."

John S. Fitzgerald's eyes half-closed.

"Men, you know the country above the post on the Missouri and Yellowstone. Clean air. So clean meat never spoils. And grass as green as paint. And pines as high as heaven. Wonderful country."

Young Jim Bridger's eyes gleamed.

"And the Crow and Shoshone squaws the cleanest gentlest God ever made."

The baritone voice of the major rose a little above the roushing basso of the wild Missouri. "In the wintertime, trapping done, you can bed down in a draw behind the mountains. There'll be plenty of sweet cottonwood bark for the ponies there, and squaw to dress your beaver and keep you warm at night, and target shootin' on the sunny side of the cliffs. And no laws around but your own."

Again the crew stirred uneasily.

"And talking about law reminds me. Mike Fink is dead."

Hugh jerked erect. Mike had been an old enemy of Hugh's. They'd once fought to a bloody draw in a no-holds-barred brawl in a St. Louis tavern. Mike had shot the heel of a Negro for the fun of it and Hugh had come to the Negro's defense. "Mike dead?" Hugh exclaimed. "No!"

"Yes, Mike is dead," Major Henry said, nodding. Major Henry told a little about it. Mike had put in a bad winter at the post and in January had gone to live with a lad named Carpenter in a cave along the Missouri River banks. They stayed off by themselves the rest of the winter, emerging finally when spring was well underway. During their hibernation some bad blood had arisen between Mike and the boy Carpenter. Shortly after they came back to the fort, the boy Carpenter became the bosom chum of a man named Talbot. This hurt Mike grievously, since Mike and Talbot never got along. Two weeks ago, Major Henry said, two weeks ago Mike and Carpenter got drunk together, and to prove there was no hard feeling between them, they agreed to an old stunt of theirs, shoot a can of whisky off each other's head at forty paces. Carpenter had the first shot and knocked the can of whisky off Mike's head well and good, but he also knocked off Mike's beavertail cap and grazed his scalp a little. This

69

threw Mike into a sad fit. It was now Mike's turn to shoot. Carpenter set the can of whisky on his head like Mike had done and shouted for Mike to hurry and take his turn. Carpenter was anxious to get back to the drinking. "I will," Mike said. "And look ye, Carpenter, my boy. That last shot ye took, that ain't the way I taught ye to shoot. You missed once, but you won't miss again." And with that, Mike fired; the ball cracking through Carpenter's forehead. Talbot, Carpenter's new comrade, witnessing the act, immediately raised a cry of "Murder!" and a few days later killed Mike with a horse pistol.

Everybody talked up at once. "So Mike Fink is dead! I don't hardly believe it!"

"Well, Mike had it acomin' sometime, I guess."

"Two more gone under. Well, well. Too bad."

Major Henry raised his hand, the long fringes on his buckskin sleeve swishing a little. "There's still more, boys." Major Henry turned to look down at General Ashley seated beside him. "General, before I tell it, I'd like to suggest something."

"Talk away, man," General Ashley said, slapping at a fly on his crossed blue knee. "I'm short of ideas as it is. We want to look at all sides of the thing."

"Well, General." Major Henry's lips thinned and his teeth gleamed white. "Well, General, I don't think it's a good idea to hang out all the wash until we know for deadsure we've nothing but friends present." Major Henry looked them all in the eye. "Men, some of us are going on. Those who haven't got the guts to stick can pack up and leave now. And go down as deserters in my book."

General Ashley jumped up. His face reddened. "Wait, Andy, wait. I wouldn't—"

Major Henry was firm. He raised his head again. "Just a minute yourself, General. I think I know what I'm doing. I just wanted to see how many men, and I mean men, we have left, is all. Men, not squaws."

"Well, I still think it's some risky to put it that way," General Ashley said again, "risky—"

"General, let me handle this. I think I know my men." Major Henry stared them all in the eye, one by one. "All right, let them who ain't of a mind to go, let them get aboard Leavenworth's keelboat pronto."

Silence and the wild Missouri rousting.

At last, with a sigh, Jack Larrison got up. He balanced on a trembling leg. "I'm sorry, Major, but I think I've had my fill of red-devil fighting. It's onhuman, that's what it is."

"If that's the way your stick floats, Jack, that's it."

Jack Larrison hobbled off and painfully stepped down out of sight.

Then Dufrain stood up. "I've had enough too, Major. I'm sorry."

"You're welcome, Dufrain. Any more?"

With sad eyes, General Ashley watched some twenty of his lads get up and slide down out of sight below the riverbank.

"Any more?" Major Henry called out. "Now's the time to speak up."

Silence again and the wild Missouri rousting.

"All right, men, that's fine. Now I'll tell you the rest of the news we just got. As you know, Jones and Immel belonged to the opposition. So that wasn't exactly a direct loss to us. But"—Major Henry's grave blue eyes searched through the remaining crew of thirty tired men—"but, we ourselves lost a half-dozen killed just a week ago. By the Blackfeet."

Again a collective sigh rose from the men.

General Ashley took over then. "Mountain men, friends, I know it's a terrible gamble. We may not only lose our shirts but our topknots as well. But if we win, we can come back rich men. You can't get rich being a fifteen-cent millionaire."

Silence. A cough. Inward looks. Fingers busy in the dry grass.

At last a tall lean man stood up. It was Silas Hammond. During the battle on the Ree sand bar, Silas had been stunned by a flying horsehoof and had been left for dead. While unconscious he had been scalped by the Rees. Yet somehow in the melee, after he came to, Silas, like Jack Larrison, had managed to escape in the night by swimming the river.

Silas removed his cap. It was a tight one made of beaverskin. The moment he took it off, his whole face sagged horribly. All eyes looked to where he'd been scalped. The crusted scar on his skull looked like a chip of black bark. The scar was healing very slowly along the edges. The scalping had cut the nerves of his facial muscles, and the skin under his eyes and off his jowls hung slack like a mournful hound's.

Silas said, "Gen'ral, I reckon I kin risk my hair again."

There was a nervous laugh.

Hugh couldn't get over it. What a man Silas was to offer his life again. Ae, what a man. And if Silas could risk his life once more, Old Hugh could too.

Hugh got to his feet. Staggering a little on his game leg and waving Old Bullthrower overhead, Hugh said, "Gen'ral, this child hates an American what ain't seen Indians skulped or don't know a Pawnee moccasin from a Comanche. I admit I've sometimes thought of makin' tracks back to white diggin's again, where the beds is soft and the wimmen white and the red niggers only a dream in the night. Ae, many a time I've sighed for the bread and beer of the old days. But then I remember fresh fleece from a buffler's hump, young cow at that, and sweet boudins just barely crimped with fire, and still sweeter beavertail. And I remember places where a child can do just as he pleases to, as far as he can see, good or bad. Where a child can sing if he wants to, or shut up if he wants to. Where meat never spoils. Gen'-ral, seein' them cowards pull out for white diggin's while our Silas here is still willin' to risk his topknot"—

the single arteries down each side Hugh's nose began to wriggle like lively red angleworms—"Gen'ral, I know what's good for this old hoss. If I have to, I'd rather be skulped by a red devil than skun by a nabob. Give me a little 'bacca, a plew a plug, and plenty of duPont powder and Galena balls for Ol' Bullthrower, and a new Green River knife, and I'm off with ee. Whoopee! This hoss can't wait to shine with fresh buffler meat. Free mountains, here I come."

General Ashley couldn't help but laugh. His red face beamed. "Hurrah for Hugh! That's what I like to hear." General Ashley laughed some more. "Though I want to warn you, Hugh, you've got to follow orders. You're not going to play balky horse again like you did up by the Rees. Each man has to do his part when the order is given."

Right behind Hugh came Prayin' Diah Smith, and then Jim Clyman, and after them the boy Jim Bridger, and quiet book-learned John S. Fitzgerald, and proud George Yount, and Augie Neill and Jim Anderson, and durable Tom Fitzpatrick, and gaunt Allen and horseface Rose the interpreter—all the lads who'd come to parley under the cottonwood.

That same night General Ashley assigned thirteen of the men to Major Henry's brigade. They would return with the major to the post on the Yellowstone and the Missouri. Among the thirteen were Hugh Glass, the boy Jim Bridger, John S. "Fitz" Fitzgerald, Augie Neill, and Jim Anderson. The other seventeen mountain men were assigned to Captain Diah Smith's party, which would leave for the Black Hills as soon as he could get supplies together.

Also that same night Hugh Glass had Clerk Bonner write a letter for him. Hugh gave the letter, along with a bundle of personals, to the captain of Leavenworth's keelboat and asked that both be mailed in St. Louis.

The letter was for Johnnie Gardner's father and it read:

Dr Sir:

My painful duty it is to tell you of the deth of yr son wh befell at the hands of the indians 2n June in the early morning. He lived a little while after he was shot and asked me to inform you of his sad fate. We brought him to the ship where he soon died. Mr. Smith a young man of our company made a powerful prayer wh moved us all greatly and I am persuaded John died in peace. His body we buried with others near this camp and marked the grave with a log. His things we will send to you. The savages are greatly treacherous. We traded with them as friends but after a great storm of rain and thunder they came at us before light and many were hurt. I myself was shot in the leg. Master Ashley is bound to stay in these parts till the traitors are rightly punished.

yr obt svt
Hugh Glass

Chapter 4

It was late August, the Moon of Plums Ripening.

On the afternoon of the twenty-eighth, on the fourth day out from Ft. Kiowa, going northwest across country and well away from the Missouri and the Rees, Major Henry sent Old Hugh ahead to make meat for the evening meal. The boy Jim Bridger and book-learned Fitz Fitzgerald were assigned to go along with Hugh. Major Henry made it a rule never to send out a hunting or scouting party of less than three men.

The three of them were mounted on good-looking ponies, Hugh on a grayblue stallion he called Old Blue, the boy Jim on a dashing sorrel he called Maggie, and quiet Fitz on a spotted red-and-white mare he called Pepper. Fitz's mare had a habit of every now and then lowering its head and snorting wildly. She had once been hit by a rattler and she was still shy of the ground. She was also extremely sensitive to Indian smells, and twice she had suddenly taken her head and galloped furiously across the prairie a mile or more before Fitz could get her under control again.

The boy Jim was tall, well over six feet, heavy-limbed, with blunt knuckles and blunt cheekbones and blunt forehead. He had the heavy elbows and large knees of a colt. He walked with a rolling, clumsy, pigeon-toed lift of foot. His hair was auburn and he wore it long, gathered up in a knot in back, with a round beaverskin capping it. He was seventeen, and for all his being a centershot and a handy blacksmith he still had the air of a greenhorn about him. Only occasionally did the beginnings of a canny Scot shine through his innocence. When excited, his blue eyes turned a very light blue, as if a moon might be coming up behind them.

Fitz Fitzgerald was a much different kind of man. Fitz was of medium height and had the slender frame of the city-bred man. He walked stylish, toes out—a manner Hugh despised and which he attributed to Fitz's having been exposed to a little schooling. For all his small size, Fitz was well-put-together, quick, fluid in motion, and was surprisingly tough. He had brown hair and the alert hazel eyes and pink cheeks of the Irishman. He was a downer and had turndown lips; was at all times quietly practical. He rarely laughed, and when he did, he roared all out of proportion to the humor involved. Hugh often noted that even when Fitz sat silent he looked restless, like a kettle about to tremble with boiling water.

The three rode well ahead of the main party, some four miles, traversing a crest of long swollen slopes overlooking Worthless Creek to the west with Glad Valley coming up ahead on the north. Far to the west reared a mesa of dull red rock called Thunder Butte. The men had been using Thunder Butte as a landmark for some twenty miles and now, at last, were directly east of it. The sun was setting upon it and gold light limned all its silhouette, while red and then rust deepened the shadow on its near side. The Butte looked like a huge mammary sliced off at the top exactly at the nipple. The Sioux claimed every passing thunderstorm struck it with lightning; that the thunder which followed always knocked down some of the dull red rock from its edges and sent it crashing to its foot. The Sioux spoke of it as the pulpit of the Great Spirit Wakantanka. The Butte was also used as an aerie by golden eagles. Around it on all sides—east, west, north, south—the long tan sloping bluffs and hills lay stretched out like languorous mountain lions.

Old Hugh had sailed all the blue oceans, from Hammerfest to the Furneaux Islands, and had seen calm seas and mad seas, and looking out from under his deep gray brows, Old Hugh saw the somber farspread oceanlike plains as another vast sea, except that it was tan not blue. The mounding waves and the hollowing troughs were hauntingly familiar. Even the occasional brush in the ravines he recognized—it was flotsam washing in the wave troughs. He also recognized Thunder Butte— it was an island volcano rising out of the black-green deeps of the Pacific. It wouldn't have been too much of a surprise to Hugh to see the Butte suddenly blow its cap and spout red lava and gray mud over the rolling expanse.

The far prairie horizons resembled sea horizons too. They undulated mistily, and mistily joined earth and sky together. Far hilltop and lowering cumulus cloud blurred off together. The earth was an immane brown dish and the sky an immense blue bowl, and where they met they blended off into each other.

Old Hugh peered out at it, gray eyes narrowed, sparkling. His lips thinned under his beard and the gray fur under his nose and over his cheeks moved.

Ae, far from kith and kin it was, with nothing but the strange new all around and ahead. And for that, perhaps, all the better. The far country was never too far. Over the next hill might be the Seven Cities of Cibola at last.

The boy Jim on his frolicsome sorrel mare galloped toward a small knoll. For one who had worked in a smithy most of his young life, the boy rode his horse well, rode it as if he'd grown to the animal. The long-shanked lad had some give-and-take in the lower six inches of his backbone. Bending Reed had made a new yellow buckskin suit for Jim, and every time the horse rose and fell in its gallop, the fringes, still long, rose and snapped with it in rustling throws. The mare's hooves beat on the hard ground in a steady rhythmic clopping gallop.

The boy Jim had barely crested the knoll when he reined in his horse sharply, ducked his head, quickly backed the horse down the knoll again. He waved his flintlock for Hugh and Fitz to come on cautiously.

"What is it, lad, varmint or red devil?" Hugh asked when they drew abreast.

"Varmint!" Jim said. Jim's young blue eyes were jumping. "Buffler."

All three swung to the ground and tied their ponies to a bullberry bush in a little draw. Crouched over, rifles ready, with Hugh limping along and Jim ambling pigeon-toed and Fitz toeing out, they crept up the knoll. The knoll was crested over with patches of prickly-pear cactus and sandy ant mounds.

"Where?" Hugh asked.

Jim pointed, fringes on his buckskin sleeve swishing.

Straight ahead of them, across Glad Valley, just at the edge of a brushy ravine, four heavy tanbrown objects moved slowly out into the open.

" 'Tis buffler at that," Fitz said. Fitz wore an old gray wool hat, and his eyes were in shadow as he looked out from under the brim. "Buffler."

"Them's my thoughts," Jim said.

Behind them Fitz's horse snorted nervously.

Hugh stood stock-still. The gray whiskers under his ears moved. Hugh looked at the four tanbrown critters and then looked around at Fitz's jumpy horse.

Jim danced pigeon-toed in the dry tan grass. "Shall we ride for 'em head on, Hugh? The wind's against us."

"Wait," Hugh said. "Wait." Hugh stared at the dark objects awhile. He watched them move across the glade. Hugh said finally, "Lads, somehow I don't like it."

"What? Hugh, old coon, you must be blind!" Jim said.

"Blind or no, I've seen sign the last mile or so."

"Sign?"

"What made them whitetail goats we saw awhile back go streaking over the hills, if humans warn't behind them? And who's in these diggin's but red devils, and the worst kind, Rees? We better wait for the rest of the party to come up, I'm thinkin', if we mean to save our skins."

Young joy fled Jim's face. Brow furrowed, hand shading his eyes, Jim looked across toward the grazing tanbrown creatures again. "But, Hugh, them critter there hain't been roused by them humans of your'n. Maybe them whitetail antelope ran because they heard us through the ground. And not red devils."

Hugh said, "Fitz, ye've growed some. What do you say?"

The down curve in Fitz's mouth deepened. "They do look a little on the big side, I'll say that." Fitz looked back at his horse Pepper; frowned. "And she smells somethin'."

"That's it," Hugh said, waggling his old gray head. "Lads, I say they're—"

Jim was still jumping. "Hugh, old hoss, ye must be blind! I say there's our meat for the major. I'm all for chargin' them." And with that, Jim clumsed back to his sorrel mare; forked her; gave her a whack with the butt of his rifle; shouted, "Hep-ah! Let's make tracks, Maggie!" and was off for the brown critters in the glade.

Hugh looked blankly at Fitz a moment and Fitz looked at Hugh.

"Now if that don't put us in a curious fix," Hugh growled. "Well, Fitz, it's kill or cure now, if them ain't buffler. C'mon, we'd better chase after the lad to see what he's got himself into. And us."

Quickly Hugh and Fitz ran back to their mounts; hopped up; rode after Jim.

The four creatures seemingly didn't hear or see Jim come at first. They grazed peacefully out into the open away from the dense bushes in the ravine.

But when Jim was almost halfway there, the tanbrown

buffalo skins on the humps of all four critters suddenly slid off and the humps lifted up and all four critters became two-legged naked Indians riding four-legged tanbrown ponies.

"Whoa!" Hugh shouted. Hugh rose in his stirrups; roared with all his great voice, "Jim, back! Back, lad, back!"

"Rees!" Fitz exclaimed, seeing the hawkbone head-dress. The hawkbones stood out on each side of the head like paired horse ears. "Decoys! Ambush! Holy son of a dog." Fitz's horse began to prance frenziedly. "Pepper was right after all."

"A war party," Hugh yelled. "And look at 'em lick it across the prairie for Jim." Hugh roared out again with all his voice. "Run for it, Jim, lad! Or you're wolf-meat sartain!"

Without breaking the stride of his pony, Jim pulled around sharply to the left and came galloping toward Hugh and Fitz again, heavy elbows working like wings, buckskin fringes fluttering.

Hugh hauled back on Old Blue; then let the grayblue stallion out a little again as he turned him about. "We'd best let Jim catch up and then make a run for it. There'll be more Rees around, you can bet your sweet life on that."

Hugh hadn't more than got the words out of his mouth when mounted Rees appeared out of the hollows, a half-dozen on both sides of them, and came galloping like mad fiends up the slope toward them. The Rees yowled. "Howgh-owgh-owgh-owgh-h!" They waved rifles and bows. Skin pennants and animal brushtails fluttered from lifted spears. All the warriors wore red warpaint; their ponies were decked with it too.

Despite all he could do, Fitz's horse Pepper suddenly bolted.

"Hold her, Fitz! Hold her!" Hugh shouted, still reining in Old Blue.

Fitz gave Hugh an odd look over his shoulder as Pepper rapidly carried him away.

"Consarn that rum devil of a horse. Fitz'd better get rid of it."

Jim quirted his Maggie and came on with a rush. His mare beat toward Hugh in a wild whirl of hooves, around and around, like two irregular wheels hitched together. Jim's face was salt white; his blue eyes square with fear.

Hugh fired a horse pistol at the nearest Ree on his left; continued to hold Old Blue to a prancing trot until Jim caught up; then gave Old Blue the quirt too. Together Hugh and Jim beat after Fitz, down the long slope toward a far hollow in the direction of the rest of Major Henry's party. They took the smoothest route across the rolling shortgrass plains.

The three Ree parties bore toward them, a half-dozen on the right, another half-dozen on the left, and four behind.

Horse heart and human heart beat furiously. Eyesight joggled; horizons wavered. Elbows clapped hard on ribcase. It was horse against horse with cunning human brain thrown in to tip the race one way or the other. The rolling clopping beat of horse hooves was loud on the hard dry ground. Pale yellow puffs of dust exploded out of the dry grass. Prairie-dog mounds came up, and the horses instinctively veered to the right or left around them.

The flying V of the Rees closed in. Arrows sailed around Hugh and Jim like quick sleet. One ticked Hugh's wolfskin cap, went end-over-end out of sight beneath his galloping grayblue stallion. Another arrow, almost spent, hit the mane of Jim's mare, stuck a moment, fell off. The mare gave a great leap; shrilled a whinny of fear; gave Jim the jump on Hugh. Shots followed; balls whistled around them. The Rees were now close enough for Hugh to see their old war wounds gauded with red clay paint. Quick cupping hands valving their mouths, the Rees howled long warwhoops. "Ohohohohohohoh! ohohohohoh!"

"Jim, lad, freeze into it!"

Imperceptibly, gradually, Hugh and Jim began to gain on the Rees. The three of them had run down from a highland to a lowland while the Rees'd had to climb part way before they could swing in behind them. The difference was just enough to give the three mountain men the edge. By the time they pounded through the softer giving ground in the valley ahead, they were well out of rifle range. And the moment they ascended the other side, the rest of Major Henry's party appeared on the south horizon, horse heads and rifle barrels and hats pricking out over the grassy edge. The Ree warriors took one look at the armed party heaving into sight, and gave up.

"Whoa!" Hugh gasped, pulling up. "Whoa, Ol' Blue."

Jim looked back over his shoulder, saw he was safe at last, and hauled up too. He rode back easily to where Hugh sat puffing on heaving foam-flecked Old Blue.

Up ahead Fitz had finally got his horse Pepper under control again, and he slowly rode back to where Hugh and Jim sat on their heaving horses.

Hugh said, "Let's blow a minute, lads. Whaugh! that was some, that was. For a minute there I felt pretty streaked, lads. Cold sweat was all broke out over me."

Jim sat breathing heavy. He didn't have much to say.

Hugh gave the boy Jim a long narrowed look. Between puffs, Hugh grunted, "So I didn't see sign, eh?"

Jim bit pink lip; flushed.

The gray beard over Hugh's cheeks worked and his pink tongue appeared and disappeared in the opening and closing mouth hole within his beard as he said, "Sonny, after this, don't run too far ahead. Always keep your eyes skinned and your ears picked for sign. Because there's always red devils about, hidin' under wolfskin or, like today, under buffler hides. Or hidin' behind cliffs or brush. They see ee every day, and it's when ye don't see any sign of 'em about that it's time to look out for devilment."

Jim held still.

"Sonny," Hugh continued, waggling his old hoar head, "Jim, lad, even if I don't always see sign with these old eyes no more, this young nose of mine dips in for me. After this, around me, wait up until my nose says for us to go ahead."

Jim said, "I'm obliged to you, Hugh. You saved my life. And I'm mighty sorry for pokin' ahead too far."

"Don't thank me. Thank your horse. Lucky for ee she was a fast critter with plenty of bottom and not just an ordinary stayer. Ae." Hugh heaved up a snort. "Lad, when I was a sull young'un like you, an' still had some green to lose—"

Fitz growled, "Oh come now, Hugh. Don't rub it in. Jim heard you the first time."

Hugh next gave Fitz a close look. "As for ee, Fitz, the sooner ye get rid of that spook Pepper the better. She may be able to smell some but she's turned old maid on ye. She'll carry ye to your grave yet."

Fitz said nothing. His turndown mouth deepened into a scowl.

They sat resting awhile, men and horses, getting their breath back. Salty smells radiated from sweated horsehair. Botflies buzzed around and under the horses' bellies.

Presently Hugh heaved a sigh. "All right. Guess we've blowed enough. Let's try again. With the major right behind, them Rees won't show again, I'm thinkin'."

With his arms Hugh wigwagged sign language to the major's oncoming party, telling them everything was all right. Then Hugh turned his horse about. "Hep-ah, Ol' Blue, let's make meat. And, lads, look sharp and shoot sharp is the word." Riding along, Old Hugh loaded his horse pistol again.

Some four miles farther on, riding up out of Glad

Valley and about to descend one of the forks of Black Horse Creek, with Thunder Butte and its long evening shadow on their left and behind them, they got their chance to make meat.

Fitz spotted them first—tanbrown movement across the fork. He held up his hand and all three hauled up short on their ponies.

"Where?" Hugh asked.

Fitz pointed.

About a mile away, in a wide low meadow of green sweetgrass, was a herd of buffalo. Light tan cows and red calves, nose down, grazed along peacefully in the center of the herd. Heavy, bulky, tanbrown bulls formed the outer rim, and one or another of them between bites kept looking up. From where the men sat, the buffaloes had the look of critters with an extra robe thrown across the shoulder.

"Buffler! And seal fat too," Hugh said softly. "About a thousand of 'em."

The boy Jim was cautious this time. "Them white varmints movin' around outside them, they ain't decoy wolves, red devils again?"

Hugh studied a moment. "No. Them's just white wolf waitin' around for stray calf or downed old bull."

"Ye sure now?"

"See them cow swallows flittin' around overhead? That's sure sign there's no red niggers about."

From underneath his wolfskin cap, Hugh studied the herd some more. Old Blue breathed evenly between his legs. "Lads, this is gonna be as slick as peeled onions. We'll ride down through that draw on the left there and come up through them plum bushes and be close enough to pull a hair out of their ear before they know we're around. And mind, no bulls. Nothin' but young fat cow now."

All three made preparations. They popped a handful of lead balls into their mouths, pulled powder horn around handy in front, jammed horse pistols in belts for easy grabbing; and then, flintlock rifle checked, set out, trotting along easily against the soft west wind and through the draw off to the left.

The moment they emerged from the plum bushes, Hugh shouted, "Hep-ah, lads! At'em and may we all make centershots!"

Old Blue had hunted buffalo before. The Sioux had trained him right. With little or no guiding, Old Blue broke through the ring of shaggy tanbrown and brownblack bulls and was into the center of the herd before the cows and calves knew what was up. Old Blue sidled up alongside a startled cow. She lifted up black nose and black eyes with a snort; then dug her hooves in and began to heave her bulk away from Hugh and his horse. Her shaggy brown hump bounded just under Hugh's right elbow. Hugh aimed for a spot just behind the left foreleg, directly over the heart, where the fur was worn off a little by the action of the leg. He fired. The sound of the shot was almost lost in the sudden great uproar of pounding hooves and bellowing monsters all around. The cow bucked up; ran on a few steps; vomited a deep red spurt of blood; and crashed heavily to the ground.

The entire thousand went into motion. Yellow dust burst up; became a pale gray ascending cloud. Red calves bawled; tan cows lowed; tanbrown bulls bellowed.

Through the sudden explosion of dust, Hugh spotted another likely fat young cow. Even as he thought of it, Old Blue seemed to read his mind and headed for her. In full gallop Old Hugh grabbed his flintlock by the barrel end, poured in a charge of powder from the horn, with a quick puert of lips popped a wet ball into the powder-acrid barrel hole, rammed the ball home by hitting the gunstock on the saddle, leveled and fired before the ball could roll out again—and dropped the second cow. Vaguely he heard the other boys firing too, dull little pops against the louder uproar of thundering hooves and bawling calves and bellowing bulls and hoarse, desperate running-animal grunting.

Firing on the run and loading on the run, on the dead gallop, with Old Blue quickly shying away after each shot, Hugh chased through the stampeding herd of brown monsters. The little arteries down Hugh's big Scotch nose wriggled red.

Hugh forgot himself, forgot he had a game leg, forgot he'd ever loved, forgot he'd ever killed Rees or any other kind of red devil, forgot he'd ever been a buccaneer killing Spanish merchantmen, forgot he was the papa of two boys back in Lancaster, forgot he'd ever deserted the boys because of their rip of a mother, forgot all, forgot he was Hugh even, forgot both Old Hugh and Young Hugh, was lost in the glorious roaring chase, killing killing killing—all of it a glorious bloodletting and a complete forgetting.

The thousand monsters moved out of the green sweetgrass meadow en masse, climbed up a slope toward dry, hard, stonestudded ground. Yellow dust continued to stive up everywhere, choking the nose and mouth, blinding the eye. Old Blue coughed, almost tossing Hugh out of the saddle. Hugh coughed, until he thought his lungs would come up. It was all a misty yellow sea moving uphill, moving incredibly swift. The rippling humping buffalo backs scudded past like clots of brown seadrift.

It wasn't long before Old Blue had chased through the entire thousand and got in among some young bulls. Here it became rough going. The young bulls ran side by side, tight, great woolly shoulders bounding and bruising together, their little ridiculous catlike tails whipping and circling and switching spasmodically. Hugh had to shoot his way out. The first bull Hugh hit made a lunge for Old Blue and the horse was hard put to it to avoid the black hooking horns. But at last Hugh made it and he pulled out to one side and on a little rise hauled Old Blue up short.

Meantime Fitz had a run of good shooting too, and got through the herd, and wound up on the other side of it.

But Jim, like Hugh, losing himself in the roaring sport of it, and having fine luck on his shots, once again got reckless. When it came time to break off, he made the mistake of cutting across the path of the last of the herd rather than easing out of it, and, despite the marvelous agility of his sorrel mare Maggie, had an old bull catch her, hooking a black horn into Maggie's belly just ahead of her back legs, deep into her milk bag, heaving her up and tossing Jim off into the air.

Jim hit the earth with a thud; rolled over on his belly; lay still while the last of the herd thundered over and past him.

Maggie screamed. In the wink of an eye her bowels boiled out of her gored belly, writhing out of her like mad pink snakes. One loop of her intestines hung down to the ground and on her third bound away from the old bull one of her rear hooves caught in it. Still screaming, she began to gallop off, with every bound tearing out her guts little by little, slowly unraveling herself. She ran until there was no more, her bowels dragging behind her like coils of fat hawser rope, and then she made one last leap for the moon, and dropped. Dead.

The buffalo herd thundered away, over the hill, down another valley, and then over another ridge, out of sight and sound both.

In the silence that followed, dust settling all around, Hugh looked across at Fitz and Fitz at Hugh. Then both looked at the prostrate form of companyero Jim and at his fallen cap and at the gutted unraveled mare.

Hugh moved first. He was off his pony in a quick twist and limped over to Jim and squatted beside him. "Ye all right, lad?" Hugh asked anxiously, cupping Jim's blunt blond face in his square hands, stroking back Jim's auburn hair.

Jim awoke, his blue eyes exactly the color of the sky above. Jim sat up slowly. He looked at Hugh, then at Fitz, then at the fallen buffalo. "Whaugh! Look at them dead buffler on the ground. Like bees after a beein'."

Hugh laughed. He looked at Fitz. "I reckon the lad's all right at that."

Fitz smiled too, his face lighting up stunningly for a moment.

"Where's Maggie?" Jim said next. He looked around. And then saw her, lying on her side some ways off. Jim paled. His breath came out in a slow expiring "Ohhh."

Hugh helped Jim to his feet. "Lad, goin' against the tide never was good sailin'."

Jim picked up his fallen fur cap; clapped the dust out of it against his leg; pigeon-toed over to where Maggie lay. He looked down at her ruptured sorrel belly; at her dirtied pink bowels; at the gathering cloud of green bottleflies.

Jim said finally, "There's no fixin' her, is there?"

Hugh said, "No. Though I've seen some stitched up again with buckskin whangs."

"Did they live?"

"As good as new."

Jim stood looking down at Maggie with sad grayblue eyes.

Hugh said, "Jim, lad, come now. 'Tis no time for funeral orations this late in the day. We've got cow down. So we'd best hurry." Hugh looked back to where a pack of dun-colored coyote and white wolves were fighting over the carcass of the very first cow he'd dropped. "Some of them sneak varmints are already helpin' themselves to the best meat."

They tied Ol' Blue and Fitz's Pepper to a nearby bush. Both horses were uneasy. They snorted at the smell of salty blood in the air; snorted at the whizzing biting noseflies.

Working swiftly, knives alternately flashing and dripping blood, Hugh and the boys skinned and butchered the cows right where they fell, on their bellies, four legs spread out to keep them upright. The cows were some five feet in height at the hump, some ten feet long from nose to tailtip. Hugh made a transverse slit across the nape of the neck and sliced off the bristly boss and laid it to one side. The boss was of the size of a man's head and it rose out of the neck just to the rear of the shoulder. Then Hugh made a cut in the bristly hide along the top of the backbone, starting at the boss and running over the hump and then down to the back to the tail. The boys, one on each side, pulled the hide outward and downward until it lay out on the grass to either side of the naked pink carcass. They cut away only the choice parts of the animal: the fleece or thin flesh covering the ribs, the broad back-fat extending from the shoulders to the tail, the belly fleece, the side ribs, the thigh marrowbones, the tongue, the tenderloin, and the hump ribs. To get the hump ribs, Hugh and the boys made a mallet out of the lower joint of one of the forelegs and broke them out using a skinning knife as a chisel. Hugh also opened the belly and cut out the boudins, the rich, smelly small intestines tight with green chyme.

The smell of blood and flesh made Hugh so hungry he couldn't resist cutting himself a nibble of liver. He salted it with a touch of gall and tossed it down.

"I see ye're throwin' it cold," Jim said, also helping himself to some of the liver. "Though I favor it with salt." Jim pricked the cow's bladder and let a sprinkle of urine whistle over his bit of liver.

"Yessiree," Hugh said, between chews on the spongy flesh. "Meat's meat, browned or not." Hugh brandished his knife. "Whaugh! Now that I've had some buffler meat, I feel a heap better and ready for huggin'."

Turkey buzzards began circling overhead. Sometimes one or another of the wolves, sitting on its haunches in a circle around the men just out of rifleshot, sometimes one of the wolves would get up and run about, whining, whisking his brush around in a fierce nervous manner. Occasionally a coyote got in the way of a nervous wolf and the wolf would snap ferociously at him, clicking his teeth.

The three men finished carving up the fallen cows just as the sun set on the far undulating horizon. The valley was suddenly levelful of shadows.

At about the same time, the rest of Major Henry's party appeared over the east hills.

Hugh wigwagged for help. And presently two men came galloping toward them with four pack horses. The two men and the boys loaded the choice meat onto the horses, left the remainder of the red ruins, by far the greater part of the animal—the hams, the shoulders, the side ribs, the head—to the wolves and the coyotes and the buzzards.

That night the mountain men made camp in a patch of deep sweetgrass near Big Meadow Creek.

Hugh and Jim and Fitz were assigned the detail of unloading the pack horses and unsaddling the riding ponies.

The moment the tamed mustangs were free of their burdens, they ran for the sand along the creek and rolled in it, snorting, four legs up playfully like big dogs gamboling, over on one side and then over on the other, sometimes balancing delicately on curved sharp backbone, deliciously grinding wet shoulder, then arched back, then volving rump into the rough, though giving, creamy sand. They whinnied in sheer delight. At last, rubbed until every nerve end had had its gratification, they rose to their feet, first up on their forelegs, then on rear legs, and shook themselves like dogs after a soaking, sand flying in all directions like drops of water. Then they ran for water in the creek and began sipping.

It was a fine herd of ponies, Hugh saw. All the colors of a hunter's kennel of hounds were there: milkwhite, jetblack, sorrel, bay, cream, piebald, irongray, strawberry-roan, bluegray, chestnut, dapplegray. Despite the wear and tear of the long four-day grind from Ft. Kiowa, the ponies still looked fresh. They were all clean-boned, strong, fast, long-winded. Most were about fourteen hands high, light in build, with good legs and strong short back, full barrel, sharp nervous ears, and bright popped eyes.

When the horses finished their drinking, Hugh and the boys hobbled and staked them, allowing each enough of the sweetgrass for a good fill.

"Tonight, before we turn in, we'll snug 'em up closer and set horse guard," Hugh said. "There's always coyote about ready to snaw your rawhide lariat when you ain't lookin'." Hugh waggled his old head sagely. "It's easier to count horse ribs than horse tracks."

Horses secured, the three hurried back to the campfire. Except for a bite of liver, they'd had nothing to eat but hard biscuit with sowbelly since early morning, and they were blowy with hunger. The thought of freshly roasted red buffalo-cow meat made them ravenous.

The spot Major Henry picked for camp was in an open glade circled by slim willows and small cottonwoods. The stream in the sandy creek was clear, though thin, and in places it trickled cheerfully over pink and brown stones.

Pierre the cook and Yount and Allen built a huge single bonfire on a patch of sand near the creek. Soft green sweetgrass circled it on all sides. The hot fire with its roostercomb flames deepened the bronze hue of the mountain men's weathered leather faces, lightened the green in the ticking cottonwood leaves above.

To the south, behind them, the nipped teat of Thunder Butte stuck up just visible over a ride of bluffs, while ahead and below lay the open-shelved valley of the Grand River. To the west, in the glowing rosebrown of after sunset, a new range of blunt bluffs loomed up brownblack and foreboding. And to the east, the coyotes and the wolves, still wrangling with each other around the bony ruins of buffalo carcasses, looked like gray and white mice gamboling around reed hampers of cheese.

Green twilight swooped down from the slumped shoulders of the hills in the east; then came rusty dusk; and then the deep purple-dark of night with crisp sparkling stars.

Jack rabbits as big as dogs presently came out of hiding and made a circle around the fire some hundred feet back, sitting on their haunches, flicking their mule ears back and forth as if trying desperately to eavesdrop on the talk of the mountain men. Mosquitoes stayed discreetly away from the roaring fire, though the horses under the trees suffered.

Piles of meat, fleece, tongue, ribs, boudins lay on blood-streaked buffalo skins. Late evening flies and a few whispering mosquitoes buzzed over the red flesh.

Jim and Fitz, and wiry brown-eyed Augie Neill and slim slow Jim Anderson, sat on one side of the fire. Across from them sat scalped houndfaced Silas Hammond. Others around the circle included proud Yount and gaunt Allen and Major Henry.

Major Henry looked tired. He had doffed his blue cap and with heavy sighs was making some entries in a gray ledger. Every now and then his eyes swept the circle of men around the crackling blazing fire, then reached out into the darkness where the ponies stamped and flailed at mosquitoes. He had the half-listening half-waiting air of a man who expected castastrophe to come pouncing on him out of the circumambient dark—and who was inwardly steeled and set for it.

Swarthy Pierre the Frenchy cook officiated at the mess. He was dressed in a long leather butcher's apron, a leather Turk's cap, heavy leather boots. He wielded an assortment of knives and forks and kettles and bottles of condiment.

Laughing, smiling, joking, Pierre worked swiftly. First he cut short pointed stakes of green willow wood, then cut alternate steaks of meat and slabs of fine fleece and jammed them onto the pointed stakes, next leaned them sizzling over the fire.

Meantime Hugh officiated at the singeing of the boudins or the intestines. Hugh emptied out the chyme—half-digested lumps of greenish-black grass—and turned them inside out and tied the ends off to keep the fat from running out. He let them sizzle in the hot red coals until they puffed up with heat, until they began to spit crackling fat. The crackling fat dripped into the fire and raised little spuming blue flames.

The buckskin boys crowded against Hugh. They sat silent, piercing eyes intent on his turning of the boudins, one or another of them occasionally licking his lips, skinning knife wiped clean on a sleeve and ready.

The smell of roasting flesh soon drew the coyotes and wolves toward the fire, scattering the jack rabbits. One of the coyotes howled like a boy with a broken leg.

With a long green willow stick Hugh continued to turn the boudins.

Presently steam began to escape from little pouches. The pink boudins began to brown, then to coil above the red coals.

"Now!" Hugh yelled, and with his long stick he lifted them away from the fire. They hung above the gaping men like browned pink snakes. The men made wild beastlike grabs for them, each slicing off yard-long sections. The men gulped them down like children swallowing strings of hot sweet taffy.

For the fun of it, Augie Neill and Jim Anderson cut off a section a dozen feet long and had themselves a race. Each grabbed a puff end and began swallowing rapidly, sometimes in their haste poking it down with a prising finger. They swallowed; they choked back laughs; they swallowed so mightily their eyes sometimes closed. Once, Augie, with a prodigious swallow, made a gain of more than a foot on Jim Anderson—only to have Jim Anderson rear back with a choked snort and jerk more than a yard out of Augie's gullet. The mountain men roared; slapped their thighs in wild laughter.

Boudins down, it was time for the next course. Pierre the cook ladled out a spiced soup made of blood and marrow and prairie onions. The men sat on the ground around the roaring pluming fire, crosslegged, and each held up his tin cup. Filled, each man took out his little private pouch of salt and pepper, sprinkled in to his taste, and slupped at the soup with eye-rolling delight.

Next came the main dishes.

The moment the alternate steaks and slabs of fleece were lusciously browned, Pierre reached into the fire with his huge iron fork and hauled them out. He gave each man a pair, slab over steak. The men gorged, chewing with fatty smacking sounds. Grease trickled down both sides of their chins, fell onto their buckskin shirt fronts.

Pierre had also impaled tenderloin on the sharp-pointed green willow sticks near the fire, and when they were done he lifted them out of the flames and jabbed them into the ground, two men to a hunk. Knives flashed as each man began cutting himself bits according to his appetite.

Next Pierre took the great kettle off its hook over the fire and found a clean place in the grass and dumped the contents out; hunks of hump ribs, tongue, bits of liver. Again the men dug in like hungry hounds.

A few of the men, fancying they needed something like bread and butter, cut themselves slices from their store of pemmican and smeared it with marrow, the trapper's butter.

Gradually the men mellowed. First there were groans of ecstasy, then grunts of pleasure, then fine eloquent social belches, and at last a few remarks.

Scalped Silas said, "Well, Pierre, now that we've had the bait, how about servin' the main part of the meal."

The boy Jim Bridger said, "Here's some more liver for ee, Hugh. Good for your beard, I hear."

Hugh laughed from behind a hump rib. "Dip in yourself, lad. It's yours which needs the manure, not mine."

Sly brown-eyed Augie said, "And I once thought pork prime eatin'. After this I'll always know it's against nature to feed on chops."

Gaunt Allen said, "Lads, I tell ye, painter meat can't shine with this."

Slim slow Jim Anderson said, "Best durn grub I ever stuffed down my meatbag."

Scalped Silas shook his mournful hound's face. "Darn this way of livin'. A feller starves all day like a mean coyote. And then at night, when he does chaw, he stuffs himself fuller'n a snake crammed with rabbit. And ain't of any account for hours after. Like a tick full a blood."

Hugh noticed his companyero Fitz hadn't said much. "Ho-ah, Fitz, bright up a little. Forget what them books ha' told ee. It ain't as bad as all that."

Fitz managed to give Hugh a slow smile. He was gnawing his way into a lump of juicy well-done fleece. Grease ran down both sides of his chin.

Hugh laughed. "Yep, when a mountain man has plenty to eat, then he's a mite cheerful. But let him starve a little—whaugh! an old grizzly is better company."

Pierre came up with some more steaming sizzling well-done hump-ribs. "Back up your cart, boys, here's another load. Bridger, my boy, come on. You ain't full growed yet and you need all you can get to catch up."

Tears of gustatory animal joy came to Hugh's eyes; streamed into his greasy gray beard. "Boys, can you beat this? And I once thought of goin' back to mush and molasses in Lancaster."

Major Henry, who had pitched into the meat with both hands, looked up at this point. "Lancaster, Hugh? Is that where you're from?"

Hugh swallowed and nodded shortly. He had made

a slip. He looked down at his half-gnawed hump-rib.
"I stayed there awhile onct."

"Who had the mush and molasses there, Hugh?"

"Nobody," Hugh snapped.

Major Henry cleaned his lips with the back of his
hand. He smiled thinly, upper teeth gleaming white in
the firelight. After a moment he nodded; gave up.

Between courses the mountain men licked their fingers and wiped their knives clean on their buckskin shirt
sleeves. Soon all the buckskin shirts were stained dark
with grease and blood.

The shirts smelled of campfire smoke and burnt
wood. Body heat and fire heat stirred up odors of other
times too—the scent of lovemaking with musky Ree
maidens, fired gunpowder, Kentucky whisky.

Soon the coffee began to boil in a pot on the cookstone. Pierre served it, the men holding out their tin
cups in turn.

For dessert, and as a special treat for good time made
so far on the trip, Major Henry ordered Pierre the cook
to break into the company's store of raisins and choco-
late drops. Old Hugh for one savored the sweets like a
grizzly delicately munching a handful of tasty red and
black ants. The treat topped off the day complete.

Finished with the feast at last, the men jabbed their
knives in the sand and wiped them on their buckskin
clothes for the last time and then got out their pipes.
They filled up with sweet honeydew tobacco from Vir-
ginia and lit up with brands from the log fire.

Each man fancied a favorite pipe. Major Henry fon-
dled a brier with slender stem and a fine bowl. Quiet
Fitz worked on a clay pipe with a stubby stem and blunt
bowl. Proud Yount fingered a brier with a long slender
stem and thimble-sized bowl. The boy Jim showed off
a novelty pipe, a huge walnut affair with paired heavy
blunt bowls the size of goat ballocks and a long rapi-
erlike stem. Houndfaced Silas Hammond fancied a du-
deen carved from hard maple—it resembled a twig with

a cluster of berries at the end. Old Hugh fancied an old ceremonial pipe he got from Bending Reed's brother—a bowl of pinkred pipestone cut to resemble a tomahawk, with a willow stem from which dangled beads and amulets and other Sioux medicine ornaments.

They sat crosslegged around the jumping flames. Some leaned back, some leaned forward. Pipe either spuming or quiet, some listened with stoic Indian gravity and some with comical gravity to the yarning and to the rambling talk. A stranger happening on them would have had to look twice, and that close, to make sure the buckskinned longhaired men around the fire were not Indians but white men.

Behind them two coyotes yowled at the skies, each in turn, howled long and loud and lonesome. In the vague light from the fire the scattered jack rabbits eddied and played over the plains.

Somehow the talk got around to the lord of the American wild, the lonely grizzly bear. A single grizzly inspired more respect in the tough weathered mountain men than did a couple of savage Rees.

Grizzlies were unpredictable. One day a grizzly might amble away from a man with an indifferent air; the next day he might suddenly attack with a rushing roar.

Gaunt Allen said, "It all depends on how hungry Old Ephraim is."

"No," Hugh said, removing pipe from mouth and looking reflectively at the jumping flames, "no, not how hungry. Old Ephraim won't eat humans. No, it's more that he's curiouser than a cat. He just naturally wants to see what you're up to. I mind me of the time when I was with the Pawnees and the Pawnees off into the Rockies for buffler meat. One Old Ephe follered me a whole day trying to cipher a white streak of clay I had on one of me leggin's. I finally had to take the dag leggin' off and hang it on a twig and let him smell it over. Then when he had it ciphered, he ran off."

"Then ye say Old Ephe warn't after your meat?"

97

"Not this old bull."

"I bet you shivered," the boy Jim Bridger said.

"Some. Though more from the chill in my game leg than from the bear. Course I admit that a grizzly love tap is about the same as a death blow. So I was careful." Hugh smoked in silence for a moment. "No, it's the ma grizzly with cubs you want to watch out for. When you see her, watch lively and mind your topknot. Whaugh! She's doom, she is, especially when her cubs ain't bigger'n little pig puppies."

Gaunt Allen said, "I still say around a grizzly it's best to shoot on sight and ask questions after. I mind me of the time when I was settin' beaver trap up a branch off the Big Sioux a couple year ago. Now that's one place you'd never expect a grizzly, let alone any kind of bear. But there was one. And was I surprised when he jumped me sudden from the rear. I hadn't seen hide nor hair of him. There he was sudden, on top a me. He fetched me a swipe and tore my pants clean off my behind. Bare as a monkey's behind, I was. I jumped for deep water fast, I can tell you. Soaked my primin', so I couldn't shoot. And there I sot, cold behind in colder water, waitin' for him to make up his mind if the water was too cold for him. And him wearin' his own fur too, and me with only my few hair. No siree, I say, shoot on sight and ask questions after. They ain't givin' you no chance either."

Hugh said, "What about the time when Reed—that's my wife—when Reed and me was playin' and swimmin' in the Platte near Chimney Rock. A grizzly peeked at us for a while from behind a rock, then all t'once jumped up and barked at us, whaugh! whaugh! scarin' the daylights out a me and Reed both, and then ran off laughin' to hisself. No, I tell you, most times they mind their own business. It's only when they get curiouser than a cat that they bother ee, and then they only want to look over your shoulder to see what you're up to." Hugh gave Allen a look of scorn. "Besides, shootin' on sight ain't always the best either. An old she-grizzly took after me once on the Niobrara, and I swear she follered me a mile after I put a ball plump center in her heart."

"Ye mean to hang your face out and tell me she had a ball in her heart and she still ran after ye a mile?" Gaunt Allen demanded. Red light from the fire made the hollows under his eyes look like small paired bowls.

"I do. We butchered her afters and found the ball bouncin' around in her heart. No, old hoss, I tell ee, you don't want to shoot at a ma grizzly unless ye hafta. They're about the toughest critter on two legs God ever invented."

Proud Yount offered a comment. "The best yet is to lay down and play dead. A man layin' down is medicine to Old Ephe. Not even the most ornery ma grizzly will tackle you then."

The red coals in the fire settled. Green twig ends in the graying red coals squealed like anguished crickets.

Cold air came down in slow fleeting puffs. Stars sparkled brilliantly overhead. Mosquitoes thickened and dared to come farther into the light of the fire. Some of the mosquitoes began to sting, and soon the men were making sudden lunging slaps at various parts of their body.

The men sat, gravely considering what had been said. Each man had his particular gesture and pose: the boy Jim Bridger with his floppy blunt-ended motion of hands when he slapped at a mosquito, his pigeon-toed feet crossed at the ankles; downer Fitz all hunched up as if about to spring, toes out; Silas Hammond squatting as sad as a kicked hound, ears holding up his face; Pierre the cook flourishing feminine finger tips when he slapped at a mosquito, smiling at anything said; slim Jim Anderson slowly drawing on his pipe and blowing smoke at mosquitoes; Yount sitting high on his haunches, broad nose high; Old Hugh occasionally waving stub-ended ham hands at mosquitoes, gray eye alternately haunting and happy; and watching, listening Major Henry scratching his dark hair, and occasionally in nervous habit, baring his teeth.

Major Henry's blue eyes narrowed in an indulgent twinkle. "Allen, next time you go beaver trapping, maybe you should put out a present for the grizzly. Maybe then he'll leave you alone."

There was an instant silence around the popping fire. All eyes fastened on Major Henry. A coyote yowled behind them.

Hollow-cheeked Allen started. "A 'present'?"

"Yes. It seems to work for the Indians. Hugh here ain't the only one who has a good word for the grizzly."

Hugh sat up slowly, old back cracking. What was this? It wasn't often that Major Henry took his part.

Gaunt Allen tried to laugh it off with a flash of blue eyes and a shrug. "I'll bite. Why should I give a low critter like a grizzly a present? Afore I shoot him?"

Major Henry clapped out his pipe on a kneecap. He refilled it slowly. His blue eyes lighted up orange as he held a brand from the fire to the bowl of his pipe.

Behind them the ponies snorted at mosquitoes; flailed whistling tails; stomped in the giving sand.

Major Henry said, " 'Low critter,' Allen? I know some Indians in the mountains who wouldn't agree with you. They think the grizzly some sort of god. One tribe I have in mind, when they need food in the winter, go hunt out the bear and bring him the best food they have left, and bow to him, and ask him to forgive them for what they are about to do, saying they know he is their friend, saying they know he wants to live up to his name as the giver of life, saying they know he wants to die for them." Major Henry puffed slowly on his pipe. His lips moved on the pipestem, thinned back to show flashing white teeth for a moment. He looked down at his free hand on his bent knees. "It almost reminds me, it does, of the way the white man, the civilized man, has treated his Lord and Master, Jesus

Christ. Civilized man had to kill him too, crucify him even, before he could become their giver of life."

Eyes fell as they always did when talk took a religious turn.

"No, we haven't advanced much on the 'red devils' as you lads call them. Fact is, one could almost claim we've slipped a little, fallen behind the red devils. The red devils sacrificed animals to live; we sacrificed humans."

This was a little too much for Old Hugh. "Major, maybe we palefaces can't shine with the red devil, like you say. Just the same this old hoss has feelin's here"— Old Hugh slapped his chest—"has feelin's here for poor human nature in any fix, while the red nigger don't care a cuss for it. They torture. They skulp a man while alive. They cut him while alive. Make a cattail out of him and set fire to him. I know. I seed it once on the Platte. They stuck my friend Clint full a pine slivers and burnt him to a crisp. That was horrible onhuman." Old Hugh shuddered. Others near him shuddered too. "This coon has made Indians go under, some, yes. But he's never skulped 'em alive. Even though he knows that scalps comes off easier warm." Hugh pointed to some hair lint, black and stringy, which Bending Reed had proudly sown into the seams of his leggings. "Every one of these scalps here came off the knob after I made sure the brains inside was dead. This old hoss says again its onhuman and agin nature what they do, and they ought to shake."

Major Henry's lips thinned and his teeth gleamed in the red firelight. He scratched his dark hair some more, vigorously. "Perhaps you're right, Hugh, perhaps you're right."

Hugh couldn't let it drop. "I say it's with the red niggers like with kids. Or like with water. If you let 'em know you're lower than they are, they'll run all over you."

There were grunts of assent around the falling fire.

Still scratching his hair, Major Henry said, "I don't know what makes it. Every night just as I get ready to turn in, my head itches like all get-out. Nerves, I guess." Major Henry's sharp eye fell on Hugh's grizzly beard. He looked at it awhile as his face hardened. Finally he said, "Hugh, I see you still haven't shaved clean yet. Like I ordered. You know that around Indians you're a marked man with that beard. They take it as an insult. And we've got enough hard doings around 'em as it is."

Another silence. All eyes flicked from Hugh to the major and back to Hugh again.

"Hugh?"

"I heered ye, Major."

"Well?"

"Don't crowd me and I'll think on it some."

"Mind that you do now. You hear? Before we move out in the morning."

Proud Yount had a question. "Major, what I still don't get is why them Rees blocked our way up the Missouri. They let us through last year."

Major Henry thought a moment. He clapped out his pipe on his kneecap a second time and put it away in his possible sack. "They said because they lost a pair of braves at Fort Kiowa. But that was just an excuse. The real reason was to keep us from trading guns and powder higher up the river to the Mandans and the Minnetarees. And the murderous Blackfeet. They want to keep the trade to themselves. That way they can keep the best rifles and powder for themselves and give the poorer stuff to their enemies. Besides making the tribe rich with the stuff they trade the ammunition for." Major Henry took off his moccasins slowly, one at a time. He wriggled his bare toes. There were streaks of black sweat between the toes. "And you really can't blame them. If they don't take care of themselves, nobody else will. Surely not the Sioux. Nor the Mandans." Major Henry speared Yount with a grayblue look. "Besides, what do you suppose we're up here for, the sights?"

Hugh said, "Feed the grizzly afore they crucify him or no, I still say some are onhuman varmints and need to be taught a lesson. Red devils."

Major Henry stood up. He stretched to his full height; yawned. "Time to turn in, boys. Pierre, put out the fire. Fitz, you and Jim Bridger lead the horses into the trees and snub them up close. Hugh, you and Yount start the watch for the night. The rest of you men take your blankets back in the trees and sleep there. Or you'll be centershots for our friends. In Indian country, supper in one place and sleep in another has always been my rule."

Without a word more, the men turned in. Each nuzzled into his favorite slumbering pose.

Gradually the fire died out. Gradually the men dropped off to sleep.

The ponies flailed whistling tails at mosquitoes; stomped in the giving sand.

Every so often Major Henry called out in a sleepy voice from where he lay, "All's well?" Sometimes he called out automatically in his sleep.

"All's well," Hugh or Yount would call back.

Stars gyrated by overhead. The soft west wind fell off. Occasionally a coyote yowled out an ancient lonesome cry.

Chapter 5

It was pitchblack dark out. A low overcast sky blotted out all the stars. Dawn was near but there wasn't a sign of it on any horizon. Mosquitoes were getting in their last bites before daylight, and the ponies flailed and stamped at them.

Major Henry and his men lay sleeping under the trees, each under a robe and each with a saddle for a pillow. Even the guards, the boy Jim Bridger and quiet Fitz, slept. Jim had slipped to his side and lay curled up against the cold, fetuslike, pigeon-toed feet crossed at the arches like flippers. Fitz also lay hunkered up against the cold, toes hooked out a little. Nearby, Old Hugh slept like a man, all stretched out, flat on his back, snoring out of a varying orifice in his gray beard. Deeper under the trees, Augie Neill and Jim Anderson, also Yount and Allen and the others, lay snoring peacefully, all well-covered by blankets.

Old Hugh came up out of inner darkness gently. Dreaming in darkness shaded off into seeing in darkness. It took him a full minute to make sure he really did have his eyes open.

He lay waking slowly. He could feel the soft giving of the fur under his back, could feel the weight of the woolen blanket on him. He wondered where the stars had gone. He heard the tussing hooves of the ponies deep under the trees, the occasional crack of a twig underfoot, the swift swishing tails. He heard the trickling of the creek water over stones.

An aftertaste of buffalo flesh under his tongue recalled him to where they were—on Big Meadow Creek, according to Major Henry's map, a spot overlooking the Grand River valley to the north. Old Hugh remembered the fallen buffaloes on the ground, lying around like bees after a beeing, as the boy Jim had said. Hugh next remembered Maggie, Jim's horse, unraveling her guts, then his own raring ride shooting down buffalo cow on every side. He remembered Jim's wild ride toward four buffaloes who turned out to be a party of Rees on the warpath.

And thinking of the Rees, Old Hugh lifted his head off his saddle, lifted it in part instinctively and in part because he was sure he had heard something sliding past him on the ground. Who could be sneaking around through camp at this hour of the night except a red devil? Where was the guard? Knifed?

Hugh felt for his flintlock Old Bullthrower; found it; carefully drew back the flint. He turned his head slowly in the direction of the slithering sound. He tried to find a silhouette against a horizon. Where in God's name were the boy Jim and downer Fitz? He and Yount had turned the watch over to them at midnight.

Maybe the boys had fallen asleep at their posts. If they had, it was going to be tough titty for them the rest of the day. Major Henry had an inflexible rule for those who slept on guard—walk all day, cactus or ants or rattlesnakes or no. And carry their own packs too.

He heard the slithering sound again, this time nearer the ponies.

Hugh rolled over slowly. His game leg ached. Other mornings he always had to warm it up awhile before he dared trust his weight on it. This time he'd have to skip it. Suppressing a groan at a twinge of pain that shot through it, carrying his rifle, he slid to where Jim and Fitz lay. He found them asleep.

Hugh shook Jim, then Fitz. He whuskered close in Jim's ear. "Lad, I hope ye're pretendin' sleep."

"Wha?" Jim said, sitting up.

"Shhh. Down, lad. Red devils around. I hope ye was pretendin' sleep. And Fitz, up, lad. Easy does it. Shhh."

Both Jim and Fitz caught up their rifles and rolled over on their bellies ready for action.

In the deep dark Hugh whispered softly again. "Ye were pretendin' sleep, weren't ye, lads?"

Neither Jim nor Fitz said anything. It was too dark for Hugh to see their faces, but from the way they moved in the dark he could tell they felt sheepish.

Hugh whispered. "I think I heard a couple of red devils crawl past, goin' for the ponies. So we'll probably have a yellin' party along in a minute to stampede the horses. Wake up the major and the men while I go back and see about the ponies."

Fitz and Jim slid from man to man; put a hand on the mouth to keep the man from crying out until he was fully awake; got the whole camp on the alert.

Hugh meantime bellied up quickly toward the ponies; got to within a half-dozen yards of them when he bumped his nose into a moccasin. The moccasin jerked away as if its owner didn't appreciate being tickled in the foot. The sole of the moccasin didn't smell white, so Hugh cautiously laid aside his rifle and drew his skinning knife. He coiled up; struck. The knife bit bone; slid off into giving flesh; sank in up to the haft. There was a cry, and a soft gush of blood as Hugh withdrew his knife.

At the cry, another form jerked up near Hugh. Hugh could just make it out against an awakening east. Hugh coiled; struck again. This time he missed. In the twink of an eye the two were wrestling on the ground like bullsnake entangled with rattler. The other stunk of acrid sweat; was naked save for breechcloth; was slippery and hard to hold. Indian all right. Quick, too. Hugh felt the point of the other's knife prick him in the back. Hugh bent away like a spring; lashed around; got his own knife arm free; struck; sank the knife home again, this time in the back, into the kidney. The Indian gave a loud cry. "Ahhh!"

At the cry every man in camp got himself behind a tree. A single rifle popped.

The delayed dawn came up fast. The cloud deck kept it gray and lowering.

Before Hugh could cry out that the horses were safe, warwhoops sounded from all sides, howgh-owgh-owgh-owgh-h! Some redskins on foot popped out of the willows across the stream; let fly a sleet of arrows, a hail of balls; quickly slipped behind trees again. Other horses suddenly thundered across the open prairie. In the rising light Hugh could make out some forty mounted Indians, faces painted red, honorable wounds on arms and legs and body painted with stripes of white and vermilion. The mounted Indians came yowling toward the mountain men's tethered ponies, cupped hand flopping over open howling mouth, ohohohohoh! Balls whizzed and plunked into trees. Arrows sailed and whacked into the grass. The mountain men, well hidden behind trees, returned fire methodically and carefully, taking good aim. They poured powder calmly, patched the ball as if at target practice, rammed the ball home as if they had all the time in the world. In through the trees the Indians rode toward them, with bodies cleverly hidden behind the horses, a heel caught on the spine and an arm hooked in a loop of hair braided into the mane. They shot from under the horses' necks.

A few of the more daring pennyskinned braves dashed pellmell into the grove, into the midst of the mountain men's tethered ponies. They fluttered colored blankets; howled horribly; waved spears; shot off rifles in the air. But with Hugh in their midst to calm them, the mountain men's horses held. Some jerked tight against close-snubbed halters; some reared and whinnied; some rolled wild eyeballs. But all held.

Balked, the mounted braves abruptly veered and disappeared down the valley toward the Grand River.

The redskins on foot vanished too, disappearing mysteriously like overnight mushrooms.

Gray dawn came up fast.

One by one the mountain men came out from behind hiding places in the willow and cottonwood brush.

"Ye all right, Hugh?" Jim called.

"Right as can be," Hugh said.

Hugh stood looking down at one of the dead Indians he'd knifed in the dark. He rolled the brave over with his foot.

Major Henry came up.

"Mandan," Hugh said, prodding the brave with his moccasined toe. "I'd know them mudhook leathers anywhere."

"Mandan?" Major Henry exclaimed. "If the Mandans've finally taken to the warpath against us then we're in for real trouble. They've never jumped the whites before."

"And all because of that dummed cowardly Leavenworth and his love-the-redskin sermons," Hugh growled. "Letting them Rees off easy last June. The whole Missouri's been a butcher shop ever since. Darn his sanctimonious hide."

Someone called behind them. "Major, come here a minute." It was Fitz. He and the rest of the party stood crowded around two forms on the ground, right where the men had slept that night.

Hugh and Major Henry stepped over.

"What is it?" Major Henry asked.

Fitz said matter-of-factly, "It's Augie Neill and Jim Anderson. Dead."

Hugh saw it the same time the major did. Each lad had a bloody rent in the buckskin shirt, just over the heart. They'd been stabbed in the night.

For a second Old Hugh wondered. And shivered. Had he done it? He'd stabbed two in the dark. He looked back over his shoulder to make sure there were two dead Mandans still on the ground near the ponies under the trees.

Hugh blinked his eyes, once, twice. Gone now was goodhearted Augie Neill who'd held out a punting pole to him in the roaring Missouri and so saved his life. Gone now was slim slow-moving Jim Anderson who'd helped him fight the Rees from behind a cottonwood log. The two lads would never again have themselves a night of loving musky Ree maidens. Let alone jollying the pretty white picture squaws back in the settlements. Nor breathe the air of the free mountains ahead.

Major Henry's brow drew tight together. "These men were stabbed in their sleep." Major Henry looked around at his men. "Who had the dawn watch?"

Jim Bridger paled. Fitz began to scowl.

Jim said, "We did. Fitz and me."

"Well?"

From under heavy beetled gray brows Hugh looked from Jim to Fitz and back to Jim again. "The boys were onto 'em all right, major. They woke me to look after the ponies and then stirred up the rest of ye. But by that time them quick devils was already through camp."

Fitz and Jim gave Hugh a look; then glanced at Major Henry.

Major Henry glared at Hugh; then at Jim and Fitz.

Hugh went on. "I couldn't see a thing either, Major. And they was crawlin' right by me. It was so blame dark."

Major Henry flashed white teeth.

Hugh looked down at slack-mouthed dead Augie and Jim. "Two more companyeros gone under." Hugh waggled his grizzled head slowly. "I suppose our turn will soon come next. Whaugh! A hard life it is."

Major Henry gave Jim Bridger and Fitz Fitzgerald a long, slow, burning look; then Hugh; then the two again; at last he shrugged and let off.

Hugh turned on his heel and went over and deftly scalped the two Mandans lying on the ground under the trees. Their scalps lifted easily. Flies and some red ants were already busy on the laggard bronze forms. One brave had a huge arched chest. He lay as if pretending death, as if he were still holding his breath, eyes rolled under from the effort.

"Pierre," Major Henry said, "Pierre, get up breakfast."

Gray dawn gave Pierre's pale face a clayish hue. He tried to smile. He said, "What'll you have, men?"

"Whisky and pancakes," Hugh said, coming back from his scalping and fastening the dripping Mandan scalps to his belt, "whisky and pancakes. Whisky to wake me up and pancakes to weight me down."

After a detail had buried Augie Neill and Jim Anderson, and after Hugh and Fitz and Jim had watered the horses and staked them out to fresh grass, the company had pancakes, coffee, and boiled hump meat. The men ate silently, soberly, every now and then looking over to where Augie and Jim Anderson lay buried, or looking over to where the redskin Mandans lay stretched out under the cottonwoods. Every man knew that within an hour of their leaving the white wolves and the gray coyotes would be wrangling over the dead warriors, would dig up the bodies of the dead mountain men, scattering the bones and skin and hair all over the creek draw.

A mourning dove hoo-hooed behind the cottonwoods. Every man shivered.

With a sad face Major Henry made some entries in his gray ledger. Yount gathered up Augie Neill's and Jim Anderson's personal possessions in a sack and put a tag on it. Later it would be sent back to St. Louis, and from there to the next of kin.

Old Hugh ate heartily. He had seen many and many a friend die. And while his eyes and lips might lament their going, his stomach didn't. His stomach had become hardened to mountain-man life. It took a power of sorrow to make his breakfast, or any meal, come back the way it went in. Once Old Hugh got his meat trap shut down it wasn't too easy opened again.

Breakfast finished, Hugh had a look at his equipment. He tested the priming of his guns, rifle, and horse pistol. He checked the powder in his horn. He made sure he had enough balls stored in the chamber of his gunstock.

Old Hugh noted that the soles of his moccasins were wearing through. He took them off and dug out a new pair Bending Reed had made for him.

Jim and Fitz looked over their footwear too. Both had bought moccasins from Bending Reed. But since Fitz was light and Jim walked Indian-style (the pigeon-toed walk was easy on both foot and footwear), their moccasins were still in fairly good shape. Old Hugh was always glad to see how well his squaw's makings outlasted most other footwear. Bending Reed knew her leathers. She always used the smoked top of an old tepee. Smoked leather was not as apt to get stiff after a soaking. Raw buckskin had a devilish way of becoming clammy and soppy in a rain and, afterward, shrinking up into stiff hard plaks. Ae, Reed was handy with the awl, she was, and her backlash Heyoka stitch could never be mistaken for another's.

Hugh and Jim and Fitz rounded up the ponies and set to work saddling and bridling them, both pack and riding horses. They lined up the pack horses in a chain, tying one horse to the tail of another ahead. The morning was well along by the time Major Henry called out, "Put out!"

Major Henry first chose a northerly course, descending the creek draw into the Grand River valley, and then, once down in the valley, struck a westerly course, following the shore of the wide, almost empty, riverbed.

Small tanbrown herds of buffalo moved grazing over the far tan bluffs. In the draws buffalo berries hung ripe red in fat dark clusters. The chokecherry trees dripped purple flesh. Every once in a while the men grabbed up a handful, stripping off the berries by letting a laden twig run between the fingers, chewing and spitting seeds as they rode along. Ocher dust stived up from the clopping hooves.

It was midmorning before the sun finally broke out. Then the horses began to sweat, sweat sudsing white their coats of hair. The men sweat too, sweat and ocher dust slowly tanning their bronze faces. Both horse and man fought the botflies. Except for an occasional curse, talk fell off completely. Eyes began to ache from the brilliant reflection off the dry ocher ground. Eyes teared over; became red-veined. Sometimes boulders bulked in the way and the leader detoured the party around them.

It was near noon when Hugh looked up to find Major Henry riding along beside him. Major Henry gave Hugh an odd hooded look, lips thinning back over bared teeth. They rode along in silence for a few moments, apart from the other men. The horse hooves hit a steady puck-pock puck-pock on the dry grass and the drought-hardened ground.

"Hugh?"

Hugh knew what was coming; said nothing.

"Hugh, in all the commotion this morning I forgot to check an order I gave last night. Hugh, I'm hoping that same commotion made you forget too."

Slowly Hugh stiffened in his saddle, and slowly he turned his old grizzly head and looked the major square in the eye. His furry neck humped up a little. Old Blue beneath sensed the change in Hugh; began to step along a little faster.

"Hugh?"

"Oh, I thought of it all right," Hugh growled.

"You're not going to obey the order then?"

Hugh exploded. "Dag it, Major, why can't I wear my face the way I want to? I don't want to look like a woman."

"We're in Indian country, Hugh, where Indians take exception to men who wear beards."

Hugh kept right on exploding. "I don't want to look like a plucked rooster, Major. I want to wear my face the way nature intended."

"Hugh, if you were alone I wouldn't care. But you're with others. What you do or what you don't do affects the rest of us. I have to think of the whole party, Hugh."

Old Blue began to step along even faster and Hugh had to rein him in a little. "Dang wimmen, slickin' us up. When we all should still be wearin' our manes like lions."

"Hugh."

"Major, I tell ee. We made a mistake when we let the wimmen talk us inta kissin' 'em, smoozlin' 'em face to face. The Indian wimmen never did it and was the better for it. And then we made a mistake when we let them talk us into shavin' so we'd look like nice little boys again. It's no wonder the country is so full of wet-behind-the ears greenhorn kids."

Major Henry couldn't help but smile a little. "In any case, Hugh, tonight you shave it off or I'll have to send you back to Fort Kiowa. Alone. Meantime, I'm taking you off the hunting detail. I'll send Allen ahead with two men this afternoon."

Hugh's old gray eyes blazed from under thick ridged gray brows. He trembled. "Major, this child's never stuck around camp for camp work. You know that. I ain't made for it. I hain't put heavy moccasins on these mudhooks"—Hugh lifted a big foot—"to help the cook."

"I'm sorry, Hugh. But what I said still goes."

Hugh said, "You said Allen and two men. Does that mean Jim and Fitz?"

"No, it doesn't. I'm taking them off the hunting detail too."

Hugh doubled a fist and hit his knee. "But why? What've they done?"

Major Henry smiled big white teeth. "Because I

wasn't satisfied with the way they handled watch last night. Nor was I satisfied with your story about your part in it." Major Henry smiled some more. "Hugh, you surprise me, sticking up for the boy Jim like that. You act like an old mule crazy over a colt."

Old Hugh's eyes opened very wide; then half-closed.

Major Henry let his horse drift away from Hugh. Presently Hugh jogged along alone again.

Hugh smoldered. He was at last really burned up. He rode along cursing under his breath.

The river valley narrowed a little. The stream switched back and forth on the sands in the wide river-bed. The wide riverbed turned from side to side too, sometimes cutting along the base of the southern hills, sometimes the northern hills. Sometimes a tight band of willows and cottonwoods bordered the stream; some-times the mud cutbanks were barren. Occasionally smaller streams came trickling in from the hills. Most such streams came out of heavily wooded brushy draws.

Huge brownblack bluffs towered over the near hills. Thunder Butte was at last out of sight, but another butte, whitegray in color and resembling a crouching wolf, which Major Henry named Wolf Butte, rose above the bluff-line in the northwest.

Magpies screamed out of low gray-leaved bullberry bushes, flying away with long black tails dragging like broken rudders. Hawks floated overhead. Above an an-gling brushy draw on the left, black buzzards circled over a down buffalo calf. Occasionally the men started up a herd of goatlike antelope, heads first cocked a sec-ond, then white tails flagging and scudding over the knolls and away. The thin stream of the Grand twinkled in the burning sun; reflected the deep blue sky above.

The party stopped for a rest at high noon. Hugh and Jim and Fitz unloaded the pack horses; watered them; staked them out to graze in some sweetgrass in a low turn in the river. The men had themselves some dry biscuits, jerked meat, fatback, and coffee. Then came a smoke and a catnap.

A wind came up. It moved in cool from the west and freshened the grazing horses and resting men. It also chased the mosquitoes and lighter flies to cover. Only the swift heavy botflies remained to torment the horses.

Far away, behind a bald hill, a mourning dove called three lonesome, clear, haunting notes: oowhee—oooo—ooo.

But Hugh still seethed inside. He was mad at Major Henry for what he thought was a womanish order. He was mad at the boys Jim and Fitz for having gotten him in the soup by sleeping on their watch. He was mad at himself for good-naturedly having stuck his neck out to save their skin.

By midafternoon, right after Major Henry had sent gaunt Allen and two men ahead to make meat for supper, Old Hugh was fit to be tied. The little paired arteries down his big bronze nose ran dark with rage. His gray eyes glittered.

The party defiled through a brushy draw coming down from the left. The party leader for the day, George Yount, had to break a way through the plum and bullberry bushes with a double ax.

In the commotion Old Hugh saw his chance to go hunting off by himself. He was last in line and could slip away unnoticed. With a sulphureous curse, and a low growled, "I don't take orders from a tyrant," Hugh turned Old Blue aside and climbed the rise to the east.

He skirted the brush at the head of the draw until he was well out of sight. Below and ahead, on his right, across the Grand River, he saw Allen and his men dodging along through a grove of cottonwood and willow. Hugh was careful to keep an equal distance between the three hunters ahead and the party behind.

It was sport to be out on one's own again, alone. The new, the old new, just around the turn ahead, was the only remedy for hot blood. Ahead was always either gold or the grave. The gamble of it freshened the blood at the same time that it cleared the eye. What could beat galloping up alone over the brow of a new bluff for that first look beyond?

The wind from the west began to push a little. It dried his damp buckskins, dried Old Blue too.

The valley slowly widened. Shelving slopes on the right mounted into noble skin-smooth tan bluffs, rose toward Wolf Butte. The country on the left, however, suddenly humped up into abrupt enormous bluffs, three of them almost mountains.

After a time Hugh understood why the valley widened. The Grand River forked up ahead, with one branch angling off to the northwest under Wolf Butte, with the other branch wriggling sharply off to the southwest under the three mountainlike tan bluffs.

There was no game. He didn't see a bird. It was siesta time. The eyes and ears of Old Earth were closed in sleep.

A wide gully swept down out of the hollow between the last two bluffs. A spring drained it and its sides were shaggy with brush. Most of the growth was chokecherry, with here and there a prickly plum tree.

Hugh felt hungry. Looking down into the draw he thought he spotted some plums, ripe red ones at that, hanging in the green leaves. Ripe black fruit also peppered the chokecherry trees. Chokecherries, he decided, chokecherries would only raise the thirst and hardly still the hunger. Plums were better. They were filling.

Before dropping down into the draw, Hugh had a last look around. A man alone always had to make sure no red devils were skulking about, behind some cliff or down in the brush. From under old gray brows, eyes narrowed against the pushing wind, Old Hugh studied the rims of the horizon all around. He inspected the riverbed from one end to the other, including each of the forks. He examined all the brushy draws running down from the bald hills on both sides.

He gave Old Blue the eye too. Horses often spotted danger before humans did.

But if there was danger Old Blue was blissfully unaware of it. Old Blue made a few passes at the dry rusty bunch grass underfoot. Old Blue blew out his nostrils at a patch of prickly-pear cactus. Old Blue snorted lightly at a mound of dirt crumbles heaved up by big red ants.

No sign of alarm in Old Blue. It looked safe all right.

Vaguely behind him, a quarter of a mile back, Hugh could hear the party coming along the river, breaking through brush. Allen and his two men were nowhere in sight ahead.

A turtledove mourned nearby: ooah—koooo—kooo—koo.

With a prodding toe and a soft, "Hep-ah," Hugh started Old Blue down the incline into the brush. Grayblue back arched, legs set like stilts, Old Blue worked his way down slowly. The saddle cinches creaked. Stones rattled down ahead of them. Dust rose. Old Blue lashed his blue tail back and forth.

The first few plum trees proved disappointing. The fruit was small; it puckered the mouth and made a ball of Hugh's tongue. Sirupy rosin drops showed where worms had punctured through.

Holding prickly branches away, sometimes ducking, waving at mosquitoes, Hugh preyed through the thicket slowly, testing, spitting. They were all sour. Bah!

The draw leveled. They broke through the shadowy prickly thicket out onto an open creekbed. Spring water ran cool and swift over clean knobs of pink and brown rock.

Old Blue had the same thought Hugh had. A drink. Hugh got off even as Old Blue began sipping.

Holding onto a rein, laying Old Bullthrower on a big dry pink stone, Hugh got down on his knees. He put a hand out to either side on wet cool sand; leaned down until his grizzled beard dipped into the water; began drinking.

Suddenly Old Blue snorted; started up; jerked the rein free and was off in a gallop lickety-split down the creek, heading for the forks of the Grand.

Hugh humped up; grabbed up Old Bullthrower; started running after Old Blue. But Hugh couldn't run much on his wounded game leg, and Old Blue rapidly outdistanced him and disappeared around a turn.

Hugh gave up, cursing. "By the bull barley, what got into him?" Puffing, Hugh took off his wolfskin cap. "Now that does put me in a curious fix. With the major already riled enough to hamshoot me." Hugh waggled his old hoar head. "Wonder what did skeer him off, the old cuss."

Hugh cocked an ear; listened awhile; couldn't make out a thing.

There was an odd smell in the air, a smell of mashed chokecherries mixed in with musky dog. But after sniffing the air a few times, nostrils twitching, he decided it was probably only some coyote he'd flushed.

Hugh stood pondering, scratching his head. "Wal, one thing, Ol' Blue won't run far. In strange country, a horse always comes back to a party. Gets lonesome like the rest of us humans."

Hugh put Old Bullthrower to one side; got down on his knees for another drink. The shadow of a hawk flitted over swiftly, touching the trickling water, touching him. Finished drinking, Hugh picked up Old Bullthrower; automatically checked the priming; cocked an eye at the brush.

Hugh worked down toward the Grand River to meet the line of march of the party.

Halfway down toward the Grand River another creek came angling out of a second draw, the water joining with the first creek and tumbling on toward the river. Hugh looked up the second draw; saw another cluster of plum trees. Ho-ah. Good plums at last. Smaller but blood ripe. Hugh couldn't resist them. He'd give himself a quick treat and then go on to meet the party along the river.

The tiny trickling stream curved away from him, to his left. He broke through low whipping willow branches; came upon a sandy opening.

"Whaugh!" A great belly grunt burped up from the white sands directly in front of him. And with a tremendous tumbler's heave of body, a silvertipped gray she-grizzly, *Ursus horribilis*, rose up before him on two legs. "Whaugh!" Two little brown grizzly cubs ducked cowering and whimpering behind the old lady.

The massive silvertipped beast came toward him, straddling, huge head dipped down at him from a humped neck, humped to strike him. Her big doglike mouth and piglike snout were bloody with chokecherry juice. Her long gray claws were bloody with fruit juice too. Her musky smell filled the air. And smelling the musk, Hugh knew then why Old Blue had bolted and run.

Hugh backed in terror, his heart suddenly burning hot and bounding around in his chest. The little arteries down his big Scotch nose wriggled red. His breath caught. The sense of things suddenly unraveling, of the end coming on, of being no longer in control of either things or his life, possessed him.

She was as big as a great bull standing on two legs. She was so huge on her two legs that her incredible speed coming toward him actually seemed slow. Time stiffened, poured like cold molasses.

She roared. She straddled toward him on her two rear legs. She loomed over him, silver neck ruffed and humped, silver head pointed down at him. Her pink dugs stuck out at him. She stunk of dogmusk.

She hung over him, huge furry arms ready to cuff and strike. Her red-stained ivorygray claws, each a lickfinger long, each curved a little like a cripple's iron hook, closed and unclosed.

Hugh's eyes set; stiffened; yet he saw it all clearly. Time poured slow—yet was fast.

Hugh jerked up his rifle.

But the Old Lady's mammoth slowness was faster. She was upon him before he got his gun halfway up. She poured slow—yet was fast. "Whaugh!" She cuffed at the gun in his hands as if she knew what it was for. The gun sprang from his hands. As it whirled into the bushes, it went off in the air, the ball whacking harmlessly into the white sand at their feet.

Hugh next clawed for his horse pistol.

Again she seemed to know what it was for. She cuffed the pistol out of his hand too.

Hugh stumbled over a rock; fell back on his hands and rump; like a tumbler bounded up again.

The cubs whimpered behind her.

The whimpering finally set her off. She struck. "Whaugh!" Her right paw cuffed him on the side of the head, across the ear and along the jaw, sending his wolfskin cap sailing, the claws ripping open his scalp. The blow knocked him completely off his feet, half-somersaulted him in the air before he hit ground.

Again, like a tumbler, Hugh bounded to his feet, ready for more. He felt very puny. The silvertip became a silver blur in his eyes. She became twice, thrice, magnified.

It couldn't be true, he thought. He, Old Hugh Glass, he about to be killed by a monster varmint? Never.

Hugh crouched over. He backed and filled downstream as best he could.

The she-grizzly, still on two legs, both paws ready to cuff, came after him, closed once more. She roared.

Hugh scratched for his skinning knife. There was nothing for it but to close with her. Even as her great claw swiped at him, stiff but swift, he leaped and got inside her reach. Her clubbing paw swung around him instead of catching him. He hugged her for dear life. He pushed his nose deep into her thick dogmusky whitegray fur. He pressed into her so hard one of her dugs squirted milk over his leathers.

She roared above him. She cuffed around him like a heavyweight trying to give a lightweight a going-over in a clinch. She poured slow—yet was fast. She snarled; roared. His ear was tight on the huge barrel of her chest, and the roars reverberated inside her chest like mountain avalanches. He hugged her tight and stayed inside her reach. She clawed at him clumsily. Her ivorygray claws brought up scraps of buckskin shirt and strips of skin from his back.

He hugged her. And hugging her, at last got his knife around and set. He punched. His knife punged through the tough hide and slipped into her belly just below the ribs with an easy slishing motion. He stabbed again. Again and again. The knife punged through the tough furred hide each time and then slid in easy.

Blood spurted over his hands, over his belly, over his legs and her legs both, came in gouts of sparkling scarlet.

He wrestled her; stabbed her.

The great furred she-grizzly roared in an agony of pain and rage. He was still inside her reach and she couldn't get a good swipe at him. She clawed clumsily up and down his back. She brought up strips of leather and skin and red muscle. She pawed and clawed, until at last Hugh's ribs began to show white and clean.

Hugh screamed. He stabbed wildly, frantically, skinning knife sinking in again and again.

Her massive ruffed neck humped up in a striking curve. Then her head dug down at him. She seized his whole head in her red jaws and lifted him off his feet.

Hugh got in one more lunging thrust. His knife sank in all the way up to the haft directly over the heart.

He felt her dogteeth crunch into his skull. She shook

him by the head like a dog might shake a doll. His body dangled. His neck cracked.

He screamed. His scream rose into a shrill squeak.

He sank away, half-conscious.

She dropped him.

Raging, blood spouting from a score of wounds, she picked him up again, this time by his game leg, and shook him violently, shook him until his leg popped in its hip socket. She roared while she gnawed. She was a great cat chewing and subduing a struggling mouse. His game leg cracked.

She dropped him.

Snarling, still spouting blood on all sides, coughing blood, she picked him up again, this time by the rump. She tore out a hunk the size of a buffalo boss and tossed it over her shoulder toward the brown cubs.

Hugh lay limp, sinking away. He thought of the boy Jim, of Bending Reed, of a picture-purty she-rip back in Lancaster, of two boy babies.

Time poured slow—yet space was quick.

The next thing he knew she had fallen on him and lay deadheavy over his hips and legs.

He heard a scrambling in the brush. He heard the voices of men. He heard the grizzly cubs whimpering. He heard two shots.

Dark silence.

Part II

The Crawl

Chapter 1

A cold nose woke him.

He tried opening his eyes; couldn't; found his eyelids crusted shut.

He blinked hard a few times; still couldn't open them; gave up.

The back of his head ached like a stone cracking in heat. His entire back, from high in his neck and across his shoulder blades and through the small of his back and deep into his buttocks, was a slate of tight pain.

The cracking ache and the tight pain was too much. He drifted off into gray sleep.

The cold nose woke him again.

And again he rose up out of gray into wimmering pink consciousness. He blinked hard, once, twice; still couldn't quite uncrack his crusted eyelids.

A dog licking his face? Dogs never licked bearded faces that he remembered.

The cold nose touched him once more, on the brow. And then he knew he wasn't being licked in love. He was being sniffed over.

Hugh concentrated on his crusted eyes, forced all he had into opening them. And after a supreme effort, the stuck lashes parted with little crust-breaking sounds. Blue instantly flooded into his old gray eyes. There was an unusually clear sky overhead. Yellow light was striking up into blue. That meant it was morning. If rust and pink had been sinking away under blueblack it would have been late afternoon. Also a few birds were chirping a little. That proved it was morning. Birds never chirped in the late afternoon in August. At least not that he knew of.

August? Where in tarnation . . . ?

With a jerk Hugh tried to sit up.

The jerk like to killed him. His whole back and his rump and his right leg all three became raging red monsters. He groaned. "Gawd!" His whole chest rumbled with it.

Out of the corner of his eye he saw a bristling whitegray shape jump back. Sight of the jumping whitegray shape kept him from fainting. That whitegray bristling shape had a cold black nose. It was a wolf.

Then it all came back to him. What had happened and where he was. Major Henry had ordered him to shave off his beard. He had refused. Major Henry had then given the hunting detail to Allen and two other men. He'd got mad and gone off hunting by himself— only to run smack into a she-grizzly.

Miraculously he was still alive then.

Holding himself tight rigid, Hugh opened his eyes as far as he could to size things up. He saw green bottle-flies buzzing around him, thousands of them, millions of them. They were like darting spots before the eyes. Every time he rolled his eyes they buzzed up from his beard and wounds and swirled and resettled. Just above him hung a bush heavy with ripe buffalo berries.

He heard water trickling over stones. He heard the wolf padding on the sand, circling him warily. The soule of a mourning dove echoed through the brush-choked draw: ooah—koooo—kooo—koo.

He had hands. He moved them. The green bottleflies buzzed up; swarmed; resettled. He moved his hands again, first his right, then his left. The right hand seemed slightly bruised; the left felt whole.

He studied the small blue marks over the back of his right hand. That was where the silvertip she-grizzly had struck him when she'd clubbed first his flintlock and then his horse pistol away from him.

Thinking of his gun, he instinctively reached for it. He couldn't find it. He pawed the sand, the dirt, the edge of a fur, over his belly. Not there. Green flies buzzed up; resettled.

He sighed. Of course. The guns were still in the bushes where the she-grizzly had popped them.

He felt of his body. The green death flies rose; swirled; swarmed around him. He found his head bandaged with a narrow strip of cloth. A huge welt ran from his grizzly cheek back past his swollen red ear and up into his scalp. The welt was a ridged seam. Someone had carefully sewn up his long terrible wound with deer sinews. The ridged welt ran up around his entire head. A few small stitched ridges ran off it. The clotted seam also felt fuzzy. Someone had also carefully webbed the bleeding wound with the fuzz plucked from a beaver pelt. Beaver fuzz was the thing for quick crust building. Many and many was the time he'd put it on cuts himself.

He ran his hand over his chest; over his gaunt belly; found everything in order. The front of him was still all in one piece. Even the leathers, his buckskin hunting shirt and leggings, were whole. Flies buzzed up angry; resettled.

He felt of his right leg; reached down too far; stirred up the red monsters in his back and game leg and rump again. "Gawd!!"

The flies began to bite him, on the backs of his hands and the exposed parts of his face and ears and the exposed parts of his shoulders.

He wondered what he was lying on. He felt around with his good left hand; found a bearskin beneath. Lifting his head, brushing away the swirling buzzing flies, looking past a crusted lid and swollen blue nose and clotted beard, he saw it was the skin of the silvertip she-grizzly he'd fought. He let his head fall back.

He felt of it again to make sure. How in tarnation . . . ? Who had skinned the she-grizzly? He couldn't have done it himself. That was impossible. The last thing he remembered was the she-grizzly lying deadheavy across his belly and legs. So he couldn't have.

He remembered hearing voices. He remembered hearing the little grizzly cubs whimpering. He remembered two shots. Ho-ah! The party had spotted runaway Old Blue and had probably heard him screaming. They had come up to help; had shot the cubs. They had pulled the Old Lady off him and had skinned her and had made a bed out of her fur for him. And they had dressed his wounds. Ae, that was it.

He smiled. Ae, real mountain men, they were, to come to a comrade's relief. He smiled. Real mountain men. They had a code, they had.

"Ae, lads, this child was almost gone under that time, he was."

No answer. Only the trickling of the brook, the buzzing of the green death flies, the padding of the circling hungry wolf.

Flies? Wolf? Silence? What in tarnation? Quickly he perked up again—and the raging red monsters tore into him.

Somehow he managed to roll over on his side, the grizzly fur sticking to his crusted-over back and lifting up off the sand. The weight of the hide tore away some of the flesh from his ribs. He screamed. Eyes closed, he caught his breath and screamed again.

When he opened his eyes once more, he saw it. His grave. Beside him, not a yard away, someone had dug a shallow grave for him, a grave some three feet deep and seven feet long.

Old gray eyes almost blinded with tears, with extreme pain, green bottleflies buzzing all around, he stared at it.

His grave.

He shook his head; blinked.

His grave.

So that was it. He was done for. His time was up.

His grave. He lay on his right side looking at it, bewildered in a wilderness.

"Ae, I see it now, lads. It's this old coon's turn at last."

Or maybe it was the other way around. Maybe he was the only one alive, with all the others ambushed, killed, and scalped.

Cautiously he rolled his eyes around. He looked at the mound of yellow sifting sand beside the yawning grave. He looked at the bullberries hanging ripe overhead. He looked at the silvertip she-grizzly hide under him. He watched the green death flies hovering and buzzing around him. He looked up at the blue sky.

Not a soul or a dead body in sight on that side.

He looked all around again as far as his eye could see; then, despite terrible blinding pain, he rolled over on his left side.

Cautiously he rolled his eyes around. Nothing there either. No horses. No men. There'd been no ambush on that side either, so far as he could see.

What in tarnation had happened? He'd been sewed up and placed on the she-grizzly's hide. Also someone had dug a grave for him. Yet no one was about.

He studied the open grave some more. To dig that the men must have thought him dead.

But if they thought him dead, why in tarnation hadn't they finished burying him?

It was too much for him to understand. His head cracked with it.

"This child feels mighty queersome," he murmured.

He felt of his skull again. Yes, his topknot was still in place, though it was ridged and seamed all over like an old patched moccasin.

He blinked; fainted. He fell back, body flopping with a thud on the fur-covered sand. Green flies resettled on him.

The wolf approached him a couple of steps; sat down

on its haunches. It watched him warily with narrowed yellow eyes. The wolf sniffed, brushtail whirling nervously. Presently the wolf got up; approached a few steps closer; sat down on its haunches again. It waited.

Chapter 2

A cold nose woke him.

His crusted lids cracked open. Blue sky filled his old gray eyes.

He remembered it. He remembered the last time he was up. Red monsters rending him. Green death flies. A padding white wolf. An open grave.

They were all there again. And this time another was waiting. A turkey buzzard. Floating on wavering three-foot wings, coasting, sometimes flopping to gain height, bald snakehead peering down at him, snakehead gaggling in and out on a long neck, it hovered over him, circling, rising, falling, floating.

The turkey buzzard meant if he wasn't dead he should be.

The green death flies puzzled him. They rarely sat on a man until he was dead. The white wolf and the black turkey buzzard had enough sense to wait until he was fully dead. Why not the green flies?

There was dead meat around somewhere then.

Well, it wasn't his, because he was still ciphering—unless the Resurrection had come and dead meat had learned to cipher . . . or he was a soul floating around outside his own dead body.

He remembered it. He'd found himself upon the she-grizzly's fur beside an open grave, his back and head sewed up. He remembered he'd fainted away trying to cipher what had happened.

The green flies continued to puzzle him. They usually never went to work until after the wolves and the buzzards had had their fill. What did he have they wanted so bad?

He woke gradually. Hearing came back; sight came back; feeling in his finger tips came back; smell came back.

Something stunk something awful all right. He hoped it wasn't himself. It stunk like a rotting buffalo carcass.

He heard the wolf padding near him. He was in part glad to hear it. As long as it kept padding, that long he was alive.

Through narrowed crusted lids he watched the turkey buzzard circling overhead. Its hooked dull-white beak worked sometimes. Its flesh-colored feet clawed and un-clawed. Its reddish-tinged neck became long, became short. Its wings shone greenblack. Its bald head gaggled at him first with one blinking eye then with the other blinking eye. It hung above him seemingly without ef-fort. There was no wind. It waggled a few times and stayed up endlessly.

He sat up; fought the red monsters; survived them; fought a faint; survived it. He brushed the green death flies away. He steadied.

He saw the yawning grave again; saw the whitegray wolf, this time two of them; saw the silvertip fur under him.

Then taste came back. Thirst. Great thirst. "Wad-der," he murmured. "Got to have wadder," he mur-mured. He was dizzy with it. His lips, tongue, roof of his mouth, all were so parched he couldn't get his tongue out to his lips. His lips felt white, felt cracked. They worked under his clotted beard. "Wadder," he murmured, "wadder."

His eyes, his ears, turned him to the sound of water. "Wadder," he murmured. His body settled forward from the hips. He rolled over. The fur hide, still stuck to his back, came up with him. "Gawd!" He undulated slowly toward the trickling stream. The stream was only a few feet away but it took him miles to get there. "Gawd!" He crawled on the sand. He hunched forward. Crawled. "Wadder," he murmured.

His good foot caught in a root. He got a good toe hold; gave himself a tremendous shove; moved half a foot. It brought him to the edge of the water trickling over clean white stones. He dug his good toe in again; gave himself a great shove again. This time his shove got his grizzled face into the water. He let it shove in. He drank like a horse with his head half under. Bubbles escaped his nose and mouth; guggled up through his beard; came out at the top of his clotted, seamed head of hair.

He drank until his stomach hurt, until it raised him a little off the white stones.

"Ahhh. Water." He shook his grizzly head. Drops sprayed off to all sides. "Ah, what is better than water?"

He drew back to a kneeling position. Again the weight of the furskin, still stuck to his crusted back wounds, tore at the flesh over his ribs. He screamed. He fell flat again.

He puffed. He waited for strength. He lay staring at the clear water directly under his nose. He saw a tiny bloodsucker waving black from a pebble. He saw a tendril of green moss waving from a stone. He saw green minnows fleeting upstream.

"Got—to—get," he puffed, "got—to—get—that— skin—off—somehow." He puffed. "Best—soak—it— in—water."

He rolled over slowly, dragging the skin with him. He slaped forward on his back until he lay with his back in the water.

The water felt cool and it felt good and it soothed him.

Presently he felt the minnows tickling him, nibbling at his crusts. He lay in the shallow waters of the stream and let the minnows lip the wounds. "The minnies'll heal me," he murmured. "Water is medicine but the minnies'll leech me. Purify the blood."

The white wolf wriggled its cold black nose at him. It sat on its haunches. It waited. The turkey buzzard gaggled its wrinkled bald head in and out and hung on its wings. It waited. The green death flies buzzed over him. A few of the flies hit the water, floated away downstream, drowning.

Ripe buffalo berries hung above him. He reached up for a cluster; put it all in his mouth, stem, skin, pit, flesh. After the fresh water he thought the bullberries had a fine grape flavor.

"Wonder where everybody is? The lads wouldn't've left me alone here."

It became high noon. And hot. His back, submerged in running water, felt fine, but his face and front sweat where the overhead sun struck him through the bullberry bushes. At the same time he was sure he was almost as hot from a fever as he was from the sun, because his back, which should have been chilled to the bone in the running spring water, actually felt warmish too. The water trickled in through the gaping rents of his leathers, around and over his turtleshell crusts, around and into the grizzly bearskin.

The minnies lipped him.

He murmured to himself. "The fur must be soaked loose by now." He reached a hand around to feel of his back. One of the red monsters awoke. He cried out. "Gawd!"

He reached around a bit further. The crusts had become soggy in the water and the fur was loosened in most places. He could feel ridges, seams, running everywhichway over his back. Someone had sewed up his back with deer sinews too. In some places the buckskin whangs had been tied into hard knots, each knot with a pair of little ears. His back felt like a patched up tepee. It was as uneven and as bumpy as the breaks in the Badlands. And probably as inflamed: burnt red, pus yellow, rotted purple. Blotched over like a case of eczema peppered with boils.

Hugh's hand came away stinking. Then he knew where the bad smell came from and why the green flies and the whitegray wolf and the hovering wrinkle-necked turkey buzzard fancied his meat.

He found a patch where the bearskin was still stuck to his back. With a pushing finger moving very cautiously, probing, he pried it off. He grimaced in pain. The beard over his mouth quivered. The pain was so terrible at times that consciousness came and went in waves.

After a rest he pried farther. The bearskin parted with little rips, from the waterlogged crusted wounds, came loose with tiny rending sounds.

He shuddered—and the last of the silvertip bearskin fell away. "Ahh!" he breathed. "Ahh." He shook his head. "Gawd! that was hard doin's! By the bull barley, that was." He sucked breath. "Gawd, I feel queersome. Like a buffler shot in the lights."

He felt better after a while. He sat up. Gray bullberry leaves brushed his brow, touched his matted gray hair. He shook his head; blinked; blinked.

"Whaugh!" he roared suddenly, and the whitegray wolf jumped back a dozen steps and the turkey buzzard overhead flopped its wings and flew in a higher circle. Hugh laughed.

The raucous laugh caught his ear. Ho-ah! His voice seemed to have changed some. Or else his ears had gone on the blink. His voice had always been heavy, a cross between a bear grunt and a deacon's growl. But now it sounded cracked and coarse. The Old Lady must've given his talkbox a whack too.

A little way from the golden mound of sand beside the open grave Hugh saw something. Ashes. A heap of them. Gray with white irregular rings. A few half-burnt twigs and branches stuck out all along the edge of the ashes like green lashes around a huge blindwhite horse eye. Around the ashes were molds and pudges in the sand where men had sat and lain.

With a grunt, and a groan of pain, Hugh lurched forward on hands and one knee. His bad leg dragged. He crawled past the grave and around the mound of gold sand. The green flies buzzed over his back. The whitegray wolf retreated a step. The greenblack turkey buzzard lifted its wing-wavering orbit above him.

He approached the ashes carefully. He studied the sand for tracks. There were many moccasin prints, most of them faint. But some of them were fresh and all of them were of two kinds: quiet Fitz's small print, the boy Jim's big-footed print. He knew that moccasin print anywhere. The two lads had bought their moccasins from Bending Reed. And there was that new contrary stitch she'd lately taken to using. The Heyoka stitch.

He circled the ash heap carefully, staying well away from it at first, and only gradually working in on it. Yes, all the fresh prints belonged to either the boy Jim or downer Fitz. And all the old prints belonged to the rest of the party: Major Henry, Silas Hammond, George Yount, Allen, Pierre the cook, all the lads.

Ho-ah! He saw it then. Ae. The major had left Fitz and Jim to stand watch over him while the rest of the fur party pressed on, going northwest and on up to Henry's Post on the Yellowstone and Missouri.

The major had probably made up his mind that Old Hugh was going to die and had asked for volunteers to keep the deathwatch and afterwards bury him decent. And the boys, Jim and Fitz, had probably chirped up because they felt they owed it to Old Hugh, after the way he'd covered up for them, covered up that they had fallen asleep while on guard duty.

Hugh looked at the shallow grave. "Decent?" Ha. A half-dozen strokes and the varmints had him dug out of the sand, tearing and gorging before he even turned cold. The lads'd sure been lax and lazy digging that grave.

Hugh shivered. He passed a hand over his hot brow.

One leg dragging, still on hands and one knee, grizzled, tattered, crusted over, looking like a he-bear in molting time after a terrible fight, he examined the sand around the ash heap, around the grave, also the spot where he had lain when he first came to. Except for the usual camp litter of broken tins and ripped paper packs and rinds of fruit and slicked bones, there was nothing. Not a thing. Neither gun, nor pistol, nor knife, nor steel and flint, nor food of any kind.

He glanced over toward the bushes where the silvertip she-grizzly had popped his flintlock and pistol. No, nothing there either.

"What in tarnation ... ?" he muttered again. "Where's the lads? They must be around somewhere."

He called out, hoarse voice more like a bear's growl than a human call, "Jim? Fitz! Hey! Where be ye?"

No answer. Not even an echo.

"Jim! Fitz! Hey!"

No answer.

"Lads! Where be ye? Jim? Fitz?"

Still no answer.

Hugh sagged and lay down on his belly. He couldn't cipher it. They'd dug his grave but hadn't buried him. Why? Indians? Red devils up on the hills? Sign? And the lads hiding in the brush?

He lay puffing on his belly.

Green flies settled on his crusts again. The wolf drew up a step. The turkey buzzard floated lower.

The stink of rotting flesh came strong to him again. It came on a rising breeze, not from his torn back. He sniffed the breeze wonderingly. Ho-ah. Something else was stinking up the gully besides himself.

The breeze felt fine on his back, warmish, and helped blow off the down-burning sun and the burning fever.

He raised on his elbows, eyes following where the nose said.

Ho-ah. Green flies in a cloud to one side of the ash heap, under a chokecherry bush. Meat then.

That same instant he felt hunger. Terrible hunger. "Meat," he murmured, "meat. Gotta have meat."

He crawled on hands and one knee and found the meat: a pile of bear ribs with scraps of rotting meat still on them, the she-grizzly skull grinning horribly at him, and a large hump of shoulder roast. All rotten. Meat the vultures for some reason had left to the green flies.

With his nails he clawed at the hump roast. Ha. Inside there was enough good meat left for a meal, even if it was a little on the prime side. He brushed off the flies.

What he needed now was a fire. Carrying some of the meat in either hand, he crawled to the ash heap. Carefully he brushed off the top ashes; carefully he shoved in a hand. Ahh! Warmth! There just might be a few live coals left. A spark or two.

Hugh scratched about under the bushes and gathered up a handful of wispy dry grass. He coiled it up into a nestlike roll, placed it carefully on the sand, piled a few leaves over it.

He turned back to the ash heap. He brushed layer after layer aside. When he got nearly to the bottom, he blew into the ashes softly.

And found it. A live coal the size of a ruby. Quickly he whisked it into the coil of wispy grass; deftly closed the wisps down over like a jeweler folding velvet lining down over a precious jewel; blew on it between cupped hands, blew on it long and slow and soft.

At last a slow twist of smoke rose out of the nest. Another long soft breath, and a flame licked out the size of a bird's tongue. He blew on it once more, long and slow, and it flashed up in his beard. Breath short, he grabbed up all the half-burnt twigs within reach, laid them on the burning grass in pyramid fashion, green spokes to a red hub. The flames grew. He laid on half-burnt branches and finished it off with bits of log. Presently he had a good fire blazing and crackling.

The flames chased back both the whitegray wolf and the turkey buzzard.

Old gray eyes feverish, Hugh broke off a long twig from a chokecherry bush; with his teeth cut a point on the end of it; jabbed on the strong hump roast; held it in the fire.

The burning sun, his rising fever, the jumping fire made him sweat like a jug in humid weather.

But he held on. Hot or not, rotten or not, he had to eat. "Meat's meat."

Lying on the side of his good leg, he turned the meat slowly in the fire. The burnt-meat smell almost drove him mad. His cracked lips worked, the gray fur over his cheeks and chin stirred.

When he thought some of the meat done, he bit in, burning his lips and nose tip, sucking, lipping up the strong fat dripping into his beard. He gnawed into it. "It's my turn now," he growled, remembering how the she-grizzly had growled and roared and gnawed into him. He chuckled as he thought of it. The old she-rip. Well, and she was flavorsome too, despite the spoilage. Ae, and filling.

He gorged until his belly hurt. The pain in his belly told him he'd probably lain without food for days. The lads must've had a time with him. Couldn't feed a man who was out of his head. Couldn't make a dead man swallow.

His belly hurt powerful. He hoped he wouldn't have to vomit. He remembered he'd always had a strong stomach. Once he got his meat trap shut down, it wasn't too easily opened again. And nature usually took its course. He hoped so.

He belched loudly, the putrid smell expelling through his nostrils. He broke wind.

He lay panting on his belly in the sand. He could

feel his stomach jumping around inside. It hopped about like a bad heart.

The fire died down to a suffing glow. Every now and then the breeze coming up the gully peeled off a layer of gray ash and exposed coals as live as flesh.

The wolf drew up a step. The buzzard came down a rung. The flies resettled on his crusts. The sun began to sink toward the west.

It came to him then. Those ashes he'd dug into for that live coal—they were at least a day old. Ho-ah! That meant the lads weren't hiding in the bushes after all, waiting for Rees to pass on so they could finish burying him. It meant that for one reason or another the lads hadn't been around for a spell.

What in tarnation? They couldn't've deserted him, could they?

Hugh shook his head. Hardly. Not Jim. Not Fitz. Not mountain men. Especially not after what he'd done for his companyeros, saving them from the major's wrath because they had slept while on guard.

No, not his lads. Certainly not Jim. And practical Fitz, for all his book learning, not him either.

What could have happened? Scalped and killed by Rees? Hardly. The lads would have been laying dead around him then. And the Rees would certainly have counted coup on him, their old enemy, too.

His gun and possibles—who'd taken them? Not the Rees, because they hadn't taken his scalp. The boys? Impossible. Not the lads.

A cracking headache set up in Hugh's head. "I feel queersome," he said.

He felt of his brow. It was slippery with fever's sweat. Ho-ah. Blood poison had set in then. Ae, rot in the blood.

He lifted his head. And wasn't too surprised to see the gully swinging back and forth like a sailor's hammock in a tossing ship. Ae, the putrid rot all right.

Slowly Hugh slipped away into delirium.

"Now boy I'll soon be under. Afore many hours. And, boy, if you don't raise meat pronto you'll be in the same fix I'm in. I've never et dead meat myself, Jim, and wouldn't ask you to do it neither. But meat fair killed is meat anyway. So, Jim, lad, put your knife in this old nigger's lights and help yourself. It's poor bull I am, I know, but maybe it'll do to keep life in ee. There should be some fleece on me that's meat yet. And maybe my old hump ribs has some pickin's on 'em in front. And there should be one roast left in my behind. Left side. Dip in, lad, and drink man's blood. I did onct. One bite."

He slept and roused and slept by fits.

"You're a good old hoss, Hugh, but we ain't turned Digger Indian yet."

Hugh's gray eyes rolled white with fever. Vaguely he saw a dozen snake-headed buzzards circling overhead; saw a dozen wolves and coyotes sitting on gray haunches around him. All were waiting.

"Where from, stranger? What mout your name be? I'm Hugh Glass, deserter, buccaneer, keelboatman, trapper, hunter, and one-bite cannibal. Anyway what's left after an old she-rip had her picks at him."

The sun sank. The narrow brushed-over gully gradually cooled.

A turtledove mourned nearby: ooah—koooo—kooo—koo.

"Oh! this looks like something now. Hellfire if it don't. The thought of it makes the eyes stick out of a man's head."

The turtledove souled again: kooooaaa.

"Hurrah, Jim! Run, lad, or we'll be made meat of sure as shootin'."

Hugh dreamt of two boys, one a blackhead like himself, the other a sunhead like Mabel his rip of a wife as was. They were looking up to him. He was showing them how to stand up to trouble like men. Point up. But Mabel was raking him from behind. Down his back.

Calling him a worthless bum. A soak who couldn't stick to a job. A poorpeter who was always getting into fights with his bosses. A tramp who was always running off to the woods. She was ripping him up and ripping him down. After a while the blue eyes of the two boys lowered in shame for him. He couldn't stand up to trouble himself, let alone teach them. She roared him; she ripped him; she gnawed him. She clawed him until he was finally cowed proper. Laid low. Under the shame in their eyes. What did the old she-rip want?

"Set your triggers, lads."

Hugh dreamt.

"Jim, lad, let me tell ee something. When the net falls on ee, there's only two things to do. Set still ontil they take the net off again. Or run off with the net and all. And never come back. Because if you make the littlest move, you just entangle yourself all the more in the law. No, lad, do like I did. Run off with the net and all."

Hugh slept.

The wolves and the coyotes pressed closer, waiting. The wrinkleneck buzzards settled on nearby branches, waiting. The flies went off into the brush for the night.

Rusty dusk flowered and faded in the west. Mosquitoes came out like vapors.

Chapter 3

A cold touch woke him. Something moved against his good side.

Hugh rolled his grizzly head to have a look. The moment he moved, the something suddenly stiffened against him; abruptly set up a loose rattling noise like little dry gourds clattering in a wind.

Rattler. Hugh forced himself to hold still. The least move and he'd have a batch of rattler poison in his blood, besides all the rot he already had in it.

Rattler? Ah! Fresh rattler made good meat.

Ae, but how to catch it.

After a while he could feel the rattler relaxing against him. It made a faint dry slithering sound. Presently he could feel it begin to crawl away. Its pushing touch slowly drew away from him.

He waited until he was sure it had crawled at least a couple of feet away. Then he moved, moved quick. He sat up against the howling red monsters in his back and rump; snatched up a heavy stone; lunged; mashed the snake's head before it could coil and strike.

He watched the snake thresh in the sand. It was a huge devil, some six feet long, and quite fat.

He found another stone, this time a flat one with a rough ragged edge like a crude Digger hatchet. With it he jammed the snake's head off at the neck. He jammed off the skin along one side a ways and skinned it. Then he cut the rattler into a dozen or so separate steaks. Blood welled over his hands.

He brushed through the ash heap, luckily found a couple of hot coals again, built himself a fine roaring fire. He roasted some of the rattler meat thoroughly and filled up. The meat was stringy, but it was fresh and fairly tasty. "Can't shine with painter meat. Or even old bull. But meat's meat when there's hard doin's."

Finished eating, and caching the rest of the rattler meat under dry sand, he crawled to the running water and had himself a long and cooling drink. He also lay in the water for a while, on his back, and let the stream and the minnies wash away the impurities.

He had no idea how long he had slept since eating the putrid bear meat. From the way his stomach felt he could have slept a couple of days. Certain it was that he had slept at least a full night because once again yellow light was striking up into blue, which meant morning.

His fever was down some, of that Old Hugh was sure too. He was still very stiff, very sore all over, and the deer-sinew stitches pulled terribly every time he moved. But the hotness, thank God, was pretty much gone away, and his eyes saw clear again, and taste had returned to his tongue.

He ran a cautious hand over his body, exploring his crusted wounds. His jaw felt much better, and the crust in his beard was already beginning to peel away along the edges. The welt up in his hair felt good too.

He explored his back. Except for one bad spot which he couldn't quite reach, he found that somewhat improved also. The near edge of the bad spot was greasy and very swollen. Green flies were still buzzing around it. He pushed his hand around as far as he could, touched it all gingerly. There was quite a gap. A flap of flesh hung down from it, and he thought he could touch bone, touch the curve of a rib.

He explored his torn rump and was surprised to find that completely crusted over. The old she-rip had taken

her biggest bite out of him there. He had expected it
to be a horrible mess.

The right leg was different. It was swollen almost
twice its size, was discolored blackpurpleblue. He felt
of it gingerly; then steeled himself as he dug in to find
the line of the bone. Halfway down, directly below
where her great teeth had bit in, gnawed in, through
the hard swollen flesh, he could feel a crack, a ridge
the size of a rim on a stone crock. He looked down the
length of the grotesquely fat leg and thought he could
see where it bent off a little at a slight angle. That
meant trouble. If he let the cracked bone knit as it now
lay, he was doomed to become a cripple. Probably never
be able to run again. Which meant the end of his prairie
days. A down bull had no business in red-devil country.

"Whaugh!" he roared. "Whaugh!" He laughed to
see the dozen or more waiting dun-colored coyotes and
whitegray wolves jump back. "G'wan, go way. You're
gettin' no free bites out a me. G'wan! What ye fancy
in this old bull is more than this child can cipher. And
I'm not sharin' any of my cache snakemeat with ye."

He squinted up at the dozen or so turkey buzzards
floating around above him. He roared up at them too.
"Whaugh!" He laughed to see them raise their wavering, gliding, greenblack circles.

It took him two full days to make up his mind to set
the leg himself.

Cost him what it might in inhuman pain, it had to
be done. It was that or give up forever being a mountain
man in the free country.

Once his mind was made up, he went about it doggedly. He crawled over to a sturdy little chokecherry
tree with a crotch a foot off the ground. Grimacing,
cursing, he lifted the bad leg into it, hooked the heel
and toe well down in the crotch, with his hands caught
hold of another nearby stubby trunk—then heaved.

Pain filled him from tip to toe. He passed out a few seconds.

When he came to, he rested a while, panting desperately.

The mourning dove souled in the gully: ooah—koooo—kooo—koo.

When he thought he could stand it again, he set himself and once more gave his leg a mighty wrenching pull. There was a crack; something gave; and he passed out again.

He came to gently, easily, up out of black into blue into yellow light.

He rested a little.

A magpie scolded a squirrel in some bullberry bushes across the brook. The squirrel skirled back.

Breath caught, he felt of his leg carefully, finger tips probing through the swollen rawhide flesh. Ho-ah. The bone had popped back into place. Ae. And now to splint it.

Working patiently, doggedly, saving his breath, he broke off a half-dozen straight chokecherry saplings about an inch thick. With his crude stone chisel he jammed off a long strip from the grizzly hide and built a tight splint around his leg. The strap of raw bearhide was still moist. In time it would shrink and make the splint fit snug.

The sun was almost directly overhead when he finished. Heat boiled out of the gully in waves. A dead calm radiated over the land. The vultures lay back waiting, wondering at all the movement of him. They turned slow wheels. It puzzled them that a stinking, filthy, hairy skeleton of a creature could show so much life.

Hugh crawled back to the stream and in the shadow of the bullberry bushes let the water run along his back. He splashed water over his face and chest and belly and legs. The water was wondrous cool, wondrous soothing.

He napped.

He dreamt. And in the dream he heard Jim and Fitz talking about him.

But while the dream was very clear and very real, the talk in it was muttery, unclear. He couldn't make out what they were saying. He could see their mouths going, and could make out it was about him, but he couldn't make out the sense of what they said.

He dreamt. And in the dream he dreamt he had died alone in a gully, his leathers and meat torn to shreds, his bones picked over by green snakenecked buzzards. He cried out in his sleep; awoke in a buzzing stupor.

Afternoon came on. Water washed him. Minnies lipped him. Afternoon waned. Water soaked him. Minnies tickled him.

Toward evening, the air cooling, he revived again. He dug up a few of the rattler steaks he'd stashed in the sand and roasted them. For greens he ate grass tips. For fruit he had some buffalo berries and chokecherries. Ripe plums hung near; they looked very inviting, but he couldn't get himself to touch them. He washed his supper down with cool spring water. The meat and the greens and the fruit and the water strengthened him.

Later, when the sun had set and the stars and the mosquitoes came out and the wolves and coyotes began padding around him on the sand, he recalled his nightmare dreams of the afternoon. Though again he couldn't make out what it was Jim and Fitz had said in the dream.

"Wonder where the lads went to? Can't understand it. There must be some reason for the lads not bein' around. 'Tis a deep puzzle to this old coon."

He rolled it over in his mind. He couldn't wait any longer for the lads to show up. He had to begin thinking about himself.

He nodded. Yes, think of himself. He had to get out of that gully and that part of the wild country soon or he was a gone goose.

He rolled it over in his mind some more. The first thing was to get back to the settlements some way. As the crow flies it was at least some two hundred miles north to Henry's Post on the Yellowstone and Missouri. And Ft. Kiowa was some two hundred miles back the other way. Either way the country was buzzing with Rees as mad as hornets. There were also the rapidly increasing number of Sioux war parties. Even some Mandans.

He thought on it. One thing was certain—he couldn't follow the Grand River back to the Missouri and then follow that back to the fort. Too many mad Rees that way. They were thicker in that direction than in any other. So if he went back to the fort he'd have to cut across the open country to the south.

He puzzled over his broken leg. He wouldn't be able to crawl on that for at least a month, let alone walk on it. He either had to lay around until it knitted or somehow drag it after him. The first alternative meant he might starve to death, if he didn't freeze first; the second meant excruciating pain.

He puzzled over his splinted leg. If he could somehow carry it off the ground he might be able to crawl along on his elbows and one knee.

He puzzled on it. And finally decided to make himself a slape—travois, as the pork-eaters called it—a pair of shafts such as the squaws hooked up to dogs and ponies to dray their possessions. He remembered seeing Bending Reed make one down in Pawnee land along the Platte.

"I feel queersome," he said, and presently fell asleep.

Mosquitoes hummed over him. A light breeze came up and tousled his gray hair.

Chapter 4

A cold nose woke him.

He made a grab for the cold nose and the whitegray wolf that went with it.

But he missed. He wasn't quite quick enough and the wolf had been a trace too stealthy. So it was no fresh meat for breakfast that morning.

He dug up what was left of the rattler and set about roasting it. He topped off the meat with grass tips and buffalo berries again, washing it all down with fine morning-cool water.

It was when he'd had his fill of water that he decided on Bending Reed and Ft. Kiowa two hundred miles away. He had to have the benefit of her cooking, her care, her potent herbs. She'd heal him. She'd put him back on his feet. Good old Reed. What a fine mate she'd made him all these years in the far country.

Calmly he set to work. He built a slape out of two long willow poles. He bound one to each side of his bad leg, starting at the hip socket and extending well out beyond his toes so that the entire leg rode well above the ground and had the benefit of the springy tips to absorb shock.

He knew there'd be a lot of prickly-pear cactus most of the way back. He had to find some protection for his elbows and arms, for his one good knee and leg. Looking around he hit on it. Cut out patches from the old she-rip. With his crude chisel he jammed off a set of patches, with tie-strings, and bound them on tight.

He sloughed off what dried fat and meat was still stuck to the rest of the bear hide and cut armholes in it and drew it on over his back.

He also collected the grizzly's four claws. Bending Reed had often lamented that while he might have counted coup on many a brave in battle and had scalps to show for it, he still hadn't counted coup on a grizzly. She wanted to see her brave decked out with a necklace of grizzly claws. Well, he'd at last got his grizzly, and in a hand-to-hand fight at that.

He laughed when he thought of what she'd do with the claws. She'd hold a victory dance around them; then string them on a deer sinew; then drape them around his hoary old neck.

He planned his trip carefully. It would be safest to crawl at night; sleep during the day. Best, too, to take a creek up one gully to the top of a divide; cross on the hogback ridge; take a gully down on the other side, and so on until he crossed the Moreau River and got to the Cheyenne. At the Cheyenne he'd be far enough south and out of range of the Rees to once again head toward the Missouri.

He began the terrible odyssey on the evening of the ninth of September, the ninth day of the Moon of Maize Ripening. The sun had just set and the high bald hills across the Grand River valley glowed like round piles of hot copper slag. Dusk came in out of the east like dark doom.

He followed the South Fork of the Grand. It veered almost directly south. He crept along the sides of the bluffs, halfway up, overlooking the meandering stream. He kept a wary eye on the brush in the draws on either side, on the trees beside the flickering stream, on the horizon rims all around.

He crept along on his elbows and one good knee. His splinted leg slaped behind him in its travois. A pair of whitegray wolves and a lone coyote trailed after him. The green wrinkleneck buzzards had given up.

Silvertip bearskin thrown over his back, bearhide guards on his elbow points and good knee, dried paws dangling from his neck on a deer sinew, he looked more like a wounded grizzly than a wounded human, looked like a bear who'd come off second best with a nest of bear traps.

A herd of antelope spotted him in the evening dusk. Curious, they approached him cautiously. When they finally got a whiff of him, they bolted over a bluff, white tails flagging.

Darkness fell slowly, changed over him like a sea of clear blue water gradually turning to black ink. Stars came out low and sharp.

He crept along cautiously. He felt his way along with his finger tips, foot by foot.

He crawled around boulders. He pushed through clumps of bunch grass. He dragged across barren gravelheads.

He ran into ant mounds, which suddenly became alive with wriggling stings. He ran into beds of pricklypear cactus, which each time reminded him of a pack of crouching porcupine. He ran into one coiled rattler, which gave him fair warning.

The first quarter mile went fine. But after that it was tough going. His wind gave out, and his elbows stung, and his one good leg tired. Oddly enough, the tiredness in his good leg set up a cramp in his bad leg.

He rested flat on his belly. He sweat. One ear on the bare ground and one ear up, he listened to the night sounds. He heard the stealthy ghostly prowling of the two wolves and the coyote. He heard the itching movement of armored beetles deep in the earth. He heard grasshoppers chawing spears of grass. He heard angleworms squirming up out of their holes and excreting rich crumbles of dirt on the surface of the earth.

The thought of being completely alone in a wild savage country, miles from any white settlement anywhere, sometimes rose in him like personified terror, like a humpnecked striking creature. He fought it, fought it, and swallowed it down.

Rees could be skulking anywhere. The two trailing wolves could at any moment multiply into a pack of wolves and make a rush for him. Another she-grizzly could be on the prowl.

One thing he was thankful for. Halfway up the bluff sides where he crawled along there were no mosquitoes to bother him. And of course in the night no green flies.

Now and then a puff-soft breeze rose out of the gullies and caressed his brow and soothed his warm itching back.

He rested flat on his belly. He thought of silent Fitz and the boy Jim.

Where were the lads? He recalled all their good points. They were fine laddies, they were, and deserved better. Gone under like the other Jim and the lad Augie.

Himself? He'd make it all right. He would play it close to the belt; cipher cautious all the way; save his breath whenever and wherever he could; sail carefully; man the rudder with a steady hand all the way into port, Ft. Kiowa, and come in loaded for bear and killing. Oh, he would all right. Old Hugh had rawhide muscles and a buckskin belly and the stretchingest a-double-s in captivity.

He crawled; rested; crawled.

Once he slept. And woke with a start. How long? How much of the cool black night had he wasted? He couldn't guess. Perhaps an hour. Maybe four. In any case he felt refreshed and rested.

He crawled along briskly again for a quarter mile.

He kept to the sides of the bluffs, in one side gully and out the other, on, on, always quartering south toward Ft. Kiowa, to Bending Reed who'd heal him with her nursing and her herbs and her soups, to the fort where the clerk would re-outfit him with a gun and possibles for the time when he'd be whole again, up on two legs, and ready to join Major Henry and the other lads up in the far sweetgrass country.

When dawn broke pink in the east at last, he was exhausted, gaunt with thirst, gray with fatigue. His fever had come back some. The red monsters had returned in his back and in his leg again.

Looking back along the bluff sides, along the highland, he guessed he'd crawled some four miles, perhaps five. A short way, yes, but for a broken man a great way. Only one hundred ninety-five miles left. Ae, he'd done better than he'd expected. There was still plenty of life left in the old gray mare. Looking back he saw, too, that by sticking to the highland he had saved himself many a weary turn alongside the wriggling meandering stream of the South Fork.

The sun was just up when he scurried down a draw toward the stream of the South Fork. He had a last look around. No sign of red devils that he could see. Good. Somehow during the night the two whitegray wolves and the lone coyote had drifted off. Also good. And overhead the buzzards hadn't come back. Ae, it looked better all the time.

The South Fork was a lively stream, some ten feet wide, a good foot deep, with a swift flow over white stones and gold gravel. He drank deep of its water, washed his face and hands and arms and as much of his torn seamed back and torn splinted leg as he could reach. For breakfast he had some grass tips, some thick wild onions he'd run across in the night and grubbed out, and a cluster of buffalo berries. He lacked meat but hoped to catch some later in the day after he'd had himself a good long sleep.

He made another careful survey around. He saw nothing.

Then he slid off under a thick cover of chokecherry trees. He spread out some dry, rusty bunch grass on the hard ground and covered it with the grizzly skin. He nuzzled in the soft bed.

He dozed fitfully for a time, at last fell into a sound and dreamless sleep.

A good day's work.

At nightfall he woke as stiff as a board.

His first thought was: "Down at last like an old bull buffler shot through the lights." His next thought was: "Maybe I should've looked more in that gully afore I left. The boys might've been further downstream. Dead or dyin'."

He didn't dare stir at first. He lay still on his bed of grizzly skin and bunch grass. The least twitch was an agony, especially in his back and down through his rump and swollen thigh. The redgray monsters still were with him.

At last, seeing how fast night was coming on, he gathered himself up into a ball of resolve and forced himself to roll over on his back.

He lay awhile, panting, very short of breath. The pain was terrible.

"Ham-bit by a bear," Hugh muttered in his dirty blood-clotted beard. "Well, at least it's no worse than bein' ham-shot."

He looked up, saw how the leaves of a plum thicket flittered in a rising evening breeze, saw how dusk was coming out of the east like a brown dust storm, saw how a pink glow from the sunset gave the oncoming brown sky an odd lilac hue.

He heard a magpie scolding down the river a ways. He heard field mice scampering over the leaves under the chokecherry trees.

He stretched carefully, starting the stretch at his toes and letting it creep up through both the good thigh and the bad thigh, and on up through his belly and chest and on out to his finger tips.

The brownblack dusk raced overhead.

"Well, Hugh, old hoss, time to turn out. There's grub to be got and sightin's to make."

With a rumbling groan he rolled over on his belly and rose to his elbows and one good knee. "Eeee! This child's sure got the miseries now. Eeee!" He gave his hoary old head a shake. "It looks like I'm gonna pay for last night's good run."

He scratched his head. Gingerly he touched his fingers along the edge of the itching healing sinewed welt running through his beard and scalp. And in scratching, for the first time missed his old wolfskin cap. Ho-ah. Coyotes probably. Coyotes'd probably fought over the smell of him in it while he'd lain unconscious after the lads'd disappeared. Probably torn to shreds.

Hugh crawled to a gray boulder and painfully lifted himself part way up, resting for a minute on his one good leg. The bad leg lay splayed behind him, dragging like the wing of a wounded quail.

He found the evening star, and then the North Star. He sighted along the bluffs to the left. Ah. The fork still angled south. Good. With squinting eyes he worked out a trail halfway up the bluff sides. In the descending darkness he made out a large sidestream gully he'd have to cross. For the rest, it was clear sailing over barren humpy ground. The bluffs seemed to be fairly clean of cactus too.

He crawled through a few bushes, picking buffalo berries as he went, and grass tips, and chokecherries. He still couldn't get himself to eat plums, rich and ripe though they might hang all around him. Something about their pudging clotted red insides was still a little too much for him.

It was almost dark when he got to the river's edge. He had himself a long cool drink. The cool water and the fruit and the grass tips made him blowy. Like a dog tilted on three legs, he urinated in the fresh green sweetgrass.

Refreshed, relieved, sore muscles slowly loosening up, he started out on the second leg of his odyssey.

He crawled along cautiously, finger tips alert for cactus and sharp stones, ears alert for night prowlers and rattlesnakes, eyes alert for the ghosts of night. One elbow forward, then the other, then the good knee, with a hunching hopscotch motion, the bad leg trailing, he lurched on through the darkness, slowly, slowly.

What in tarnation had happened to the lads?

A night wind came up and began to push. It blustered around him; whipped his hoary hair; buffeted his bad leg; filled the air with stinging dust and sand.

He talked to himself. "That's it, old hoss, hold your noddle steady. South by west. South. South by east."

The wind parched his lips. His lips dried; became cracked; hurt.

The wind tugged at the bearskin over his back; stung his wounds with sand. It rattled the bearpaws dangling from the deer sinew around his neck.

The wind whipped up varying streaming veils of dust. The wind was cold. Sand bit his skin like a million pushing cold needles. He shivered and snuggled under the bearskin.

He lay down to rest, flat on his belly. He gasped for breath through a dry throat. His tongue lay in his mouth like a dry thumb.

"Wadder," he whispered, "wadder. Got to have wadder soon or this child's gone under after all."

He came across a bed of prickly-pear cactus. He broke off an ear; removed the needle-long pricks one by one; nibbled carefully, spitting out fuzz pricks; chewing slowly, making the meat and moisture in it last as long as possible. The prickly pear tasted a little like a geranium smelled.

He crawled on. He found a bed of dwarf wild roses in a dry swale. Finger tips wary of pricks, he fumbled out a handful of seeded fruits. He chewed each carefully, crunching the soft orange peel and the seeds into a fine thick paste. It was strong but it was food.

The wind blew cold, numbing his skin, fluttering the tatters and fringes of his buckskin.

He came across a trickle of water in a side gully. He took a sip. Bah! Bitter with wild salt and alkali. He spat. Ptt. Wild salt and alkali gave a man the bad skitters.

He napped. And dreaming, dreamt of dying in a lonely gully, dreamt of Jim and Fitz sitting around a jumping fire, dreamt they were talking about him.

"Jim? Fitz? Where be ye? Ye didn't desert me, did ee?"

He woke with a start. His head buzzed with a sudden terrific headache.

It was the dream. It seemed to have burnt flesh in his head. It had exhausted him. He lay resting.

He tried to think what it was he'd dreamt about. He wormed around through his head trying to find it. He had a feeling it was important. He pinched his old eyes tight trying to find it. But somehow the dream was always just out of reach.

He rested in the driving wind until dawn broke rusty over the eastern rim. He had just enough strength left to slide down the base of the bluff to the water's edge.

He drank a swallow at a time. He rested and panted. He drank a swallow.

He couldn't find it in him to hunt for food, neither for grass tips nor for bullberries.

He dragged himself into a chokecherry thicket out of the wind. He stretched out on dry ground and snuggled under the bearskin. He gave a last look around. Dust rode high in the sky above him. It was a hazy brown world. A bad day for butterflies. And a poor day's run for him. At most but a mile.

He fell asleep too tired to brood on what might have happened to the lads.

*   *   *

A sound as of faint distant continuous thunder awoke him. He opened his eyes, cracking apart stuck lids. He listened intently, heart bounding up wildly in his chest. There were no clouds overhead and the sun was halfway down the sky in the west. Thunder in a clear sky? He couldn't cipher it, unless. . . .

He turned his head a little and put his ear flat on the ground. There was a faint drumming in the earth all right. Buffalo? War party? Antelope? Mountain men?

He rolled over on his side. Near the root of a choke-cherry he spotted a gopher hole. Ah. That would tell him. He hunkered over and put his ear into the round dusty opening. And heard it. The clear steady drumming of hundreds even thousands of pounding hooves. Buffalo herd on the move. Coming his way too. Maybe red devils herding them into a surround to make meat. Wild thoughts sparked through his head. So that was to be his fate—scalped and left for wolf meat, or tromped to death.

With a wrench and a groan, and a curse at his sad fate, he got to his elbows and one good knee, drew the grizzly hide over his head, quickly skedaddled into the thickest part of the chokecherry brush. "It's kill or cure now."

They were on him before he had time to think of the redgray monsters in his back and rump and leg. They came up over the bald tan bluff from the north-east and roared down toward him and the river, mostly cows and calves at first, the cows tan in color and the calves red, lowing and bellowing, eyes strained and bloodshot, panting hot and hard, short tails whipping about like toy wood windmills, by tens by hundreds by thousands. They crashed through the chokecherry thicket to either side of him. They poured into the gully and poured out. Dust and sand stived up; hid the sun. Grass, tree leaves, twig bits, branches, pebbles spretted all around him. A few of the cows and calves bounded down into the South Fork and splashed across to the other side.

Hugh hunched up. As best he could he got his splinted leg under him and tried to protect it with his body. He waited for the inevitable. There was nothing to do but wait. Gray head bowed, gray bearskin-covered back bowed, he waited it out.

Then the young bulls came through the gully in waves, huge hairy, blowing, snorting young bulls, eyes wild, black head and black horns lowered, black shaggy humps and foreparts bouldering along, small tan afterparts skipping, each young bull for all the world looking like an overgrown black bull up front and a nervous tail-whipping silly tan heifer in back, one after another, by tens by hundreds by thousands, solid black walls of them, bellowing, blowing, roaring, wilder even than the cows and calves.

Hugh hunched over, waiting for eternity to come calling.

And at the last, the bulls once more, the old ones who always formed the rear guard of any large herd. They pounded through the gully as old men might, with heavier grunts, with more rasping breaths, with strange knocking or popping sounds in their joints, all of them dark black both up front and in back, brulling more than bellowing, old legs stilting more than bounding, a solid wall of them three deep, packed hide to hide, with behind them an occasional half-fleeing half-chasing whitegray wolf and dungray coyote following after—and at last they too were gone.

Hugh hunched over, waiting, waiting, waiting for the pound of horse hooves to come along next, and Indian yells, for the sleet and strike of arrows, for the pop and drill of the ball.

Nothing happened. Dust slowly drifted off. Dust slowly settled. Dust cleared away.

Hugh looked up. Gone. But not as if they'd never been.

Every bush, every chokecherry, every tuft of grass, every wild plum, every bullberry had been tromped into the sand, shredded to bits, blasted to tits. Everything. Even the ground had been relandscaped. What had once been a sharp-banked gully was now but a slow dip in the land.

Everything . . . except the small cluster of chokecherries where he sat hunched under. Somehow the three waves of rolling thunderous tons of buffalo flesh had parted to either side of him.

Hugh couldn't understand it until he threw back his grizzly skin for a better look around. The touch of the silvertip fur told him. The first buffaloes had mistaken him for a grizzly and in parting around him had set a pattern for the rest of the herd to follow.

It made Hugh smile a little. The old she-rip was turning out to be of some use to him after all. He was making the old she-rip pay him back in more ways than one: first as food, then as elbow and knee guards, then as a robe, and then as a disguise.

The excitement of the stampede died away and Hugh gradually came back to himself and his troubles. All that cow meat flying by, and buffalo cow at that, made him hungrier than ever. One look at his hands and arms told him he was getting thin a little too fast. "Got to have some meat soon or I'm bound for the boneyard sartain."

He crawled to the water's edge. The few buffalo who'd splashed through the stream had muddied it up. He waited until the water changed from brown to tan before he took a drink and washed his hands and beard.

The drink of water gave him a momentary feeling of well-being.

He decided to crawl on a ways. Farther along the buffaloes might have veered away from the South Fork and left him something to browse on. The sun was still high, and he had plenty of time before dark to find some grass and bushes.

He worried a little about what might have stampeded the buffalo. But look around as he might, he couldn't find sign of it. Probably just a whirlwind.

The stampeding buffalo had churned up the ground into fine floury yellow dust. He padded across it. He left an odd trail in the yellow dust: two long tracks, a round dent, and a pair of trailing wriggling marks. Hugh smiled a little when he thought of it. Let some trailhawk try to cipher that one! Ae. Either a three-legged two-tailed whangdoodle or a monster varmint from another world.

He was glad the wind was down and the late afternoon sun warm.

He crawled along steadily, staying well away from the meandering South Fork, cutting across from one lazy looping turn to the next, keeping to level ground above the first drop-off and beneath the line of bluffs to his left.

His arms and one good leg seemed to be taking it better. They were probably getting used to the odd navigation. The hip of the bad leg felt better too. The hip socket didn't ache as bad as before, and occasionally he found he could let a little of his weight rest on the willow slape. Probing a hand around behind him told him his rump was healing very well. The only spot that was still questionable was just out of his reach. It was above the loose flap of flesh on his back. The edges of it were greasy and Hugh's hand always came away from it stinking.

A mile farther along he saw where the buffalo had all veered across the river. They'd leveled its banks, rearranged the bed of the stream, destroyed a stone-cropped ford. It was amazing to see how in a few thunderous minutes a herd of buffalo could change the face of a country.

Ahead too were chokecherry and plum and bullberry bushes again. Ah. Grub at last. He hurried forward.

But he found another herd had been there before

him. They'd cleaned off all the leaves and berries within reach. They'd grazed off what little fresh grass there'd been. They'd even chewed off some of the tender twigs.

From his crouch Hugh looked up at the ripe black dripping berries out of reach overhead. "Doggone my skin, if that don't beat all." He shook his grizzled head. "Now how am I gonna get them berries?"

On hands and knee Hugh groused around until he found a long stick with a hook at the end. "Ah, now I've got ye. Come to Old Hugh." Hugh reached up the long hook and pulled down the springy tops of the cherry and bullberry bushes and helped himself. "Should a thought of this before. The best and ripest are always out of reach at the top."

He also dug up some tender roots: wild onion, bunch grass, wild lily, and wild turnip. In digging out the roots he came across a dozen or so white grubs. To his surprise the grubs tasted somewhat sweet, a little like stale white-sugar candy. And last he uncovered a nest of mice, a mother and two wee ones. He caught them each with a pounce, skinned and gutted them, ate them raw. "Meat's meat," he growled with an inner smile to himself.

Quickened, refreshed, he set out once more. The sun was almost down. Red began to bleed across the entire western horizon. The bald hills across the South Fork rose up into the falling red sun like lifting thunderheads. The bald hills on his side of the river sank away like the huge round waves of a falling sea.

He was just about through the thicket when he spotted it. A red buffalo calf. Hugh's old gray head reared up like a suddenly alert grizzly's. Food. Real food. Tender calf meat wasn't quite as good as young cow meat, but it was a lot better than old bull. And a whole lot better than raw mice fries.

The red calf had its head buried under some brush, its rear end sticking up grotesquely. Something had scared it, probably the other stampeding herd, and not finding its mother immediately, it had gone into what it thought was hiding. It made Hugh laugh even as he plotted to catch it and kill it.

Elbow by elbow, slowly, just barely inching along, looking a little like a huge gray humping grubworm, Hugh crept toward it. A dozen yards. Then only eight. Then four. Carefully Hugh picked up all the sticks and loose stones in his path and laid them to one side. There couldn't be a sound or the calf might bolt. Calves sometimes stayed hiding, head down like an ostrich, until their ma sought them out or until they heard another sound. Hugh knew of cases where calves had almost starved to death waiting for the old lady to get them, so deep was it set in them to play possum.

Hugh was almost within reach; he had settled back on his good knee and partly on the slape, his huge hairy hands open, when the willow slape creaked. The creak was enough. The red calf jerked; looked up, red eyes wild and a rolling white; saw him a grizzly rampant and ready to pounce; and then was off, already betraying in its double-motion gallop that it would someday be a front-heavy buffalo bull.

Hugh cursed. He watched it vanish over the bluffs ahead. "By the bull barley! that dummed leg. All set to dip in when whutt! away he goes. Lickety-split." Old Hugh shook his head sadly. "The luck of Old Hugh is enough to set the devil himself to weeping like an old woman." He shook his old gray head. "Yessiree, there went supper, dinner, and breakfast all combined. Besides a nice red cap for my head. And maybe even a pair of soft moccasins for Reed the old lady."

Night came up over him black and cold. There was no wind.

He crawled on, a lurch and a roll and a lurch. He kept well above the fork.

Chilly night air pressed down on him. It got colder by the hour.

Hugh shivered under his grizzly hide. His fingers numbed and he had trouble picking out a path through the prickly-pear cactus beds. He worried that he might fumble onto a nest of rattlers.

"Looks like we're in for some frost by mornin', sartain sure." Hugh blew white breaths in the black night. "Just so it don't snow. That's the main worry now. That, and more grub."

Eight hours later, when he came to the next zigzagging side gully, he stopped to check his bearings. He found the Big Dipper above him; then the North Star. In the faint starlight he traced out the meandering glittering surface of the river below. Just ahead it veered off sharply to the west. Ho-ah! The time had come for him to leave the stream and follow a gully south up through the bluffs and climb to the top of the first hogback watershed ridge. That meant no water and no berries ahead for probably some twenty miles. He'd have to fill up all he could right where he was, get himself a good rest, and hope to have enough reserve to make it over the top and down a gully on the other side until he hit the Moreau River or an angling branch of the Moreau.

Dawn broke red over the earth's east rim. Light spread over the tossing kneaded land very rapidly. Lightblue sky in the east pushed back darkblue sky in the west.

It was time to take on grub and hole up again for the day.

He sat puffing like an old gray ganted dog. His breath blew white in the pink dawn. He heard the first frost of the year moving up the side gully. He heard green leaves slowly crispening.

Shivering in the hoarfrost morning, Hugh supped on bullberries, and chokecherries, and tipsin roots, and white grubs, and a couple of slow armored beetles. The first frost had sweetened the buffalo berries, made them almost rotten ripe. Hugh had himself an extra-large helping.

He drank water from an ice-wrinkled South Fork. He washed up, crystal clear spears of ice catching in his matted beard.

Before he turned in, under some brush in a side hole in the side gully, he had a last look around. No sign of varmint, either two-legged or four-legged. Good. He'd had a good day's run, his belly, though blowy, was full, and he had a warm fur to sleep under.

He slept. He dreamt of stampeding buffalo herds. He dreamt of a red buffalo-bull calf playing crouch tag with him like a playful puppy. He dreamt of prickly-pear cactus beds advancing on him like droves of porcupine. He dreamt of glass-clear beardtips cracking in the gray frost of morning. He dreamt of inch-long white snakes emerging from the wound in his back and from between his bare white ribs. He dreamt of seeing Jim and Fitz being torn limb from limb.

Chapter 5

A cool evening breeze woke him.

Opening slow eyes, Hugh rose out of rolling dreamland into a land of ragged ocher gullies and bald gravelhead bluffs and wind-streaked skies.

One long look at the ragged gullies and Hugh let himself sink back into torpor. Why live? Ae, what was the use?

For a little while Hugh let himself drift through a fur-scented purgatory, between a state of dreamy sweet death and a state of prickly sour life.

But his stomach and blowy belly had other ideas. "First things first," it said. "Turn out, you lazy white nigger, and round us up some grub. There's work ahead. And sweet revenge after that. Turn out, old hoss!"

Hugh heard his stomach talking so clearly he was sure he was at last out of his head, had at last gone loco.

"Turn out!"

"Ae, ae, master. I heard ye the first time."

And half-smiling, half-afraid of the whimsy, Hugh threw back the heavy stiff silvertip grizzly fur and, with a groan, rolled over on his belly and rose to his hands and knee and had a look out of his hole.

The sun was almost down, sinking clear and yellow across the South Fork. That meant another striker of a cold night. It made him shiver to think about it.

He cleared his throat, hawking up balls of night spit.

He stretched his limbs as much as the redgray monsters in his back and bum leg would allow.

In methodical fashion he set about getting his meal. He had himself some frost-sweetened bullberries, and wild turnip or tipsin roots, and a couple dozen white grubs, and fresh water.

He was washing up when he spotted a gopher. Like an Arab about to pray at sunset, it sat on its haunches at the edge of its hole, paws folded across its chest.

Hugh's old predatory eyes narrowed. Fresh meat. Ae. But how to catch it.

Almost immediately he had an idea. Fix a snare with deer sinew. He snapped off a couple dozen whangs or fringes from the front of his buckskin shirt, tied them together into a good sound leather string about three feet long. He made a slipknot loop at the end.

The moment he advanced, the striped yellowgray gopher vanished tail-whipping into its burrow. Hugh placed the snare carefully around the edge of the hole and then lay back, waiting, the end of the string looped around a finger.

He waited.

He watched the sun hit the horizon in a vast explosion of clear yellow light. He watched shadows race in from the bluffs across the South Fork.

After a while the gopher couldn't resist it. It had to have a look, if not a last peek, at the fading day. Its head popped out an exploratory second; popped back in. Then it popped out its head again for a longer look; then a still longer look—and that instant Hugh jerked the snare and had himself some squealing fresh meat. It had a strong wild taste, naturally salty, and he relished it.

Fortified, quickened, he began the long climb south, up, up, toward the divide on the hogback. The going was rough right from the start. The gully zigzagged sharply, sometimes cut very deep to either side into the sloping land. It was cold, bitter cold. The higher he went the thicker the prickly-pear cactus became, the more numerous the anthills. The heavy bearskin soon began to weigh like a lead sheet on his back. For every three feet he crawled forward on loose dirt, he slid one foot back. Soon too he hit gravelheads with sharp cutting little pebbles. Occasionally in the dark he rammed head-on into boulders, scaring the wits out of himself, making him think for a moment he'd run into another she-rip of a mother grizzly.

The higher he climbed the colder and more brisk the northwest wind became. Another frost was due as soon as the wind let up, and this time a sharp one, maybe even a good freeze. It would be a hard night on hands and knees. It would also be a hard night on a broken leg with poor circulation.

He was glad about one thing. The old she-rip fur might hang heavy on his back but it was warm. Maybe its weight did cut down his traveling time but it more than made up for it by the comfort it provided. Hugh snuggled under it as he struggled along.

The stars came out crisp white. The wind veiled black dust across his path. The gully became shallow; at last lifted up and became a low draw with thick clumps of bunch grass and occasional beds of prickly-pear cactus.

Gradually Old Hugh tired. His good leg trembled with quick fleeting cramps. His elbows quivered from the ache and pain of various stone bruises.

He rested, panting; slept awhile, ganting; awoke with a start, shivering; crept on, bad leg slaping behind; rested some more, puffing; slept.

He dreamt of dying alone in a gully, cold and blue and bloated with snakenecked greenblack turkey buzzards circling hungrily overhead.

He woke with a jerk; crawled a few yards; rested; slept.

He dreamt of Jim and Fitz sitting around a jumping fire and arguing about him.

Cold and shivering, he again woke with a guilty start; crept on a ways; rested; slept.

He dreamt of his two boys, the blackhead and the sunhead, dreamt of the old she-rip tearing him up and down his back.

And creeping along in the black night, he fell into a small washout. He was so exhausted when he hit bottom he didn't bother to see if his bad leg had tumbled down with him. It was too cold to bother. "I feel queersome," he murmured. He curled up as best he could, snuggled under the heavy grizzly hide, and fell asleep.

He slept through dawn and on through a sunny glinting day. Rusty dusk lay over the sloping land, and over the bald tan bluffs and small red teat mesas forming the ridge to the south, and down in the far valley of fall yellows behind him to the north, when he at last poked his head out of the small washout.

"This child's slept a hole in the day, 'pears like."

He stared at the brown evening. He blinked bloodshot eyes. His bowels rumbled with hunger. "This child needs meat." He began to puff just thinking of the work ahead. "And this child needs wadder too."

Stiff-limbed, with one of the redgray monsters raging again, the one in his back, he clambered out of the washout.

One good look around and he knew he was doomed to go without either grub or water for that day—unless he ate rusty dead bunch grass and drank his own urine. There was nothing, not a bush or a tree or a trickle of water.

Like a dog digging for gophers, he scrabbled some dirt out from under a thick clump of bunch grass. Ae. Nothing but dry hard dirt. In digging, dirt packed in under his fingernails and he sucked them clean in his mouth. The dirt had a sour flour taste.

He pinched in his brain to help quiet down his growling stomach. He worked up some saliva to wet his throat and lips. He hoped the wind would stay down during the night. Wind dried one out.

Just before black night swooped down over the long swinging land he had a last look around. From the spot where the sun had set he plotted his course for the night. The course lay between two small red crumbling mesas directly south. He saw that his climb during the night previous had lifted him fairly high out of the South Fork valley. He also saw that the rest of the way to the top of the hogback divide lay smooth and undulating ahead of him. Even the incline was much more gentle.

There was no sign of redskin or varmint in the god-forsaken drygrass country. The land was clean of green grass and running red meat. The sky above was clean of flying flesh. There was nothing but himself and the twinkling stars above and the rustling dried bunch grass below. He was alone. Solitary. There was only himself to feel sorry for himself. There was only himself to tell he was himself. Only he knew that he knew. He was alone.

"These parts make this child so lonesome for company he's about ready again for huggin' with a she-grizzly."

He shivered in the cold. "But I'll say this for the frost. They won't be any more mosquitoes this fall. Or green bottleflies."

He found it in him to go on without food. Some little energy had seeped into his well during the night. For a little while there was enough to work the pump.

He laughed grimly to himself when he thought of the trail he was leaving across the country: two long tracks, a round dent, and a pair of wriggling marks—a three-legged two-tailed whangdoodle for sure. Ae, and maybe even Old Wakantanka himself at last come down to earth to play a Christ's role.

He crawled on slowly like a three-legged dog dragging a stinking gamy leg and walking on sore pads.

Thrown stars moved across the black skies.

"Wadder," Old Hugh murmured, "wadder. Got to have wadder."

He looked up at the star-flying skies. "Don't it ever rain in this godforsaken country? I'd catch me some fresh rain water in me bearskin." He wetted his cracked lips; tried to work up some saliva for his parched throat.

"Wadder," he murmured, "wadder. If I only had wadder I wouldn't mind goin' without meat."

The closer he got to the two little red teat mesas the stonier the terrain became. Bunch-grass clumps became more sparse. Even the cactus beds became rare. Rough blackred stones began to shred his bearskin elbow and knee guards. Prickly brush tore at his buckskin shirt-front as he straddled over them. Old Hugh cursed the country. Much more of it and he'd have to cut up his bearskin for clothes and guards.

He stopped to rest on a long flat rock. Before stretching out he felt around first to make sure there weren't any rattlers around.

He panted, mouth open, beard floofing in and out of his cracked lips.

He panted. It was hard doin's, all right. Ae. And probably the death of him at last.

He thought of the gamy death smell that'd been hanging around him a bit stronger the last day. He explored his back under the bearskin. Some of the scab had come off the sinew-seamed wounds. In a couple of places he could pull out the deerskin stitches. The stitches came out easy, greasy, like old hairs pulling out of rotted follicles. He pushed his arm around farther to touch the open sore above the loose flap of flesh and bared white ribs. Still slippery with pus. He felt of it gingerly. His hand came away stinking. Bah!

He found the open wound hadn't rotted through to his lung. He was done for if it had. Ae. He'd seen men rot away into slow death once the corruption got into their bellows.

He explored it carefully again. He felt the bare bone of one of his ribs. He felt the string of a loose tendon. Or was it a blood vessel? There were also odd squirming bits in the middle of it.

Squirming? Ho-ah. Maggots, then. Ae. So he was rotting away like an old down buffalo in a wallow like he feared.

He lay down flat on his belly. Just about dead before he'd even crossed the first divide, he was. With at least one more big divide to go and a long raft ride after that down the Cheyenne and then the great Missouri itself—and the raft ride probably the toughest part of the trip.

Why live? Ae, what was the use?

He wept.

He dipped into sleep and dreamt of campfires. There were many of them and they all were one. Around the jumping flames sat Jim and Fitz still arguing about him. He himself lay stretched out on his belly, his back blooming with little bloody plum trees. But once again he couldn't make out what Jim and Fitz were saying.

He called out, "Jim? Fitz? Where be ye? Come clost so I can hear ee."

The roar of his own voice woke him from the flame-jumping nightmare.

His head buzzed. A terrible headache cracked in his skull. When he looked up at the stars, they became streaks of light rushing from east to west, and when he looked ahead, the pair of red mesas blurred off into a dancing mountain range.

He dipped into sleep and dreamt again. This time he was back in Lancaster. Back with his white wife Mabel and his two sons, blackhead and sunhead. There was a final supper of some sort, a supper which for once had begun with jolly joshing, with the boys happy that Pap and Ma for once were getting along a little. It was the night he'd come home with a new hunting rifle, a Lancaster model, instead of coming home drunk as he usually did. The food was good, though somewhat skimpy. The talk was pleasant, though somewhat chaffy. Hugh was glad Mabel was smiling some again. He liked seeing his boys happy. And Hugh had just begun to think maybe Mabel was actually having a change of heart, giving up her notion that he should get a better job, accepting his notion that they should move farther west so he could hunt for a living, giving up her airish notion of rising in the world—when somehow, he didn't know just how, somehow it happened that he dropped a family heirloom of her mother's, a prize hand-painted bowl, breaking it to a thousand smithereens. That set it off. To the sad horror of the lads, he and Mabel were at it again. She threw things at him: mops, pails, pestle, breadboard, coffee grinder. He might have accepted all that, but she spotted his new Lancaster gun. She picked it up by the barrel end and rushed toward him, intent on smashing its butt over his head. That was too much for Hugh. Let her break his new gun over his own noggin? Never. Not on your life. He jumped up and wrestled it from her. Enraged that he should dare show physical resistance, she slugged him. In a flash Hugh balled his own fist and hauled off and hit her smack in the face, hit her so hard she spun across the room and landed in the woodbox. There was a terrible silence. And in that silence it came to Hugh at last, finally, that he could never live with that she-rip of a woman. She was just too much for a man. There'd never be a living with her, of any kind, no matter how much he loved his lads, Blackie and Sunny. So he deserted. Deserted the lads even though he heard them calling after him, lonesomely, "Pap! Pap! where are you going, Pap?" But Hugh hardened his heart; pretended he didn't hear them. "Pap! Pap!"

Their shrill boyish voices calling him woke him with a start from his dream. He looked around wildly as if half-expecting to see the lads themselves.

Again his head buzzed with a terrible cracking headache.

He shuddered. What awful dreams he was having lately.

He lay flat on his belly, possessed by the after depression of the nightmarish dream, lay possessed by a dark sense of guilt, so dark he shuddered again involuntarily.

Deserted them, that's what he'd done. What a miserable coward he was. Maybe Mabel was a rakehellion she-rip, ae, but the boys were still his boys, of his own flesh and blood, that's a fact, and good boys too, boys who deserved to have a father. It hadn't been their fault that he and their she-rip of a mother hadn't been able to get along. Not at all.

Deserted them. Ae. Too cussed independent he was.

He said it aloud the first time. "Maybe that's how come it's this child's turn to be deserted. Bein' paid back in kind, he is."

The saying of it aloud startled him.

Deserted? He deserted in turn? The lads Jim and Fitz desert him?

Impossible. Not his lads. Impossible.

He turned his head over and rested on the other cheek. He pushed the thought angrily from his mind.

He lay puffing.

The dark aftereffects of the dream persisted. It weighed down on him. It haunted him.

He couldn't get rid of the idea that maybe he'd been deserted after all. Thinking on it, a man could see how it explained everything—no dead bodies around, no horses, no gun or possibles, no hunter's or trapper's truck about.

Oh, but the lads wouldn't't've left him behind to die the hard way. Impossible. He put it from his mind. There was work to do.

Crumbling with weakness, parched and cracking with thirst, cells sucking with hunger, somehow he found it in him to rise to his elbows and one good knee and crawl on.

Crawl on. Creep on. Nose on. Past stones. Around boulders. Through rocky defiles. Over cutting jagged outcroppings.

He stopped to rest. He lay puffing, ganting.

Deserted? could his companyeros Jim and Fitz have deserted him?

He considered the two lads, each in turn.

Jim now. Jim was too goodhearted to pull a stunt like that on his Old Hugh. Jim had good upbringing. Not Jim. No.

He puffed; rested.

And Fitz? Fitz, well, Fitz was a horse of another color all right. Fitz was hard, practical, cautious. There was no room for peedoodles in him. Fitz never laughed. Something wrong with a man who never laughed. And then all that book learning of his. Anybody knew that reading made a puffball lighter in the head. Reading filled the head with excuses on how not to be a man in a fix. On how not to be a brave buck. In a fix a bookman sat down and told over all his ideas afore he got to work and shot his way out of a fix. In a fix a man hadn't ought to have but one idea—and that was how to get out of a pretty fix pronto. Concluded to charge—did so. That was what true mountain men did.

Fitz? Yes, Fitz might think on it in a close fix.

He crawled on, crept on, nosed on.

Twice he scared up mule-eared jack rabbits. Another time he flushed up a herd of fleeing flagging white-tailed antelope.

Once he almost had a jack rabbit. The jack had cowered until he was on top of him. In the starlit quartermoon-lit night Hugh saw it first as a round gray stone. Its roundness in the midst of the tumbled coarse jagged rock attracted his feeler hand as something to rest on in relief. He put his hand on it. There was a giving of soft fur and flesh. And a startled squeal. And then before it occurred to him it might be meat to eat, before his hand could instinctively close on it, the jack rabbit squirted to one side and, in a huge shrilling bound, was gone.

"Meat," he muttered, smelling his hand and recognizing the warm milklike rotted-clover smell of the creature, "meat."

He rested, puffing, cheek resting on a hard cold rock.

The dark thought wouldn't leave him alone. The tougher and grimmer the crawl up the hogback became, the more he became convinced, even possessed, with the idea that his lads Jim and Fitz had deserted him, that Fitz had somehow talked Jim into it.

Deserted. The lads had deserted him. That Irisher Fitz had done it.

Damned Irish. Never was any good for anything except run away from a fix. A fighting Irishman usually meant an Irishman afraid of being called a coward. They could talk forward faster and walk backward faster than any other dummed two-legged creature on earth. He'd sensed it in Fitzgerald from the first. Too practical, too cautious. Hard front and soft back. And the boy Jim, though a Scotchman like himself, too young to know better. Damned Irish. That's what a man got for learning life out of books.

Deserted.

A wave of hate swept over him. If there was one thing Old Hugh hated, it was cowardly deserters. Amongst mountain men alone in a far wild country full of enemy varmint there just wasn't room for cowards, deserters, or they would all go under. In red-devil country mountain men had to stick together. It was the code. He himself had often risked his topknot to save some comrade left behind in battle. Many a time. He didn't deserve to have this happen to him. Especially not at the hands of his own lads, Jim and Fitz. Not after the way he'd saved their skin from the major's wrath.

How could his own lads have come to it?

He crawled on. Nosed on. Crept on.

But the dark thought was back again the next time he lay flat on his belly to rest.

Could they really have deserted him? His lads?

He couldn't shake the notion. He remembered too well how the lads had let him cover up their sleeping on guard, remembered how they had not talked up like men to say they were guilty of negligence, that they had indirectly caused the death of Augie Neill and Jim Anderson. If they could be cautious once, they could be cautious twice.

Cautious. Ae. Too cautious. "Ae, and you can lay your pile on it that it was Fitz's idee too. He talked Jim into it. Poor lad."

But Jim was a coward to let Fitz talk him into it. The blackhearted bugger. Leaving him to die the hard way.

"If this child ever gets out of this alive, the first thing he's gonna do is track them cowardly cautious devils down and kill 'em. Inch by inch. Slow torture 'em. Skin 'em alive. Fry 'em alive. Punch pine needles and pine slivers in 'em like the Pawnees did to Old Clint and make torches out of 'em. At the same time, so they can watch each other go up in smoke." Hugh ground his teeth; clenched and unclenched his fists.

Another wave of hate passed over him. The cowardly snakes. The cowardly squaws. Leaving him to die the hard way. Alone.

"Oily cowards. Someday this old coon will have a showdown with ee, lads."

Those two devils who called themselves mountain men had a code all right. Deserter code. Ae.

Well, he had a code too. A code which said a man had a right to kill deserters. It was a crime before God and man both to desert a man in a wilderness full of howling red devils, taking his possibles away from him, leaving him without food, with nothing but his naked hands left to fight off the varmints. Leaving him without a last bullet to kill himself with in case of unbearable pain. Or in case of capture by red devils. The lads knew a hunter always saved one last ball for himself in case of a pinch. If he could help it, a hunter did all he could to avoid torture by Indians—like Old Clint suffered at the hands of the Pawnees.

Leaving him with a ripped-up back and a broken leg. Ae, he had a code too, and it said to kill deserters on sight.

Waves of hate flushed over him. He ground sand in his clenching fists.

"Them oily cowards. If it's the last thing I ever do, I'm gonna live long enough to kill the both of 'em. The major is gonna know too. They're maybe laughin' to themselves right now, thinkin' they got away from it, not buryin' me, playin' me for a sucker, and runnin' off with the best rifle this side of the Ohio. But they'll have another think comin' someday."

He got to his hands and knee and crept on. He crept until he couldn't anymore.

He stopped. He lay ganting in a long crack in the rocks. He watched the quartermoon sink orange then slow red into the gold-dusted black rim of earth.

"Meat," he said, "gotta have meat. Or there'll be no sweet revenge for this child."

The long crack in the rocks reminded him of the grave the lads had dug for him back in the gully.

He lay puzzling about the sandy grave. If he was dead, why hadn't the lads buried him? And if he wasn't dead, why had they dug it at all?

Open grave. His grave. Place for his old bones to molder in.

While they were at it, why hadn't they dug it at least a decent six feet deep? They didn't have the excuse that the ground was too hard or too stony. The sand was soft and deep.

The more he thought on it, the more he became absolutely convinced he'd been deserted. The lads probably began to dig his grave; saw he wasn't going to die after all; were in a hurry to catch up with the major; took to their heels. Ae. Took to their heels, grabbing his gun and possibles. The very lads he'd befriended and protected. Fitz and Jim. Lads he'd come to love. Lads he'd always chosen as his hunting companyeros. He could have chosen Augie Neill and Jim Anderson, but he had chosen Fitz and Jim. Jim had asked special for the privilege the first time and he had agreed. Augie and Jim Anderson didn't care. They were too full of fun.

Fitz and Jim. Why should they desert him when he'd never done them any harm? He'd never deserted them.

Lying in the long crack in the rocks, the rock edges cutting into him cruelly in the long lonely dark night, Hugh brooded on their ungratefulness. He turned it over and over in his mind. It burned in him. Seared. Ungrateful devils. And that after he'd stuck his own neck out for them.

He'd get them if it was the last thing he ever did. If the Lord didn't get them first.

He got up on his hands and one knee and crawled out of the long crack in the rocks and nosed on into the darkness ahead.

He crept on until he couldn't anymore; stopped.

He let his head hang heavy from his bulky shoulders, too exhausted and too tired to slip forward on his belly, too weak to weep.

When he found it in him again to look up, he discovered dawn was just beginning to gray the east. He also discovered that in the dark, while he'd been busy with dark deserter thoughts, he had crawled between and beyond the pair of teat mesas. Ho-ah! That meant he was over the divide, that he had nothing but downhill going until he hit the Moreau.

Something in the sloping and far resloped landscape caught his eye. It was the silhouette of a great butte. It came up out of the tardark earth and reared over the graying horizon and against the sky like some altar of sacrifice. Its flat top glowed faintly pink where the first shafts of predawn red caught the dark red rock. It glowed a little as if the coals and bones of some sacrifice were still glowing on its flat place of fire.

Hugh's old bleary eyes stared at it. Where had he seen it before? He was sure he'd seen it before. Sartain sure. Ae. The red dark reality of its rearing up before him and the vague red dark memory of it in his mind kept changing places, swinging around like a double-arrowed weather vane on a single pole.

Thunder Butte. Ae, that was it! Thunder Butte. Thunder Butte. Ae. He was seeing the back side of it. On the way up from Ft. Kiowa with Major Henry and the lads he'd seen the front side of it.

The seeing of it overjoyed him. The seeing of it brought Ft. Kiowa closer. What with downhill going ahead and good old Thunder Butte at last in sight, he was sure to make it now. Because once he'd crawled far enough to leave Thunder Butte out of sight behind him, he'd be on the Cheyenne and floating down on river currents.

He sighted down the long slope below him. The channel of a creek or a river angled off in front of him toward the southeast, angled just to the right and south of Thunder Butte. Was that the Moreau at last?

He looked beyond the angling zigzagging channel. Far over a low sloping he saw another channel. The second channel was deeper and wider, more pronounced, with a still further hogback ridge beyond it.

Hugh nodded. Ae. The first was probably only a good-sized creek and the second the Moreau itself. The creek probably joined the Moreau on the other side of Thunder Butte.

Hugh mapped out his trail. He'd take that gullyhead off to the left there and follow it down to the creek. The Thunder Butte creek would have water and wild roots and berries. Once on the creek, he'd cross it and follow it a ways until he got to that pass just south of the Thunder Butte, then crawl over the creek ridge to the Moreau. And at the Moreau he was sure to find a lot of water and good grub.

Dawn came up fast. It burst over the east rim of the earth in a vast racing explosion of pink then saffron then white clear light. The detail of the valleys stood out clearly in the strange zigzagging streaks of light and dark.

Hugh examined the rocky plateau around him. Nothing. Not a spear of grass. Not a stir of life. He'd have to go on without food again.

He found a hollow in the rocks and curled up under his silvertip bearskin.

His last thought was the hope that a rattler might crawl in with him. A rattler was dangerous, ae, but a rattler was meat. Sweet meat.

He woke by midafternoon in blinding sunlight. His first thought was of Fitz and Jim and of how sweet revenge would be.

His next thought was of his belly and of how hungry he was. "This child could right now eat the wild hairs out of a bear, he could. A she-rip at that. Gladly."

And his next thought was of how refreshed he felt after the sleep. It amazed him that his old creaking beat-up body could come back like a young man's after a good sleep. "This child's been in many a tough fix, with his body all in one piece and no bones broke, and it carried him out on two legs. But I'll be dog if this don't beat all the way it's carryin' me out this time."

To quiet his belly he jammed a piece off his buckskin shirt; pummeled the piece to shreds; chewed it until leathery juices revived his saliva buds. " 'Tain't exactly buffler boudins but it'll do until I catch me some."

He made a final sighting down the long undulating rock-cropped slope toward the creek ahead with Thunder Butte as the mark to go by.

Compared with the day before, the going was wondrous easy. There were still many sharp stones and rockjuts the first ways, but it was all downhill, and most places he could slide and coast.

The gullyhead widened into a ragged irregular gash. Volcanic ash showed black ribs in the pinkyellow clay cuts. Soon clumps of rusty red bunch grass began to appear; then cactus beds; and then anthills again. He had himself a few geranium-flavored acrid cactus ears, munching and chewing them thoroughly to get out every last drop of moisture and sustenance. He thought of having another but was afraid of getting the misery skitters. The misery skitters could weaken a man faster than a double dose of galloping consumption.

He crawled along steadily.

He was halfway down toward the Thunder Butte creek when night began to race in a dooming black from the east. The sun went down in a brilliant throw of colors, an explosion of yellows and whites and peony-pink glories, limning the whole irregular, jagged, scissored horizon from far southwest to high west to low northwest with a glowing white-hot gold.

Despite his terrible hunger, his emaciation, his parched throat, the nauseating pervading stench of his rotting back, Hugh couldn't help but marvel at all the spectacular colorings. "With a little salt and some pepper to flavor it, a man might almost make a feast on it."

He hurried on, every now and then looking out at it, and finding himself strangely exalted by the swift transformations of the marching, retreating, rioting glories, by the violent struggle between the shafts of light and the clouds of darkness.

At last darkness won out, absolutely, except for twinkling stars and a lazy recumbent quartermoon in the west.

With darkness, too, came easier terrain. Keeping well away from the gully and taking the ridges along the falling sloping draw, Hugh found the ground smooth again and easy to crawl on. If it weren't for badly shredded knee and elbow guards, a stranger might think him out on some picnic lark, part of some three-legged sack race.

He crawled steadily all night long. Carefully he nursed what little strength he had. He stopped to rest and puff; once slipped off into a restless nap; crept on, slid on.

It was almost dawn when he hit the creek. For once he didn't bother to make sure no Indians or she-grizzlies lurked in the brush along the creek banks. He plowed straight through the yellowing bullberry bushes and down into the little stream of running water, wading out into the middle of it, bad leg and all, and gulped water and splashed his face, all the while murmuring little talk to himself in his feverish joy at finding water, hinnying like an old boar happy to be at his favorite trough again.

Hugh drank until his belly hurt him.

He ate frost-ripened bullberries, and wild onion roots, and a few white grubs.

The sun was just up when he slid under low plum bushes in a short receding draw away from the creek.

A good day's run. Almost ten miles. He was moving at last.

Again he woke in midafternoon, in brilliant lemon September sunlight.

This time, however, even though he'd had something to eat the night before, and had water and food again on rising, he didn't feel refreshed. Going without food on the first hogback was finally catching up with him.

There was something else too. His back stunk worse; his brow felt feverish. And no matter how much he drank, the dry fur lining in his mouth wouldn't wash away.

He checked over his bearskin elbow and knee guards; found he needed a complete new set. With a crude stone chisel he jammed out three new pads and bound them on.

He checked his bum leg; discovered the cords binding his splint were slack. Ho-ah. The cracked bone was knitting then and the swelling was going down. Or could it be he was generally getting thin from lack of meat?

Rusty sunset had just fallen when he set out on the next lap home. He crossed to the right side of the creek and followed it down, always holding the black silhouette of Thunder Butte in sight dead ahead in the southeast.

The bronze quartermoon had just set when he ran into the remains of a Sioux warrior. Sewed up in a skin bundle, lying out full length, some six feet above ground on a scaffold of dry saplings, it swayed slack and lonely on four upright posts, black against the star-pricked sky. The tattered edge of a skin snapped in the slow night breeze. Little rawhide memento bags tolled in the slow breeze too.

Looking up at it, Old Hugh found himself suddenly lonesome for Bending Reed and the rites of her tribe, found himself lonesome even for the old days on the Platte with the Pawnees. The decaying leathery remains of the unknown warrior brought tears to his eyes. The white man might sometimes bury his dead kin six feet under, as deep as he made his privies, but the red devil placed his dead six feet above ground for all men to see, out of reach of varmint, as high as he would carry his head in the happy hunting grounds of afterlife. Ae, there swayed the honorable end of a free brave's life on Mother Earth, reared up out in the open so that his gross dark ignorant body could be given back to the powers of heaven and to the four quarters of the universe and to all the rains and to the wingeds of the air and to the little people of the earth. Ae, the red devil still knew the old and true religion. He still walked with Grandfather Wakantanka on the bosom of Grandmother Earth.

Looking up at the swaying recumbent reposing body, watching the little memento bags belling in the breeze, and imagining the penny-skinned hawknose face composed in stoic calm and peace, Old Hugh found himself hating cautious Fitz and the boy Jim with redoubled fury. Even in the midst of the most precarious existence, the Sioux tribes had time to give their fallen warrior a decent and an honorable burial. But his two friends had not only deserted him, they had left him unburied.

"If I ever lay hands on those two low-lived snakes, them oily cowards, not even their bitch of a mother is gonna recognize 'em after I get through with 'em. I'll tear 'em limb from limb, and then feed 'em hunk for hunk and rib for rib to the coyotes and turkey buzzards, and then collect their bones and burn 'em and dump the ashes in a whorehouse privy. I will. If it's the last thing I ever do. And may God forget to have mercy on their souls."

Looking up at the peaceful body of the Sioux brave withering away in the slow cool night wind, Hugh vowed he'd at least live long enough to exact his sacred vengeance.

"And when I've finished with 'em, I'm quittin' whiteman diggin's. I'll join up with Reed and her tribe, beargrease or no, like I've always had a hankerin' to. I'll make the Ree my true enemy, not just a low-lived red varmint like I've always said. The red devil has a code. We ain't."

He nubbed on, hand for hand, one good knee and one bum leg sliding along.

From the dead Sioux brave on, he didn't see one solitary tree or bush. There was nothing but raw clay cuts, and rough stones, and wide islands of floury sand. There wasn't even cactus.

All night long, with hovering Thunder Butte's silhouette black against the southeast horizon, he kept thinking of Moses and his anger at the Israelites in the

wilderness at the foot of Mount Sinai, kept thinking of
Job and his tribulations in the wilderness at the foot of
the treeless mountains of Arabia.

In the fury of his hating he got good mileage out of
his torn old hulk of a body, some eight, nine miles
across wicked terrain, until he hit a small spring coming
down out of the rugged hills on the right.

The little spring had fresh cool water and a cluster
of willows and plums. He drank the water; ate a few
bitter willow twig tips; finished off with the hated
plums. Then at dawn slept the deadsleep of the dead.

There was more brilliant lemon September sunlight
in the afternoon when he awoke. Along with it came a
wailing jerking wind that eddied sand around his body
and half-buried his bum leg and made his eyeballs grind
gritty in their sockets.

The first thing he saw on looking around was towering altarlike Thunder Butte hovering high in the southeast skies. He thought he could make out a pair of
eagles circling it. The whole jagged tossing country
seemed pegged down and held in place by the massive
redstone butte.

He drank morning cool water; ate a few bitter willow
twig tips; munched down a dozen ripe plums.

He felt burnt out when he began his crawl again.

"Meat," he murmured, "meat. Gotta have meat soon
or this hoss can fold up his wings and call it a day."

Why live? Ae, what was the use?

" 'Cept that if I let myself go under, cautious Fitz
and that boy Jim'll get away with lettin' me die the hard
way. Desertin' me. Them low-lived cold-bellied snakes.
If it's the last thing I do, I'm gonna ring their necks
and hang 'em out to dry for turkey-buzzard bait in
the winter."

His burning hate finally revived him enough to get
him going for the night's crawl ahead.

The bed of the creek straightened and widened, and

every quarter mile it became easier going for him across the soft fanning silt aprons. The creek continued shallow and aggrading, playing from side to side in the gorge, building layer of sand and silt upon sand and silt, alluvial fan upon alluvial fan.

Hugh stopped for a sip from the creek now and then. Gradually it turned bitter to the taste, became sharp with wild salt and alkali.

"This child's gotta have meat soon," he murmured, "meat."

But watch and prey as he might, he found nothing, found nothing, neither night mouse nor coiled rattler nor vested vulture.

It wasn't until dawn that he hit another spring trickling out of the hills to the right of the stream. A few yellowed bullberry bushes grew along its cut. He drank greedily of the cool fresh water; ate greedily of the half-dried half-rotten bullberries.

He had a last look around before crawling off to sleep. Thunder Butte loomed high over him, a massive red altar of sacrifice waiting a little off to the north of him, east by north. At least so it seemed. He had looked at it so often and so long, had dreamt about it in nightmare so often, he wasn't sure any more of his sense of direction, or his sense of size, or his sense of distance.

The dry fur lining his mouth and covering his tongue felt thicker.

"What this child wouldn't give for a peaceful pipe of 'bacca to improve the taste in the mouth ain't fit for sayin'."

But the fury of his hate had carried him another eight, nine miles closer to Ft. Kiowa and Bending Reed.

He slept the sleep of the unborn child.

When sleep receded and his old gray eyes uncracked, he found the wind down and the blue skies streaked with faint white mare's tail.

He also found that it was the misery skitters which

had awakened him. Plums and the half-rotted bullberries. Or maybe the wild salt and alkali at last.

He groaned out of the midst of his miseries.

Why live? Ae, what was the use?

"Dig out the grave again, lads, this child's headin' that way, he is. His hash is settled at last."

Seven times the misery fits convulsed and possessed him. Seven times he was sure he was dying on the spot. Miserably. Head low. A gut-shot skittering coyote. And yet seven times he revived enough to think of going on to get his revenge.

Up on one knee, bad leg trailing in the willow-twig slape, hanging onto the brittle limb of a dead willow, he had a look down the creek to the east.

"Gettin' a little too clost to Thunder Butte and parts east to suit me, lads. Any closer to the Missouri and I'm liable to stumble onto a nest of Rees."

He surveyed the rise of tan bluffs to the south. The little spring led up a gully, and the gully in turn led up toward the low pass over the hogback, the same pass he'd spotted way back on the first divide.

"It'll be hard doin's again climbin' that, even if it is a low one." Hugh shook his old matted grizzly head. "But what's to be done is gotta be done, skitters or no. This child don't dare go any farther east. It's sail south or nothing."

He had a good drink and started in.

Twilight came red; night came rusty with halfmoon illumination.

Up. Up. And the misery fits seven times seven.

The trials and tribulations of an old broken man swollen with pus and hate.

"Job and his boils had nothin' on this child and his sores."

Powerful weak.

Meat. Meat. Meat.

Where did his old beat-up body get the guts to go on?

"A whangdoodle at that. Only a whangdoodle could make a go of it off a nest a maggots in his back and rot in the blood."

A ravening gut worming its way across a tan wilderness.

"My bowels boiled, and rested not: the days of affliction prevented me. I went mourning without the sun: I stood up, and cried in the wilderness. I am a brother to dragons, and a companion to owls. My skin is black upon me, and my bones are burned with heat."

He looked back over his shoulder. Thunder Butte loomed high, flat top first wavering close, then far, then close.

Up. Up. And the crest in the low pass gained at last. And dawn a lovely wildrose blossom.

"Meat. Meat. Gotta have—"

Ho-ah. What was that circling wheeling in the dawn-pinkened valley below? beside the twinkling Moreau? Not turkey buzzards?

He peered down the falling tan slopes.

Yes, buzzards. And this time it wasn't his meat they were celebrating. It was some downed critter's meat.

A surge of final ultimate energy sent him skedaddling down toward the meandering silvering Moreau River.

He scrabbled downhill until he came to the last drop-off. Cautiously, head raised like a grizzly predator he peered past a final rock.

A dozen greennecked buzzards circled and squawked just out of reach of a dozen white wolves. The white wolves were working on a red four-legged critter down on a sand bar, their tails whisking about lively as they struggled with each other for the spoils. Around them in a ring, waiting their turn, sat a dozen impatient howling dun-gray coyotes.

"Buffler! A down young bull calf! Maybe the one I missed back in the hills!" Hugh cried. "Meat."

With a roar and a rush, silvertip grizzly bearskin lifting a little from the speed of his rush, dried grizzly paws bangling from his neck, willow slape careening on stones and loose gravel, gravel avalanches rushing ahead of his running elbows, Hugh charged through the ring of coyotes and into the boiling mass of snarling white wolves. "Whaugh!" he roared. "Whaugh! Hrrrach! Get! Getouttahere!"

At the roar and rush the bloody-mouthed white wolves leaped back. One look at Old Hugh's grizzly head and grizzly covering and they fled the sand bar, the coyotes slinking away with them. But fear a grizzly as they might, they didn't run far. They turned at the edge of the sand bar and sat down on their haunches. They watched him. They whined and got up and sat down. They licked blood off their snouts and paws, licked them slick and clean. They howled outraged at the intrusion. The vultures overhead retreated too, raising their wavering crying circles a rung or two.

With bared teeth and clawing fingers, Hugh tore at the raw red partly mutilated flesh, pulling fleece away from the underbelly, ripping off strips of soft veal from the hindquarters, sucking up dripping still-warm blood. With a gnawed-off leg bone he broke out a few ribs. With a stone chisel he jammed off a slice of fatty hump. He also had himself a couple of coils of boudin.

He'd become so thin, his teeth hurt at the least bite. Bits of raw flesh got caught between his incisors deep in the sunken gums.

He ate until he couldn't any more. He drank deep of the shimmering silvering Moreau, drank until his guts ached.

He ate and drank and slept all through the day. He ate and drank and slept all through the night. He slept on the sand bar, one arm laid protectively over the half-eaten red bull calf. When the wolves and coyotes and the vultures threatened, he fought them off, roaring and gesticulating wildly. Sometimes hunger woke him. Sometimes slavering snarling wolves woke him. A full belly always put him back to sleep.

Chapter 6

Hugh never did remember how long he slept and ate and slept and ate beside the down buffalo-bull calf on the sand bar. Time was measured solely and only by how often his stomach needed refilling and by how often the wolves and vultures dared to approach him.

Perhaps it was the third day, or the fifth day, or the seventh day—he never did know which—when one morning he noticed the circling prowling wolves and coyotes and the wheeling wrinklenecked vultures were suddenly gone.

It made him sit up. Besides his own mangled hulk there was still some buffalo-calf meat left. The meat was getting to be a little on the strong side, but for that reason it should have been all the more appetizing to them. Something was wrong. It was sign red devils were about.

Quickly Hugh packed what he could of the bull-calf meat, buried the rest of the carcass in the sand so that Indian dogs wouldn't give him away, and backing off, erased his tracks with a willow switch. He scurried into a thick fringe of yellow-leaved cottonwood saplings along the east shore of the Moreau.

And just in time. He had just comfortably stretched out his bum leg and was adjusting the grizzly skin over his back, when he heard a pony nicker across and down the river. Two other ponies whinnied in answer.

Hugh lifted his matted grizzly head for a cautious

look. Ho-ah. Coming up across the Moreau were red devils with hawkbone headdress like horse ears. Rees then. Some forty braves, all armed with rifles and all riding ponies, rode ahead of a whole village on the move, squaws, children, dogs burdened with travois, ponies weighted down with slapes of supplies. Pale clay dust rose in swirling clouds above and behind them. Sometimes one or another of the dogs sat down to howl at his lot in life, at his sore feet or sore back. Immediately one of the squaws, either afoot or riding, laid on with a stick, cursing, to get the dog up and on the move again. Small babies in tight bundles rode atop pony packs, little berry eyes alert and bugged at all the bustling show. Skin pennants hung slack and torn; skin panniers hung empty and bedraggled. The whole tribe looked beaten and hungry.

Ae, the very Rees he'd helped Ashley fight on the Missouri back in early June. Hugh guessed they'd probably been on the move and scavengering off the dry countryside ever since Leavenworth had let them escape from their fortified villages on the Grand.

At the head of the motley procession and a little off to the side, as a general might hold himself apart, Hugh spotted gnarled old Chief Elk Tongue on a black stallion. Bronze arrowhead nose pointed ahead, the old chief rode along calmly and arrogantly, a couple of flashy eagle feathers pluming and dipping in the slow wind, skin pennants dangling from an upright spear.

Hugh shivered. He remembered the chief as the most ferocious paleface-hater of them all. Looking at him, Hugh could see that the chief had aged, that he seemed more embittered than ever by the endless uprootings of his tribe. Dark savage eyes flicking from side to side, seeing everything, Chief Elk Tongue was truly the old-style arrogant tribal patriarch.

Chief Elk Tongue and his wandering raveling Rees were the first humans Hugh had seen since he broke away from Major Henry's party to go off hunting by himself. Old Hugh hungered with tears in his eyes for the friendly sound of a human voice. But he knew that to call out now for help was suicide. Any other tribe and he might have chanced it. Hugh bit back his tongue, clamped down on his lips, for fear some sound might escape him.

Ae, one little squeak from his hideout and the Ree braves'd come raging and whooping across the river and he'd be made a riddle of before he could say his name. And if not a riddle of, then a torture-stake victim. Hugh wished with a terrible wish that he had pistol or rifle with at least one ball left so he could make an end of it should the Rees suddenly discover him anyway. In his broken state he knew he didn't have it in him to stand the elaborately horrible tortures Plains Indians performed on hated captives.

Hugh hoped old Elk Tongue hadn't put flankers out across the river on his side. If he had, he was wolfmeat sartain sure.

One thing Hugh was glad for. Every dog in the tribe had been put to work, and they were too busy dodging squaw blows and howling over their sore feet to sniff him in his hideout or to sniff out what remained of the calf carcass in the sand bar.

Hugh waited. The yellow leaves of the cottonwood saplings claddered softly overhead.

He skulked down as low as he could. He took breath in little shallow soundless sucks. His heart beat loud and shook his chest. Hugh steadied his hands in the soft drifted sand under the saplings to keep from trembling.

Lean emaciated squaws continued to belabor lean emaciated dogs. Lean starved babies stared bug-eyed at the passing barren land. Rib-hard ponies cantered along head down and snorting. Surly thin-bellied braves looked from left to right.

Slowly, noisily, the pennyskinned tribe crossed before Hugh not forty feet away and trotted out of sight around a bend in the river bottom.

"Whaugh! that was a striker of a close one, that was. One sight of this child and they'd a known him like they'd a knowed their old dead chief Grey Eyes. The day I watchdogged when General Ashley's boys diddled their squaws they'd never forget. Let alone seein' me be the last to run for the keelboats."

Old Hugh watched the dust settle around the bend. When Old Hugh's thoughts returned to himself, he found fear's sweat had broken out all over him. "A close one, that was. Too clost for this old hoss. Whaugh!"

From his hiding place he studied the sky, and all the tipping rims of the horizon, and all the angling river bottoms, and a clump of tall cottonwoods up the river.

"Ae, a striker. And this old hoss is caching right here until night comes around again. Best to get some sleep anyways. And from now on, keep an eye peeled and an ear picked for sign. Dummed friend stomach almost got me in a sad fix that time."

He slept fitfully. And dreamt of having been caught by the vengeful Rees. The braves had tied him to a stake and with pine splinters were puncturing him full of holes; the squaws had torn out his privates by the roots and were roasting them over a fire; the berry-eyed children like dogs had fouled his legs and were tugging at his beard. Then the flames leaped high around him and he saw his old companyero Clint crying over his sad fate and pleading with the Pawnee chief to let him go free. The roaring, searing flames leaped high and Hugh screamed.

The scream woke him.

He lay awake awhile, thinking, shivering, as he passed the dream before his mind again. The wind tossed the fall-yellowed cottonwood leaves in lifting flutters. Sunlight twinkled over his face. He heard the waters of the Moreau sliding softly over the sand bars.

He slept fitfully.

*　　*　　*

He woke after dark.

A bullying wind was out. It whipped the sapling cottonwoods about and moaned sadly through the gullies and ruffled the streaming Moreau.

In the dark he fed on the calf meat he'd quick grabbed up when the Rees broke in on his feasting on the sand bar. He drank from the wind-whacked waters of the Moreau.

He checked the splint on his leg. The tie-straps over the thigh were loose, and he tightened them. He felt of the swelling around the cracked bone. The flesh of it seemed to be softening some.

He checked his back and seat. He was surprised to find that the scabs had fallen off at last. Baby-tender skin had replaced them. Ho-ah. He was healing then, he was. Ae. There was only the hole in his back left to heal.

He set out, following the banks of the Moreau, heading slowly southeast. In the moon-lit dust-riding night Thunder Butte loomed over him almost directly north. The butte wasn't getting any smaller with the distance, but it was moving back.

The dark bullying night wind wouldn't let him alone. It got stronger every minute. Once it made a sail of his bearskin and almost carried him off a high bank into the river. Only by quickly grabbing a willow sapling did he save himself from a dousing. Another time a particularly savage blast scooped up what seemed like a flying sand bar hitting him with a million billion drilling stingers. Hugh had to duck under the grizzly skin to keep from choking. It took him a good ten minutes of careful prying with a finger to get the sand particles out of his eyes.

After a couple of miles of it, with the wind continuing to blow mean and vicious, and at last turning cold too, Hugh gave up.

"Burnin' up too much of that good meat fightin' it,"

Hugh muttered in his old beard. "Best to save it for a good day and better goin'."

Ahead in the varying dust-riding moonlight, Hugh spotted a big creek coming out of a valley on his right. A heavy grove of cottonwood and willow and wild fruit fringed it where it joined the Moreau. The sight of all the growth waving back and forth in the raging night wind gladdened Old Hugh's heart.

"Now that begins to look like somethin'. Cover for both man and beast." Hugh studied it for sign. "Yessiree, cover. An' this child's cachin' in it for the day, he is." Hugh cocked his head to one side as if listening to something, someone in his head. "Do ee hear now, lads? Cover ahead an' the old carcass mendin' as slick as a peeled onion. My deal is comin' soon now. Best set yourself for bad doin's, lads."

He had another drink of water, this time from the big creek, and had another cautious look around for sign, and then, without eating, turned in behind a thick slash of dry canebrake.

A cold nose woke him.

Two pairs of furred slanted yellow eyes glittered down at him out of a very bright blue sky. One pair of narrowed eyes glittered very close. Dogs. Indian dogs gone wild. Strays from the Rees who'd passed by the day before. Or the advance guard dogs of a second Ree village on the move.

Hugh snapped up both hands; caught the dog around the furred neck; choked it with a frantic fanatic grip. The other yellowgray dog leaped back. The caught dog struggled, and doubled its neck around to snap at his hands, and dug its claws into his leathers trying to get away, and rasped piteously for breath.

"You devil! So you and your companyero thought you'd make a meal of me, did ee? Well, you've another think a comin' on that. It's me who's gonna eat, not you."

Hugh hung on. Gradually the dog's struggles weakened; ceased altogether; and at last the wild cur fell slack across his belly.

"Fresh meat is good meat," Hugh grunted. "Even if it ain't prime calf meat."

He sat up slowly. His limbs and back cracked like dried rawhide.

In the midst of the dry canebrake he found a heavy white stone the size of a bowling ball. With a quick stroke he crushed in the wild dog's head. He found another stone, this time a flat one with a rough cutting edge, and jammed at the dog's tough furry neck until the jugular began to spout blood. "Nothin' like a bucket a blood to start the day."

He skinned two of the dog's legs and gnawed them down to the bone. The meat was tough and flat. He chewed until the roots of his old teeth hurt him again.

He noticed after a while that the other dog had disappeared. That Hugh didn't like. It meant the two dogs probably hadn't been wild after all, that they belonged somewhere.

Grizzly predator head rising slowly out of the canebrake, bright afternoon sunlight silvering his matted gray hair, Hugh surveyed the river valley all around, east, west, north, south. As he'd noted the night before, he had nested down in the midst of a considerable grove of cottonwoods and willows and a few wild fruit trees. The heavy yellow cottonwood leaves clattered briskly in a wind coming out of the west. Some of the cottonwood leaves let go and spun around and around until they hit water or sandy ground. The pink willows were tougher and less noisy. The red plum leaves fluttered softly. From where he crouched Hugh had trouble telling the leaves apart from the drying wrinkled plums.

Less than a dozen yards away the waters of the big creek joined the fanning washing Moreau. Both streams ran clear and clean over gold-sand deltas and occasional beds of pebbles, beds dull orange and speckled with bits of black and flecks of white.

Up from both sides of the Moreau the land rose in thrown slopes of grassed-over clay and gravel. To the north still loomed omnipresent dull-red Thunder Butte. To the south rose the first smooth slopes of the Fox Ridge bluffs. While out of the west and into the east the bottoms of the Moreau swung and angled along.

Hugh was about to settle back in the canebrake when his quick eye spotted the other wild dog. Pink tongue out and puffing, it was sitting on its haunches in front of an old ragged patched-up tepee, exactly across from him on the other side of the river and up on a low bench of gravel.

Hugh ducked down and began to sweat. He swore softly to himself. "Right in my eye practically and I missed it. That dummed stomach of mine is gonna get me in trouble yet."

Hugh puffed. "Red devils, no doubt. Ae. And they've probably spotted me too."

He sat crouched and very quiet for a long time. He listened for the sounds of approaching stealth in the whistling tossing canebrake.

When nothing happened, he cautiously and noiselessly wormed his way to the edge of the canebrake and parted the last few stalks and looked out from a spot low near the ground.

A tepee all right. And the wild dog too.

But it was only one tepee, and an odd one at that. It looked Sioux but it wasn't Sioux exactly. It looked like a tepee made by a Sioux and then traded to a Ree who'd made it over to fit his ways of staking and decoration.

For a half hour Hugh studied the tepee and the dog, never once moving from his prone position at the edge of the canebrake. During all that time he saw nothing moving in and out or around the strange tepee. And in all that time too the wild dog sat in front of the tepee doorflap, pink tongue out and calmly puffing.

Hugh couldn't understand it. Had the Rees left some old crone or brave behind to die? They sometimes did when on the move. In hard times, when the old became too weak to travel, tribal custom sometimes said they had to be left behind. In fact, the old often asked for the privilege themselves. Bending Reed had once told him that her own old brave of a father had made such a request. "My children," the old wrinkled penny-skinned sack of bones had said, "my children, our nation is poor and we need meat. Think not of me, but go to the country where there is meat. Go, and leave me to what lies in store for me. My eyes are dim, my legs no longer can carry my body, my arms can no longer bend my bow. I wish to die. Go, my children, go make your hearts brave and forget me. Go, I am good for nothing and my days are done." With a catch in his throat Hugh remembered Bending Reed's telling of it. After his desertion by the boys such memories were like searing heartburns.

That was it, all right. An old brave left to die. With a few provisions to last out his days. And his favorite dogs left to watch over him, and maybe, gone wild, to eat him if the wolves didn't get him first.

Hugh waited another half hour before venturing out of his hiding place.

The dog in front of the old tepee took one look at Old Hugh's grizzly aspect as he emerged from the canebrake and ran howling into the brush behind the tepee. It made Hugh smile. "He ain't forgot about what this grizzly did to his companyero. No siree."

Hugh waded on elbows and knee through the river, bum leg in the slape trailing after like a wetted plew of beaver on a sled, and boldly approached the tepee. Still no one in sight, still no wild warwhoop out of the yellow brush and the yellow grove to indicate the tepee was an ambush.

Hugh lifted the flap and peered in past a dangling medicine bundle.

He was right. An old one left to die alone. An old withered crone. She was lying prone on a fur beside the ashes of a fire in the center of the tepee. A striped blackred woolen blanket covered her. Her eyes were closed. But she was still breathing. She was incredibly old and wrinkled.

Somehow she looked familiar, Hugh thought.

Hugh crawled in for a closer look.

A white weaselskin amulet hanging from a stick thrust in the ground behind her head finally helped him identify her. Hugh sucked in a breath. Ho-ah. It was the old mother of Grey Eyes. Hugh's flinty eyes rolled. When the Rees fled their villages above the Grand on the Missouri, Pilcher's boys had been instructed to set fire to the villages. Just after they'd fired it, they found the old mother left behind in a mud-covered round lodge. Hugh clucked his tongue. The Rees must have snuck back into the burning village to save her from a fiery and ignoble end. And in their subsequent raveling over the country, they had managed to take her along this far.

His quick old eye fastened greedily on the paunches of food left at her side. A small bag of rich pemmican, soft enough so the toothless withered old lady could mouth it down; a cake of cornbread, also soft and easy on the gums; and a bladder of fresh water—all provisions for the rest of her journey here on earth and for the first of her journey into the new spirit world.

Hugh pounced on the pemmican and cake. Human food for his poor old stomach at last.

There was a quiver in the wrinkled oldpenny eyelids. The old woman's eyelids parted and old blackcherry eyes tinged with a deadskin-gray looked up at him.

Hugh held still, eyes furtive in bushy face.

Her old wrinkled leathery lips moved. "——face."

The old word whispered out of an old throat gave Old Hugh a pause. The old word said in Arikaree he readily understood. He knew a little Ree—it was a cousin language to the Pawnee which he knew well. Face. Paleface. She didn't see him then the way the dog saw him. Paleface. Ae, with the long beard he now had he was a paleface sartain sure. Major Henry was right that it stuck out.

The old black eyes brightened and the dead skin on the eye slid to one side like the winking nictitating third eyelid of an old hen. One of the withered bony arms stirred under the striped blackred blanket. Her old leathery voicebox harsed low again. "Meat."

The second old word jolted Hugh. He dropped the bag of pemmican and cake of cornbread.

Once more the old throat harsed an old word. "Water."

Hugh's eyes filmed with tears. He couldn't help it. Poor old soul. He knew what it was to be left alone to die. Ae. He knew.

"So it's water ye want, is it?" Old Hugh's voice cracked. "Well, Old Mother, water it is ye'll have. This child can't begrudge ye that."

He angulated his body and leg over and sat beside her. He cradled her old head in an arm and, with his other hand, held the mouth of the bladder of water to her lips. Her old black braids fell across his soiled leather sleeve.

She drank slowly. Some of the water pulsed down her throat; some of it spilled and ran down the wrinkles cutting back from her stiff leathery lips. When she finished, he laid her head carefully down on the tanblack buffalo robe again. Hugh had the feeling that if he hadn't been careful, her head could very easily have parted from the spine despite the old tangle of veins and sinews and leather skin holding them together.

She thanked him with filmy eyes; then her eyes closed. She puffed slowly, with long pauses in between. Sometimes the puffed breaths came so far apart Hugh was afraid she'd breathed her last.

"Poor old soul," Hugh said, eyes tearing over again.

"No, there's some things this child won't do, no matter how far his stomach's made him backslide. I can't skulp a live red devil, or desert a friend, or take orders from a tyrant, or hurt Indian wimmen. Pa'tic'ly old red-devil grammaws on their last legs."

She heard him. Her old filmy eyes opened and cleared for another slowly brightening live look. "Meat."

"Ae, an' meat ye shall have too, Old Mother." He held up the pemmican. "This suit yer taste?"

She tried to shake her head; roved her eyes back and forth instead. "Meat."

"Ae, so it's live meat ye want. Well, in that case, this child'll have to go back to the canebrake for that dog he killed."

Saying it, it occurred to him. It was one of her dogs he'd killed. Unbeknownst he'd taken meat, and favorite meat at that, from a dying critter. All Indians thought dog meat a great delicacy. Unbeknownst. But yet done. "Ae, Old Mother, meat, live meat, ye'll have."

He heard a noise outside the tepee. He jerked erect, tense, eyes fixed on the doorflap. Rees come back?

It was a sliding noise, a noise of something being dragged, slaped, over the sand. With a quick surging roll of a grizzly he lunged for the doorflap. He peered out.

It was the still-live dog dragging the dead carcass of his companyero dog. The live dog apparently had been trained to retrieve. Good. The live dog had saved him the trouble of getting the carcass himself.

Hugh was careful not to scare the live dog this time. The live dog might come in handy later on. But careful as he was, the live dog again bolted at the sight of him.

Hugh shagged the partly eaten dog into the tepee.

"Now, Old Mother, did your companyeros leave ye any fire-fixin's maybe?"

He searched and found flint and steel in a leather

bag near her head under the fur she lay on. He also found an old knife, worn back almost to the haft.

Hugh rubbed his gnarled hands in joy. "Hurrah! Old Mother, good meat it'll be. I hope ye'll allow the cook a taste." Old Hugh winked at her.

The wink wasn't lost on her. Her old leathery lips tried to form a smile; made what looked like a grimace of terrible pain instead. Hugh thought it one of the finest smiles he'd laid eyes on. "Ae, Old Mother, I'll bet ye was a merry lass in your day, wasn't ee? Ae. The pennyskin Rees was always said to be the best on the Old Missouri."

Old Hugh found dry twigs; hustled up firewood; with flint and steel soon had a blazing fire going Indian-style. With the old woman's knife he skinned the dead dog. He impaled it on a slender green willow rod; placed it in the forked ends of two stakes set at either end of the fire; began barbecuing.

When it was finally done, the dog meat tasted wonderful. Hugh fed her first, fed her like he might feed a baby, mashing the flesh with a stone and giving it to her in thin strips. Between feedings he couldn't resist licking his fingers now and then.

Presently she indicated she'd had enough. She thanked him with another flowering of brightness in her old filmy black eyes.

"Don't mention it, Old Mother. I'd do the same for me own mother, God bless her, departed as she is from this valley of trials and tribulations." Again tears popped in Hugh's eyes. He blinked them back, inwardly a little ashamed of his gullishness.

Sure that she had enough, Hugh pitched in himself. The meat had been turned to a fine brown fare-thee-well. It was crispy on the outside and tender on the inside.

The live dog outside couldn't resist the wonderful smell of singed browned flesh either. It poked its twitching cold black nose in through the doorflap, warily, irresistibly drawn.

Hugh smiled until his whiskers moved up his cheeks. He tore off a piece of meat and tossed it to the cold black nose.

The half-wild yellowgray dog slipped into the tepee and with a single vulsing swallow snapped it down. Its eyes begged for more.

"A friend it is I want ye to be, pooch. Me and the old lady here may have need for ee in time to come. One way or another." Hugh tossed it another strip of well-done flesh. "Dip in, pooch." Hugh winked at the dog.

Again the dog downed the browned meat in a single pulsing swallow.

When Hugh turned to see if the Old Mother was enjoying the humor of it with him, he found her dead. She'd been so far gone that the first stir of her stomach became a stumbling stone for her old heart.

"What? So soon, Old Mother?"

Hugh stared at her for a minute; then burst into tears. "What? an' we just friends?"

Gently he closed her eyes, first one, then the other.

Eyes streaming, he stared down at her. "Ae, at least ye had the luck to ha' a human around to close your eyes. But who'll close the eyes of this old hoss when he goes? He ain't got nobody back in the States to remember him. My lads'll have long forgot their old man. Ae. The old she-rip'll ha' seen to that."

That night, after the filling moon had come out, with all the land in silver shine, Hugh with his bare hands dug out a grave for her in the sand bar and held a brief but decent paleface burial service. He mumbled a few words from Job over her. " 'Man that is born of a woman is of few days and full of trouble. He cometh forth like a flower, and is cut down: he fleeth also as a shadow, and continueth not.' " As an afterthought Hugh also spoke over her as a good Ree husband might. "Now go, my child, go to the land of souls, go to where many of your friends and relatives are already waiting for you. Do not turn back, but look ahead, and soon you shall find them who love you and who are waiting for you. Go, do not turn back, look ahead, and you shall be happy." Sadly he lowered her into a deep hole he'd dug for her. Waggling his old head at the sad turns of life, he covered her over with sand. Then, also Ree style, he took a handful of sage and rubbed it up and down his arms for purification against what had killed her.

A last look at the mound, and then at the tepee, and he was off, bladder of pemmican, corn cake, what was left of the barbecued dog, blackred striped woolen blanket, knife, flint and steel, and his own grizzly skin over his shoulder. He left the tanblack buffalo robe for the wolves to tear up and devour.

He whistled up the half-wild dog and started across the Moreau. The dog followed him warily, some dozen yards behind, yet always there.

He crawled hard all that night. He took the big creek straight south, away from the Moreau, holding his noddle steady on Rattlesnake Butte towering above the Fox Ridge divide, with Thunder Butte directly behind. The dog followed.

At dawn the next morning he came to where the big creek turned west. Ahead were the hills of the next divide. He ate heartily of the pemmican and corn cake and roast dog. He shared some of the roast dog with live dog. He went to sleep in a thicket of whistling willows.

He awoke late in the afternoon scratching like fury.

He sat up, still scratching. What in tarnation—? Had the live dog given him a batch of fleas?

He examined the seams of his leather clothes. And swore. "As I live, graybacks! Lice." Ae, lice from the Old Woman. A giveaway present. Rats desertin' a sinkin' ship. Who'd clumb aboard one that was not going to sink yet awhile.

"Well, there's nothin' for it I guess but to find me an anthill."

He found a tub-sized hill of lively ants. He carefully stripped down to the skin except for his bum leg. He laid his buckskins near the anthill. "Friend ant will carry off all the seam squirrels and the nits. Ae, afore I finish the rest of the pemmican and corn cake, I bet."

He smiled. He remembered Clint his old companyero had once asked him how he could tell when the ants were finished with the job. He remembered too his reply. "When the ants start bitin' ee, that's when."

The half-wild dog sat nearby. It whined as he worked on a piece of cold roast dog.

"Here, pooch, have a bone. Eat while ye may. To-morrow it may be your turn."

Presently the red ants began crawling over him, and he knew they were done with the cleaning job.

Chapter 7

Hugh climbed steadily toward Fox Ridge.

The country changed. It became smooth and rolling with league-long slopes, some rising, some falling, with a sky so high under sheep-white cirrus it made the breath short, and all of it cut in the far valleys with deep eroding ocher gullies.

It was shortgrass country: good soil, little or no cactus, very few stones; a minimum of wild salt. It lacked only rain, and rain at the right time, to become the Garden of Eden at last, the wild lily of the valley of men's dreams.

Between crawls, while resting in slanting evening sunlight, Hugh sometimes brooded on the lonesome country. While it might be a mite too wild for him at the moment, the condition he was in, the plains country was surely coming to a time when all of it would someday become settled too, just as the wild coasts of the Atlantic had at last become the States, just as the wild valleys of the Ohio had at last become settlements, just as the Indian village on the banks of the Mississippi where the Missouri came in had at last become St. Lou. It was bound to come.

It made Hugh sad to think on it, all the she-rips and their cubs coming in and destroying a hunter's paradise. The white queen bees would come in with their tame worker bees and build honeycomb towns and cities just as the real queen bees already were taking over the wilds just ahead of the oncoming settlements. Ae, the enslavement of both land and man was coming here too. Ae.

Hugh could just see it, the henpecked men coming in, still thinking they were men, and free men at that, and saying to each other as they looked over the virgin stretches for the first time, picking up a cloud of dirt and crunching it, and fluffing it in the palm of their hands and letting it sift out between the fingers: "Smart chance for corn here all right." "Corn? Naw, not corn. I expect we hadn't ought to raise nothin' but wheat and rye here." "Corn or no, it's still the biggest clearin' I ever did see." "And no sour soil." "Yep, I can't wait till we all start eatin' our own hominy and johnnycake raised right here."

Between crawls, in the rusty dusk, Hugh also thought of the lads, cautious Fitz and the boy Jim. Where were they now? Probably snug and safe at Henry's Post on the Yellowstone and Missouri. He hoped they'd made the post safe. It would be a dirty trick if fate dealt out the cards so that Rees counted coup over them before he did. If the red devils got to them first, the lads'd die thinking they'd pulled one over on him.

Remembering how he'd been taken in by the lad Jim, Hugh shook his grizzled old head. "Crazy as a mule over a colt, I was. Yessiree. Jest sick for a colt of my own. I swear. Well, howsomever, I larned, I did. And it's never again for this old hoss. No siree. From now on, after I've had my revenge, it's me noddle in me own business and nobody else's. Strict. Hugh for Hugh."

Between puffs, in moonlight as silver as a little boy's milk-blond hair, Hugh worried a little that Thunder Butte behind him didn't get any smaller. In almost two days of crawling south away from it the dull redstone butte still seemed to loom over him as lofty as ever. It just wouldn't recede and sink away into the horizon. Part of it he knew was due to his crawling up out of the Moreau River depression. The higher he climbed up Fox Ridge the more both Thunder Butte and the ground he crawled on was apt to stick out above the surroundings. But at the same time Thunder Butte should have got smaller in size. Distance should have shrunk it some.

The butte began to haunt him. Old Hugh was hard-headed and he knew it was puckerstopple to think of the butte as an altar of sacrifice, an altar such as Old Testament sages might have used for their offertories. Yet he couldn't help wonder why it hung so stubborn and high in the north.

Maybe it was the fever. Fever could have ruined his sense of distance. He'd known cases where sickbrain hope had completely addled a man's judgment. Maybe he wasn't crawling across the country as fast as he thought. Could be.

The possibility of an early blizzard worried him too. He'd seen a foot of snow in early October in the Dakotas many a time. A blizzard catching him before he got to the Cheyenne would put a bad crimp in his plans. Crawling across snow would be well-nigh impossible. His arms'd freeze. Let alone freeze his stilled leg in the splints. Ae, an early fall blizzard could wreck it all.

"Hugh, lad, best face it. Ye're in a fix if it snows. No two ways about it."

He studied stubborn Thunder Butte; sniffed the slow wind drifting in from the northeast.

"But, Hugh, lad, ye've just got to last it. Got to. And ye've not only got to last, ye've got to get your work done."

Ae, last. Get the work done. That was the end-all and the be-all of a man's whole life. His purpose here on earth. The driver that sat behind a man's stomach. And his driver had a whip. Hate.

"Lads, I'll get ye yet," Hugh muttered, looking over his shoulder at looming omnipresent Thunder Butte. "Old Hugh will serve right and make ye pay for your wrong."

* * *

Child Hugh crawled hard all that night. Always the wild dog followed him a safe distance behind. Using the North Star as his lodestar, Hugh bore hard on, going east by south, headed straight for coiled-up Rattlesnake Butte.

A great round moon followed both him and the ghost-yellow dog. It watched his wormings across dry-grass country, first from its rising in the east and then from its setting in the west. The turning moon cast a thin fine fog of silver light over the sleeping sloping land. In it the rusty tips of the dead bunch grass resembled yellow day lilies. In it the dull red rock of Thunder Butte resembled a sunflower. The great round moon filled the silver valleys with rivers of milk.

He made up his mind not to look back at Thunder Butte for a while. Maybe the next time it would look smaller.

More and more he began to use his bum leg. The swelling around the cracked bone was almost gone. Tight splint fixed firmly in springy willow slape, he could bear part of his weight on it on occasions. He was beginning to crawl more on his hands than on his elbows, and more on his awkward slape and good knee both than just on the good knee.

What amazed him was the way his body had taken to going on all fours like any four-legged creature of the wild. Even with the leg in the slape he got around very handily, could even run a little if he wanted to. The run, when he tried it, wasn't just an awkward one either, but a run that coursed, a run that lifted him off the ground a little, that gave his carcass a coasting motion all its own, like some rowboat with four oars flailing water.

It gave Hugh a peculiar insight into how the four-legged animals felt as four-legged beings, an insight so sharp that his first impulse was to sniff at the thought of it instead of smile at it.

It also gave him a peculiar insight into the curse God

had put on Nebuchadnezzar, the King of Babylon. God had changed Nebuchadnezzar's heart from that of a man to that of a beast and had him driven from among men and made it his portion to eat of the grass of the earth like an ox. And God caused Nebuchadnezzar's body to be made wet with the dew of heaven till his hairs grew out like eagle feathers and his nails grew out like bird claws.

All that night Child Hugh crawled hard, and at dawn found himself at the foot of Rattlesnake Butte.

Time to sleep again. Also time to have a look back at Thunder Butte to see if at last it hadn't shrunk a little in the distance.

But it hadn't. When he looked back it loomed as holy, solemn, and high as ever. Looking to either side Hugh could see that he had crossed the crest of flat Fox Ridge. Crawling the last had been easier going too; so he knew the land was tipping down and away from the red rock altar, knew the horizon should have risen enough to have hidden it from view. But it hadn't.

Mirage, that was it.

Or else he'd gone loco at last. Maggots in the head as well as in the back.

"This child can't cipher it nohow. Maybe if he slept on it some, maybe it'd turn out to be just a bad dream."

Thunder Butte.

"Well, howsomever, first we'll have us some meat afore we go to sleep."

But the wild dog was gone. Sometime during the night it had drifted off, sometime during the interval when he'd resisted looking back at Thunder Butte, it had left him. Hugh missed the dog; could almost taste it as roasted meat on his tongue.

"Tarnation! Just when I needed him most."

Hugh looked around at the countryside. Nothing but dry bunch grass. No cactus beds, no berry bushes, no twig tips of any kind. And no water.

"Fresh roast dog. I swear. Nebuchadnezzar had green grass, he had, but not Old Hugh. Well, I guess there's nothin' for it but to bite in and hold on until I hit water below."

In the flooding light of a red-clover dawn, Hugh studied the fall of land below to the south. Once again he could make out far valleys angling from west to east, with the near one shallower than the far one, with a low hogback between them. The first was a big creek, he decided; the second was the Cheyenne River itself. The first valley had smooth grassy hills, with a few trees and shrubs that looked like chokecherries, with here and there a poplar. The big creek doubled around like the contorted flow of a stepped-on snake and finally joined the Cheyenne far in the southeast. The far valley had rugged stony hills, jagged horizons, and its flow was wide and deep and much more direct.

Hugh nodded to himself. The second valley was the Cheyenne all right. Get there and a man could float in to Ft. Kiowa.

To the left of Rattlesnake Butte a gullyhead began its cut in the grassy slopes. Hugh saw where it eventually ran into a dry creek. Here and there brush fuzzed out in its slow turns.

Hugh went on all fours to the gullyhead and burrowed out a flat place in sand and clay and snuggled under the bearskin and curled up to go to sleep.

It worried him that the wild dog had disappeared. He hoped it didn't mean red devils around. The dog might have sensed Rees before he did. Maybe a pair of daring young Rees were right now watching him curl up for the day's rest. Well, if they were, he would soon know it. He'd wake to shrill warwhoops and the crunch of a stone club on his noggin. And thinking about it, and his stomach rumbling with hunger, and the open wound in his back itching—whether from healing or from wriggling maggots he couldn't make out—Hugh drifted off to sleep.

*   *   *

A cold nose woke him.

For a second, lying on his belly with head to one side, as he rose out of the motherwort magma of the unconscious, Hugh was back on the forks of the Grand, thinking the cold-nosed wolf was back again. He screwged his eyes around at the blue sky expecting to see wheeling wrinklenecked turkey buzzards overhead too.

But the sky was clean. There was neither gaggling greennecked buzzard nor laughing red-tongued wolf. Instead there was a looming silvertip, a huge *Ursus horribilis*, a he-grizzly with a black piglike snout snuffling him over.

The shock came so quick he had no time to show fear. He just lay. And hoped he'd stay scared enough not to show it. A man lying down was medicine to the grizzly bear.

Old Ephraim stood huge over Hugh. One of his forepaws rested on the ground not three inches from Hugh's eyes. Hugh could see sunlight glinting on the silvertipped hairs over the great gray hooked claws. Hugh could also see, so close was the forepaw, skin dust and powdery dandruff in the deeper dark fur.

The huge creature snuffled at Hugh slowly, warm breaths pouring over Hugh regularly. The breaths had the faint decayed odor of dog's breath.

Old Ephraim snuffled at Hugh's grizzly hair, at his crooked hairy arm, at his grizzly neck, at the grizzly bearskin over his back.

Hugh understood it. Old Ephe had, at first sight, mistaken him for a dead companyero grizzly. But then it had got a sniff of man in the bearskin and had come over for a closer look.

Hugh smiled. The gray beard over his cheeks moved.

Old Ephe spotted the movement; quick sent a cold nose to explore it. The bull-huge beast shifted its weight to smell the better. It's forefeet moved with a soft heaviness. The ground under Hugh's ear resounded dully with the sound of it.

Hugh held the smile until his face ached.

Old Ephe cocked his great dog's head from side to side, watching.

It made Hugh laugh, a laugh he was careful to keep inside, and a laugh that was in part both a laugh of fear and a laugh at himself.

The idea of Old Ephe giving him a going-over, trying to make out whether he was a dead she-grizzly or a man in bearskin clothes reminded him of blind Isaac in the Old Testament feeling Jacob over, a Jacob in sheepskin pretending he was an Esau.

The thought of himself as a Jacob, Old Hugh didn't fancy too well. He wasn't a Jacob. The Jacobs were the Rebekah favorites, the mama boys, the she-rip sissies who stayed behind in the settlements to do squaw's work, the smooth men back home who ran shops and worked gardens and ran factories. No, if anything he was an Esau, a hairy man and a man's man and a cunning hunter, a man of the prairie and the mountains. It was the other, the man who'd probably married his old she-rip of a Mabel back in Lancaster County, who was the smooth man dwelling in a shingled tent. Ae, Old Hugh was Esau, the first, who'd come out red all over like an hairy garment. He was no Jacob coming out second and taking hold of an Esau's heel. Like an Esau he too had sold his birthright in Lancaster land to another, to the Jacob who probably right that minute was enjoying a ripping up and down his back by a she-rip Mabel.

Old Ephe apparently knew Hugh for what he was at last. For suddenly, with a single deft swipe of forepaw, the grizzly tore the grizzly skin off Hugh's back.

Hugh sucked in a breath of fear. Ripped up again?

But Old Ephe wasn't a she-rip ripper. Old Ephe was only a male curious about an odd smell coming out of

Hugh's back. The next instant Old Ephe was licking Hugh's open wound.

The licking tickled Hugh, tickled him horribly. He wanted to burst out laughing. The terribly funny tickling almost drove him crazy. With all his will power, he held back hysterical laughter.

As abruptly as he began, Old Ephe left off licking, and with a tumbler's tremendous heave of body, turned to one side and ran off, hump high and rolling, small Indian-ball-sized ears flicking back and forth nonchalantly, grampa rear waddling along.

When he was sure Old Ephe was gone from the gullyhead, Hugh rolled over on his side and sat up. He felt around behind his back. And feeling, he found the last crusts gone around the wound and the center of it slick and clean. The grizzly had cleaned out the maggots just when their work was done.

Then Hugh did laugh hysterically. The grizzly, like all grizzlies with a sweet tooth, apparently had been fond of maggots and by God, dead she-grizzly skin with a man's smell in it or no, was going to have some.

An hour later, when he himself began to wonder where his next meal was coming from, let alone treats like sweet maggots, Hugh pulled an Old Ephraim himself. He'd often seen bears stick a forepaw in an anthill, wait until the angered scrambling ants covered it, then lick them off, obviously considering them a delicacy as well as good food. Hugh found an anthill, stuck his paw in it, held it in the hill even though the ants stung him a little, and then, paw and forearm covered, withdrew it and forced himself to eat ants. Surprisingly they tasted very good. Tart, sharpish, but curiously like salted sugar.

He was about to set off for the night's run down the hill, when, looking over his shoulder, he saw Thunder Butte was gone.

Gone. But not as if it'd never been.

Chapter 8

Wild geese were flying south in great trailing wavering V's by the time he reached Cherry Creek valley. It was October, the Moon of Leaves Falling.

The wild bullberries had pretty well dried up and gone. But the wild root crop was plentiful and the green glades abounded with squirrels and gophers. Old Hugh fed right well on them.

When he reached the deep stony valley of the Cheyenne, Old Hugh greeted the sight of the swift-flowing yellow river glinting in the morning sun with a shout of joy.

"Hurray, lads! Old Hugh's made it at last. As good as. It's all over but the shouting now. Best get yoursel's set, because Old Hugh's on the warpath. If the red devils ain't got your topknot by now, Old Hugh soon will."

He unbound the willow slape from his bad leg, took off the splints, and gave himself a thorough scrubbing in the slightly alkaline Cheyenne River. He rinsed the bum leg gently, rinsed out his scalp, rinsed as best as he could the torn corrugations across his back.

He splashed in the shallow waters along the sandy shore, singing, shouting, for a little while heedless of lurking red devil and she-rip grizzly.

Flowing water meant life. It meant fish. It meant drink. It meant cleansing. It meant travel. Yes, land was important. Ae. But land was the given. Like a mother, it was there to begin with. It was water men craved, not land. Men loved land for the water it had just as children loved a mother for the milk she had.

He soaked his calluses, those along the bottoms of his forearms from the heel of the hand to the point of the elbow, and the broad warty one on his good knee. With handfuls of gritty golden sand for soap he scoured out the dirt.

Cottonwood leaves as yellow as buttercups fluttered high overhead. The morning sky was a deep gentian blue, was clean and serene. The stony bluffs to either side bulked up sharply. Here and there the bluff cheeks were bearded out with spine cactus. Far down the slowly twisting river valley perspective faded off into a hazy aven-blue.

He was dizzy with the joy of being alive. Dizzy with it. He rested beside the rippling, wrinkling, flowing yellow waters of the Cheyenne. He lay down on a grassy sward beneath a huge towering cottonwood. The smell of fresh waters and falling autumn leaves and green grass restored his soul. His cup ran over.

The spot beneath and around the great cottonwood tree was like a park, Hugh thought. Buffalo and antelope had kept the grass close-cropped. Buffalo and antelope had trimmed the lower portions of all the trees and bushes to an even height. Sitting under his tree Hugh guessed he could see more than a mile in any direction under the level line of trimmed-off leaves. Approaching friend or enemy would have been spotted on the instant. Late fall flowers bloomed in the short deep green grass. Yellow poplar leaves and pink willow leaves fell in showers.

God's park, he called it. And he Adam without an Eve.

One day he found an old Indian middenheap on a knoll. The moment he saw the low mound he got an idea. He found himself a sharp-pointed ash stick from amongst the driftwood along the Cheyenne's banks and began to dig through the heap. He found a few broken water bowls with angular black and white designs, a few broken potsherds, a few clay pans. He found a hand-made bone fishhook. He found a broken stone hatchet. He found a small piece of flint. He found a smudged flat cookrock.

With the bone fishhook and his ash stick and a slender grapevine, he fished the Cheyenne. He caught channel cat almost as fast as he could throw in the hook.

With Old Mother's much worn flint and steel, and milkweed down for tinder, he built himself a small fire and fried the catfish on the cookrock.

He fished. He ate. He slept. He restored his soul.

He swam and it refreshed his torn corrugated body. His bad leg floated gently and easily and without pain in the swift-flowing yellow waters.

He fished. He ate. He slept. He healed.

It wasn't long before he tried standing on both legs. Holding onto the huge cottonwood to steady himself, he got up on his good leg and slowly shifted his weight onto the other. The bad leg hurt but it bore up. The knitted crack in the bone stung, yes, but it didn't buckle. Ae, in a month he'd be going around on two legs regular again.

He found a small ash sapling with a V-shaped fork. With his broken stone ax he cut it down, shaped himself a crude crutch out of it. From then on, taking his time, between frequent rests, he went about upright once more. He was a human critter again, not just a four-legged varmint.

Exploring the poplar-shaded valley to all sides, he one day came across a down cottonwood beside the river. It had a trunk three feet through.

The big tree trunk gave him another idea. He had been thinking of making raft out of driftwood and grapevines. But why not make a dugout instead? He had a crude hatchet, a knife, and the firemakings to do it with.

No sooner thought than done. He set to work. Firing carefully, he burnt out the insides. A couple of times the fire threatened to eat in too deeply, and he had to quickly roll the trunk over into the stream to put it out.

When the insides were too wet from the soaking, he chipped and chopped away on the outside. The chopping was the hardest. It went very slowly. A day's work at it hardly showed results.

After two weeks of steady firing and chopping he at last had himself a crude dugout some fifteen feet long, two feet wide, and a good foot deep. It wasn't a beauty, but it floated.

He loaded in his grizzly skin, his necklace of grizzly claws, the red-striped blanket he'd taken from the old Indian crone and which he now used to cover his back, his bone fishhook, his flint and steel, his crude stone ax, a supply of gutted half-dried channel cat, and a long poling stick.

He made a trial run the first day and found only one thing to complain about. And it was bad enough. The dugout was somewhat unstable. In swift rough water he had trouble balancing it.

He muttered, fussed about it some. "Must've dug it out on the wrong side of the log. A child has to sit exactly in the middle and breathe out of the middle of his mouth if he don't want to capsize the dummed thing."

It was early November, the Moon of Deer Rutting, when he set out for the fort. It was evening and the sun had just set in the gorge to the west in pale jewel-weed pallor. The wind was in the west too, a swift lifting wind that made a man breathe deep to get enough of it.

Hugh sat exactly amidships with the long pole balanced across his lap, ready to dip in on either side to keep the crude prow headed straight downstream.

The Cheyenne ran swift, steady, with a sound at

times as of a low hissing skink and at other times as of boiling water. The Cheyenne swung right, swung left, playing through the stony yellowgray valley like a manipulated yellow hemp rope. Within the banks the main current followed a swinging course too, often a course of its own contrary to the bed, zigging when the bed zagged, sometimes hugging the shore on the left when the bed indicated right, sometimes agreeing with the bed to a point where it overswung it and undercut the bank.

In the falling rusty dusk Hugh watched the land go by: cottonwood-studded points, rock-cropped headlands, flat green vales, thick groves of willows, shallow sandy banks coming down to streaming fords.

"This child's never had it so good," Old Hugh murmured to himself. "After what me and my bum leg went through, this is paradise at last. I've been a keelboatman off and on all my life and I've floated down many a river I first pushed up, but never as sweet a river as this one. Never."

The water flowed along and he floated down. He swung to the left. He swung to the right. He rode the swift main current. He watched the country go by, the stony land and the swampy land, the clearings and the canebrakes, the parklike pastures and the jungle groves, the dry gullies and the swift straight creeks. He floated down.

"Don't mind if I never see ee again," Hugh said. "It's good-by for now and I hope for good. You may be home to some critters but not for this one. I'll be glad to get back to Reed and her pot."

The Cheyenne churned through its winding channel. It boiled whirlpools. It spread calms.

"It's like I always said. Best to have a little grief first and much joy afters than the other way around."

He watched the bluffs turn by.

"Lads, Ol' Hugh is comin'. He's on his way. Best prime your pans and set the flint. Ol' Hugh's a-boilin' along. It won't be long afore ye'll feel mighty queersome in your lights. It's six feet and under for the both of ee."

Darkness flowed into the stony valley like a low black fog. Overhead the high tops of the spine-bearded bluffs and the headlands still glowed plantain purple.

" 'Tis a wonder. There's nothin' like runnin' water."

He held his leg and ticked off the miles he saved crawling. He held his leg and watched the bends swing into view, come toward him, hold under his eye, swing past, slip behind and out of sight. He couldn't get over how wonderful it was that except for an occasional dip to the right or the left with his pole he could sit on a soft folded grizzly skin and let the river do all his crawling, all his walking, for him.

Ae, the birds were going south for the winter and so was Old Hugh.

Twice during the first night he had close calls.

Once it was a large Sioux village camped beside the river on the north shore. He saw the cluster of cone tepees coming. A fire glowed under trees ahead, lighting up the near shore and the tall cottonwoods and the near tepees, and limning the vague outline of the south shore. The Sioux were celebrating some kind of victory. A quarter-mile away Hugh could spot the braves bending and stomping and kicking as they danced around a set of fresh scalps up on spears off to one side of the roaring orange-titted bonfire. Circling them sat young maidens watching the show. Deeper in the shadows lounged old meditative bucks and collapsed old squaws.

Hugh ducked down flat in the dugout, hiding his long pole alongside his body. He hoped they'd be too busy whooping it up to notice the dugout floating past, hoped that if they did look his way they'd mistake the dugout for a piece of fat driftwood.

But not all the maidens were watching the show. Two were bent on cleanliness. They were wading in the shallows near the village. Light from the fire glowed brown on their naked supple bodies. They were chattering and laughing together, splashing each other, dipping in and out like pennyskinned mermaids, their faces open and gay, their titties as lovely as four full moons.

Then they spotted the dugout floating downstream across from them. They ducked down, only their heads showing. They watched with intent berry-round eyes.

The Cheyenne turned a little in front of the village and the turning saved Hugh. His dugout, without his pole to keep it headed downstream, slowly revolved in the turn, revolved just enough to present the blunt back end of the cottonwood dugout, the end which still looked a little like a round log. The maidens studied it; looked at each other questioningly; let it pass.

Hugh let out a great sigh once he was out of sight of the village. "They might have been friendly Sioux. Maybe even relations of Reed. But they just maybe might not have been either. A white man alone is fair game for even friendly red devil."

The other close call came when, shooting through a narrow channel, where the just risen milk-silver full moon couldn't shine, he ran full tilt into a sawyer, a fallen behemoth of a cottonwood, presenting its sun-flowerlike mat of roots straight at him like a vast maw. Hugh saw it in the dark as a gathering tangle of trouble. Quickly he volved the boat a quarter-turn around and then punched his pole into the matted roots. Ordinarily he could quite easily have poked or poled his way around it. But his boat was top-heavy and it took all his skill as an old seadog to keep the boat level and moving around the down cottonwood.

He was glad when morning came. Though for once he was far from tired. Just sleepy. He pulled for shore and hid his dugout in a thick canebrake at the mouth of a slow creek.

He fried a channel cat aboard the dugout; washed off the fish smell; drank long and thirstily; curled up on the grizzlyskin; drew the blackred striped woolen blanket over him; and slept the sleep of the justified.

The second morning, coming around a turn, coasting out through an avenue of arching poplar, the wild Missouri opened before him.

After all the barren bluffs and clay gullies and rock outcroppings and stony hogbacks he'd seen, Hugh thought the river a grand ocean. Majestic, sweeping wide, the tan sheet of seething water flowed eternally into the south. Anon and anon and anon. With occasional running whirlpools and sawyer eddies breaking its surface. With whole trees—majestic cottonwoods and umbrella elms and gnarled fierce oaks and slender ash and delicate maple—surfboating along and bobbing up and down in the water like gigantic sea serpents armed like octopuses.

On the nearside, great dead snags with limbs thrust to the skies like praying skeleton hands rolled over and over, slowly, forlornly. In a backwater on the far shore some snags lay piled up two deep, broken, tangled, cracked off, looking for all the world like a dinosaur boneyard.

Squinting, narrowing his eyes, Hugh could just make out a herd of antelope grazing on the far bank. Behind them reared a sloping hogback where it came down into a long turn of the wild Missouri.

Gray haunted eyes burning silverish under tufted gray brows, bush of grizzly hair hanging down to his shoulders like a long gray parted mop, Hugh sat looking at it all until the sun felt warm, even hot, on his burnt black nose and high cheeks. The old seadog awoke in him for fair. There was challenge in the turbulent seething sheet of tan waters, and he liked it. With himself as both captain and crew, he was anxious to test his craft against the wild Missouri, even if he did have a wobbly top for a boat.

"But not for now," Hugh promised the rolling brown

flood, "not for now. Tonight maybe. After Ol' Hugh's had his beauty sleep. I'm rich now, I am, and can afford sleep and sailor's rest."

Hugh spotted an acre of waving cattails along the lee shore across the Missouri. He poled across easily and with a hard shove sent the dugout rustling into it. The tall cob-topped cattails hid him and the boat completely. He breakfasted on channel cat he'd dried the evening before, and washed up, and lay down to sleep out the day under the striped blackred blanket.

He slept. The wind soughed up from the south and tossed the heavy cattail cobs back and forth.

He slept. The November sun shone gently and revived the green grass in the low sloughs.

He slept. The wind soothed softly and rustled the ocher leaves in the rushes.

He awoke to the sound of squealing squirrels. The tree squirrels were gathering acorns under some oaks behind the cattails, fighting with crows over who was to store what provender where. Everybody was getting ready for the winter ahead.

Hugh washed his eyes in river water, pushed the dugout to the edge of cattails, studied the fleeting coffee waters and the far shore and then the near shore for sign, went about making supper out of the last of his dried channel cat.

Restored, refreshed, body relaxed, body sweet with a long night's rest, he swung his stubby unstable craft out into the main current of the wild Missouri and began rushing home to Ft. Kiowa.

"Ae, lads, it's comin', that queersome time when Ol' Hugh with a quick snip of the knife parts ee from your scalp. Best get your prayers said now."

Hugh smiled when he imagined the look on their faces when he'd step up to them and ask for his fixin's.

That look alone, whatever it would be, would be worth almost all the horrible suffering he'd gone through.

"Reed, get the pot ready and fill up with the best buffler cow in the fort. Ae, and don't forget your medicines. And your fresh leathers. That steel awl I bought ee is gonna be hot for usin'. Your old man needs an overhaulin' from his crow's-nest on down."

The wild Missouri rushed him south. It rushed him past the mouths of Okobojo and Chantie Creeks, past Medicine Butte, which in the full round moon loomed up like a broken shattered Thunder Butte, past the mouth of the stinking Bad, past Antelope and Medicine and Cedar Creeks, and around the looping Grand Detour.

"It's whisky and pancakes for me again for breakfast. Whisky to wake me up and sharpen the taster. Pancakes to weight me down and cover the ribs."

Ae, the wild Missouri rushed him south.

It was almost dark when he saw the Stars and Stripes snapping in a cold northwester over Ft. Kiowa. There'd been snow flurries during the day, and the bluffs towering high to either side above the river plains looked like sleeping flocks of albino leopards.

Hugh approached the west shore warily. His limbs shivered with trembles. He found it hard to believe he was home at last.

Squinting in the falling pink dusk, the tan waters turning redbrown beneath him, Hugh soon saw there were no sentinels out along the bank. That meant there were no rampaging red devils about. It also meant no war party could cut him off from safety at the last moment.

The dugout hit the mud bank under the loading dock with a giving thud and rode part way up it. Hugh stood up; stretched; sighed. He gathered up his possessions. He slipped the necklace of grizzly forepaws around his neck. Like a chief he folded the blackred blanket around his body. He threw the grizzly skin over an arm.

He picked up his crude ash crutch and, upright, hobbled out of the dugout and up the path and onto the plains before the fort.

He limped past the lone great cottonwood under which General Ashley and his men had met in early August to plan the fall trapping campaigns. Today neither bird nor leaf fluttered from the tree's ocher twigs. Huge thick branches tubed up into the dogbane skies like white-hot stovepipes.

Swatches of fresh snow made the going underfoot slippery. Hugh hobbled along on all three cautiously. He was going to make sure that no last-minute accident would ruin the homecoming.

Before the fort gates was the usual Sioux village on a trading visit. Skin pennants dangled in the wind from the highest pole sticking out of the tepee smoke hole. A few children raced and played with half-wild dogs. Before the doorflap of one tepee, the tallest and the best, stood a solitary chief wrapped in a grayred blanket, his nose-sharp face as expressionless as a redstone hatchet.

The sentinel in the gate hailed Hugh. "Where you from, stranger?"

"The Grand," Hugh said, his voice a strange deep bass. Hugh recognized the sentinel. It was Old Childress, Old Childress once a mighty hunter but now too full of aches and pains to pursue antelope and buffalo. "The Grand, that's where."

Childress viewed Old Hugh severely through the little wicket in the main gate, his flintlock aimed true into Hugh's right eye. Overhead other sentinels on the rifle walk and in the corner blockhouses watched Hugh narrowly too. "Where's your companyeros?"

"I'm alone."

"From the Grand? And what mout your name be?"

Hugh laughed at Childress. "Why, Childress, old hoss, what kind of a come-on is this?"

"What! Hugh, old coon! I thought ye were gone under!"

Hugh snorted. "Well, this child was mighty nigh losin' his hair at that, he was."

"Ol' Hugh! That beats, that does." Old Childress slowly lowered his gun.

"Open up, Childress. I'm half-froze for hair."

"That beats, that does," Old Childress repeated, gray eyes dawing wide.

"Open up that dummed gate afore I think you're a snake-eyed nightmare."

"Will so."

The gate opened and Hugh hobbled through and into safety.

Hugh said, "Got any 'bacca?"

"Have so. Fresh."

"Give us a chaw."

Childress handed Hugh a leather pouch, eyes still wide with awe.

Hugh took a good wad, lifted it, straggly ends and all, into his hairy maw, chewed solemnly a moment, spat to one side. "Got any whisky? I've got a bad dry too."

"Have so. English and the best. Also some Taos lightning."

"I'll take a horn of English."

Childress said, "Come with me. There's plenty in the men's quarters tonight." Childress hollered up at one of the watching sentinels on the rifle walk. "Melette? Get down here and mind the gate till I fix up this travelin' bag a bones with a snootful."

"You don't need to come," Hugh said. "I know my way around."

"No, I'll take ye. I'm glad for the break." Old Childress looked up at Hugh with awe still in his eyes. "So ye're alive, Hugh. Fitz said you was dead."

Hugh jumped. "Fitz? Fitzgerald?"

"Yes, old hoss. Major Henry sent him down to tell

227

Ashley he and the boys'd made it safe to the post on the Yellowstone and Missouri. All except you, that is."

Hugh chewed slowly. He spat to one side. "Is Fitz here?" Hugh's fists worked like buzzard claws.

"No, Fitz's gone. Left with Jed Smith a month ago. For the Black Hills and beyond like was planned. He'll join up with the major in the winter somewhere near the Big Horns."

Hugh slowly relaxed. The great time hadn't quite come yet.

Old Childress led the way across hard-packed ground. Hugh limped after steadily on all three.

A sound of shouting and singing and fiddles and drums came from the loghouse men's quarters. The door was open and Hugh could see a leaping fire. Some twenty souls, leathered mountain men and bearded river roughnecks, were gathered around the flames. The walls shone ruddy behind them.

"What's going on in there?" Hugh asked.

"An old-fashioned breakdown. A keelboat's just in from St. Lou."

"Keelboat? I didn't see one out on the river."

"It's floated down ten mile to pick up some fresh buffler meat."

Hugh looked at the festivity and stopped. "No," he said.

"What's the matter, old hoss?"

"No." Hugh leaned on his crutch. Something in him balked at the idea of sitting down all of a sudden in the midst of old friends and their raillery. They were good men, ae, lean hard men, meat eaters who didn't run to settlement fat, and friendlier than a tail-wagging puppy too, but—"No."

"We've just finished chuck, Hugh. But there's java on the fire."

"Coffee?"

"Sure. C'mon, Hugh, you must be starved for men and meat."

Hugh continued to lean on his crutch. In the falling smutdark dusk he surveyed the interior of the walled fort. He looked particularly into the black shadowy corners.

Old Hugh said, "Where's Reed?"

Old Childress hauled up short. "Don't tell me ye want squaw afore meat!"

"Where's Reed?" Hugh said sternly.

"Yonder. Ahindt the clerk's shop."

Hugh jumped for the second time. "That oily Bonner ain't taken her as his squaw?"

Old Childress laughed, showing toothless gums, and slapped his bony knee. "Old hoss, you do want squaw afore meat then! You wild old goat you! Hee hee."

"Has he?" Hugh asked fiercely in a hoarse bass voice.

"No, no. No, it's just Reed in one of her sour fits again. She's in mourning."

"What?"

"Sure. For ye, old hoss."

Hugh stood still. His eyes softened.

"Old Hugh, for an old hoss you surprise me, hankerin' after squaw so." Old Childress shook his gray head. "Take me, now. I hain't had squaw for seven year now. Though I admit I never thought squaw prime company taken alone." Old Childress shook his head some more. "Squaw? For many a year I packed one along. Bad was the best, and after she was gone I tried no more." Old Childress thumped the ground with the stock of his flintlock. "I never did understand why to some men the squaws look whiter and smell sweeter with every passing week away from white diggin's."

Hugh looked in at the door of the loghouse again. With every passing second the roar of the shindig increased in tempo and volume. Whisky flowed; spirits rose; talk became shrill. A few Sioux squaw, the wives of mountaineers, strutted about through the melee proud of their display of beads and fofurraw, their deerskin dresses jingling with bells and bangles and their

faces bedaubed with St. Lou paint. Against the walls
stood lonely Sioux warriors, lean, wrapped in tanblack
buffalo robes, too proud to sit down at the fire and fun
without invitation, also sulky and uneasy to be so close
to white scalps without being able to do anything
about it.

"No," Old Hugh said, "no, it's me for Reed first, in
mourning or no. See you, Childress."

Hugh found Reed's tepee behind Clerk Bonner's
shed. With a flickering fire inside, the tepee glowed like
a pumpkin with a candle in it. At the flapdoor Hugh
let his crutch fall to the ground, held a moment on his
own two legs, then dropped to his knees and crawled
in. Reed had put fresh sweetgrass in the bedding, and
the tepee smelled very sweet with it.

Bending Reed was sitting before the fire, legs folded
to one side. Hugh saw right away that she was in
mourning like Childress had said. She'd cut off her hair
again. She'd blackened her face, diagonal lines running
from the bottom of her eyes to her neck, the lines rep-
resenting the paths of her tears. She'd also daubed her
deerskin dress with various mourning paints.

"Reed," Hugh said.

She heard him and looked up. Her shiny cherry eyes
glittered at him over the ruddy fire. Then her mouth
opened in surprise. And also in surprise her hand
snapped up and covered her mouth.

"Reed, it's your old man. Back from the wars. Have
ye cow meat handy?"

Reed stared. Slowly she took her hand away from her
mouth. Slowly she crossed her hands over her heart and
hugged them close.

Hugh smiled under his beard. He recognized the Indian sign for love.

He tossed her the dried grizzly claws. "Here, Reed,
here's for you. Special. Ye can dance for joy now, Reed.
I'm a brave at last."

She picked them up; looked at him wonderingly.

"Don't ye believe me, lass? Here, look." Hugh showed her the scars in his beard and scalp, tossed off his striped blackred blanket and showed her the terrible corrugations across his bare back, drew back the torn leather around his bum leg and showed her beartooth marks. "It's grizzly all right."

She stared at the scars, at the dried paws, at his grizzly face.

"So Heyoka's still got your tongue, eh?" Hugh's voice continued rough and harsh, though he intended nothing but tenderness. The hoarseness, he decided, came from lack of use during all the lonesome days crawling. "Still balky and contrary, I see. Well, Reed, lass, sit then. Old Hugh'll make for himself, he will. He's been doin' it for nigh on three months now. Three months of plain hell."

Then Bending Reed's dark glittering eyes snapped and she got up.

It wasn't long before Old Hugh was salved and greased from head to foot, and filled to the neck with fresh buffalo cow and pemmican.

It made Hugh laugh to see Reed gloat over the dried grizzly claws.

Part III

The Showdown

Chapter 1

Bending Reed plied her flying awl and within a few days Old Hugh had a new skin suit. From the smoked top of an old tepee she made him leggings and moccasins. From freshly tanned antelope hide she made him hunting shirt and breeches and big halfmoon-curved mittens. And finally to complete it all, she made him a new cap from a well-cured wolfskin.

Next, from a private hoard of smoked skin and sinew she made an extra dozen pairs of moccasins and leggings, all of them marked with her characteristic backlash Heyoka stitch, and these Hugh sold to the river roughnecks who had come up on the keelboat *Beaver*. Cash in hand, Old Hugh went to hard-eyed Bonner the clerk and bought a used flintlock, powder horn, bullet pouch and mold, flint and steel, skinning knife, tobacco and pipe, and some salt. Hugh also bought a gray woolen capote—a blanket long enough to cover most of his body, with a hood to cover the head and face in case of a storm. The capote was expensive and Hugh had to charge part of it. Old eyes twinkling in comical gravity, Hugh told Bonner the clerk, "I'll give you so much cash down and a slow note for the balance."

With an old razor Hugh whacked off part of his beard, changing the appearance of his face from that of a shaggy poodle to that of a fierce tomcat. Hugh also whacked off some of his gray hair so he could get it decently under his new wolfskin cap.

Bending Reed thought her husband, Chief White

Grizzly, a very handsome brave in his new get-up. His fresh yellow leathers were in pleasing harmony with his crisp gray whiskers and the mahogany parchmentlike color of what could be seen of his cheeks. His old gray eyes snapped like in the old days: Indianlike, wild yet watchful. The trembles in his fingers vanished.

A week of warm weather flooding in from the south helped too. When Hugh wasn't exercising his knitting leg, he lay on a fur robe on the sunny side of the tepee, stretched to the full, soaking in the sun. The warmth and the leisure, the slow firm churning of his stomach, the healing itch in his back and leg and lopped-off lobe of his seat, the sound of Bending Reed's humming and chatter as she filled his hairy ears with the latest fort gossip plus the latest from her tribe of Lakota, the spieling of some comrade mountain men happening by, the warm womblike safety within the tall cottonwood fort walls—all worked as medicine on him, medicine made sweet with old remembered aches and travails.

Occasionally the sap of returning health rose so sharply in him that he couldn't sit still for doing; then he got to his old limbs and, flintlock in hand and powder horn and possible sack slung over a shoulder, stumped out through the fort gate and out across the plains, for all the world as if he were going to course a score of miles if need be to bring down meat for the fort.

He never got farther than the base of the first sleeping bluff to the west just two miles away. His just-knitted leg couldn't take it. He came back each time limping and blowed, and as ugly as a soretail grizzly.

Bending Reed plied him with affection and food and happy squaw chatter. And at night, warm together under furs, she offered him her body.

Her body he didn't care for. That part of him hadn't come back.

"Has my husband forgotten?" she asked, teasing him,

Siberian eyes slanted and mischievous in the low glow of the falling fire.

"This child ain't forgotten," Old Hugh growled, voice a deep monotonous bass. The new heaviness and slowness of his voice always startled him a little. "No, this child hain't forgotten a-tall. And that's the trouble."

Bending Reed's eyes opened wide. She clapped a hand over opened mouth. "Heyoka," she whispered after a moment.

Old Hugh spoke as if he hadn't heard. His voice continued to roll out in a slow monotonous bass tone. "If it's the last thing this child does, he's gonna catch them oily cowards and skin 'em alive and feed 'em to the dogs."

Bending Reed nodded to herself. "Heyoka."

"What?"

Chapter 2

Heyoka or not, Old Hugh was soon hot on the trail of the deserters Fitz and Jim. It was December, the Moon of Deer Shedding Horns.

Patron Joe Bush, bourgeois of the keelboat *Beaver*, decided to make a run for Ft. Tilton higher on the Missouri before the river froze over. Hugh offered his services as hunter. The *Beaver* was already full up, and Patron Bush wasn't too anxious to take on an extra mouth, let alone a trouble-making cripple, but Hugh's fierce insistence and his reputation as a centershot finally persuaded Bush.

The *Beaver* made good time up the Missouri. Cordelling, sometimes sailing, most times pushing with poles, the river roughnecks prowed it through tan waters, past dirt-brown banks, up around the Grand Detour, up past the Bad and Cheyenne and Moreau Rivers, up past the Grand River where the ferocious Rees once thrived, up past the Cannonball and the Heart, and at last came within sight of the Knife where the friendly Mandans lived and where Ft. Tilton was located.

Because he felt himself in the way, and because not once all the way up from Ft. Kiowa had he brought down any meat to pay for his keep, Hugh offered to hunt across the bend and meet them at Ft. Tilton.

Hugh and Patron Bush stood in the prow of the boat, looking up river. Bleak gray blanket clouds drove at them from the northeast. It felt like snow.

Behind the two, burly sweating keelboatmen groaned

as they humped the boat up the river. A walk or passe avant ran along both sides of the *Beaver* and a dozen men worked each side. At the leader's cry of "raise poles" the men ran backward from aft to fore along the walks, and at the cry of "lower poles" the men jammed the poles into the river for a new purchase. Huge shoulder cupped around the knob-end of a pole, facing the rear, the men began shoving and walking toward the aft end of the boat again. Working in smooth unison, the keelboatmen literally walked the boat up the river.

Patron Bush was loath to let Hugh go off alone. Patron Bush was a heavy squat man with scowling features and a pessimistic air. Patron Bush hated frontier life and was going to get out as soon as he'd made a quick killing in the fur trade. " 'Tain't safe, Hugh. There's Rees about, I hear."

"Who said?" Hugh watched the *Beaver* slowly gain on the dirt-brown shoreline.

"A runner told about it."

"How kin that be when these old eyes saw them headin' west along the Cheyenne." Hugh noted how rubber-ice was beginning to edge the shoreline.

" 'Tain't safe, Hugh. I don't recommend it."

Hugh stuck out his stubborn chin. "It'll take your boys three days to get the *Beaver* around the bend. I can cut across in a day. Easy. Even with meat to weight me down."

Patron Bush scowled up at Hugh. "What's the hurry?"

"Booshway, I can use them two days."

"But why?"

"Booshway, send me and there'll be fresh meat waitin' for you at the fort."

"Hugh, what's got into you? You out to make more trouble?"

"Booshway, it's December already, and the way I'll have to hump it to the mountains afore the big snows come will take the gristle off a painter's tail."

"Hugh, you ain't ready for wear yet with that bum leg. Hugh, there's somethin' wrong with you. You act like you're out to get even with somebody. Or somethin'. Like the boys back at Fort Kiowa said."

Hugh hid his eyes. He watched the keelboat swerve around a bobbing sawyer in the moiling tan waters.

Patron Bush's little brown pig eyes wrinkled up into two narrow slits. "If I had your excuse, you'd never catch me leavin' a warm fire and a lovin' squaw, let me tell you.'

Hugh hid his eyes. He recalled all too well the snug comfort of Bending Reed's tepee, a round nest snug in the snows within the fort walls. Hugh stared down at the backlash Heyoka stitch in the seams of his moccasins. Ae, a well-built tepee had it all over frame houses in the winter. It wasn't drafty; everything one needed lay close to hand; and it kept easy. It was truly, as Bending Reed believed, a world in itself, in itself a world in image. Ae, but what were all these advantages as long as certain white devils, two of them, were still loose in the world and their desertion of him unavenged? In Bible times vengeance might be the Lord's but not in Free West times. In the free mountains vengeance belonged to him as had a right to it and could get it.

Hugh said, "Well, does this child take the shortcut and make meat for you, or don't he?"

Patron Bush pointed to the low snow-dappled bench lying within the bend. "You'll break a leg crossin' that greasy stuff."

Hugh abruptly stuck his gray bristle face into the patron's. The red rivulets down the sides of Hugh's big Scotch nose began to pulse a little. "Booshway, it's my life. Get out the skiff."

"All right, go then!" Patron Bush suddenly said, eyes quailing, spitting a great gob of tobacco juice over the side into the tan Missouri. "And be durned to ee, too! I know I won't see ee alive again, that I won't."

Patron Bush ordered the anchor dropped and the

skiff readied. And a quarter-hour later Hugh found himself on the west bank of the wild Missouri, alone, all his worldly possessions on his back.

The northeast wind whistled in the riverbank willows and snapped the ocher twigs of the cottonwood saplings. The wind was cold and wet and occasionally streaked with a flake of snow. Hugh drew the hood of his thick gray woolen capote close up around his head and face.

Swinging his powder horn and bullet pouch within easy reach, and waving his rifle at Patron Bush to show he was all set, Hugh started northwest across the low bench.

A thin blanket of snow lay on the gray frozen ground and it made the going greasy just as the patron had predicted. In some places, around anthill breather holes and fresh badger mounds, the snow had melted away. Grass tufts poked through every few steps.

Hugh limped along steadily, choosing his footing with care. His just-knitted limb felt surprisingly strong. He swept the white horizon with keen gray eyes. His big nose reddened in the mean wind.

He looked across to where the Missouri curved off to the northeast. Low sloping whitegray bluffs pushed back into the same horizontal crevice from which the low streaking graywhite clouds came.

Except for the brush close along the Missouri's bank, not a tree and not a bush was in sight. It was mounded monotonous country.

He limped across the highest part of the bench in the great bend without seeing so much as a field mouse. "A crow'd hafta carry grub to fly this godfersaken country," Hugh growled to himself. "Howsomever, meat or no meat, walkin' it to the fort will be that much time saved."

Dusk had just begun to sift down through the gray blanket clouds when Hugh started down the west side of the bench. Ahead the Missouri came curving out of the east again, coming around in a grand looping sweep and heading directly toward the base of a cutbank plateau. The bluffs on the far side looked like a coil of puffed-out bowels.

Then he spotted smoke rising from the plateau. Looking closer he saw certain blisterlike mounds on the plateau and recognized the first of the Mandan villages. Ah, fire and a little food. Tarnation with making meat that probably wasn't there in the first place.

He looked longingly toward the earthen lodges. Only a mile or so away, the sod-covered lodges had the appearance of huge kettles upsidedown. Above each lodge pricked spears dangling with skin pennants and medicine poles fluttering with scalps. Smoke rose from the many smoke holes in thin gentle wavering plumes barely discernible against the graywhite horizon.

Hugh hadn't yet seen many Mandans but he'd heard they were almost white the way they lived. And compared with the Sioux they were paleskinned. Some of the Mandans even had the blue eyes and the blond hair of Danes. To top it off, the Mandans also believed in the theory of a Great Flood and how an ark saved all living creatures.

Ae, with the bum leg stinging like a bee-bit finger it would be good to get in out of the mean wind.

Between him and the village on the plateau ran a little creek. Willows fringed it on either side. Hugh's wise old eyes swept it, swept it again, and came to rest on a curious gathering of gray in a thick clump on the side nearest the Missouri. In the cloudy gray dusk it was hard to make out just what it was. Antelope? Elk? It was grayish and could even be an Old Ephraim.

Just to be on the safe side, Hugh picked his flint, set his trigger, and crouching low, stalked noiselessly toward it, moccasined feet feeling out a safe course through the snow-covered sweetgrass.

The gray bunching became two gray whorls, then

became two gray creatures, then became two squaws wearing weather-grayed leathers.

Hugh blinked to clear his old eyes. Mandans? Out to get some sweet creek water?

Just then the two squaws turned and saw him. And they recognized him at the same time that he recognized them. He was the feared Chief White Grizzly and they were Rees, the exact same Ree squaws that Augie Neill and Jim Anderson had diddled on the Grand.

Hugh dropped to the ground and tried to duck behind a low mound of dirt cast up by a badger.

Too late. The squaws set up a howl and began running toward the Missouri. The squaws were young, and with their deerskin skirts girded up, they ran like the wind.

Hugh glanced toward the willow-fringed Missouri and spotted what they were heading for—another red-devil village, this one with low mud lodges. Just like those he'd seen on the Grand last June. Rees all right. A whole nest of them. He was caught. "A shortcut always turns out to be the long way home," Hugh groaned to himself.

Hugh's heart suddenly struggled in his chest. He panted. The single arteries down each side of his nose wriggled like lively red angleworms.

"There's nothin' for it but to see if these old legs of mine'll still run a little," he said, and suiting action to the words, leaped up and forced his cracking old pins into a flailing spiderlike run. He grunted in pain each time his bum leg hit the frozen ground. He ran with a princing nincing run, hoping he wouldn't fall on the greasy terrain and rebreak his leg. He brushed through the willows; leaped the narrow creek; headed up toward the Mandan plateau.

The cries of the squaws roused the whole Ree village. Heads popped out everywhere. The chief of the village hit the bloodied pole and sounded the alarm. Warriors with paired hawkbone hairdress and naked save for gun and breechcloth swarmed after him. They gained on him swiftly.

Old Hugh saw the landscape dancing. Starlike spots before the eyes blurred his vision. "It's gone under for this old hoss this time for sure."

But a sentinel sitting atop one of the upsidedown kettlelike Mandan mounds saw the commotion along the creek and he in turn sounded an alarm. Quickly two Mandan braves stripped down for battle, leaped on their ponies, one a spotted red-and-white mount and the other a jet-black, and raced toward him. Manes and braids and tails flagged out stiff as they came on.

Hugh scrambled along as hard and as fast as he could.

The running Rees formed a V as they gained on him. They came within gunshot of him. One Ree settled on a knee and fired a ball. It sailed harmlessly ahead of Hugh. He could see it skipping along across the frozen ground, kicking up little white explosions in the snow.

The Mandan braves galloped furiously toward him, pennants snapping from bow tips. The Mandan brave on the spotted pony gained on the other, and made a sweeping turn around Hugh, placing the body of the pony between Hugh and the pursuing, whooping, firing Rees. The Mandan on the jet-black pony galloped directly for Hugh; hauled up hard and short; helped Hugh clamber up behind him on the rump of the pony; beat the pony into a heavy encumbered gallop back toward the Mandan mounds on the plateau. The Mandan on the spotted pony meanwhile artfully and carefully kept himself and his horse between Hugh and the Rees.

Ree balls whistled all around them. The Rees howled with rage when they saw their hated enemy escaping them.

The Mandans galloped back to the plateau; shot through the opening in the picket fence; came to a jouncing halt dead in the center of the village.

When Hugh, panting, exhausted, got down from the

horse, he found himself surrounded by a melee of laughing cheering Mandan braves, squaws, children, and barking dogs. Two feather-decked chiefs stepped forward and solemnly embraced him. They hugged him so tight he could scarcely catch his already gone breath. Vaguely in his mind Hugh remembered hearing that the Mandans believed in hugging friends so that the heart might be felt.

The elder of the Mandan chiefs invited him to a feast already in progress. Hugh accepted.

That night he heard that the Rees had ambushed the *Beaver* and had killed every man aboard. Patron Bush had been right that he would never see Hugh alive again.

Hugh murmured to himself, musingly, " 'Pears like the Good Lord had it in mind to save this old hoss for His revenge after all."

Chapter 3

That same night too, after smoking a pipe of peace with the Mandan chiefs, during which they assured him their attack on Major Henry's party in August had been a mistake, that same night Old Hugh went on to Ft. Tilton a short ways upstream on the Missouri. The same brave on the jet-black horse who'd saved him, brought him in safely.

At the fort, Hugh made his report on what had happened to Patron Bush and the *Beaver*; asked for and got extra provisions—dried meat, pemmican, salt and pepper, coffee, a tin pot, a pack of tobacco, horse pistol, powder, balls, flint—asked for and got an extra gray woolen blanket.

Hugh also asked for a horse.

Bourgeois Tilton shook his head. In the candlelight his glossy black hair shone like polished black lava. "I've only got one. And that I have to use for the business. You know."

Flintlock under an arm, restless eyes taking in the array of goods hanging from pegs stuck in the log walls, good leg itching to get going, Hugh said, "You say it's smooth humpin' all the way up to where the Little Missouri cuts in from the south?"

Bourgeois Tilton lifted amazed button-black eyes. "You fixin' to leave yet tonight?"

"Tonight."

The candles flutted, and for a second the log-walled supply room darkened. Bourgeois Tilton's eyes darkened too, with concern. "Oh, Hugh, you don't mean it. You're only joshing me, I know."

Hugh headed for the log door. "This child does mean it. Sartain."

"Hugh, you've lost your sights! Get in a good night's sleep first. At least." Bourgeois Tilton shook his head as if he couldn't believe what he was seeing. His long black hair lashed around. Bourgeois Tilton snorted nervously. "Hugh, you can't go it alone all that way! If the Blackfeet don't get you, the wolves will!"

"Booshway, them Rees'll know afore mornin' that I'm here at the fort. So I've got to leave by then. Otherwise I'll never get away. They'll watch this place night and day till they get me."

"What's so all-fired—?"

Old eyes half-closed, Hugh looked back over his wide sloped shoulder. "I have to go. I've had sign."

"What sign?"

"That I must a been saved special."

" 'Saved special'?" Bourgeois Tilton snorted. "You must be teched. For what?"

"To get revenge." Hugh let the door close behind him, and alone in the black night, he set off up the river. "Saved special I must a been. Otherwise why did He let everybody aboard the *Beaver* die and me live? To me that's sign the Lord saved me for special doin'. To get revenge on the lads."

Hugh walked steadily all night long. He made good time despite his bum leg and the run he'd made earlier in the evening. When dawn came up pink and glorious over the slopes of crisp white snow, he found he'd covered some fifteen miles.

"Chosen," he said to the sun. "The Lord chose me."

He built a fire in a deep draw; warmed up the dried meat; had some coffee; had a pipe of tobacco; and, after a last look around, curled up in his capote and woolen blanket on a bed of willow twigs.

"Just so the snows'll hold off till I get to Henry's new

post," he said, nuzzling in the woolens. "Somewhere in the Big Horns."

The sun rose and warmed him. He felt drowsy.

"Chosen," he said. "And lads, best get your prayers ready and said. Ol' Hugh's comin' with the Lord's revenge. I've been chosen. I've had sign. I have."

For twenty-five days, all the way into early January, Hugh trudged steadily west, crossing the Badlands at the mouth of the Little Missouri, crossing the mouth of Shell Creek coming down from the north, and had good luck with the snow and cold. The weather held fair and, for that time of the year, even warm.

When the provisions he'd bought from the bourgeois at Ft. Tilton gave out on the White Earth River confluence above the Blue Buttes, he shot and killed a ten-point elk and, after he'd had his fill, fire-dried some of the meat to carry with him.

"Chosen," he said. "To help the Lord get His revenge."

At the Little Muddy he awoke one morning to find a small herd of wild mustangs pawing the ice along the edge of the Missouri trying to get a drink.

"Ho-ah," he whispered, "ho-ah, maybe this old hoss can ride the rest of the way."

It was open country all around, making it tough for him to sneak up and catch even one of the slowest mustangs; so he tried an old stunt he remembered from down in the south country. Taking a bead on the leader, a grey-maned milkblue stallion, he creased it just above the shoulder. The milkblue stallion fell, just as Hugh planned, while the rest of the herd scampered and whinnied shrilly away.

Quickly Hugh made a halter out of his belt and a strap; sat astride the prone pony, fully expecting it to get up after a minute or two, as well-creased ponies always did. But when the mustang stallion didn't stir after some ten minutes, he examined the wound under the gray mane. And shook his head. Too bad. He'd creased it too close to the spine. He'd killed it.

Hugh stroked the beautiful milkblue coat a few times. A pretty critter if ever there was one. Ae, too bad. Hugh shed a few tears over the noble beast; then, with a sigh, left it to the wolves.

"For the Lord," he said. "To get His revenge."

At the fanning confluence of the Yellowstone and Missouri, Hugh came across the abandoned fired remains of Major Henry's first post. It made Hugh curse softly to think that the major and the lads Fitz and Jim had once been on the spot. Well, just so Fitz and Jim were with the major in the new location in the Big Horns. That's all he asked. One chance to get his hands on Fitz. And the boy Jim too. For the Lord.

Hugh surveyed the land from a knoll on the north ridge. The major had picked a good spot for the old abandoned post all right. The site was on the first bench on the north side of the river and was clean of trees. The site not only provided a sweeping view of all the country around, it also commanded all traffic up and down both rivers. The Missouri, much tamer at this point, and also much cleaner, drove quietly out of the northwest, while the Yellowstone, rightly named for its flowing sands and clays, doubled on itself out of the southwest. Both rivers drove through wide flat valleys, with falling banks of gray clays and yellow gravels, with shifting gritty beaches and sand bars, with highlands behind them cropped with shortgrass and sage, and with finally a spear-shaped bench of yellow clay rising between them. The cutbanks of both rivers were sharp and fringed with cottonwood and willow and river ash.

All of it was crossroads country for the Indians: the sometimes friendly Assiniboins, the ever devilish surly Blackfeet, the usually shrewd Minnetarees, the mischievous humorous Crows.

Old Hugh wondered why hard-mouth Major Henry

had left the site. It could only have been the pesky Blackfeet. That, and a lack of beaver.

Hugh trudged on.

"Chosen," he said. "Lord's work."

Below Blue Mountain to the east he shot and killed two small whitetailed deer. He came up on them behind a grove of dark green cedar, a whole herd of them, all of them watching two young bucks sparring. The sparring fascinated Hugh. The two bucks fought like tavern brawlers. Erect on their rear legs, front feet windmilling a mile a minute, soft bluebrown eyes one moment fierce and startled and the next moment half-closed and blinking, keening a little, they battled around and around in the snow, over sagebrush, into a little draw, beside a pyramid of red-streaked gray rock, against and through red willow brush, going it for a full quarter-hour—until Hugh remembered he was out of meat. With rifle and horse pistol he shot them down before they knew what happened. The rest of the herd bounded away like jack rabbits, gone in a wink, kicking up little puffs of dirt mixed in with snow.

"Lord's work," Hugh said.

Opposite the mouth of the Powder River, Hugh ran across a small herd of buffalo. These too he ambushed, from behind a thicket of alder saplings; brought down a fat young cow.

After making sure there was no sign of Indians around—he was still in dreaded Blackfoot country—he set about having himself a feast.

From underneath the thin cover of snow he scratched out a handful of dry forage grass and screwed it into a nest. He lit his punk, made from a pithy bit of pine, and placed it in the nest. He closed the grass over it and waved it in the air until it ignited. Quickly then he placed dry kindling over the little spitting fire. When the fire was going good he added cottonwood branches, pyramid-style. He stood a moment to warm his hands over the merry crackling fire.

He skinned the young buffalo cow in the usual mountaineer fashion. The handling of steaming, bleeding flesh warmed his hands and face more than the fire did. All the while he butchered and nibbled, his roving restless eye kept a wary lookout for sign. It was noon of a clear blue day and, with the plains and low hills an endless expanse of snow, he could see for miles. The cow had fallen in an open glade on the west side of the Yellowstone, and the only cover for enemy was the fringe of alder saplings he himself had used to sneak up on the buffalo. He watched the alders carefully, the rest of the sloping and resloping white horizons carefully. Oddly enough, over toward the Little Sheep Mountains and the higher Big Sheep Mountains were what Hugh often called sheep clouds. It gave him a chuckle to think on it.

After he'd had his fill of freshly roasted hump rib and prime steak, topped off with a dessert of boudins, Hugh packed some of the choice cuts and set out once more for the Yellowstone and Big Horn, where he hoped to find some evidence of Major Henry and Diah Smith and their trapping parties.

"Vengeance," Hugh said, smacking his lips, still savoring the crisp roasted flesh. "The Lord's chosen, this child is. Gifted special for it."

He'd limped on but two miles with his burdens and his guns when he spied movement in the cedars on the second bench to the north. Quickly he scurried behind some silvergray sagebrush.

Wild eyes wicking, flicking back and forth like the searching eye of an albino, Hugh studied the clotting and unclotting dots on the far terrain. More buffalo? Could be. Horses? Likely. Blackfoot war party? Also likely. They'd probably seen the dark dot of his body moving across the white snow.

"Chosen," he said, setting his triggers. "I carry a duty and've gotta get through in one piece." Shrewdly, swiftly, he laid out a plan of defense. No movement until found—and then a centershot into the chief, with the horse pistol in reserve to put himself out of misery if need be. His gray old eyes wicked wild out of his bristly leathern face.

He knelt in the snow and waited, peering out from behind the sagebrush. They would see his tracks in the snow behind him. The ponies would smell out the blood and fresh cuts. Hugh nodded. Ae, he was done for.

When he looked up again he saw it wasn't Blackfeet at all. It was just a band of wild mustangs, some forty of them, of every color of the rainbow: blood bay, deep chestnut, nutmeg roan, white with black skin underneath and showing through a smoky gray, paint, sorrel with a white star and white stockings and yellow mane. The band was led by a pair of pacers, a stallion and a mare. The pacing stallion was blue, left foot stockinged, with a white blaze streaming down his face so that he seemed to be drinking it. The pacing mare was a dun, or a claybank buckskin, with a primordial streak down its back like a skunk stripe. The mustangs were big, much bigger than the mustangs he'd seen on the Platte and on the Sante Fe trail. These seemed to be almost fifteen hands high—an unusual height for mustangs.

Watching them from his covert of aromatic silvergray sagebrush, Hugh noticed something about the two leaders. The dun mare seemed to be as much queen or bell mare of the band as the whiteleg blue stallion was king. Also the dun queen mare had odd lines. She was more throwback than ordinary mustang. Curiously enough the whiteleg blue stallion resembled her somewhat, mostly in his motions, especially the way he paced. Looking closer, Hugh saw it. The blue whiteleg was a son of the dun throwback mare. Ae, that was it. That accounted for the two being boss together. As queen she was bringing him up to be king.

Though the band came within a hundred yards of where Hugh lay skulking, they never sensed him. The wind was from the south and in his favor. Luckily, too, they crossed ahead of him and not behind him where they would have spotted and scented his trail.

With a flourish of tails, with a directing whinny from both the throwback skunk-stripe mare and the whiteleg crown prince, they whirled over and down the cutbank and onto the sandy beach of the frozen Yellowstone River. Steam rose from the spot and Hugh guessed there was a breathing hole in the ice—probably from a warm spring. In the frosty air the horses blew breaths as big as spade beards.

The whiteleg crown prince ran down the stream a few yards, turned stylishly, and had himself a hearty and private bowel movement. Hugh smiled. It was the finest display of good manners he'd seen since he'd left white diggings.

He watched them take turns drinking at the breathing hole. They drank in an orderly fashion, each in his or her proper place according to an established nipping order, the dun queen mare and the blue crown prince standing guard and acting as police.

"If this child could only catch one of them critters," Hugh murmured to himself in a low gruff monotone, "what fun he'd have ridin'· in the rest of the way." Hugh waggled his old head. "Yessiree. Somehow this old hoss's got to catch him one of them ponies."

Even as he muttered to himself behind his bush, the dun skunk-stripe mare sensed something, probably his low voice, and with a great shrill yell almost twice human in volume, a great brood-mother call, she turned the entire band away from the bank. Nipping first one rump and then another, she got them thundering down the stream along the beach and then away over the cutbank, with herself and her son in the van, pacing, silver tails streaming and flowing, heads up, sharp nervous ears erect and flicking back and forth.

"Consarn ee, ye old she-devil!" Hugh growled. "Too

smart, you are. But I'll get ye yet, I will. This child's doin' Lord's work and he can't be balked."

Hugh came out from behind his brush and walked down to the cutbank to have a look at and maybe even have a drink from the breathing hole in the ice. He found tracks everywhere, old as well as new, especially many old, which told him the band made a daily call on the winter watering place. He glanced over to where the blue crown prince had comported himself in such stylish fashion. Aha. That wasn't the first time the young fellow had been polite. The still-steaming fresh droppings were only a small part of a huge frozen pyramidlike pile. Hugh laughed. The blue crown prince already fancied himself a king. Only king stallions allowed themselves private privies. The frozen pile was another proof that the band made regular calls on the breathing hole, that like all animals they had certain hours for watering.

Directly above the hole, leaning out at an angle from the cutbank, hung a single huge ocher-barked cottonwood.

The big tree gave Hugh an idea. He set to work immediately to execute it. He went back to the cow-buffalo carcass, rolled it over, finished skinning it. He spent the rest of the day and part of the next morning carving out a lasso, a halter, and reins from the hide, each a braid of four leather strips.

The next afternoon when it came time for the band to return for their watering again, after hiding gun and possible sack and reserve meat, Hugh tied one end of the braided lasso to a fat limb on the land side of the cottonwood and, with the other end in hand, he shinnied up the slanting tree until he was directly over the breathing hole. He got behind the thick trunk and sat back on a limb, waiting, loop open and ready. The spot he'd chosen was a good one. He had a good clear space between the branches to swing out and cast. Hugh knew that he'd have but one chance, but one throw, at the wild ponies, and he had to make that one cast good. He couldn't miss or he was done with that particular band of mustangs. The skunk-stripe queen and her blue crown prince would never forget.

Soon the band came on in a long orderly string, kicking up light puffs of snow, the dun skunk-stripe queen and the blue crown prince in the lead, pacing, silver tails streaming. They came on without sensing him behind the tree trunk, without seeing him skulking above the watering place. The wind was again in Hugh's favor.

He set himself. He made up his mind to catch the dun skunk-stripe mare. Something about her drew him. She'd probably be the toughest to catch, but he had to have her. It was the mare or nothing.

She prinked in under him, whinnying at her band in reassuring fashion.

She had most of the band lined up for the water hole—when she suddenly sensed him. She lifted her head to smell the better. That moment Hugh swung out the loop and made his cast. It fell whirling, and it fell exactly and completely around her head and neck. She ran on it, up the cutbank, and threw herself on the hard frozen ground.

That same instant the blue crown prince became king. His great male roar, loud and deep-chested, something between a raging buffalo bull's bellow and a ferocious wounded mountain lion's roar, broke out over the shrilling throats and thundering hooves and snapping tails. The whole band reacted to it like iron filings to a magnet. They arranged themselves in an orderly stream, head to tail, and all shot out of the hole and up over the cutbank and bounded away across the white plains toward the Little Sheep Mountains.

Hugh meanwhile had his hands full. He scrambled down the cottonwood trunk. Quickly he slipped the braided hide halter over her head. He saw that skunk-stripe had knocked herself out momentarily and he swiftly went over to cut the braid lasso near the cottonwood and secured it to the halter. He loosened the loop around her neck to let her get her breath, used the loop to tie her feet in pairs, and stood back to await developments.

Developments were not long in coming. When skunk-stripe, or Skunk, as Hugh now named her, came to, she bounded straight up into the air above his head, once, twice, thrice, each time higher than before.

"Dag me if she don't mean to make an ascension!" Hugh ejaculated.

She shrilled; she cried; she screamed. She danced; she bounced. She curvetted; she caracoled; she pirouetted. She put her head into the folds of her behind; she put the folds of her behind around her face.

"Dag me if she don't mean to reverse her innerds!" Hugh marveled.

She did it all with her feet tied in pairs, and with Hugh hanging on for all he was worth and occasionally getting a free hoist into the bargain.

Even with her feet hobbled, the dun throwback mare might have gotten away if Hugh hadn't retreated to the cottonwood and snubbed her up close. He drew her up until he had her kneeling.

He let her rest. He let himself rest. Both stood panting on the wide white plains and under the high blue heavens.

After a while he approached her, foot by slow foot, hand by slow hand.

Skunk didn't like his smell. She showed him her teeth.

Hugh persisted.

She resisted, turning up her nose at him again.

At last he got close enough to breathe into her nostrils, to breathe his ghost into her. He rubbed her nose. He passed his hand over her eyes as if he meant to close them in death. He stroked her ears, her forehead. He breathed his ghost into her nose again. He hummed to her; sang to her; cajoled her.

She trembled; she shivered her coat. She cried; she lamented the wild she'd lost.

He petted her; soothed her. He breathed his ghost into her again.

She had a lovely wild smell. He loved her.

Then of a sudden he was astride her. She tore away on her sets of two legs; hit the end of the lasso; fell heavily, with Hugh rolling easily to one side.

Again, after a time, he got astride her.

Again, quick as a fox, she bolted and threw both herself and Hugh.

Hugh went back and got his gun and reserve meat and his possible sack. From the sack he selected a bit of salt. He held the salt out to her in the palm of his big hand.

She hated him for offering it. Yet she couldn't resist it. She was so hungry for good salt she couldn't help herself. Table salt was ever so much sweeter than wild salt. She nibbled it. And he had her.

Presently after cutting her hobbles, he managed to get astride her again with all his plunder of gun and possibles and meat slung over his back. He leaned over to cut the lasso—and they were off.

She jumped. She bolted. She set herself for what she thought would be the inevitable fall at the end of the braid lasso. She stumbled when it didn't throw her. Then, regaining her stride, she set off across the wide white plains under the domed blue heavens.

Hugh let her go. She ran and ran and ran. The country was open and he let her run.

"Run, you she-rip you! Run! Every jump is a dozen steps saved for this old hoss. Run, you she-rip you."

He knew that the quickest way to tame a wild horse was to get it away from its usual haunts, so that as time went on it would rely more and more on its master.

She galloped. She galloped a good ten miles before she gave up exhausted.

That night Hugh staked her out. He knew she feared the braided hide rope, knew she would behave.

She grazed on grass she pawed out from under the snow.

The next morning she was as tame as a pet mouse.

Also the next morning he found her bag full of milk.

That struck him as odd—until he ciphered out that she'd probably just foaled, that the foal had been a male, and that the blue crown prince had killed it as a rival.

Hugh milked her in his tin pot and drank heartily of the sweet white steaming treat. It made Hugh grimace to think he'd taken the place of the dead brother stallion.

Two nights later, January began to live up to its name as the Moon of the Seven Cold Nights. It froze so hard it cracked.

But the meat, the blankets, and the wild skunk-stripe mare pulled Hugh through.

"See?" Hugh said with a waggle of his shaggy old head. "See? Sign again. It *is* the Lord's vengeance now. An eye for a tooth and a tooth for an eye."

Chapter 4

Thirty-eight days after he left Ft. Tilton, in February, the Moon of Pairing, he spotted Major Henry's new post on the Yellowstone and the Big Horn Rivers. The fort stood in a parklike meadow, with here and there a tall umbrella cottonwood, on the first bench of land on the east side of the Yellowstone. It overlooked both rivers, and a sentinel in the gate tower could spot movement for miles up and down either stream. The clean blue waters of the Yellowstone, now frozen over, came in from the west, and the dirty brown waters of the Big Horn, also frozen over, came in from the southwest. Both rivers ran through wide valleys edged with cedar-crested rimrock. Behind the fort, to the southeast, certain rocks resembling a white castle rose out of creek-dissected hills. The hills were tipped with arrowsharp pines. It was all Crow Indian country, and safe. Hugh nodded. Once again Major Henry had shown good judgment in selecting a post site.

It was dusk, the end of the day, when Hugh rode up the trail across the parklike meadow beneath the occasional cottonwoods. Skunk was tired and hungry, and so was Hugh. The snow was belly deep in the drifts. The cold was tight, and the hood of Hugh's capote was frosted all along its inner edges. The wind was mean, and Hugh turned his shoulder into it and his face away.

There was a sudden smell of roasting. Meat. Barbecued meat. Skunk smelled it about the same time Hugh did. To the pony it meant hay; to Hugh it meant simply meat.

"Hep-a," Hugh said, giving her a heel in the ribs. "We're safe now, Ol' Skunk." But the kick was hardly necessary. The dun throwback of her own accord quickened her pace along the hoof-pocked trail.

It was deep dusk when the sentinel hailed him from the log tower over the log gate. The Bull Mountains beyond the rimrock to the north lay white like vast blue snowdrifts. Castle Rock gleamed clean white against the oncoming blueblack night.

"Where from, stranger?"

Hugh drew Skunk to a stop. "Whoa, lass." From underneath frost-edged capote hood, Hugh glowered up at the weathered log tower. Hugh couldn't quite make out the blunt face peering down at him from a gun port. But the voice was familiar. It was young and it had a Scotch crust. Hugh set the trigger of his flintlock.

"Where from, stranger?"

"Fort Tilton on the Missouri," Hugh said in a deep bass monotone.

"You alone?" The young voice sounded uncertain.

Hugh didn't miss the irony of it. "Not to start with. But I am now."

"Red devils?"

" 'Tis so. Rees took their hair. After an old she-rip grizzly clubbed them down."

"Who went under?"

"Jim Bridger and Fitz Fitzgerald. On the forks of the Grand."

There was a loud gulp above him; then the blunt face came out for a closer look. Even in the deep dusk Hugh could see the face quite plainly. It was the lad Jim Bridger and his young face was chalkwhite.

"Not—Hugh—Glass!"

"Ae, Hugh Glass, my lad, ae," Hugh said, throwing back the hood of his gray capote and lifting his flintlock menacingly. "And open up afore I give them red curls a your'n a second part, you oily coward."

Jim Bridger hung out of the gun port as if petrified, mouth open.

"Yes, Jim, my boy. So you thought I was gone under, did ee? Well, lad, I ain't dead yet, not by a long shot. Open up and hand over Ol' Blue my hoss and Ol' Bullthrower my gun."

Jim gulped again; then jerked his head in. A moment later Hugh heard him running down the steps on the inside. Hugh set himself for the face-to-face encounter, fully expecting Jim to open the gate.

But when the cottonwood log gate didn't open after a minute or two, Hugh realized that Jim hadn't run down to let him in after all, but had probably gone to rouse the garrison, maybe to report him to Major Henry in person.

That burned Hugh. And it burned Old Hugh even more to realize that while he'd been talking to Jim there'd been on the tip of his tongue, and certainly in his mind, the impulse to say something kind and friendly to the poor lad.

"This time it wasn't dummed friend stomach that almost threw this old hoss either. It was just bein' plain lonesome, it was."

Hugh cocked his head to one side. "The lad's still a coward and a bad 'un, he is, not comin' down to open up to Ol' Hugh."

Hugh slid off the dun throwback mare and, leading her by the reins, strode up to the gate and began banging thunders on it. "Open up, consarn ee, you cowardly dog you." The little arteries down Hugh's nose wriggled red with fury. Mean devils gleamed out of his great gray eyes. "Vengeance is mine, the Lord says. And Ol' Hugh's come to put it on ee. Open up."

The thunder on the gate awakened the dogs within the stockade and they began to yip and bark furiously.

Men came running. A horse whinnied and Skunk lifted her head and replied with a shrill hinny of her own.

A voice cried out, "Hold on out there. Help's comin'."

"About time," Hugh growled, letting off and checking his trigger.

The log gate opened in the middle and parted, one half to either side, creaking in its wooden slots, and directly before Hugh, with a flaring smoking pineknot overhead, with an armed mountain man on either hand, stood grim-mouth Major Henry. Behind the blue-capped major pressed other faces, faces Hugh remembered like old portraits suddenly come to life: gaunt Allen, proud Yount, hound-faced once-scalped Silas Hammond. But there was no Jim or Fitz.

Major Henry took one look in the flickering light and then exclaimed. "Good Lord! it *is* Hugh Glass." The major stepped up, holding the flaming pineknot closer as he peered into Hugh's face. "Good God, yes. Hugh, two men testified that you were dead! That they'd buried you on the forks of the Grand!"

Hugh laughed a short crazy laugh. " 'Men,' you say? Cowards, I say. Cowards. Boys asked to do man's work."

Major Henry's lips thinned and his teeth gleamed white. "A miracle if there ever was one."

Hugh didn't like the kind of attention he was getting. He had planned it another way. He looked at the bearded faces, at their skin suits so well worn it took a close look to see what they were made of.

Hugh handed Ol' Skunk's reins to the nearest pair of hands. "Hold her ready for me till I get back." Hugh pushed the major aside. "Make way for vengeance. This child's the Lord's chosen and he's got a dirty job to do."

Major Henry quickly blocked Hugh's path. "Whoa, there, old hoss! Where do you think you're going?"

Hugh looked the major up and down. Devils gleamed in his gray old eyes. "To drag out that coward Jim from wherever he's hid himself." Hugh spat to one side on the moccasin-packed snow. "And get that cowardly downer Fitz out from wherever he's hid too."

"Where do you think that is?" Major Henry snapped.

Hugh saw gaunt Allen and hound-faced Silas slowly shaking their winter-reddened faces. At a gesture from the major the two tall leather-clad guards raised their rifles at ready.

Hugh let out a snort. "Why, where else but in your quarters, Major? Under your bed where all cowardly dogs go to hide."

Grim-mouth Major Henry slowly shook his head. The major's deep eyes took on the blueblack of his state militia cap. "Fitz ain't here."

Hugh growled like a frustrated bulldog. "Where is the oily coward?"

"Gone to Fort Atkinson. Took a dispatch."

Hugh swore and spat in the snow again. "That's the second time that cautious coward's got out of it by bein' a messenger. That dummed lucky dog." Hugh glanced around at his open-mouthed listeners. "The boy Jim's under your bed though, hain't he?"

Major Henry smiled faintly. "All right then . . . my quarters it is. I'm as curious as the rest of the men to hear what happened." Major Henry gestured curtly at the tall buckskin guards. The long fringes on his skin suit rustled. "Take his guns. And his knife." Major Henry smiled wide white teeth. "We'll hear both your stories, yours and Jim's, before we get to your revenge."

"It's not my revenge, Major. It's His vengeance, it is."

" 'His'?"

"The Lord's. I been chosen." Again Hugh spat in the snow to show his defiance and independence. "And this child ain't givin' up his guns."

"Then you're not comin' to my quarters."

Hugh stepped back, jerking his rifle away from the guard who'd taken hold of the end of it. "But, Major, how do I know but what you'll lock me up till that cowardly Jim makes his getaway?"

Major Henry grimaced, showing fierce white teeth. "Come now, Hugh. You know I always deal fair and square with my men. You'll get your chance to accuse Jim all right. Face-to-face."

Slowly Hugh let his wrath subside. "All right," he said, "all right. I'll give up my guns." Hugh handed over his flintlock, horse pistol, and knife. "But mind ye, Major. This hoss'll be in a queersome fret if you don't let the Lord get his vengeance."

Major Henry gave the others a warning look, and then, pineknot flaring a smoky orange, guards and old mountaineer friends Yount and Allen and Silas following, he led the way across the frozen snow toward his quarters under the far wall of the fort. Stars twinkled almost within reach. In the men's quarters light from hearth fires and candles glowed irregularly through oil-paper windows. Someone with a monotone voice sang an old mountaineer ditty. A voice growled, "What's trump an' whose deal?" Another voice answered, "Don't crowd me an' I'll tell ee."

As they walked along, moccasins singing at each step in the frozen snow, Major Henry sought to mollify Hugh a little. "You're a walkin' miracle if there ever was one, Hugh."

Hugh said nothing. His old eyes glittered under heavy gray brows. He knew salve when it was being applied.

"How a man could live after the mauling you got, bones sticking out everywhere, head and back and rump ripped open"—Major Henry shook his head and sucked his teeth in sympathy—"how a man could live after that is beyond me."

"Meat never spoils in the mountains, Major." A trace of a smile crinkled in the corners of Hugh's eyes. His leather-red cheeks moved. "You know that."

Major Henry laughed. "That's true enough."

They came to the major's quarters. Major Henry held the log door open for Hugh and the others. They entered.

A merry pine fire spat and glowed in the stone hearth. The smooth-barked cottonwood walls glistened red. A welcome wave of heat breathed Hugh in the face. Hugh blinked his eyes at all the sudden light and warmth.

Hugh took off his halfmoon fur-lined mittens and his woolen capote. He loosened the thongs at the collar of his deerskin hunting shirt. He stepped over to the fire in the shimmering stone hearth. After briefly warming his hands and face, he turned around and hauled up his hunting shirt to warm his seat and aching back.

The major's quarters were small, some fifteen by eighteen feet. The floor was of halved cottonwood logs and the sloped ceiling of ash and pine branches and wide flats of cottonwood bark. Opposite the fire hung a tattered much-fingered map. A huge rough table dominated the room. Two candles in a tin plate flickered pale moons to the hearth fire's fierce sunlike luminescence. Rough ax-hewn three-legged chairs circled the table, except at the head where the Major had a four-legged armchair, also rough-cut.

Yount and Allen and Silas stood waiting for the major to seat them. The two guards flanked the door.

Hugh's eyes gradually adjusted to the light from the red fire and the low pale-moon candles. And gradually, too, something drew his attention to a shadow behind a low fur-robe bed in the far corner. Hugh leaned forward to see better. And when he saw clearly what the shadow really was, he let go another snort.

"Just like I said. The cowardly dog's under your bed."

Hugh strode over and looked down at the boy Jim Bridger sitting in the shadow of the bed, knees drawn up under his chin and arms around his legs. The lad Jim was dressed in fringed leathers and wolfskin cap like all the other mountain men.

At a gesture from the major the two tall guards quickly stepped forward.

Hugh let go still another snort. Then, with a moccasined toe, he kicked the boy Jim lightly in the ribs. "C'mon, Jim, lad, get up and wag your tail. I wouldn't kill a pup. You know that."

Jim's blue eyes rolled up at Hugh. He quailed, ashen, at the touch of Hugh's toe. Then Jim flushed red and hid his eyes. He trembled as if about to burst out of the seams of his leathers.

"Get up," Hugh said. "Get up, and be a man for once."

Jim got redder in the face; looked down; trembled.

The silence in the log-walled room suddenly hummed. Hugh felt it but ignored it. "C'mon, get up, you cowardly dog. 'Tisn't every day you get a chance to repent black treachery."

When Jim still kept his blunt face hid, Hugh gave him another kick in the ribs. "C'mon, you cow—"

Jim suddenly leaped up, red boy's face in a rage, huge hands balling and unballing. "Damme, Hugh, but I can't let you kick me like that." Jim loomed over Hugh.

Hugh backed a step. It amazed Hugh to see how the lad towered over him. The lad had grown since he'd last seen him. He no longer looked up to anyone.

Jim caught the amazed look in Hugh's eyes. It gave him courage. And suddenly, before Hugh could get up his guard, Jim let Hugh have it in the face. The blow was a haymaker, picked up off the hip, and it caught Hugh flush on his big Scotch nose and jutting chin. There was a sickening crack and Hugh's wolfskin cap flew off.

Hugh staggered back; fell against the table beside the major. Hugh would have fallen to the floor if the major hadn't grabbed him and held him up.

Jim came forward a long lunging pigeon-toed step and clutched up the front of Hugh's leather shirt and twisted it tight across his chest. "And, Hugh, I can't let you go around callin' me a pup either. Because if you do, so help me God, I'll give you such a beatin' it'll make what the she-grizzly gave you look like mouse nibbles."

Old Hugh lay stunned, half against the major and half against the ax-hewn table. The lad's wild swing had been more than a mere man's punch. It'd been a regular giant's, it had. The Lord's vengeance wasn't prospering very well.

Then Hugh remembered all the days of his vengeance and of how he'd crawled through hell itself for this chance at a showdown with the lads, Fitz and Jim. The memory of the crawl rallied his long-nourished hate, and with an oath, and a violent twist of his body, Hugh tore free from Jim's grip.

Hugh roared, "So ye'd hit a companyero, would ee? Hit a companyero ye'd already deserted and left for dead, would ee? A companyero who'd always thought of ee as his own kin, would ee?" And before Major Henry could prevent it, Hugh, head lowered, arms flailing, charged Jim. Hugh decided a buck in the belly'd knock the wind out of the lad and so maybe give Old Hugh the upper hand again.

But Jim was too quick, too young, for Hugh. Jim sidestepped the rush; whacked Hugh over the back of the head with a heavy blacksmith fist; hit Hugh so hard Hugh saw the old dark come rising up all around him once more.

Hugh caught himself; turned to face Jim again. He ganted for breath. The gray beard around the edges of his mouth fluffed in and out on each puff and breath. "So it's tricks, is it? All right, let's see if tricks'll help you this time." Arms wide, Hugh approached Jim warily. Suddenly he rushed Jim; got his huge arms around Jim's middle; shoved with all his power; and down both went beside the fur bed, Jim's fur cap flying off.

Hugh was astraddle Jim in an instant, and automatically, like in the old brawling days back in St. Lou, Hugh's thumbs sought out Jim's eyeballs.

Sitting on Jim, however, was not like sitting on a horse, broke in or not. Young Jim was supple, and he had hands, and while with his left hand he tried to defend his eyes, with his big right hand he sought out a hold under Hugh's thigh. When Jim finally got the hold under Hugh's thigh, he squeezed with all his might. It was as fair a hold as Hugh's. An eye for an eye.

Hugh gritted between clamped teeth, "Desert a man who thought of ye as if ye were his own son, would ee? Would ee? Well, we'll see, now, we'll see."

Each held the other in an ever-tightening clutch of final mortal pain. Jim's blue eyes began to rise up out of their sockets and approach each other across the bridge of his nose; Hugh's thigh began to burn searingly and a spear of pain shot far up into his belly. Neither would let go; neither could let go. Jim's mouth stretched open in agony; Hugh's belly humped up in agony.

Jim finally left off defending his eyeballs with his left hand; instead he began to hit Hugh in the nose again and again with all he had. Jim hit and hit, hit with mashing sodden whacks. And all the while, with his right hand, he tightened up the twist he had on Hugh under his thigh.

Right in the middle of all the clutching and twisting red pain, Hugh abruptly remembered his lads, his sons back in Lancaster, remembered Mabel his she-rip of a wife, remembered how he'd deserted the lads and her, remembered how he'd become a roamer, a buccaneer even, and a killer. Who was he to cast the first stone? Who was he that he should gouge out the eyeballs of a lad who could easily have been his son?

Black regrets and old gray biles churned around and around. There were whirls and whorls of red pain. Hugh's head buzzed. He felt a faint coming on.

Ae, ae, who was he to cast the first stone? A bigger man would forgive a mere boy.

Hugh gave one final dig with his thumbs, and then heaved a huge sigh, and let his shoulders sag, and let go his hold.

Surprised, Jim let go too.

They stared at each other a moment or two, and then, breathing loudly like maddened bucks who'd been forced to part, they slowly got to their feet, and picked up their caps, and clapped them on.

Major Henry stepped up then. "All right, you two. That's enough now. Suppose we sit down and talk this over like sensible men. Jim, you sit here, at my right. Hugh, you sit here, on my left. The rest of you down the line on either side." Major Henry took off his blue cap. He grimaced, showing white teeth. "And take off your caps. At my table you have some manners."

Grumbling, glaring at each other, the two sat down on opposite sides of the table, Jim rubbing his eyes and knuckles, and Hugh rubbing his thigh and nose.

Major Henry beckoned to one of the guards. "I think this calls for a drink. John, go get us a bottle of brandy."

After they'd all had a shot from a tin cup, and fresh tobacco had been passed around, tension eased somewhat and tongues loosened.

Watching Hugh scrounge around ill-at-ease on a three-legged teetery chair, hound-faced Silas Hammond said with comical gravity, "What's the matter, old hoss? You been ham-shot or somethin'?" Silas's scalping scar gleamed in the red light from the roaring pine fire.

"Yeh, Hugh," gaunt Allen said smiling, taking up the cue. "Sittin' there you act as oneasy as a gut-shot coyote."

Hugh grumbled in his gray whiskers. "I can't seem to get myself squared to this seat. That ten-prong buck I shot under the Blue Buttes wasn't done sucking when I last sot on a chair. Why don't we sit like men afront

the fire there, Major? This thing's wilder'n my throwback mare. And rides harder'n an iron statue."

Everybody laughed. The major declined the sugges-
tion. And the men relaxed still more.

The bald cottonwood walls glowed red and pink by
turns in the firelight. The mountain men's winter-burnt
faces took on a deep scarlet hue.

Presently Major Henry signaled for Hugh to begin
his side of the story.

Stubborn Hugh shook his head. "And let the boy Jim
here take his picks on what I tell? Not this child."

Again young Jim Bridger flushed, and after a moment
of inner boiling found it in himself to speak up to the
older man. "Damme, Hugh, don't call me boy neither.
Or so help me Hannah, I'll—"

"Here here!" Major Henry said soothingly over his
pipe. His blue eyes sparkled ice-gray in the pale-moon
candlelight. His Missouri state militia cap on the table
took on a deep blueblack shade. "Hugh, suppose you
treat Jim here like a full-grown man till you've heard
his side of it. At least." Major Henry licked a trace of
sweet brandy from his lower lip. "The truth is, Hugh,
after what Jim did for us this winter, if there ever was
a man, Jim here is it."

Hugh held back a snort. His old gray eyes opened
looking at Jim. "Oh?"

"Yes. Jim here's spent most of winter looking for
beaver all the way to Colter's Hell. Alone."

Hugh's opening mouth made a dark hole in his gray
whiskers. " 'Alone'?"

"Exactly. And a man's work it was, I say."

Proud Yount agreed emphatically from his end of the
table. "That's right, Hugh. And we're all going to make
our pile on what he found."

Gaunt Allen said, "What the boy here done alone I
know I couldna with an army behind me. That's a fact,
Hugh. You can put your pile on it and feel safe. He's
a reg'lar hivernan now."

Hugh wriggled his big red nose. It still hurt. "Wal, if he did it alone. . . ." Hugh gave Jim a doubting look. "Tell me, lad, what was the Indian there?" Hugh took a slow puff on his old pipe, narrowed eyes watching Jim.

Jim mumbled a vague answer around the stem of his pipe.

"What? Speak up. And take that dummed pipe out of your mouth when you talk."

Jim fired up. "Snake. Blackfeet. Some Flathead."

Hugh's brows lifted. "You've learned to read sign then, I see."

Jim said, "I learned it from the best, Hugh. From you. You know that."

"Hrumpp!" Hugh put pipe to mouth again and blew out a cloud of smoke.

Major Henry said, "Well, Hugh, do we hear it yet tonight? or what?"

"Let the lad tell his side of it first," Hugh said, gesturing with his spuming pipe, still trying to make himself comfortable on his teetery three-legged chair. "This child's just as curious to hear it as you." Hugh glowered across at Jim. "Because this child still can't cipher how come you birds quit a friend. Deserted him."

Jim burst out. "But Fitz and me didn't quit you, Hugh. We didn't."

"Not?"

"No."

"Go on. Tell it then. I'm listenin'," Hugh said grimly, biting the stem of his pipe. "With all three ears."

. . . Jim's story took up where Hugh's memory left off, just after the she-grizzly fell across Hugh's mangled body.

Allen and Silas were the first there. They saw the bloody, incredibly ripped-up body lying under the dead she-grizzly. At first glance they thought Hugh gone under. The two young grizzly cubs stood near, smelling at their dead mother and growling at Hugh's body. Allen and Silas shot the cubs. Then Allen and Silas pulled the great she-grizzly off Hugh's body.

Major Henry and Jim and Fitz and the rest of the party came galloping up. Just as they leaped down off their horses, Old Hugh let out a great agonized groan. Everybody jumped. And shivered. It was the first they knew he was still alive. The major took one look at Hugh and ordered the camp to be made beside the body on the sand in the gully.

Jim said, "Lookin' at him made me bawl like a big baby, so torn up he was. I couldn't help it."

Both the major and Fitz, with Jim helping, washed Hugh's wounds with fresh water from the nearby stream. The major next assigned Fitz to the job of sewing up Hugh's wounds, Jim helping again. Fitz was very careful with the awl and deer sinew, and when he had done the major pronounced it a good job.

"All the while he sewed I bawled like a big baby," Jim said. "Especially the times when Fitz had to punch the awl through the skin. It was like sewin' up a skin suit again after the hounds had chewed it to pieces playin' with it."

Fitz and Jim skinned the grizzly. The cook Pierre butchered the cubs and the grizzly, and the camp had bear steak for the first time on the trip. Hugh had at least done that much for the party. He'd maybe disobeyed orders but at least he'd made meat where Allen and his two men hadn't.

Fitz and Jim offered to hold the deathwatch through the night. It was the least they could do for Old Hugh now.

Hugh groaned and talked out of his head most of the night. Fitz and Jim took turns wetting his lips with brandy. They expected him to die hourly.

Just before the major went to sleep, he ordered Fitz and Jim to dig a grave for him and have it ready by sunrise. Both the Rees and the Mandans might be down on them again at dawn, the major said, and the party had to be ready to fly at a moment's notice. This Fitz and Jim did, dug the grave down some three feet before they hit rock and hardpan.

Sometime during the night, Hugh's horse, Old Blue, came back to the party. An inquiring nicker announced his presence.

When dawn opened pink over them at last, Hugh was still miraculously alive and the party hadn't been attacked by red devils.

They had breakfast, mostly bearmeat, a few biscuits, with coffee and a pipe of tobacco. Not a word was said.

After breakfast, Major Henry squatted beside Hugh and studied him.

Hugh was still unconscious. Sometimes he moaned pitifully. His big chest heaved unsteadily. He tossed restlessly on the grizzly skin. Each breath looked like it might be his last. His mauled black-and-blue face was hot and his big body raged with fever. Every now and then he groaned. Once he mumbled incomprehensibly. His wounds had stopped bleeding.

"Still alive," Major Henry said.

Fitz nodded dully. "It's his heart. He always had a young heart."

"Well, we'll give him a couple hours more. To either come to or go under."

Fitz said, "If he comes to?"

"Well . . . I don't know then. We can't carry him the condition he's in."

Proud Yount came over and stood looking down at Hugh and listening to the talk. He spoke up finally. " 'Twere best for everybody all around if he died."

Major Henry and Fitz said nothing.

"I bawled like a big baby seein' him fightin' it without knowin' it," Jim said.

At noon Major Henry finally made up his mind. "Mountain men, we can't wait any longer. We're dead ducks sitting here like this. We've got to move on."

Silence beside the murmuring creek.

"Since we can't move Old Hugh, we'll have to leave him here. Who'll volunteer to stay with him till he either dies or comes to?"

Silence on the heat-seething sand.

"I know it's asking a lot of you men. But we've got to do something."

Yount said, "It was the dummed fool's own fault he got mauled. He disobeyed orders."

Silence in the midst of the flittering plum leaves.

"We can't go into that now," Major Henry said at last. "That's water over the dam and gone."

Silence under the high blue dome of heaven.

"Who'll volunteer?"

Finally Jim raised a hand.

"You know the hazards?"

Jim nodded. If the red devils caught him it was torture and sure death.

Yount said, "But what for, Major? He's just a dead man who's sure to die."

"Well, Jim?"

"I'm stayin'," Jim said, trembling. Jim didn't have it in him to leave the old man to his fate. He liked the old man and the old man had been kind to him. The old man had taught him a lot about how to survive in wild red-devil country. And the old man had also covered up for him when he and Fitz had slept on guard duty the night before.

"You sure you want to stay, Jim?"

"Yes."

The major smiled a little. Then he looked scornfully at the others sitting around the dying body of the old grizzled man.

"Looks like I don't have any other men about to do what turns out to be a boy's job," Major Henry said sarcastically. Major Henry got out pen and gray ledger to make a few entries.

"I guess it falls to my lot too, Major," Fitz said then. "The three of us were together most times on this trip."

The major relented a little. "I suppose at that I am asking too much." The major brooded over his gray ledger. "Tell you what. We'll take up a collection. As a reward."

"I don't need no reward," Jim said.

"Nor do I," Fitz said. "I'd never take it."

"Yount," the major said, "take up a collection anyway. And Fitz, since you're the oldest, and you've had the most experience in these parts, I'm putting you in charge. You're to stay until Old Hugh dies, and then you're to bury him decent. Or, if he lives, until he's well enough to be moved."

Major Henry and the rest of the party rode off for Henry's Post on the Yellowstone and Missouri, heading almost straight north to bypass Black Butte and the Little Missouri Badlands. The major gave Fitz and Jim a last wave of the hand from the top of the brown bluffs across the north fork of the Grand. And then Fitz and Jim were left behind with sad Old Hugh Glass and their sad thoughts and their wondering horses, Fitz's, Jim's, and Hugh's Old Blue.

They waited.

By turns they wetted Hugh's lips with brandy, with water, with bearmeat soup. They took turns standing guard on a nearby brush-cropped high point. This time neither came close to falling asleep while on watch.

Twice the first day they were sure red devils had spotted them. Each time, they had mounted their horses and set off after the major, when they discovered it was only buffalo and not a war party. Each time they got down off their ponies ashamed.

Hugh's old body hung on stubborn.

The second day Hugh seemed to sink a little. They made ready to go. Jim even worked up a prayer to say over Hugh, a prayer such as Diah Smith might have said.

But Hugh's old torn carcass hung on.

The third day Hugh looked better, and Jim began to hope that maybe they could move him after all, take him along to Henry's Post up north. Toward evening, however, after a terrible hot day, Hugh turned pale purple and began to sink again.

Still Hugh's old ripped-up hulk clung to life.

The fourth day Hugh began to stink, and white wolves and gray coyotes padded in silently from the hills. This was the worst day because Jim couldn't stand the thought of the old man being torn up and eaten by the wolves and coyotes, which was what surely would happen to him no matter how deep he and Fitz might bury him.

And yet Old Hugh's body hung on stubborn.

The fifth day, in the evening, around a campfire, small flames jumping in the rusty dusk, Fitz and Jim broke out into a violent argument. Jim was a young lad and Fitz was a realist.

Fitz said, "We've been waitin' five days now for him to die. We've done more than our duty. I say we move on."

Jim said, "But we can't leave him like this! He's still alive, man!"

Fitz said, "There's sign all around, Jim. We're wolf-meat tomorrow for sure if we don't pull out now. And you know yourself we still can't carry him."

Jim said, "But we can't desert a live man, Fitz! He's still alive."

Fitz said, "Better that two get out alive and him what's gonna die anyway left behind, than all three of us die. Every day we wait the major's gettin' farther and farther away and it'll be that much the harder for us to catch up."

Jim said, "But we can't desert Old Hugh! We can't! Not as long as he's still alive."

And then, for the first time, though he was still un-conscious, Old Hugh spoke up clearly. "Lads, don't lose your topknots over this child. I'm dead, I am. Or as good as dead. Which is the same thing. Run for your lives. Every day the major and his party're gettin' farther and farther away. Run, lads."

Both men turned pale at the sound of his voice.

"By that time this child was past bawlin'," Jim said. "Lookin' at him torn there, and groanin' and him not knowin', just couldn't make me cry no more. But I felt worse."

When it came time for one of them to turn in, Fitz and Jim had another wrangle.

Fitz said, "Jim, I tell ee, he ain't got the chance of a whistle in a whirlwind of livin'. He's a gone goose. There's nothin' more we can do for him except bury him. C'mon, lad, grab holt his toes there and let's lower him away."

Jim said, "But, Fitz, he just talked to us less'n an hour ago."

Fitz said, "Jim, lad, that was the death rattle. I know that anywhere. I've heard it a hundred times if I heard it once. He's gone under. He ain't breathed for at least a half-hour. Hurry, grab holt his toes or it'll be too late. The Rees are breathin' down our neck."

Jim said, "I'm sorry, Fitz, but I can't. You bury him then. Old Hugh was good to me. I ain't sure he's dead, and until I am, I can't."

Fitz said, "Well then, be damned to you and your sentimental hide, I'm leavin'. Ye can bury him by yourself."

Jim said, "But, Fitz—"

Fitz said, "Jim, I know this: if we stay another five minutes, the three of us are gone under. If we go now, right now, two of us 've got a chance to get out of this alive."

And once again Hugh spoke up. It was as if he'd heard all their wrangling, though of course he was still out of his head. "No, lads, no! Don't leave me here to die alone in this gully! Don't let me die the hard way!"

"See!" Jim cried triumphantly. "See! he's still alive!" They stayed.

Later that night Hugh began to talk more. He talked so much both Fitz and Jim believed he was about to come to at last.

Hugh's talk was religious, which surprised them. He talked about Esau and Jacob, about how he was Esau, the first, who'd come out red all over like an hairy garment, while the other fellow was Jacob, the second, a smooth man, Rebekah's favorite. He talked about how he too had sold his birthright in Lancaster land.

He also talked about a Mabel and two boys and about how a low-lived coward had deserted them back in white diggings.

Fitz said, "Don't it sound to you like he's talkin' about himself?"

Jim said, "If he is he won't be the first then."

Fitz said, "Meanin' what?"

Jim said, "Meanin' we've already done it a dozen times in thought with him."

Fitz shut up.

Toward dawn Hugh talked again, this time quite clearly. "Now, boy, I'll soon be under. Afore many hours. And, boy, if you don't raise meat pronto you'll be in the same fix I'm in. I've never et dead meat myself, Jim, and wouldn't ask you to do it neither. But meat fair killed is meat anyway. So, Jim, lad, put your knife in this old nigger's lights and help yourself. It's poor bull I am, I know, but maybe it'll do to keep life in ee. There should be some fleece on me that's meat yet. And maybe my old hump ribs has some pickin's on 'em in front. And there should be one roast left in my behind. Left side. Dip in, lad, and drink man's blood. I did onct. One bite."

Both Fitz and Jim shuddered at the awful words.

Fitz managed to say, "You're a good old hoss, Hugh, but we ain't turned Digger Indian yet."

Hugh said, trying to sit up in his delirium, "Where

from, stranger? What mout your name be? I'm Hugh Glass, deserter, buccaneer, keelboatman, trapper, hunter, and one-bite cannibal. Anyway what's left after an old she-rip had her picks a him." Hugh's wild glazed eyes stared at them from between puffed up eyelids.

Jim said, "What—did—he—say?"

Fitz said, "He said 'one-bite cannibal.' An' he asked us to dip in."

Jim said, "Oh! that sounds terrible. Hellfire if it don't. The thought of it makes the eyes stick out of a man's head."

Hugh said in his delirium, "One-bite cannibal. That's what I said. 'Twas on the Black Prairies by the Brazos. 'Twas this way. I'd come back from a hunt and there sat my companyero Clint eating meat. 'Dip in,' he says. 'I shot us a wild goat.' I took a bite. 'Twas the toughest meat this child ever set teeth to. Couldn't seem to swallow it. Then I saw the butchered feet ahind a bush. Ten toes. Clint'd killed our guide, a miserable red-devil Comanche who couldn't get along with his people. I shoulda knowed there was no antelope on the Brazos. Ae, and Clint paid the Lord for that too. In full. With his life. The Pawnees stuck him full a pine splinters and made a torch out of him."

Fitz said, " 'Cannibal.' "

Jim said, "He didn't know it! You can't help what you don't know! Clint lied to him!"

Hugh shouted up, "Hurrah, Jim! Run, lad, or we'll be made meat of sure as shootin'." Again Old Hugh tried to sit up, glazed eyes staring at them.

Fitz held him down. Fitz said, " 'Cannibal.' 'Tis hard to believe. 'Cannibal.' "

Jim said, "He didn't know it, Fitz! And he said he had trouble swallowin' it! Even when he didn't know it! That's as deep as it was set in him."

" 'Cannibal,' " Fitz said.

Hugh tried to sit up again. "Hurrah, Jim! Run, lad, or we'll be made meat of sure as shootin'. The red devils is everywhere. Ahind the hills and down in the sloughs."

Fitz pushed Hugh down once more. " 'Cannibal.' "

Jim said, "He didn't know it, Fitz. He couldn't help it, Fitz. You heard him."

Hugh shouted, "Set your triggers, lads."

Jim said, also trying to hold Hugh down, "Now, now, Hugh, old hoss. Hold still till we get the bridle on."

Hugh said, voice suddenly fallen, confidential-like, "Jim, lad, let me tell ee somethin'. When the net falls on ee, there's only two things to do. Set still ontil they take the net off again. Or run off with the net and all. And never come back. Because if you make the littlest move, you just entangle yourself all the more in the law. No, lad, do like I did. Run off with the net and all."

Hugh slept.

The next morning Fitz saw them. A war party of some hundred Ree braves. They were well-armed and loaded for bear. They were led by ancient Chief Elk Tongue and the ferocious brave Stabbed. They were across the river. There was no time to lose. The two of them just didn't have a tinker's chance in a hot tin pan against them. Their only chance was to make a run for it and hope their ponies were faster than the Ree mounts, for once they were caught they were in for horrible tortures. The red devils were fiends for knowing just where the tenderest parts of a man were. Looking at the Rees across the river and at Hugh beside him, Jim was so terror-stricken and conscience-stricken, both, he couldn't move.

"Let's go, Jim," Fitz said.

"I can't," Jim cried.

Fitz's hazel eyes were calm. He looked down at Jim; then at Hugh. Then Fitz reached down and took Hugh's guns and skinning knife and possible sack and flint and steel.

"Hey there! What're you doin'?" Jim cried. "Gonna leave him without any way of pertectin' himself?"

Fitz said, "You don't think I'm so foolish as to leave them guns and possibles for the Rees, do you? To kill us with later? Only a fool'd do that. You've got to be hardheaded about such things, Jim."

Jim cried, "But the wolves?"

Fitz said, "C'mon. We've done our full duty. Only a fool'd want to do more. You've rubbed the fur the right way long enough. C'mon."

Jim said, hiding his face, "I can't, Fitz. Hugh was my friend. He stuck up for me."

Fitz clambered his pony and grabbed hold of the lead rope to Old Blue. All three horses were snorting at the Ree Indian smell coming toward them on the wind across the river. "C'mon, Jim, get aboard that horse."

Still Jim couldn't get up.

Fitz held a gun on Jim. "Dammit, Jim, get aboard that horse. That's an order. Somebody's got to have horse sense around here." Fitz waggled his gun at Jim. "Don't you see, Jim? If we go now, the red devils'll chase us and so maybe even leave Hugh in peace."

"In peace for what? The wolves and the vultures?"

"Get! That's an order!"

Then Jim got up on his horse. Jim's face was white, numb.

They rode off lickety-split, the Rees chasing after them. And, just as Fitz said, in chasing after them, the Rees missed finding Hugh. . . .

Jim's young hoarse voice quit. Silence. Hearts beat quick and fast. Pineknots snapped in the fireplace.

Major Henry's eyes, Jim's young eyes, Yount's eyes, Silas's eyes, Allen's eyes, all were on Hugh.

Hugh said in a low monotone, "Major, did Fitz really sew me up?"

Major Henry nodded slowly, solemnly, blue eyes grave on Hugh.

Hugh trembled. The single arteries down each side

of his nose pulsed dark in the light from the red pine fire. "I feel mighty queersome," Hugh said.

Major Henry grimaced, baring white teeth. Major Henry took up pen and gray ledger and prepared to make another entry.

Hugh rubbed his sore nose. He knew that every man there was thinking about his confession that he was a one-bite cannibal.

Hugh said suddenly, "He that is without sin in this matter, let him be the first to cast a stone!"

No one said a thing.

"The first. Because, not knowin', you'd've taken that first bite too."

"Suppose we admit that," Jim said, looking Hugh square in the eye. "Ain't we even all around then?"

Hugh said, rubbing his nose some more, "I still think what you and Fitz did the most littlest thing I ever heard anybody do to a friend." Hugh gave Jim a searing look. "And tellin' the major here that you'd buried me decent when you knew it was a lie—that was littler still."

Jim glared right back. "Littler'n what you did to Mabel and the boys? Littler'n all the killin' you did when you was a buccaneer?"

Silence.

Hugh couldn't hold his eyes up to Jim's. He said slowly, "All right, Jim. I'll let you go for now. But remember. Your life is mine on loan until I hear what Fitz has to say about your black treachery."

Jim jumped up on his side of the table as if he meant to take another swing at Hugh.

"Now, now," Major Henry said, getting up too. "Now, now, we still ain't heard Hugh's story yet, Jim. How he managed to get here." Major Henry smiled at both Jim and Hugh. "And I'm oncommon curious to hear about that."

Chapter 5

Some weeks later, refreshed by plenty of food and rest, and feeling as spry as a spring rooster again, Old Hugh volunteered to deliver an important message to Ft. Atkinson on the Missouri just above the Platte.

Major Henry accepted the offer.

Major Henry knew what he was doing. Hugh was tearing mad to go, was going to go anyway if an excuse weren't given him, because Hugh believed downer Fitz was at Ft. Atkinson. The major knew that revenge, or the Lord's vengeance as Hugh persisted in calling it, was still seething in Hugh's breast. And that need for revenge, plus Hugh's remarkable daring, was sure to get the message through.

The major had been talking to a friendly Crow chief. The chief told about beaver south of the Big Horn and Wind River Mountains. "So thick and so tame," the Crow chief said, "your men won't have to set traps. They can club 'em over the head and get all they want." Major Henry trusted the Crow chief and decided to move his entire camp south. Spring trapping time was rapidly approaching and after that came trading time at the summer rendezvous. And General Ashley would have to know about the change in plans because the general was coming up with fresh supplies and provisions and trading materials for the rendezvous. So the urgent need for a competent messenger.

The major assigned four men to accompany Hugh: Dutton, More, Marsh, and Chapman. The major also made a private messenger out of Dutton. To Dutton he gave the job of warning General Ashley what Hugh had in mind for Fitz. Dutton was also told to put Fitz on guard should he get the chance. The major swore Dutton to secrecy and then sent him off with Hugh.

Hugh and his men put out for Platte early one balmy morning in March, the month of the Sore-eye Moon. They traveled straight south down the valley of the Little Big Horn, cut between the Wolf Mountains to the east and the dark shouldering Big Horn Mountains to the west, crossed over the highlands to the southeast until they came to Crazy Woman Creek, then took the Powder River straight south again. In the valleys the country was barren. When it wasn't white with late snow it was silver with sage. There was little game, less water, and only sparse patches of dead prairie grass. Up in the highlands the country was greened over with pine and greasewood. It was land red devils would avoid in the winter and, therefore, fairly safe.

Twice the men had the good luck to run onto small herds of lost buffalo in rolling bald country, once on the Salt River below Pumpkin Buttes and the other time, also on the Salt, below Teapot Rock. It was poor bull at the Pumpkins, but at the Teapot the lads had a fairly young cow.

"This cow beats painter," young Chapman said with satisfaction. They were all seated around a fire, each working on a fine morsel of hump rib. Chapman was eating his carefully, like a St. Lou dandy might nibble at a quartermoon of melon. Chapman had black snapping eyes and a humorous manner. His hunting coat of fringed elkskin, compared with the greasy clothes of the others, was almost as spotless and yellow as the day he put it on. Chapman usually saw the light side of things.

Hugh nodded, smacking his lips and cleaning off his whiskers, "Good, that it is. But cow tastes better later in the spring. After she's had fresh sweetgrass for a month. Then you can't beat cow."

Twice, too, the men had the good luck to find water just when they needed it most, once where the Powder River turned west and once near the source of the Salt. At the Salt the men had even given up trying to chop down through ice to get at water.

"She's frozen solid," More announced, throwing his ax aside disgusted. More had the haunted look of the tall misfit, the look many mountain men had, except that where others had open faces like Jim Bridger's, he had a sinister-appearing face.

Hugh scoffed at More and got down on his knees in the snow and ice chips beside the green-edged hole. Hugh took out his skinning knife and with a downward stabbing motion plunged the knife into the very point of the hole. There was a slicing sound in the ice and then water welled up around Hugh's hand and in a moment the green hole was full of water.

"See," Hugh said.

"Well I'll be a son to a mule if that don't beat all," More exclaimed, smiling surprised from out of the hood of his gray woolen capote. "And here I thought I'd already dug up sand bottom."

"You did," Hugh said, "but that's just where the water sometimes still runs. Through the sand under the ice."

When they hit the Platte below the Sweetwater River, just across from the Haystack Range—a range that kept rising like black doom as they approached it—they had more good luck. The weather turned warm and the snow vanished almost overnight, revealing that they'd moved from grayyellow land to land bright with pink outcroppings and green rabbit brush and tender bright-green sweetgrass. There was also budded cottonwood. After a long drygrass diet the ponies relished the sappy cottonwood bark.

Further down the Platte, across from the Laramie Range, they came upon bright red rimrock crested with green cedar. The contrast of green cedar against red soil raised involuntary sighs. There was hard work to be done, always, but as they rode along, the men sometimes couldn't resist looking for long moments at the green foliage growing out of red land. Faces brightened; voices lifted; blood pulsed sweet and clean. They were true men of the wilderness. They'd lived for the ever-new in the wild and their senses had become as sharp as a pregnant squaw's. The sky was blue—it hurt the eye like a bright light. The air was fresh—it stung the lungs like a sweet ether.

They crossed the Platte above the Guernsey Hills. And still they had good luck.

Dutton said, "This can't go on." Dutton was a gaunt hollowcheeked blond with big floppy ears and big knuckles. He tended to look at the down side of things. Sudden greening spring seemed to gnaw at him instead of exhilarate him.

"What can't go on?" Hugh asked, looking up from where he rode along on swaying sure-step Skunk.

"This breeze of luck we're having, that's what."

" 'Tain't luck," Hugh said, wise old eyes looking out at the land by themselves.

"What is it then, a gift from somebody?"

Hugh's smile moved his whiskers. " 'Tain't exactly a gift, no. Though it's bein' given us. Because of who we are."

Dutton stared at Hugh. "You're not arguin' we got this comin'?"

"I might. A child can't help but have good luck as long as he's doin' Lord's work."

Dutton fell silent and his pale blue eyes slid to one side as if afraid that the private knowledge he had might be revealed in them.

"This child's been chosen, that's why. I've been gettin' sign all along."

Dutton said nothing.

" 'Tis so," Hugh said. "Spring grass can't shine too soon for me and the Lord."

They followed the North Platte in a southeasterly direction, with always a wary eye out for Indian sign, always and ever studying the varying and lifting and falling horizons, the pinkish rimrock and bold Laramie Peak to the south and the Rawhide Buttes and Spoon Butte to the north.

They were well into the wide bowl of Goshen Hole, just above Scotts Bluff and Wild Cat Ridge, and the sun had ascended into April, the Moon of the Ducks Coming Back, when Hugh first noticed it. His throwback dun mare, Skunk, began to sniff the wind and act restless.

"Ho-ah," Hugh said. "Skunk smells something." Hugh held up his hand and the party trailing out behind him in single file immediately stopped.

"What? Hugh?" Marsh called out. Marsh was in charge of the pack horses heavy with beaver plew meant for General Ashley. Marsh was a laugher. His face was always either in the grip of a laugh or on the brink of a laugh. When he wasn't laughing there was a look on his face as if he expected to be told something that would make him laugh. The laugh, and the expectation of the laugh, had, over the years, finally creased his face with an indelible smile. Marsh resembled a merry gargoyle atop a medieval castle wall. Marsh considered Old Hugh one of the most comical men he'd ever seen. This annoyed Hugh. Hugh liked being a wag now and again, like any man, but at the moment he was all business.

"What? Hugh?" Marsh said again, face sobering down to a mute smile.

"Skunk's got her nozzle onto something." Hugh stood up in his saddle and peered intently into the bowl of Goshen Hole. "And this child got a whiff too."

Marsh looked around and studied the pack horses, some ten of them, each with a pair of balanced packs on its back. Marsh studied the horses of Dutton, More, and Chapman. Marsh's smile continued to fade a little.

"The other horses are quiet. Skunk's probably just in heat, is all."

"All the more reason to believe her," Hugh said shortly, old gray eyes wild yet watchful on the bowl below. Hugh took off his wolfskin cap to hear the better.

Dutton rode up. "What's up, Hugh?"

"Shhh."

Hugh studied the terrain carefully. They were riding on a south rim of land overlooking Goshen Hole. The North Platte drove straight across it from northwest to southeast. The whole of Goshen Hole looked like the scooped-out bed of an ancient lake. Across the river, some miles away, rose the whitegray chalk sides of the Box Butte tableland. A few wild cedars and scrubby pitch pine clung to the upper chalk edges. Black and gray sage and sweet cactus and rabbit brush dotted the bowl bottom like a poor man's scraggly beard. Below and ahead beside the river grew a thick grove of willows. The willows were already reddish brown with rising sap. Grama grass had just begun to green the baked sands and shakes of the shores and islands of the swift river. Tucked into the crevices and sun-warmed pockets of the ravines leading down to the river were the first yellowgreen sprouts of saxifrage and sour dock and windflower and beardtongue.

It was a clear day with occasional mare's tail clouds fanning by overhead. The sun had climbed to almost high noon and it fell warmly on the backs of Hugh's hands. A few hawks had come out and were riding the updrafts along the rim. A picket-pin gopher sat motionless. It too was busy looking out over the far country below in Goshen Hole.

Marsh said, "Nothin' north of us that I can see."

Hugh got down off Skunk and took her nose in his hands. He had the feeling she was about to whinny. Her ears were flicking back and forth like a nervous mule's and she had her head up like a checked pacer's.

Then she took a deep breath, fluttering her nose, and Hugh grabbed it just in time. "Damme," Hugh said, "but there must be something."

"Where, Hugh?" Chapman said, riding up, face for once concerned.

Hugh shhhed them.

Hugh studied the red willows along the river. Hugh said, "Ain't seen a single critter either, wing nor foot, except for that picket-pin gopher. And he's watchin' like Skunk is."

"Hawks flyin' overhead," More said, face drawn into a deeper scowl than usual.

Hugh snorted. "That don't mean nothin'. They'd fly in droves over a battlefield."

They sat and looked and listened.

Presently other picket-pin gophers came out of their holes. Then a flock of wild geese V-ed in from the south. Hugh and the men watched the wild geese intently. The great longnecks drove straight for the river, made two long looping 8-shaped passes at it, and slanted in for a landing. They hit the water and kicked up sprays like falling shot. The men all heaved a huge sigh.

Dutton said, "Can't be anything down by the river at least."

Hugh grunted. He watched Skunk and was relieved to see that when he let go of her nose she reached down and began to crop at sparse bits of spring-green bunch grass. "Maybe the wind's shifted and she can't smell it anymore."

"But the geese hit the river, Hugh," Dutton said.

Hugh put on his wolfskin cap again. "This child still don't like it. I mind me of the time I didn't heed Ol' Blue and the next thing I knew I was halfway down a she-grizzly gullet."

The landing of the wild longnecks brought Marsh back to his accentuated smile again. "Well, Hugh, what'll it be, meat by water or meat up here on the hill?"

Hugh got on Skunk. "The ponies need water," he said shortly. He patted Skunk's silver mane. "Hep-a," he said, giving her a heel in the ribs, "hep-a." And in a moment all the clopping hooves of the pack train were going again.

They rode down to a ford in the Platte where the water fanned and spilled across spreads of sand. Marsh and More unsaddled the horses and watered them in the ford and staked them out to green. Chapman and Dutton got up the chuck.

Old Hugh did sentinel duty. He climbed up on a nearby pink rock outcropping and sat looking north across the swilling fanning river. Behind him the red willows swayed in a soft south breeze. The willows were thick, and he cast an anxious eye at them now and again.

Hugh was repriming his rifle and checking the load and was in the act of forcing down the ball with his long hickory wiping-stick, when the opposite shore was suddenly red with Indians. The Indians saw Hugh and his party and commenced to gesticulate enough to frighten Old Nick himself. Individual braves could be made out very plainly across the running water. Hugh saw the familiar hawkbone headdress resembling paired horse ears and instantly knew them—the same Rees he'd seen on the Moreau the fall before while crawling to safety to Ft. Kiowa. Elk Tongue's band. Somehow they'd roved across Cheyenne Indian country below the Black Hills and through the Badlands.

Old Chief Elk Tongue sat easily on a spotted pony at the head of the band. He was dressed in full battle regalia, an honorable target for the enemy. Behind him sat some forty warriors all painted red for battle and armed with rifles and bows and tomahawks and shields. Despite the still chilly spring weather all were naked save for leathern breechcloth.

"Look up, men," Hugh called down from his pink rock. "Red devils across the river."

Every hand dived for his rifle.

"Wait up," Hugh said, jumping down. "No shootin'. Let's see what they want first. See what they have to say."

Presently two warriors came forward across the swilling ford. Their ponies came on splashing and prancing.

Hugh stepped to the shore to meet them. Gravel crunched under his moccasins. He held up his hand when the two braves were almost across.

Hugh instantly recognized the leading warrior. It was Stabbed, the same Ree brave who'd served as policeman with him the day General Ashley had parleyed with the Arikaree chiefs on the Missouri above the Grand. Hugh had killed his brother Bear Mouth for playing grizzly with Aaron Stephens' body.

Stabbed stared at Hugh; stared at the armed men behind Hugh; stared at Hugh. Stabbed's sensitive mobile mouth drew up into a ferocious poutlike grimace. The pennyskinned muscular giant's wild eyes wicked and glittered with hate. Stabbed's red-streaked cheeks moved menacingly with the grimace. Like his dead brother, Stabbed was high-shouldered and he went about naked save for breechcloth, hawkbone headdress, and a necklace of grizzly claws. An eagle feather in back fluttered in a light breeze.

Hugh began the parley, using the expressive ancient gestures of the Great Plains Indian sign-talk. Right hand lifted and waggling, Hugh said, "How."

"How."

Hugh waggled out the sign for peace pipe, then for bow and arrow. "What do you want? Smoke pipe? Make war?"

"Rees smoke pipe with Chief White Grizzly."

Hugh then answered in Pawnee, sister language to the Arikaree. "Tell your chief I thank him very much.

But we are in a hurry to see our Great White Father. Tell your chief we cannot visit him."

Stabbed's eyebrows went up. He answered in Ree. The Ree sounded like Pawnee spoken with a twist of the tongue and with the syllables dragged out a little. "That is too bad. Chief Elk Tongue hopes you will not fork today. Chief Elk Tongue hopes his friend Chief White Grizzly will visit his lodge."

"We thank Chief Elk Tongue. But we must hurry to visit our Great White Father."

"Chief Elk Tongue says he loves his friend, Chief White Grizzly."

Hugh shook his head. "Tell your great chief that we cannot visit him today."

"Are you squaws to run? What have you got for presents?"

Hugh turned to his men. "I guess one of us had better go and hold a parley with the old red devil." Hugh sighed massively. "And I guess that'll have to be this child. Maybe if I give him a few presents, some 'bacca, pony beads, maybe he'll let us alone."

Dutton said, worried, "Whatever you say, Hugh. You know them. We don't."

Hugh said, "They're all great swimmers and horsemen. If we make a run for it they'll be after us like bees after a honey thief. And we can't run with all that beaver."

Dutton said, "Whatever you say, Hugh."

Hugh looked at his men. He wished he were alone. He'd know what to do then. But here he had men, beaver, and a message to worry about. Hugh had come to like his men. They were his first command and he had begun to feel an officer's, a mother's, love for them.

Hugh said, "I'll go over on Skunk. Keep me covered as best you can from here." Hugh filled his pockets with tobacco and beads, jammed his horse pistol and skinning knife in his belt, saw to the priming of his flintlock, and climbed aboard.

Hugh motioned for Stabbed and the other Ree to lead the way across the river. He splashed after them through the shallow swilling ford.

When Hugh rode up the opposite sandy shore, Chief Elk Tongue had already gotten off his spotted pony. He was an old man, like Hugh, but also like Hugh he was still very spry. Hugh got down off his horse in the midst of howling swirling dogs and yelling berry-eyed children. High-shouldered warriors looked at him with wild ferocious eyes. Squaws, old and young, watched silently.

But Old Elk Tongue seemed to mean what he said through his messengers. Long gray blanket rustling, he approached Hugh with a smile on his old mobile lips, a beautiful smile for even his old dark face, and embraced him as if Hugh actually were his brother.

Hugh suffered him. The smell of the old red devil suddenly made him homesick for Bending Reed. Hugh longed with a great longing to be back in her tepee at Ft. Kiowa.

Golden eagle feathers fluttering, Old Elk Tongue took Hugh kindly by the hand, led him toward a rocky knoll.

They crested the knoll and then Hugh saw the village. The knoll had been just big enough to hide the entire Ree village from view. Skunk had been right. Immediately behind the village jutted a low rimrock. It protected the lodges from cold north winds at the same time that it trapped the sun's heat. There was a huge blazing fire in the center of the village and around it flittered a few withered witchlike hags.

" 'Tis now for the woolly wilds," Hugh thought to himself, eyes alert for some sign as to what it might all lead to.

Old Elk Tongue surprised him then as they walked along. Old Elk Tongue spoke in Ree. "My people are happy that Chief White Grizzly has honored us. My brother, it was no small thing that you have done."

" 'Honored'?" Hugh ejaculated in Pawnee. "You 'honored'? How?"

Old Elk Tongue smiled benignly on Hugh, though the warriors behind the old chief continued to scowl with wild blackcherry eyes and to fumble nervously with their rifles and bows. Each warrior had the part in his hair painted with vermilion; each had his old wounds painted garishly.

"With the white man's burial ceremony. White Grizzly is our brother because he prayed as a holy man for the spirit of the mother of Chief Grey Eyes."

"Ho-ah!" Hugh said then. "This child sees now, he does. Somebody spotted him on the Moreau with Grey Eyes' dyin' old she-rip then. Whaugh!" Hugh smiled and nodded, careful not to stare the old chief in the face.

Old Elk Tongue led Hugh toward his skin lodge, members of the band following. Skin streamers and the smoke flap fluttered from the tepee poles above the smoke hole. A medicine bundle hung over the door. The door faced east, the place of the long-winded sun, and the source of the light of the universe.

Old Elk Tongue held the leather flap aside for Hugh, beckoned for him to enter.

Hugh was about to do so when an old squaw grabbed him by the tail of his fringed elkskin hunting shirt and jerked him back with a yell. Before Old Elk Tongue could stop her, she spat in Hugh's grizzly face. She taunted him, saying, "Dogface, I throw filth at you. Coward. Squaw. Wait till the council with the great Chief Elk Tongue and Chief Stabbed is over. I shall dance over your scalp yet." She broke into a long wailing lamentation.

Hugh managed to maintain his calm. He held still so that Old Elk Tongue could rebuke her and push her away.

Old Elk Tongue said, "The old mother is sad because

White Grizzly killed her son. In the great battle by the Grand."

"What was her son's medicine?" Hugh asked.

"The great spirit of the fierce grizzly. He ate enemy like grizzly."

Old Hugh's eyes opened a little. "Bear Mouth. Brother to Stabbed. Sure. Mimicked a grizzly and carried what was left of Aaron Stephens around like he meant to tear him to bits."

Hugh said, "Tell her White Grizzly is sorry. Tell her he has presents for her to help her forget her grief."

The moment Hugh finished speaking, the old witch quit howling and held out her hand.

Hugh had to laugh inside his whiskers. With a chuckle he gave her a handful of bright pony beads, white and red and blue. She clutched the beads in her pale cracked palm and ran.

Again Old Elk Tongue beckoned for Hugh to enter his lodge. Hugh bent down and crawled in. Old Elk Tongue and a couple dozen braves followed. Each naked Ree brave, including Elk Tongue, deposited his weapons, both knife and gun, by the door. Hugh deposited his weapons too, his rifle and horse pistol, but in the bustling of each man finding his rank and place to sit, Hugh managed to hide his skinning knife in his shot pouch. Hugh was sure that one or another of the warriors had an extra knife hidden in his breechclout. They sat in a circle against the wall, against the dew skin, and out of the reach of the cold draft coming in under the tepee's bottom edges. Hugh sat at Old Elk Tongue's right hand in the place of honor at the back. They sat with buttocks on the ground, knees out, and ankles crossed against the crotch.

A fire crackled in the middle, throwing warm blasts of air against their faces. A pipe of peace, a red pipestone affair with a long willow twig for pipestem, lay against a stone altar. Behind the circle of men stood twelve short poles, six on a side, with a sacred bundle hanging from each pole. The bundles represented the twelve tribes of the Ree nation. Hugh had once heard that the sacred bundles were the Book of Genesis of the Arikarees.

A holy man took up the tribal pipe of peace from the altar, lighted it with a coal from the fire, and performed a rite over it—offering the pipe to the six powers: the west, the north, the east, the south, the sky, the earth. Then he smoked it and embraced it and passed it on to Chief Elk Tongue. Elk Tongue offered the pipe to the six powers, too, and smoked it and embraced it and passed it on to Hugh. Hugh likewise offered it to the six powers and smoked and embraced it and handed it on to the naked warrior next in line.

When the pipe got to the giant Stabbed, there was a silence.

Old Elk Tongue looked up from his musing. "What is wrong that Stabbed does not smoke the pipe of peace with our brother White Grizzly?"

Stabbed looked at the wild young warriors near him. Muted sunlight coming through the skin walls and the smoke hole above gave Stabbed's folded arms and ferocious face and raised knees a rich penny color. His eyes glittered and rolled. Stabbed said, "Stabbed feels very heavy in his heart. He has great grief."

"Yes?" Old Elk Tongue said patiently.

"White Grizzly does not speak with a single tongue. He smokes the pipe of peace as a friend but his heart is black toward us. White Grizzly has killed many of our braves."

"How! How!" The high-shouldered young braves grunted approvingly, sensitive lips scowling.

Old Elk Tongue gave Hugh a sad look. He shook his head, black-and-white eagle feathers at the back of his head rustling, gray blanket opening a little in front. "My young braves are angry because White Grizzly has no presents for them." A louse chased down one of the long braids of the old wrinkled chief. "No presents no friends."

Hugh smiled under his whiskers again. And once more he dug into his present sack, this time giving each brave in the tepee a handful of tobacco. Every brave except Stabbed accepted the gift.

Hugh said, "Let Stabbed tell White Grizzly truly what he wants to help him forget his grief."

Stabbed said, blackcherry eyes darting with hate, "What present can White Grizzly give that will bring back to his lodge Bear Mouth my brother?"

Elk Tongue interposed. "White Grizzly, my braves are wild. It will take much to keep them from attacking White Grizzly. Maybe Elk Tongue should adopt White Grizzly as his blood brother."

Hugh's old eyes whirled around, flashing graywhite. Blood brother to the Rees when he already had a Sioux squaw for wife?

Elk Tongue explained. "My brother, you have honored the Rees with your white man's burial ceremony and also our Ree ceremony for the mother of Grey Eyes. My brother, that was no small thing you have done. Chief Elk Tongue wishes to adopt you and make you his blood brother."

Stabbed broke out with anger. "Stabbed can never look upon White Grizzly as the blood brother to Elk Tongue. Never. Never until blood has been shed for his brother Bear Mouth."

"How! How!" The young braves grunted approvingly.

Elk Tongue explained further. "Bear Mouth and Stabbed both came from the belly of the same mother. Bear Mouth and Stabbed both came from the society of the same grizzly clan. Bear Mouth and Stabbed came from the same dog society." Old Elk Tongue shook his head sadly. "Dog soldiers are our police. When the police are wild, the chief can not promise peace."

The little arteries down each side of Hugh's big nose began to move. Stabbed was bent on trouble, that was certain. Quietly Hugh opened his shot pouch. If it came to a fight he'd whip out his skinning knife and bring down at least one brave with him.

Elk Tongue continued to shake his head sadly, his eagle feathers rustling. "My wild braves are hard to hold. My wild braves are not happy since the great battle on the Grand. Their heart aches with many bad memories."

Hugh said slowly in a deep heavy bass monotone, "White Grizzly says it again. Let Stabbed tell truly what he wants to help him forget his grief."

Stabbed looked toward the leather flap door where all the weapons lay. "Stabbed will take White Grizzly's rifle and pistol."

Hugh slowly shook his head. "White Grizzly is sorry. White Grizzly must return the rifle and the pistol to his Great White Father. They are the Great White Father's to give and to take."

Silence. The curving eaglebeak nose of every brave in the tepee quivered. Small eyes, already screwed up into gimlets by sun and wind, became smaller. Some of the braves slowly bared their teeth. The teeth, though yellow, looked white against the pipestone skin.

Stabbed suddenly gave the sign of his bear society. He grunted like a grizzly. "Whaugh." Then he leaped up, knife in hand. Like Hugh, he too had secreted a skinning knife on his person.

And, as suddenly, Old Elk Tongue, despite old bones, was up on his feet too. He placed himself between Stabbed and Hugh. The two Rees glared at each other, each proud, haughty, imperious, like great noble eagle cocks.

Old Elk Tongue said, "White Grizzly is my blood brother. What he did was no small thing. He buried the mother of our great chief Grey Eyes. He spoke the white man's sacred ceremony over her. He prayed for her spirit like a Ree holy man. A great thing that was. He is my blood brother."

Stabbed said, "White Grizzly's blood or his guns. Stabbed's tongue is short; his arm is long."

Old Elk Tongue continued to glare at Stabbed. Stabbed glared right back.

When Elk Tongue saw he could not cow the younger Stabbed, he slowly opened the folds of his gray blanket, dropped his breechcloth, and put his hand under his thigh, and said, "By my power, and by the power of my ancestors, White Grizzly is now my blood brother."

The Ree braves in the lodge gasped. They clapped their hands to their mouths in surprise. Dropping the breechcloth usually meant grave insult. But here their old chief had turned it around to mean sacred power. The old chief had never before appealed to such great medicine.

Stabbed couldn't look Old Elk Tongue in the eye then. He sat down again.

Slowly Old Elk Tongue looked each brave in the eye, still holding his power in hand. Then, after a long solemn moment, Old Elk Tongue let go, and drew up his breechcloth again, and folded his gray mantle, and sat down beside Hugh.

But wily Stabbed wasn't through.

Later, when the council broke up in Old Elk Tongue's tent, as they were crawling out through the flap door, he invited Hugh to his lodge for a feast.

Hugh presented an absolutely calm face. But inwardly his mind raced. And raged. If he didn't accept the invitation, Stabbed as dog soldier and policeman would take it as an insult, and raise an uproar, and so throw the already mad-as-bees Arikarees out of Old Elk Tongue's control.

Hugh decided to put on a bold front. Bluff was sometimes exactly the right medicine with the touchy bird-brained red devils.

Hugh said, "Chief Elk Tongue is my blood brother. If Stabbed will invite Chief Elk Tongue, then White Grizzly will accept."

Stabbed quivered with suppressed fury at Hugh's neat gambit. Hugh's request was an honorable one and Stabbed had to accept it, just as Hugh'd had to accept or suffer the consequences. Stabbed sulked audibly, like a male prairie grouse about to fight.

Hugh managed to suppress a sigh of relief within his beard. At least he'd gained that much. If Elk Tongue really honored him as a blood brother for having honored the dead mother of dead Grey Eyes, he had a chance to come out of it alive.

Just before Hugh crept into Stabbed's lodge, he asked permission to sign-talk with his men to tell them he was stopping for a feast. Stabbed gave assent, though he had to work at it. Hugh went to the rocky knoll that lay between the village and the river and wigwagged to Dutton and the others not to worry, that he was halfway finished with what he considered a successful council, but in any event they should remain armed to the teeth.

Once again Hugh crawled through a doorflap, and deposited his guns at the door with the others, and sat in a circle with select warriors, knees out and legs crossed at the ankles. Each man sat according to his rank, Stabbed and Hugh and Elk Tongue in the place of honor at the back. Ree police guarded the door outside.

Right from the start, while they smoked the red pipestone calumet, Hugh saw sign that this was one feast which was not going to end up with the customary full belly and sense of well-being. To whet the appetite, supposedly, Stabbed's young buckskin-clad squaw, Wild Lily, handed out tidbits of pemmican. The way she did it—eyes stiff and bugged in an immobile face instead of in the usual merry manner accompanied by a lewd jest now and then—was enough to set Hugh's teeth on edge. But it was the pemmican itself, full of hair and gravel and maggots, which told most. Even Old Elk Tongue had trouble getting it down, while the high-shouldered fierce young warriors glimmered at the joke that Hugh was obliged to eat rotten food at a feast that was supposedly in his honor.

Hugh next happened to notice that Wild Lily had not killed one of the tribe's best and fattest dogs for the feast. The dog he saw in the stewpot over the fire in the middle of the lodge was one of the meanest and scrawniest he'd ever seen.

Outwardly Hugh seemed calm enough as he solemnly chewed on the rotten pemmican. But inwardly his mind continued to seethe as he wondered how he was going to escape this new pinch.

The pipe of peace was making its second round, and Old Elk Tongue's mobile lips were curving and uncurving as he mused to himself—when Hugh heard a child squeal behind him.

Hugh turned his head just enough to make out that the squeal came from a stubborn two-year-old boy. The boy was persistent in wanting to join his father Stabbed at the feast. Hugh saw Wild Lily clap a hand over its little mouth; saw her bundle the child away. Hugh's eyes opened. Ho-ah. The decks were being cleared for action.

Hugh saw there was nothing for it but to make a break for it. There wasn't even time to jump up and quickly grab up his rifle and pistol.

Suddenly Hugh doubled himself up into a ball and rolled over backward. He kicked up the side of the leather lodge; rolled out; bounded to kis feet. Then he leaned forward into a swift run, dodging in and out through the village, around and behind and beside various conical tepees standing between him and the low rimrock to the north and farther away from the river.

There was an immediate shout, then a great roar of voices, then a shot. Then came a great whoop of rage and fury and a flurry of shots.

Hugh threw a quick look back over his shoulder and, past the slant of a leather lodge, caught sight of Stabbed picking up a handful of dust and flinging it in the air.

It was the ancient summons to battle. Hugh knew then it wouldn't be just his scalp and life they were after, but also those of his men still across the river. Most of the braves would be across that river like a shot, swimming or riding, and would have the men cornered and captured before they got a quarter-mile away.

A pang of anguish, of sympathy for the men, a pang not unlike a heart attack, gripped his chest so that he could scarcely breathe. It was terrible, it was too bad, but the way the dice rolled, it probably had to be. Hugh only hoped that the men had heard the uproar and the shots in time so that they could get at least a little head start on the Rees and so maybe miraculously escape them after all.

Hugh ran past the last lodge, then past the village middenheap, then hit for the nearest point of the low whitegray rimrock to the north. Hugh spotted a slanting hole some ten feet up. His heart leaped when he saw it. "If this child can make that afore a red devil comes around that last lodge, this child's got a sucker's chance." Hugh leaped up with all his might; caught hold of the top edge of the ledge; chinned himself up with powerful gripping grabbing scrabbling hands and arms; got a leg over; climbed in; ducked down. Looking about, he spotted a slatelike slab of rock off to one side. He gave it a jerk; found it loose and lighter than he expected; pulled it over him and covered the hole like a cook might cover a pot or kettle.

Just in time too. The dirt had hardly stopped falling when, looking past the edge of the stone cover, Hugh saw a dozen whooping hawkbone braves led by Stabbed come legging it around the last tepee and heading straight for the low rimrock hellbent for revenge. Their paint-striped faces were horrible to behold, drawn up as they were into ferocious grimaces, mouths open with bared yellow teeth and uling, wide red throats screaming and shrilling, flintlocks and bows and arrows windmilling, and legs in violent run.

Hugh groaned. Stabbed had seen him duck into the slanting hole. He was gone under, sartain sure at last.

Hugh took knife out of shot pouch and set himself. He would bring down at least one of the red devils with him. Stabbed if possible.

But Stabbed and his braves bounded up the whitegray rimrock and right on past him.

Hugh gave a massive sigh of relief. Ahhh. Stabbed hadn't seen him after all. Stabbed must have thought he'd somehow climbed out of sight farther along the rimrock.

The dozen Ree braves were barely out of sight and hearing, when Hugh heard a curious whizzing underfoot. He looked down. There, in the darkness, on green mossed-over rocks, was a slowly writhing brown diamond-flecked design. Rattlesnake. Still too full of winter cold to rattle properly, or coil and strike, it was not too cold to be harmless if a man was careless enough to place a moccasined foot directly in front of its mouth. Hugh whirled; reached down; stabbed around until he sliced head from body. Before he was done cleaning out the slanted hole he found and killed seven others.

Again Hugh peered out from behind the stone slab cover. And what he saw then evoked another series of stabbing pains in his chest.

Three of his men had been captured, the laugher Marsh, and elegant Chapman, and misfit More. Some twenty Rees, led by the brave who accompanied Stabbed across the Platte for the parley, had quickly caught up with them. Marsh, Chapman, More, each of them, had their hands tied behind them and then had their hands tied to a horse's tail. The very first jerk had unsprung arms from shoulder sockets. That first jerk must have been terrible. The snorting ponies dragging the men half-turned about to look at the drenched half-drowned dirt-bedaubed things bouncing irregularly along in the dust behind them.

At the sight of the hated whites captured and bound,

the whole village went into a wild joyous frenzy, the braves howling out their spite and vengeance like coyotes, the musicians beating drums and blowing eaglebone whistles and bangling medicine rattles, the squaws giving the tremulo. Dogs chased after the rolling bouncing forms of the men, dashed in for a bite, howled and barked. Little Indian boys ran after the victims too, target-practicing with their little boy-sized bows and arrows. Little girls and young squaws and old squaws also ran after, cursing, swearing, mouthing the foulest and the lewdest of insults, all the while gesturing what they meant with their fingers and hands. The squaw who had spat on Hugh was right up in front with the rest. She was in an ecstasy of revenge and joy.

Hugh couldn't find Dutton. It made him hope that Dutton had somehow managed to get away. Probably on one of the horses.

Then followed the most awful part of the victory ceremony dance. Three braves, led by Stabbed's companyero, stopped the horses, and with cries of savage triumph, went over and counted coup on the still live men, and then scalped them, cutting out the whorl or crown below which, as the Indians believed, lay the seat of intelligence, cutting it out with a single twist of the skinning knife and lifting it with a jerk. Once scalped, the braves turned the bodies over to the squaws, who promptly, with equally sharp knives, castrated them, disemboweled them, dismembered them, stabbing them endlessly, and doing it all so fast that life and consciousness hardly had time to escape before the mutilations were finished. And last followed the fearful awful blood-curdling coyotelike howl of the death whoop.

Gone was the laugher, Marsh. Gone was the cheerful dandy, Chapman. Gone was the haunted one, tall misfit More. And where Dutton was only God knew.

Hugh cried.

"Too bad Old Elk Tongue couldn't hold his braves. But I guess they was too much for even him."

The braves, again led by Stabbed's companyero, held a dance of the scalps around the huge blazing fire in the center of the village. They two-stepped, they howled, they beat drums, they beat their chests, they recited their coups and exploits, they howled execrations at the hated white man. "Hay-ah-hay! Hay-he-ah-hay. Hay-ah-hay." "Ow-owgh-he-a! Ow-owgh-he-a-hi!" "Hi-hi-i. He-he. He-he-a. Hay-a-hay."

Hugh cried.

Meantime Stabbed and his braves, who'd missed finding him in his slanting hole and who'd run beyond the rimrock, at last came back. Stabbed cursed and ranted and raved that his prize, Chief White Grizzly, killer of his brother Bear Mouth, should have somehow got away. Stabbed was so mad he refused to join the scalp dance around the blazing fire where his companyero was parading about proud as an eagle cock with Hugh's gun and pistol. Stabbed howled and swore. The worst was Stabbed sat on the very slanting stone slab under which Hugh lay skulking.

Hugh didn't dare shiver, much less take a relieving breath of any kind. He thought to himself: "I'm just barely out of one scrape, when, wingo! I'm plumb smack in the middle of another. If that ain't somethin' to grind on then my name ain't Ol' Hugh Glass." Hugh bit on his teeth. "My stomach may be empty but it's a dead cinch my brain ain't."

When night finally fell over the village and the river and the rimrock, sulky Stabbed at last got off the stone slab and climbed down the rimrock and joined the dance.

Hugh breathed easier.

Chapter 6

Hugh had himself a time penned up in the snake den.

He didn't mind eating raw rattlesnake meat—after eating it during his ordeal of crawling to Ft. Kiowa, it was in the way of being an old treat. He didn't mind the lack of sleep—like a dog he could make that up later. He didn't mind the lack of water—it wasn't hot out, and the little he did need to survive he got by licking a wet mossy rock on the shadow side.

But he did mind the tight narrow cramped quarters. The need to stretch his legs almost drove him crazy. Experiment as he might, he just couldn't find the room to get his legs stretched out straight.

The need to stretch his legs to the full became an obsession with him. He tried every position and angle imaginable. He scrounged around like a bitch about to pup and needing a comfortable nest to pup in.

He didn't dare allow himself the luxury of shoving off the stone cover for a few minutes in the dark of the night. As long as both he and Dutton were still at large the Rees were bound to have sentinels out and on the alert for the least movement.

Finally, three days and three nights later, the Rees, like a flock of unpredictable crows, suddenly took off one morning for parts unknown. At a signal from Old Elk Tongue, the squaws began to take down the lodges and load the ponies and dogs, and by high noon the whole village was gone. Hugh wondered if Old Elk

Tongue hadn't probably guessed that he and Dutton were still in the area and had decided to give them a chance to escape by moving everybody out.

When Hugh was sure they were safely out of sight, he pushed the stone cover to one side and crawled out. And immediately stood up and stretched, high up on his moccasined toes. "Ho-ah! This child was about beat for stink. All alone in a tight hole a man makes mighty poor company for himself. Another day of it and I'd've been just another dead snake in a full privy."

Hugh searched both banks of the North Platte River for sign of Dutton. But look as he might, and call out as he might, Dutton seemed to have vanished with the dew. Except for the dusty Ree trail, not a track led away from the area.

Hugh took stock of his situation. He'd lost his rifle and horse pistol, yes, and all of his plunder, but he still had his skinning knife and flint and steel. Looking at the three, a slow wise tortured smile moved under his whitening whiskers. " 'Tis so. These little fixin's still make a child feel quite rich, quite pert, even though he is two, three hundred miles away from anybody or anywhere, all alone among the painters and wild varmints."

Hugh decided his best chance was to head straight for Ft. Kiowa, some two hundred seventy miles to the northeast. It was the nearest settlement, and it was some hundred thirty miles closer than Ft. Atkinson. Also, to follow the Platte down to Ft. Atkinson would have been suicide. The Pawnees, tribal cousins of the Rees and his one-time enemies and captors, still lived on its banks.

Ae, Ft. Kiowa it was. Hugh looked forward to seeing Bending Reed again. She would fix him up with a fresh supply of leather wear. And Clerk Bonner might just possibly let him have a little more credit and give him a new rifle and horse pistol. Then, too, he might just possibly catch an early spring boat going south to Ft.

Atkinson where the downer Fitz was supposed to have gone.

Hugh once again took his latest miraculous escape from the Rees as sign that the Lord meant to preserve his life for a special reason. " 'Tis so. The Good Lord has something special in mind for this child. 'Tis to get His vengeance on Fitz for having deserted this child on the forks of the Grand."

Hugh trapped a rabbit and skinned it. He revived one of the dying Ree fires with a few armfuls of dead willow twigs. He barbecued the rabbit to an aromatic fare-thee-well. He relished it to the bone. He drank from the river. He washed his whitening whiskers, took a last look around, and set off.

The weather held steady and he made good time. As he'd done before, he slept daytimes, traveled at night.

Hugh had always been a great leg, and with his limb and seat and back completely healed, he once again could cover ground on foot like a tireless mule with the smell of home in its nostrils. Hugh was one of the few mountain men who could outwalk and outdistance any horse, wild or tame. He had a great chest, powerful legs, a tremendous reserve of energy, and when he set his mind on it, a will as tough as buckskin. He never gave up. It had been Hugh, more than Clint, who willed the two of them through to life on their weary ordeal walking up from the coasts of Texas to the Platte, where the Pawnees caught them.

He crossed the source of the Niobrara River; climbed over the Pine Ridge divide; unerringly hit the source of the White River. He followed the White northeastward. It wound about and meandered through rolling ochergray land with pines in the distance on the buttes and ridges. Cottonwood, ash, willow, chokecherry fringed the stream.

The farther he went down the White, the more chalky and dirty-cream white it became. He drank white; he shat white. And sour? The wild salt and alkali in it puckered the mouth to a bee-hole and crimped the gullet to a wasp-hole. It was like drinking salty chalkwater. Instead of assuaging thirst it increased it. Luckily a late spring snow fell, and for a couple of days Hugh could suck white snowballs for water to go with his red meat, mostly gopher.

Hugh followed the White all the way into a yellowwhite eroded country, an ancient open terrain, called the Badlands. The White dwindled, and thinned. Sometimes there was hardly enough water to connect the pools at the turns. Hugh said, "The way it looks here, the White ain't gonna have enough water to make the Missouri."

A full moon followed him every step of the way. At night, the Badlands country was an eerie wonder world, silvered over with muted luminescence as if all were in dream and he a bearded bad conscience.

A south wind followed him, too, blowing up the valleys in long hooing drafts and whistling in the cedars on the yellowwhite cliffs. Sometimes the wind moaned in the rock crevices; sometimes it rustled softly in the first yellow grasses of spring. It was a lonely and an old land.

The sooing south wind was especially haunting. It made him cry sometimes. It played old harps in his head. It made him wonder at the good of it all. What did a man really live for? Today's meat? Tomorrow's journey? Or what?

It was a cinch there was no life if a child sat still and failed to eat and sleep. There was life only if a man was on the move, ae, on the run even. Crawling, walking, running. Journeying, journeying, journeying. Always on the go. Heading toward a Somewhere that always and ever in the end turned out to be a Nowhere. For what? For a God? For a Devil? For a Man? For a Beast?

Or was it merely for Mister Stomach and his ability to beget other Mister Stomachs?

" 'Tis so. Friend stomach has little patience with

309

queersome notions. This child's seen it. Little patience."

What about the Lord's vengeance he was supposed to be getting for Him? Or, for a fact, his own private revenge?

Hugh didn't know. Sitting in the moonlight on a rock overlooking a gutted saffron valley of a million acres, with Vampire Peak and Cedar Butte rearing up over the far wall beyond and the driving south wind playing organ music in the great pipes of the deep earth, Hugh didn't know.

"Maybe it's neither one that shines. Neither the Lord's vengeance nor this child's miserable revenge. This child feels queer, he does, like a buffler shot in the lights, thinkin' on it. I've knocked about these free mountains from as far north as Missouri's head to as far south as the starvin' Gila, and I still don't know. And if life deals fair a-tall, this child'll pro'bly never know." Hugh slowly tolled his white hoar head in the moonlight. "Maybe the ants *has* the answer, as the Good Book says. Dig, eat nits, and hide in the dark when somebody steps on the mound overhead. 'Tis so."

The rock he sat on was perched on the very tip of the south wall. Wind and rain had honed it into the shape of a crude grampa's chair, with a high back and wide armrests, and a rough footstool beneath. A stunted wizened cedar, clinging to a crevice, rustled beside him like a nervous green parrot ruffling its feathers.

Overhead, the full moon moved through the silverblue skies of night. Below, shadows replaced shades, shades chased shadows; points of light replaced spots of white, spots of white chased points of light.

After a while the moon seemed to stand still in the fantastic valley, while the moonwhite peaks and the ghostly spires and the trembling pinnacles moved, began to sail by, all of them like silent icebergs lost in hard open land.

Hugh saw old ships, three-masters and four-masters,

sail serenely by. Below and hard on the right, chasing a prize Spanish galleon, drove Pirate Lafitte's favorite ship, *The Pride*. Hugh shivered at the likeness. It brought back haunting memories of butchery and murder, rapine and looting. The fluttering silverwhite sails of *The Pride* seemed to be gaining on the ghostly sails of the three-decker Spanish galleon. The sea even rippled with whitecaps.

Hugh blinked, and in an instant the scene was no longer a sea but a city with gold-walled castles and delicate white minarets and soaring towers and serrated battle walls. The Seven Cities of Cibola at last? He could see priests and men, duennas and maidens, and all dressed in silver-trimmed black, strolling through the streets.

Hugh blinked, and in another instant he was looking upon a vast graveyard with a thousand kingly monuments of polished white marble. There were tombs for nobles and sarcophagi for popes and single lonely dazzling white pillars for virgins and lofty pyramids for long-dead Egyptian Josephs.

Hugh blinked, and in still another instant he was looking upon a sea of faces. There was the old she-rip Mabel, mouth wide in a bellow for him to take up the harness and support her and the lads. There were the lads themselves, still looking to him for a way of going in a woman-run world. And that crook Jacob and fair-haired Esau. And Pirate Lafitte dressed in black and his gang of scarred cutthroat buccaneers. And Clint, eating an antelope with a Comanche face. And Clint again, besplintered on the Platte and screaming the minute he became a flaming torch to the delight of the Pawnees. And Augie Neill and Jim Anderson, lips moving in soundless appeal for help. And sweet lad Johnnie Gardner, so full of holes he was made a riddle of before he was dead. And the laugher Marsh, with his neck broken and his head askew and hanging down his back, smiling ludicrously at his own fleeing. And the boy Jim Bridger

ready to strike with his great fist again, at last a man.
And blackhearted Fitz, still enjoying a life he no
longer deserved.

"Yes, Fitz, enjoy life while you may. This child's
comin' to get you."

Hugh suddenly caught himself trembling and sweating.

"Whoa there, lad," Hugh said, jumping up. "Steady
as you go. You've got to hold your noddle steady on
Reed and Fort Kiowa, lad, or by the bull barley it's
over the hills and far away for you."

Hugh climbed down from the high place, walked east
along the rim of the wall.

" 'Tis a bad place for a bad conscience, it is."

Walking, he watched the changing shapes and shadows, the lights and whites, moondaft and marveling to
see still other mirages parading past.

" 'Tis a place where the Lord is likely to come to a
man in a visitation. Or come to wrestle with a child
and touch him on the hip and change his name from
Jacob to Israel."

Walking, he watched a certain draw rise and fall between the thinnest of parallel fluted columns, a column
colored rose and a column colored cream and a column
colored milkwhite. " 'Tis a church, it is. A church to
stand silent in while waiting for the Word."

He swung on, intending to cut away from the rim of
the wall, yet not being able to, irresistibly drawn by the
old shattered hulks riding at anchor in the graveyard of
the Heavenly Shipwright.

"I feel clean," he said, pulling on his whitening
beard. "Clean."

Walking, he watched another ship ride by, in full
sail, jib flying, spanker rattling, mizzen royal popping,
a triumph of building genius and a glory of the seas.

"Steady, Hugh. It's time to ask what's trump and
whose the deal."

Then, like an Indian at parting, he walked away from
it without waving good-by.

*　　*　　*

One dawn, just south of White Clay Butte, where the Little White River came swinging in from the south, Hugh saw some fresh grizzly tracks. They were headed down river too.

That gave him pause.

He studied the tracks carefully. The prints were huge, and they dragged. There were no cub prints about. A he-grizzly. An Ephraim both old and huge.

The land about was bald save for a little patch of tufted buffalo grass growing on either side of the White. The grass was of a pale green hue and had short shriveled blades. Beneath the grass, in the roots, would probably be a few white grubs, perhaps a few ants, and maybe even a gopher or two. Ho-ah! That meant both he and the grizzly would soon begin eyeing each other as fair game, with the grizzly better armed. Lonely he-grizzlies rarely attacked man unless they were extremely hungry. But hard barren ground could have only one effect on the grizzly—kill the first thing it saw moving.

At the same time Hugh saw that he couldn't very well leave the White for, say, the Bad River to the north. He'd have to cross hard-pan stone-cropped prairie every bit as cracked and dry and merciless as the hogbacks between the Grand and the Moreau, and the Moreau and the Cheyenne, and he'd had enough of that kind of travel, even if he did have full use of both his legs again.

Hugh decided to sleep on it. It was day; he had walked a full long night, and he needed a rest. So he drank a few swallows of chalky salty White, caught a gopher and roasted it, and crawled into a shadowy cave under the north riverbank.

He woke well before sunset. And he woke feeling queersome. Something had altered while he slept.

Cautiously he crept out of his hole. He looked up river and down river. He searched the opposite bank. He examined the bank behind him, casting uneasy glances toward White Clay Butte. There was nothing so far as he could see.

Yet he was conscious that something had altered.

He thought on it awhile, watching the sunlight slanting lower and lower across the running dirty-cream water, and finally decided he couldn't wait on something he couldn't see. "What this child don't see he don't know."

He elected to follow the river again and so willynilly had to follow the grizzly tracks. He hoped Old Ephraim had rambled on right lively during the night and so had left him far behind. Or else had turned aside, either north or south, across the country.

A mile down the river he came upon a prairie-dog village. It was all torn up. The grizzly'd had himself a feast. He'd cuffed and clubbed out about an acre of mounds. Gray dried pelts and dry clots of blood and freshly dug-out mounds of pale gray dirt lay in every direction.

"Ho-ah! So Old Ephe's et, has he? Maybe now he won't have a hankerin' for this child's liver."

Hugh tromped over the torn up sour soil. It was a small village and such live prairie dogs as were left were cowed and had skulked deep in their burrows. The yellow sun was almost down and each pale gray mound cast a grayblack shadow.

Off to one side he found a half-dead prairie dog that Old Ephe had missed. Hugh pounced on it. Meat.

He skinned it and built a small stinking fire out of driftwood cast up on the treeless shores. While he ate, the live prairie dogs behind him at last dared to come out of their burrows. They scolded him furiously. Their wifelike yapping made hirn feel uncomfortable.

When he set off for the night again he noticed that the grizzly's tracks led directly from the prairie-dog village to the river, and then vanished. Hugh crossed the river twice, going both up and down stream on both sides of the river, but still couldn't find trace of which way Old Ephe had gone.

Hugh decided not to worry about Old Ephe until he should meet him face to face. "What this child don't see he don't know. Reed's only four, five days away now."

He tramped on. The earth turned away from the big sun, and yellow light became rusty dusk, and stars came out to belittle man and all his worming trails.

He tramped on. The earth turned toward the full moon, and soon darkness became silver luminescence again, and stars paled in the silverblue sky.

The riverbanks and the sloping sides of the White valley held bare. There were no trees, no bushes, no carpets of grass. If there hadn't been occasional Dakota prickly-pear cactus underfoot and the moon a hanging ball of pure silver in the eastern heavens, Hugh could easily have mistaken himself for that first interstellar traveler at last wandering across the face of the moon, afoot and musing in its lifeless valleys.

He'd had a good long drink from a fresh spring, miraculously spilling out of the north wall of the White valley, when he noticed it. And for a few seconds he thought himself back in the wind-hewn grampa chair overlooking the valley of the Badlands with its draws full of riding ghostships and its sea of phantasm faces. Because what he saw when he looked back was a silver shape walking along behind him in the silver light in the silver valley of the White. And the shape was only a score of steps behind him.

Bewitched and gone loco at last, he was. It was one thing to make imaginary ships and faces out of fantastic eroded land, ae, but it was another to have one of the silver shapes crawl out of the Badlands valley and follow him down the White. Ae, he'd gone loco, he had.

He wished for his rifle, Old Bullthrower. A flying pill from Old Bullthrower would soon settle whether it was a ghost or critter or companyero or what.

Worse yet, the shape resembled a silvertip, a grizzly

the size of a great bull. Had Old Ephraim, who yesterday preceded him down the White and who plundered
the prairie-dog village, had he got scent of Hugh and
so taken to pursuing him?

Hugh decided to test his senses.

Hugh took a step toward it, and stopped. The silver
shape backed a step, and stopped.

Hugh blinked. Who ever heard of a grizzly playing
follow-the-leader?

"Best hurry to Reed afore it gets worse," he murmured within his white whiskers.

He turned his back on the silvertip and once again
headed for Ft. Kiowa.

A hundred steps later, Hugh looked over his shoulder. Companyero Old Ephe was still a score of steps
behind him, following him slow step for slow step, a
silver shape in the silver light in the silver valley of
the White.

Hugh stopped dead. Ephraim stopped dead.

" 'Tis a mirage," Hugh said aloud. "Like what this
child and his companyero Clint saw on the Brazos after
Clint helped himself to that antelope with a Comanche face."

Hugh started up again. Gravel rattled underfoot. The
shape started up again. Gravel rattled under its claws.

"Ho-ah!" Hugh said aloud. "Now I see a different
light."

Hugh took a dozen steps to his left, toward the white-
yellow cliffs to the north of the river. Old Ephraim took
a dozen steps.

Hugh took a dozen steps to his right, toward the
riverbank. Old Ephraim took a dozen steps.

Hugh stood facing the silver shape.

The silver grizzly stood facing him.

"What be ye? Shape? Critter? The devil himself
come to haunt me in a bearskin?"

The silvertip lifted its flat snout and sniffed the air.

" 'Tis a critter," Hugh said. He trembled. He preferred the haunt.

There was one other test. He could ignore Old Ephraim.

He tried it. Resolutely, without a backward glance, his back a continual shiver of flesh, he began marching down the river, the fringes of his elkskin hunting shirt threshing gently at each step. Gravel crunched underfoot. Sand crinched. He walked across bars of gray silt, and beaches of sand, and up banks of flour-fine loess, and across sunbaked flats of wild salt.

He looked back. Step for step, bar for bar, beach for beach, the silvertip—or was it a silver shape?—had followed him all the way, its front feet padding along dog-fashion and its rear feet lifting along grampa-style.

He shook. With all his talk of Lord's vengeance, maybe at that the Lord Himself had come down to make him a visitation, to teach him forcibly that he was not an Esau after all but a Jacob, that after he'd wrestled with the silver shape until break of day, against which he would not prevail, the silver shape would touch the hollow of his thigh and he'd be cripple again.

"Let me go," Hugh cried.

"Go," the valley answered.

"What mout your name be?"

"Be," the valley answered.

Again Hugh faced ahead, and led the way down the White.

They came to a thick grove of cottonwood, brush, saplings, old boles. A stream of fresh water fed the trees. In the silver night the leaves tingled silver.

"Ah," Hugh said, "maybe now I lose him."

Ten minutes later he emerged from the grove. When he looked back, the silvertip—or was it a silver shape?—had vanished.

"Ah," Hugh said, "he's run across a better scent. Good. May it be a dozen antelope so he'll have more than his fill."

Dawn broke pink, and he supped on gopher, and drank fresh water from the stream, and went to sleep in a bed of leaves under a bullberry bush.

When he awoke in midafternoon, after he'd break-fasted on gopher, he found the grizzly tracks again. The tracks were headed straight for Ft. Kiowa.

Then Hugh had enough of it. He decided to kill the grizzly. He drew his knife.

He tracked Old Ephraim carefully, following him along the winding riverbank, across sand bars, through groves of cottonwood, skinning knife flashing in the evening sun.

At the third grove he lost all track of him. The claw prints trailed clearly up to a little spring, then disap-peared as if tracks, grizzly and all, had been washed away into the White.

Hugh couldn't cipher it. The little spring poured out of a rock some forty feet from the bank of the White, and trickled flashing across a flat bed of gold sand and beneath a grove of stately cottonwoods, and dropped splashing a few feet into the river. No matter how often he surveyed both sides of the sparkling streamlet, he couldn't find a trace of where Old Ephraim had left the stream.

"Another Ascension, that's it," Hugh said smiling to himself. "Or else a grizzly finally climbed a tree."

He was about to go on when his eye caught move-ment ahead. Some twenty feet on the other side of the streaming spring lay the fat bole of a fallen cottonwood patriarch. The old tree was at least four feet through. Looking carefully Hugh noticed that the edge of the whiteocher bark along the top seemed blurred, as if somehow it had grown silver fur which a breeze was ruffling.

Fur?

Hugh stood puzzling.

Just then, with a snort, with a grunt like a laugh at having been discovered, Old Ephraim jumped up from his hiding place and galloped away down the river. Every now and then Old Ephraim tossed his big dog-head this way and that as if he couldn't get over the humor of it.

Hugh said, "You know, to play a joke like that on me, Old Ephe must've liked me." Hugh looked from the fallen tree to the flowing spring and back to the fallen tree again. "He must've jumped all of twenty-five feet."

Fifteen days after he'd climbed out of the snake's den beside the Platte, in May, the Moon of Planting, Hugh reached Ft. Kiowa on the Missouri.

His moccasins were worn to shreds. He was gaunt. He was white.

When Hugh stuck his old hoar head into Bending Reed's tepee, Bending Reed clapped a hand to her mouth, slant Siberian eyes stating in surprise at the pure white of his whiskers. "White Grizzly," she managed to get out at last.

"'Tis white you see all right, Reed. White. But it ain't a grizzly robe like last time. It won't pull off. This child's still an Esau." Hugh humphed to himself. "He hopes."

"Heyoka?"

"No, not Heyoka," Hugh said. "Esau." Then Hugh added, "Reed, put on the pot. Tomorrow I catch me a boat for Fort Atkinson. I've been saved special again."

Chapter 7

Gen'ral, my minds made up. You're not going to talk me out of gettin' Fitz next time I see him." Hugh banged a big hairy fist on a buckskin knee. "That's my right."

" 'Right'? 'Rights'?" General Ashley exclaimed, mild blue eyes suddenly snapping blue sparks. "The only rights you have are those I allowed you when I hired you."

The two were sitting alone in the officers' brick quarters in the center of Ft. Atkinson. It was almost noon, and the sun coming in through the oiled paper which did for glass panes gave both their wrinkled brows a lardlike texture. It was also very hot and sultry out, and both men were sweating profusely. The general's blue Missouri state militia uniform was blotched with black rings, especially under the armpits, while Hugh's yellowbrown leathers were spotted with acid-edged dark brown rings. Ashley sat on the forward edge of a four-legged handhewn chair, facing Hugh, who also sat on the forward edge of a chair. Beside them on a table was a half-empty bottle of whisky and two tin cups still partly filled.

Hugh raised his white head as if he were a predator grizzly about to jump Ashley. "Then I quit your consarn. Here and now. So I can take that right."

"But why?"

"Because I've a right to it."

Outside a mule brayed on the parade ground.

"But why? Are you God or something?"

"No, not quite God. But I've had sign He saved me special to get Fitz."

"Oh that's nonsense. Preacher's rubbish."

Again Hugh lifted his bushy white head as if he were about to tear into Ashley. "Gen'ral, out here in the middle of nowhere, full of red devils and varmints, mountain-man code says I've got that right."

"Wait, wait, Hugh!" Ashley held up a slim soft hand, blond face an anxious red and kind mild blue eyes crinkled with worry. Ashley moved forward to the very edge of his teetery chair. "Hugh, I know just how you feel—"

"Gen'ral, you're a liar. You don't know how I feel. Because if you did you'd take my part." Hugh picked up his tin cup from the log table, and angrily swilled the brown liquor in it around a few times, and finished it off in a single throw.

Ashley jerked upright, sat back in his chair. "I'm a what?" A quick shrewd look passed over his blond face. "So you've quit my concern, eh? All right. If you've quit, then I'm turning you over to General Leavenworth of the U.S. Army."

Hugh sat risen with whisky and hate. He hadn't wanted to talk to Ashley, knowing what Ashley would say. But Ashley had insisted, promising Hugh good whisky as well as some back pay due him, and so Hugh had consented. Hugh knew that Ashley would use every means in his power to block his vengeance.

A mule brayed outside on the parade ground.

Hugh set his empty tin cup on the table. He sat twisting his wolfskin cap around and around on his buckskin-covered knee. The white whiskers around his mouth moved as he ground his teeth together. His restless old gray eyes glowered stubborn at Ashley. Hugh knew what he was up against. Either a man belonged to a fur-trading firm or the U.S. Army had control of his movements. No unattached white man could hang around or travel in Indian territory unless he had a permit. If he killed Fitz as a member of Ashley's firm, Ashley would punish him. If he killed Fitz as a ward of the U.S. Army, the U.S. Army would punish him. Hugh cursed inwardly. He boiled at the thought of Ashley sitting in his way. Inwardly he railed at the whole business of interference by the settlements of the East and their laws. Until the big fur companies and the Army had moved in, he and his companyeros, the free trappers, had been free to render right as they saw fit, according to horse sense and the code of the free wild. Hugh wished now he hadn't shown up at Ft. Atkinson. Fitz hadn't been there when he arrived, and ever since everything and everybody had worked to forestall his and the Lord's vengeance. And rumor even had it that Fitz wouldn't be around until late in the summer, when he was expected to come in with the spring catch of beaver from both Captain Diah Smith and Major Henry. It meant a whole hot summer of lying around doing nothing. And yet, where else was he sure of catching up with Fitz but at Ft. Atkinson? He was trapped, blocked, crossed all around.

"Hugh," General Ashley said, softening his voice and putting a soft small hand in friendly fashion on Hugh's leather-covered knee, "Hugh, like I've said before, why don't you go back up to Fort Kiowa? You'll be happier up there with Reed and hunting for the fort. And along with that you've got my proposition."

"What proposition?" Hugh snapped, brushing the general's white hand aside. "That I spy on Astor's boys for you? Not this child. I wasn't meant for such skunk's work."

General Ashley flushed. "I'll make it worth your while, Hugh."

A great snort exploded from Hugh. "Hire Fitz for such work, why don't you? He's the kind of sneak who'd do a good job for you."

General Ashley flushed very red and fresh beads of sweat broke out all over his fairskinned face. "Hugh, you've got Fitz all wrong. I don't know just what did happen on the forks of the Grand, but I'm sure Fitz must have his side of the story too."

"Gen'ral, are you callin' this child a liar?"

"No, no. Not that at all. Just that I can't conceive of Fitz doing such a thing. Not my Fitz. Why Fitz's been like a rock to me. Without him and a couple of others I can name, like Diah and the major and Tom Fitzpatrick and the lad Jim Bridger, I don't know what I would have done. The whole concern would have flopped long ago without them. Fitz all alone brought in an important message from the major at Henry's Post on the Yellowstone and Missouri. Then last winter Fitz brought another message from Diah, south of the Big Horn, to the major, north of the Big Horns. And still later he brought me still another very important message from the major, all the way from the Big Horns there to me here on the Missouri. And then, mind you, and then he turned right around and offered to lead a pack train back to the Wind River Mountains for the rendezvous which the boys are probably holding right now this very minute." General Ashley shook his head slowly, tollingly. His blond hair slid forward out of its smooth combing. "And then, there's all that book work Fitz does for me. Untangling accounts I just can't make head nor tail of. And that makes Fitz doubly valuable to me. He's a first-rate mountain man plus being a first-rate bookkeeper." General Ashley took out a big white linen handkerchief and mopped his brow. "No, Hugh, Fitz's been a rock to me. Simply a rock. And all I can say is, he must've had his reasons for doing what he did on the Grand. And I'm standing by him."

Hugh sat stubborn, swollen. Hugh hated the mention of Fitz's proficiency as a bookkeeper. He begrudged Fitz his education. "Why did he lie to the major then, Gen'ral, if he was so smart and had such a good reason to leave me die alone?"

"Oh, now, Hugh, be the bigger man in this. Maybe

Fitz did make a slight mistake there on the Grand,
but—"

" 'Slight mistake'? Fitz left me to die alone, and you
call that a slight mistake?" Hugh exploded, white brows
lifted, eyes wild.

"I mean," General Ashley hastily added, "I mean, a
man's allowed—"

"He deserted me, Gen'ral, and this child ain't for-
gettin' it. I'm killin' him on sight."

General Ashley sat very still in his chair. "After all,
Hugh," he began slowly, "after all, Hugh, you left the
party against orders when you went hunting alone. It
was really your own neck after that. Everybody knew
that. And certainly Fitz did. It was more or less your
own fault when you got mauled by the grizzly."

Hugh burned. The mahogany color of the skin over
his cheeks turned black. "Suppose I did disobey orders,
Gen'ral? Does that excuse a man for desertin' a companyero? When the night before the same companyero
covered up for him when he and Jim slept on watch?"

General Ashley's mild blue eyes opened very wide.
"He and Jim slept on guard?"

"Yes they did. And I covered for 'em. There was no
harm done, not much anyway, and so I did it. You know
what the major would have done had he caught 'em."

General Ashley gave Hugh a long searching look.
Slowly he shook his head. "Then maybe you're doubly
to fault."

"How so?"

"You should have turned them in. Another mistake
like that and it might have cost you all your lives."
Ashley shuddered at the thought of it.

"But it didn't, Gen'ral. And Fitz and Jim owed me
that much at least."

Ashley sighed. He picked up the bottle of whisky and
refilled their tin cups. "Hugh, have another on me."

"Thanks. I will."

They both drank up.

A mule brayed lonesomely out on the fort's parade ground.

Ashley licked his lips. He looked at Hugh soberly for a while; finally said, "Hugh, when are you going to shave off those whiskers?"

"When my beard turns black again."

"Hugh. Hugh. What a stubborn mule you are. With that bush of white grampa bristle should also go the wisdom of a grampa. Hugh, act the forgiving granpappy to the boys. You came out of it alive. So what do you care?"

"And forget how I woke up lookin' at buzzards? Forget what it felt like looking at my own open grave? Forget how I burned and suffered crawlin' back to Fort Kiowa? Forget that Fitz stole my gun and flint and steel and knife from me? Forget how he deserted me and left me to die the hard way? Forget all that?" Hugh leaped to his feet. The little arteries down either side of his nose ran deep red. He towered massive and grizzly over gentle, mild General Ashley. "Gen'ral, what in tarnation are you askin' this child to do? Give up everythin' he is?" Hugh slapped his huge chest. "Gen'ral, this hoss has feelin's here!"

General Ashley's mild blue eyes held up to Hugh. "Hugh, those feelings you say you have, are they nothing but hate?"

"What?"

"Don't you have any feelings of kindness to go along with those feelings of hate? You have no forgiveness in you at all? You've never made a mistake you couldn't help?"

Hugh's eyes opened very wide. Hugh remembered a mistake he couldn't help all right. There was that time when he'd been a one-bite cannibal with companyero Clint. But Hugh pushed the memory down. And instead he said, "Gen'ral the trouble with you is, you didn't crawl from the forks of the Grand to Fort Kiowa like I did."

"Hugh, it's too bad you never had boys of your own. Then you might have been more tolerant. Like a good father should be. Who'd know his boys were bound to get into some kind of trouble sooner or later."

Then Hugh also abruptly remembered the two sons he'd deserted back in Lancaster—and, trembling, shut up.

General Ashley stood up slowly. He pulled down the coat of his blue uniform. The gold braid on his shoulders gleamed dully. "Hugh, I saw men die. My men. And what did they die for? For me. For me and my money. Just money, just me. I'll never forget that. Not till my dying day. My conscience is heavy with it. That's why I'm trying to save all the life I can. Fitz's life. Your life. The lives of all my men."

Hugh swelled with an involuntary deep breath. The tremendous breath made him dizzy and he almost fell over. A pain like a heart attack exploded in his chest again.

Hugh righted himself by gripping the back of his handhewn chair. He checked a terrible impulse to pick up the chair and hit the general with it.

Suddenly he turned and clapped on his wolfskin and picked up his rifle standing at the door and went out.

Again a mule brayed out on the fort's parade ground.

Fort Atkinson was the largest military outpost on the Missouri north of St. Louis. It had been built on a high flat bench on the west side of the river. The north end of the high flat bench squared off into a cliff known as Council Bluff. The whole bench afforded a commanding view of the river.

The location was strategic both commercially and militarily. It was at Council Bluff where the Omaha and the Pawnee and the Dakota tribes already in old times met in council to settle their differences or to declare war, and where Lewis and Clark conferred with various Indian tribes early in the century. It was at the fort that General Leavenworth got the news of Ashley's defeat at the hands of the Rees on the Missouri just above the Grand. It was at the fort that trappers and hunters got their last provisions before striking out into the unknown, either north up the river or west to where the Platte came in from the Rockies.

The flat bench fell off sharply into cliffs on three sides: on the east directly into the sudsing tan waters of the Missouri, and on the south and the west into a draw called Hook's Hollow. The steep cliffs, along with a stockade across the north end, made the fort impregnable to all Indian attack.

A wagon way led up from the dock on the rushing Missouri, climbing up toward the southeast corner of the flat bench, going past a blacksmith shop and lime kiln on the right and a brickyard and the mouth of Hook's Hollow on the left. The wagon way headed directly for the gate between a commission house and a long soldiers' barracks, and once up on level ground, curved past a well, a flagstaff, the brick officers' quarters, crossed the parade ground, and ended in front of the cookhouse on the west side. The cookhouse and more soldiers' barracks formed a fine defensive angle on the northwest corner of the parade ground, and the artillery barracks and a hospital formed another excellent defensive angle on the northeast. Beyond to the north were the stables, and then came the stockade. The fort even boasted a school for the officers' children, and a library for the studious, and a confectionery for the sweettooths.

A mile to the west the land lifted into a considerable ridge, from which reared a flagpole above a lookout. From the lookout tower a sentinel could see many miles in any direction: west out to the endless flat tableland prairies along the banks of the Platte, north out to where the rushing tan Missouri came doubling and redoubling out of bluff-ruffled gray loess terrain, east out to where rolling loess lay cut by raveling streams, and south out to where the Missouri pushed relentlessly through more bluff-rimpled valleys.

The late June sun struck straight down into the fort. There were no shadows along the north sides of the whitewashed brick buildings. Grass had long ago dried to wisps. A faint haze of dust hung in the heat-simmering air. A company of blue-clad riflemen drilled on the center parade ground, the silver shako plates on their high bell-crowned leather caps glittering in the sun. Near the cookhouse, carters were busy hollering and hawing at stubborn ringtail mules. Near the stables, fox-eyed traders were swopping for both the joy of it and for a living. Between the soldiers' barracks and the cookhouse on the southwest corner, hunters came in through the open gate carrying limp carcasses of elk and deer and wild fowl. Trappers in greasy leathers and pulldown hats argued over traps and pelts. Solemn Indians watched everything that moved, with sun-narrowed glittering dark eyes. The fort was a perfumery of various hide smells, beaver and elk and deer and buffalo and bear; and a color fair of buckskin browns and yellows and warpaint greens and vermilions and soldier blues and silvers and flannel reds and jean blues and boot browns; and a soundfest of men bragging and swearing and mules braying and hinnying and horses blowing and stamping and dogs barking and roaring.

Outside the fort, below the southeast corner of the drop-off, like ants busily scratching in and out of mounds, men scurried back and forth from lime kiln to brickyard to lime kiln again. Still others hurried like ants in and out of sawmills and rock quarries and grist mills, intent on doing yesterday's and tomorrow's work today.

It was into this lively hurlyburly that Hugh stepped when he left General Ashley in the officers' quarters. The sight and the smell of it made him feel both savage and weary.

He stopped on the bottom step, a halved log, and inwardly growled at it. What was the good of it, the bustle and the doings, as long as he hadn't gotten his rights? The general had given him some back pay, had outfitted him with a second-hand rifle and an old mule, and had fixed him up with a job hunting for the fort; but such things were trifles as long as he hadn't squared accounts with Fitz, and the lad Jim who still had his life on loan to him.

It made Hugh burn all the more to learn that Fitz had taken over his friend and favorite, Old Bullthrower his rifle, and his companyero of the trails, Old Blue. The nerve of the skunk almost made Hugh jump for rage. Ae, Fitz would get his all right, all right, come time he showed his face in the fort.

Hugh let out a great blast of breath. "If that snake Fitz was standing here in front of me right now, I'd centershoot him on the spot, and then go to my bunk and have myself a long restful sleep. I would."

Hugh let out another breath, and then headed for his old mule. He walked past a group of keelboatmen just in from St. Louis playing euchre and seven-up, around a quintet of bareskinned Omaha bucks playing a game of hand on the bare parade ground, and at last came to the hitching posts near the southwest gate beside the soldiers' barracks where his old mousegray mule, Heyoka, drooped sleeping on her feet.

"Hep-a! Heyoka, ol' girl!" Hugh said, slapping the contrary old bag of bones on the rump, "hep-a! We'd best mosey on, ol' skate, and get us some more meat, or the gen'ral'll pasture us both out to the wolves." At the clap on her rump, the old mule woke up and automatically lashed out with a flicking, surprisingly swift rear hoof. The hoof missed Hugh because, like always, he allowed for it. "Still up to your old tricks, eh?" Hugh gave the old skeleton another clap, hit her mangy mousegray fur so hard he raised skin dust and dandruff. Old Heyoka's deer head came up, her huge jack-rabbit ears lay back as if set to run, and her roached mane shivered and rippled nervously. This time, instead of lashing out with a hoof again, she suddenly reared up, snapped her hitching strap, and was free.

Old Heyoka didn't waste time. She wheeled around, began clopping lickety-split for the open fort gate and for freedom out on the open plains. Hugh's mouth fell open, watching her go.

There were joshing loiterers at the gate. One of them, a peachfuzz pigeon-toed greenhorn just in from Kentucky diggings, and still as goodhearted and helpful as the day he left ma, jumped up and in two long leaps blocked Old Heyoka's path. Ears down, the old mule tried to shy past anyway. But she wasn't quite quick enough. With another tremendous leap, the pigeon-toed peachfuzz caught hold of what was left of her leather hitching strap and hung on. And, heels digging in, dragged her to a stop just outside the gate.

Hugh's mouth clapped to, and he strode over to repossess his mule.

Hugh was hardly in the mood to thank anyone, let alone a boy greenhorn. He grabbed hold of the mule's bridle, whirled on the peachfuzz, and like a she-grizzly giving her cub a claw to put it in its place, snarled, "What's it of your concern if my ol' skate breaks? Maybe she had a free day comin'."

The youth's light green eyes and red mouth opened like morning glories. "Whaaat?"

"Listen, you darned pigeon-toed greenhorn you, when you see a man's mount runnin' off, don't stop it. Let it go to the devil if it wants to. It ain't your'n, so let it go."

"But I thought—"

"Never mind what you thought. It's what I think that counts this time." Hugh stuck his old white face into the lad's young peachfuzz face. "And let me tell you somethin' else. If'n you're intendin' to make a go of it out here in the middle of nowhere, stick to your own business. Like when you see a man's possible sack fall off his saddle on the trail—don't tell him. He'll find out soon enough. When you get to camp, if you ever do, still keep your meattrap shut. Why? because you're a greenhorn. When the cook needs water and wood, help him, but don't get in his way or say a word. If the horses need hobblin' or waterin', do it, but don't brag about it. Just do it. And shut up. When you set down to the fire, get out your pipe and smoke it and shut up some more. Don't ask questions. Follow that advice and you'll pass."

"But I was only—"

"Shut up!"

A familiar voice broke in then. "Well, well, look who's orderin' people around now." The voice was slow and cracked. It came from a voicebox that hadn't been used in a long time.

Hugh turned slowly on his heels. Coming toward him off the open green prairie was a haggard black-bearded man with floppy ears and sun-blackened knobby hands. His buckskins were in tatters and his worn-out moccasins flopped around his ankles and his feet were red and cracked and bleeding. His eyes were great round moons of suffering. He carried a rusted gun and an empty shot pouch and a dangling powder horn.

"Don't you remember me, Hugh, old coon?"

"Dutton, old hoss! Down here?" Hugh exclaimed, glad to change the subject, and for the moment joyfully relieved that at least one of his men had come through. "And I was sure you'd gone under with the rest! Marsh, More, Chapman."

"Wal, at that this child was mighty nigh losin' his hair, he was."

"Still lookin' at the downside a things, I see."

Dutton's shoulders hung sloped down and away as if they'd been folded against his body like bird wings. "I'll allow to havin' my green rubbed out a little." Dutton tried to smile. "A little."

Still hanging onto the hitching strap of Old Heyoka, who'd fallen asleep again on her feet, Hugh said, "Come along. I'll take ye in to the gen'ral. I'll bet you're half-froze for meat." Hugh looked the walking scarecrow named Dutton up and down. "Lad, ye must tell me about the whole consarn."

Dutton hung back. A private thought of some kind lurked far back in his gray-ringed haggard eyes. "Thanks, Hugh, old hoss. I've made it alone so far, so I think maybe I can make it alone the rest of the way."

"Ho-ah! another contrary hoss, I see."

"No, still half-beat and not yet ready to square off to a chair. I want to get used to bein' here alive and safe first."

"How did you come? Down the Platte?"

"Did so." Dutton's voice, as it warmed to the task of talking again, slowly lost its cracked edge.

"And the Pawnee didn't catch ee?"

"Hunkered past 'em in the night."

"What was grub?"

"Grass and gopher."

" 'Twas the same by me. All along the White."

"The White, was it?"

Hugh nodded. "Yep, and wild salt it was mostly too. Tell me, old hoss, how did you get away when the Rees came swarmin' across the river?"

"Your Ol' Skunk broke from the Rees and I boarded her and did it."

"Ho-ah! I knew she had leg. Where's she now?"

Dutton rubbed his hollow belly. "Et."

" 'Et'?"

"Yep. Just afore I hit the Pawnee."

Hugh shook his head sadly. "Too bad. She was a good horse once I tamed her."

Dutton looked up at Hugh wonderingly, with still a certain private thought lurking far back in his eyes. "Hugh, old coon, ye've turned white since the last time I seen ee. What happened?"

Hugh shrugged. "Yep, it's white I am now all right." Hugh laughed a half-laugh at himself. "The gen'ral's even takin' to callin' me granpap."

" 'Granpap'?"

"Yep." A dark thought flitted across Hugh's old gray eyes. "Yep, he wants me to forget Fitz's dirty black treachery."

"Then Fitz ain't here?"

Hugh hauled up short. "Hey? What? Oho! So that's the way the stick floats, does it? You was to warn Fitz afore I got to him."

Dutton blinked. Still slow of tongue and also slow of thought from the long ordeal of hiking across the barren flats of the Platte River bottom, Dutton barely caught on he'd made a slip. "Now, Hugh, I didn't mean harm. You know that. I was only askin'."

Hugh's old rage returned. "So this is how I'm practiced on, is it? Treachery and snakes all around. If it ain't Fitz and Jim, it's downside Dutton honey-fuggling the booshways."

"Now, Hugh, here now."

Hugh turned his back on Dutton. He climbed aboard the still sleeping Old Heyoka, and tucked his rifle under an arm, and kicked the old mule in the ribs. "Hep-a! Get! Let's make some meat."

"Hugh!" Dutton called after him.

"Hep-a!" Hugh growled again, digging his moccasined heels into Old Heyoka's underbelly. "Hep-a! Get!"

Old Heyoka was going before she finally opened a great dull purple eye. She switched her ringtail as she stilted slowly and laboriously away.

Some time later in the summer, as he was riding back to the fort across the prairies, Hugh saw another bearded scarecrow come stilting out of the shining shimmering west. Except that this walking scarecrow was more ghost than a pair of crossed sticks and old clothes. Hugh was in a prairie pothole, trying to flush out partridge, when he first saw him.

The gaunt man came on, head down, stumbling, shufflingly. His buckskins were in tatters and were bleached a dry hard leafbrown, and his feet were bare and cracked and bleeding too. The varnish on the stock of his gun had worn off and it was as bare as a weathered board. The gun barrel was rusted.

Hugh held Old Heyoka in. Fitz? At last? Hugh set his triggers.

The bearded gaunt man looked up. He gazed east, longingly, forlornly.

All at once the gaunt man seemed to see something electrifying. He raised a hand and croaked a strangled shout. It wasn't Hugh he was seeing because Hugh was to the north of him and still hidden in the pothole. And then the gaunt man swooned and fell to the ground.

Hugh glanced to the east to see what there was to see. Beyond the farthest edge of the waving windstroked yellowing grass, against the blue, the Stars and Stripes fluttered above Ft. Atkinson. The flag was all that could be seen of the fort lookout above the horizon. Hugh understood. He gave Old Heyoka a kick in the underbelly. "Hep-a. Get! Fitz or not, that hant needs help. Hep-a."

By the time slow Old Heyoka gained the rim of the grassy pothole, the gaunt man had got to his feet again, had faltered ahead a step, had fallen again. Twice more he got up and twice more he fell flat on his chest.

"Poor devil," Hugh muttered. "C'mon, hurry up you, you ol' skate. Hep-a!" Hugh hit the old mule with his quirt. "Mule or no, you probably wouldn't run even if it was your own colt staggerin' in, would ee?" Hugh let down his triggers.

The gaunt man finally gave up. He sat. He sat looking east toward the fluttering Stars and Stripes. Pus-streaked tears streamed down his weather-blackened terribly hollow face. His long dark brown hair hung to his shoulders. He was bare-headed. His hunger-hollowed face made his already large doming head look like a great skull crowned with a poorly fitted wig. His small dark blue eyes burned.

Hugh reined in the old mule and slid to the ground. Holding the reins in one hand and his rifle in the other, Hugh approached the sitting haunt with high light steps.

The bare brown-haired skull turned slowly. The dark blue eyes burned at Hugh; looked through him; focused behind Hugh's head.

"Jim!" Hugh suddenly exclaimed. "Jim Clyman! Here, lad, let me help you up."

"It's Hugh," Jim Clyman hoarsed. His voice, like Dutton's, was so unused to speech it hardly more than croaked.

"Yes, lad, Hugh it is. And he'll help ye get to the fort and meat."

Clyman's eyes continued to run slow painful pus-stained tears. Clyman shook his head to say he didn't want help. "I—just—stopped—to blow a—little."

"You is grit, you is. And them's the sort as kin have anythin' I got. On the prairie. Come, let me help you up on my old mule."

"Just—stopped—to—blow—a—little."

"Poor devil," Hugh said, as he caught Clyman under the arms from the rear and boosted him up on Old Heyoka. "A bag a wind couldn't weigh more."

"Just—stopped—to—blow—a—little." Gradually Clyman's voice began to lose its cracked catchy edge as it warmed to the task again. "I'll—be—all—right."

"Sure, old hoss. That's it. I know just how you feel." Hugh hit Old Heyoka on her dusty tail to set her into motion. "Hep-a! ol' skate. 'Tis a mercy run this time."

Clyman slowly turned his head and looked down at Hugh holding him up. "I—ain't—dreamin'?—Them—is—the—Stars—and—Stripes?"

"They are, lad. Fort Atkinson."

"Thank—God—for—that."

"Yes, thank God for that, lad."

Hugh continued to hold Clyman in the saddle as he walked beside the mule.

Clyman couldn't help talking, slow as it was. "You're—white—Hugh."

"That I am."

"And—you're—alive."

Hugh laughed shortly. " 'Tis so. Though there be some who've wished I'd stayed dead there on the Grand."

"Who?"

"Fitz and Jim."

Clyman glanced down at Hugh. Slowly he shook his head. "Not Fitz—and—Jim—Hugh.—Not—them."

Hugh said nothing. Instead he gave slow-stilting Old Heyoka another clap on her dusty ringtail rump.

When Hugh finally got Clyman into the fort, and up on a leather bed in his quarters, he wondered a little if he'd come along in time after all. Because Clyman looked like an old man, a huge hairy skull sitting in the midst of seemingly crumbling bones with only his small dark blue haunted eyes still alive.

But Clyman surprised him. Soup and whisky, and bread and buffalo hump, and a shave, soon revived him. Within a week's time he was able to walk from his leather bed to the mess room and back again three times each day. And within another week he could talk normally again. And he seemed to shed the aged look too, the first week regaining middle age and the second week his youth.

"Tell about the whole consarn," Hugh said one day as they sat smoking their pipes on the halved-log steps in front of their quarters. A saffron-bright September sun slanted warm upon them. Hugh was in his old leathers while Clyman leaned back in a fresh set of yellow fringed buckskins. The fort yard swarmed with busy carpenters and draymen and trappers. A mule brayed at a hitching post near the gate.

" 'Twasn't much," Clyman said slowly, sucking deep on his corncob pipe.

" 'Twas fair enough to kill ye," Hugh said, blowing out a little fog of smoke.

" 'Twas my own fault," Clyman said, looking beyond Hugh.

The mule honked again.

The sun warmed the backs of their hands as they held pipe to mouth.

Hugh said, "Who said it wasn't?"

Clyman blinked.

"Don't tell me that Fitz deserted you too?"

"No, not Fitz. He wasn't in it. No, 'twas Tom Fitzpatrick who was with me. Though 'twas myself that was foolish."

"Tell about the whole consarn," Hugh urged again, old gray eyes drawn up shrewd and wondering.

So Clyman told about it. How he and Tom Fitzpatrick scouted ahead of Captain Diah Smith's party packing beaver plew bound for the States; how they went down the Sweetwater looking for a place to cross; how, when they found a shallow place in the river, Clyman elected to stay with their plunder while Tom went back to guide Smith and company to the spot. Clyman built a bower in some willows and holed in. A few days later he heard voices and, looking out, spotted a war party of Indians. He didn't feel safe, so he left horse and plunder and walked backward from the place across open sands and hid in some rocks some distance from the stream. He hid out some eleven days waiting for the Indians to move away and for Tom and Diah Smith to come along. When he finally climbed out of his hideout, he found his horse and plunder gone. When Tom and Diah still didn't show up, he decided to follow the Sweetwater to where it flowed into the Platte, and then take the Platte across the long prairies to Ft. Atkinson on the Missouri. All he had to do was follow the river and he was sure to get in safely. It was summer, there was plenty of buffalo and game around, and he was well armed. And all would have gone well if he hadn't run into a Pawnee war party, who robbed him of everything except his gun and a little powder and a few balls. From then on Clyman gradually weakened into the stumbling cross Hugh had seen out of his prairie pothole. Clyman said he saw numerous bands of wild horses, and even creased one, but, like Hugh, had shot too low and had killed it. Clyman saw buffalo and managed to kill one. But the nearer he came to the fort the more barren and desolate and game-forsaken the country became.

"What was grub?" Hugh asked, between puffs on his pipe.

"Mostly grass and gopher."

" 'Twas the same with me. All the way to Fort Kiowa. And then along the White."

The mule brayed again.

Clyman looked at Hugh. "Drinkin' the White give you granpap hair, Hugh?"

Hugh's lips twisted and his white whiskers moved over his cheek. "Might have. Except a spook played with me all of forty mile."

Clyman nodded. "I've seen them too."

Hugh laughed. "If that grizzly got a good look at me he saw one too."

Clyman nodded some more.

Hugh said, "So it wasn't Fitz who deserted ye then?"

"Like I said, Hugh, 'twasn't Fitz but Tom who was with me." Clyman scowled. "And I wasn't deserted. Tom done his best and done right."

"Ye're sure?"

"As sure as I'm sittin' here." Again Clyman scowled. "Hugh, ye've sure got desertin' on the brain, ain't ye?"

Hugh fell silent.

Clyman clapped out his corncob in the palm of his

skinny bony hand. "Hugh, you've forgot you was young once."

"Meanin' what?"

"Meanin' we all left the States for a reason."

Hugh thought on it awhile. "What was your reason, Jim, if I may be askin'?"

Clyman also thought on it awhile. He sighed. "A woman. And a hankerin' to see the West."

"And why see the West?"

"Because it was out there. Because it drawed me. Because I wanted to be where I'd never been."

Hugh fell silent.

Clyman said, "And yours, Hugh?"

Hugh bit on his lips within his bush of a white beard. The white fur over his cheeks moved.

Clyman said, "Course 'tain't really none of my business, Hugh. I was just wonderin'."

Hugh saw them all right—Mabel and the two sons he'd deserted back in Lancaster. And seeing them clearly again in his mind's eye, he shivered.

Clyman seemed to read his mind. Or else he'd been talking with General Ashley. Clyman said, "It's too bad you never had kids of your own, Hugh. Then maybe you might have been able to take their side a little."

Hugh jumped to his feet. His voice was suddenly in a rage of agony, "But goddam it, Jim, I just can't seem to forget what them two miserable cowards done, stealin' my gun and knife and leavin' me to die alone! And lyin' to the major!"

Clyman put his pipe in his possible sack. He looked up at Hugh, looked through and around behind him. "Hugh, it's like I say. You've sure got desertin' on the brain, ain't ye?"

Keeping the fort supplied with meat kept Hugh and two other hunters humping every day of the week.

After they beat out the brush near the outpost, they

gradually extended their forays up and down the Missouri breaks.

Some days Hugh had to ride out more than twenty miles before he saw game at all. A couple of times he was gone for three days, riding out to a chosen spot one day, hunting the spot the second day, and coming in with the meat the third.

One of these chosen spots, and known only to him, was in a ravine some thirty miles up the river. The ravine ran back from the Missouri about a mile. It was some hundred yards wide, with steep sides some two hundred feet up, and heavily brushed over with prickly ash and wild gooseberry and mean blackberry and tall ash and slender elm. Like a park, the bottom of the ravine was comparatively treeless, with each tree grown out to its full umbrella potential. All of it was grassed over like an Eden. Through it meandered a flashing trout stream, running as clear and as pure as new glass over yellow black-speckled sands.

Hugh liked the place the first time he saw it, and so did his old mule, Heyoka. Hugh liked it because it was peaceful, with little or no sign of struggle, and because it reminded him vaguely of another time. Once Hugh even allowed to himself it would make a good place in which to build a log cabin come time he needed to settle down. And Old Heyoka on her part liked it because the grass was succulently tender and green, and the water fresh, and the shade cool. She also liked it because it was the one place her master allowed himself to loll on the grass hours on end. This gave her a chance to do what she most enjoyed: stand dozing on her feet in between feedings, her old dull purple eyes closed and long jack-rabbit ears folded down and ringtail switching automatically at an occasional passing fly. Because the spring ran briskly, and because there were no potholes or bogs around, there were no mosquitoes. Hugh called it Hidden Spring.

One day Hugh had bad luck. Somehow he just

couldn't seem to scare up a single blessed deer or rabbit. Even the usually busy squirrels were gone for the day. It made him wonder if he should read it as sign that red devils were about. And he might have considered the idea too if Old Heyoka had shown signs of uneasiness. Mules had a great sense of smell, especially for Indians, whom they seemed to fear more even than mountain lions and other varmints of the wild. But since Old Heyoka stilted along serenely and in her own slow way, and because the air was suckdry, which could account for the caution of wildlife, Hugh put the thought of danger from his mind. Besides, he was busy brooding on other matters.

The bright October sun had just passed high overhead when he gave up the hunt for the day. They were following the high west bank of the Missouri, going north. To the east lay the immane expanse of the rushing muddy river, some of its waters sheeting swiftly ahead, and some of it standing still, and some of it eddying backward. To the west of them, between the edge of the brown bankcut they stood on and the high bluffs a mile away, spread a thick fall-yellowed grove of ash and cottonwood and prickly brush.

" 'Tis no use, ol' skate. The critters has dug in, they has. Best wait until sun sets, when they'll all come out for that one last stretch afore they go to sleep. Or wait till mornin' for a new day and better chances."

Old Heyoka poked along, flopping first one ear and then the other.

"We'll camp out in Hidden Spring for the night. It's along here somewhere."

Old Heyoka plodded along, flopping first the other ear and then the one.

"Hep-a! let's head for it then," Hugh said, clapping her on the rump and hawing her half-around. "I see the openin' to it across the brush there." They headed into the grove.

Old Heyoka seemed to sense what was up. Both her

ears came up and her dull purple eyes opened full. She began to canter stiffly along.

Hugh glanced from left to right as they swung along. His triggers were set; his eyes naturally alert for the least movement. His eyes moved ceaselessly, noting the least tipping of a leaf, or passing mosquito, or far falling branch.

Every now and then, like hot water boiling over for a few seconds until the pressure was off, thoughts bubbled to the surface of his mind and broke into talk and gestures, meant for no one in particular, not even for his own ears.

"Someday, when this country gets settled up, long after my bones has fallen through my coffin, this country'll be just like all the rest of the white settlements east a here. And that's a miserable pity, that is. Such purty park country. But it's a comin'. Look where St. Lou is now."

Old Heyoka stroked along. The shade of a fluttering saffron-leaved cottonwood passed over them like a cloud shadow drifting over.

"Deceit. Selfishness. And the white girls looking and acting too much like pictures. Thievin'. Lyin'. One man set over against another. With the she-rips sittin' on top. No, this child don't want it nohow. As soon as that skunk Fitz shows, and I've had my right of him, this child's headin' upriver again. To Reed, and maybe beyond. No, there's nothing like life in the free mountains. This child considers it against nature to leave buffler and feed on hog."

Old Heyoka clopped along. The shade of a lemon-yellow ash darkened them for a dozen steps.

" 'Tis true, out here a man's time and his gone under is just ahead and around any turn, but this child still favors the free west." Hugh waggled his old head sharply from one side to another, almost shaking off his wolfskin cap. " 'Tis so. When I go, to show the kind of life I've lived in her, I'm gonna ask them to bury me standin' up. This child never yet looked up to any man, not in his day, and after I'm dead, I don't want anybody lookin' down and sayin', 'Here lies Ol' Hugh Glass.' No siree, not by the bull barley."

They entered the ravine. The brush up the bluff sides was stroked over with scarlet and eggyolk yellow. The spring trickled along briskly, the grass was still springgreen and as tender as pink-tinged lettuce, and the milkweed was flossed out with silver hair.

Old Heyoka slowed now and again to crop a mouthful of fresh grass.

"Hep-a," Hugh said, slapping her gently. "Up to the head there, lass, where's soft sand for this old back to lay in."

It was as warm as a barn in the little valley. It was silent. Senses slept.

Hugh hauled up just below where water welled out of the ground near the foot of a towering saffron fully umbrellaed cottonwood. In hot summer he would have dismounted in the shade, but in autumn, October, both mule and Hugh instinctively stopped in the open sunlight.

Old Heyoka began to sip the cool swift water even as Hugh took off her saddle and apishamore. She shivered at the delight of free skin again.

Hugh knelt beside her and drank too, cupping up the water to his bearded mouth. He drank with the mousegray old mule until she'd finished, then he got up and staked her out some distance away.

Hugh opened his grubsack and had himself some dried jerky and fort biscuit and a pack of raisins. He had come to like raisins and ate them with real relish, one by one, biting each through and sucking juice and flesh until it had melted away.

He had a pipe of tobacco and then lay back in the soft warm sand near a patch of close-cropped grass, legs crossed over each other. His rifle lay within reach. His skinning knife was ready in his belt.

He closed his eyes. It was warm and red behind the eyelids.

He lipped a few puffs on his pipe; slowly let it smoke itself out.

Half-thoughts, half-notions, memories as fleeting as motes, lusts as evanescent as fireflies, passed through his mind. Being became a running stream.

He would have fallen asleep if a last fly of the year hadn't come along and bit him a bee of a bite on his big red Scotch nose. The bite brought him up. He rubbed his nose energetically.

After that he stayed up. The fly bite touched off a chain of thoughts, one link leading to another, until he hit on the subject of Fitz, and then a quick hot flush of rage suffused him, making the hairs on his skin prick up.

"That miserable cowardly skunk! The Lord's vengeance is mine and this child's gonna get him. Someday."

He sat up, and refilled and relit his corncob pipe.

"And what's wrong with a little revenge may I ask? The Bible and the old times are full of it."

He blew out clouds of smoke.

"Well then, Fitz, just why did you lie then when you told the major you'd buried me decent?"

Hugh swore, and Old Heyoka perked up one of her big fluted tube ears.

"One-bite cannibal or no, and all the rest, I still have my rights, Gen'ral."

Hugh hit the soft sand beside him with the flat of his hand, so that it plaffed up over his leather buckskin leggings a little.

"You dummed Irisher you. So that's where your book-larnin' has brought you—to where you can make up fancy excuses for desertin' your companyeros."

Hugh tore up some nearby tufts of grass by the roots.

"Yessiree, Major, I ain't restin' until I count coup on Fitz, the miserable cowardly skunk."

Hugh blew up puff after puff of smoke. They rose to the heavens like miniature Indian smoke signals.

"What I ought to do afore I kill ee, Fitz, is torment ye a little. Tell ee I'm handin' you over to your conscience. I was once given over to a one-bite cannibal conscience and ye can see the results. Ha."

Hugh sucked his pipe until it crackled like fat frying over a hot fire.

"My conscience. Ha. So full a hant sons I keep seein' them over and over again, no matter how downright onhuman the she-rip mother of the first two was." Hugh scratched his big red nose. "Just full of 'em. There was my boy Clint. And then came my boy Johnnie Gardner. And then my boys Augie Neill and Jim Anderson. And then my boy Jim Bridger. Ha. Just an old mule crazy for a colt, like the major says. Well, that's what a bad conscience does for ee all right. Grows hants. First thing you know I'll even be thinkin' on Fitz as one of my boys."

Hugh drew on his pipe until the fire in it went out. Then he clapped out the corncob and put it away.

"One thing this child is gonna make sure of. I'm gonna get my Ol' Bullthrower back for sure. Comes to my rifle, I'd as liefsomer lend a man my wife. Or my heart's blood. She shoots center she does."

Hugh swore.

"What? I don't have it in me to kill the skunk? Ye'll see, ye'll see. Just let him cross my path just once more. An eye for a tooth and a tooth for an eye, that's what I say."

Hugh swore twice.

"And then that money that the major collected, Fitz, for you and the lad Jim to stick by me—what'd you do with that Judas money? Ha?"

Hugh jumped to his feet.

"It's more than a man can stand, thinkin' on it, day after day. C'mon, ol' skate, best we get a move on and hunt us up some meat. Afore I mistake ee for Fitz and let you have it in the lights."

Hugh was about to untie Old Heyoka's hitching strap, when he heard a commotion outside the gate. He looked up, saw blue-clad riflemen and leather-clothed trappers bustling around a common center, voices full of excitement and surprise.

"What mout the trouble be out there?" Hugh called to a tall blue-clad guard on the riflewalk over the gate.

"Heard say there's another scaresome skeleton in from the mountains," the guard said, looking down.

Hugh let his hand slip off the knot of the hitching strap. Instinctively his hands picked up his rifle and set the trigger. "Another? Who is it?"

"Said he was part of Captain Smith's party."

Hugh felt queersome. It was probably Fitz.

The commotion of men came slowly through the opened gate. A second blue-clad guard led the way. Riflemen and trappers continued to boil around a common center.

Rifle in hand, and standing behind Old Heyoka, Hugh watched the walking scarecrow go by. It was no surprise to Hugh to see the scarecrow carrying Old Bullthrower, his old friend and rifle. It was downer Fitz at last.

Fitz walked along stoutly. His deepset haunted eyes looked quietly out at the world. His pink Irish cheeks, now burnt black by the Platte prairie sun, were only partially sunken, and his brown hair, where it showed from beneath a wool hat, was still untouched by gray. His step was still quick and his movement fluid. His turndown lips had worn back to a cold hard scimitar of determination. His chin was darkly bearded, and his leathers in tatters.

Hugh saw him; fingered the trigger; thought: "Should I shoot him?"—and then let him go. Hugh turned his back on him and said to his old mule, "This child can wait till he's had meat and rest. I want Fitz as full as a wood tick afore I mash out his miserable life." Hugh untied the knot and got aboard Old Heyoka. "Hep-a. We'll go make meat for him to feed on. Soldier's rations is poor grub for mountain men."

Two days later, just back from one hunt and ready for another, with his hand again on the knot of Old Heyoka's hitching strap, a voice of an old time hailed him.

"Hugh, old hoss, I hear you're lookin' for me."

Hugh stiffened; slowly turned. His hand slid automatically from knot to gun, automatically set the trigger.

"Hugh, the gen'ral tells me you've got a stick to shave with me."

It was Fitz, coming toward him from the general's quarters. Fitz carried Old Bullthrower. Two days rest and meat and new leathers had worked wonders for him. He looked like a new man. His eyes were bright, his shaven jowl pink, his turndown lips lifted a little.

Hugh stood looking at Fitz and slowly felt himself fill up, swell up, until he thought he'd burst. He thought: "Should I shoot him? Now?"

Fitz said, "I've got somethin' for you too. Your favorite rifle. Ol' Bullthrower. I kept it for you through thick and thin. Kept 'er greased and primed."

Hugh stared. His heavy gray brow raised, and white circles grew around his old gray eyes. He stared at his old friend the flintlock.

"Here, take it, man, it's yours, ain't it?"

Hugh let down the trigger of the second-hand gun he had in hand and set it against the hitching post. He took Old Bullthrower. Without thinking, out of old habit, his hands took their old familiar hold on the rifle and raised it to his shoulder and his eyes sighted along it.

"First-rate rifle, Hugh. A centershot if there ever was

one. I know why you favored it. It's saved my life many a time."

Hugh cradled it in his arms.

Fitz said briskly, "And as for Ol' Blue, your hoss, I lost him to the Indians beyond the Fiery Narrows. Too bad. I meant to keep him for you too. And them same Indians got your hoss pistol and your old skinning knife."

Hugh raised his old gray eyes from Old Bullthrower and stared at Fitz. He thought: "Should I shoot him? Now? Even though he's probably never been a one-bite cannibal like me?" Old Heyoka switched her scabby ringtail beside him.

Fitz said, "Hugh, the gen'ral tells me you harbor a grudge against me and Jim. Well, Hugh, if I was in your shoes, I can't say as I'd much blame you. But, Hugh, we boys intended you no harm. No harm. We did what we did the best we could at the time. You'll just have to take the will for the deed."

Hugh continued to feel full-up inside. He thought: "Now?" He set the trigger.

Fitz said, "You know how I work. Practical. Try not to let feelin's color what I see."

Still Hugh said nothing. His hands held tight onto Old Bullthrower.

Fitz said, hazel eyes looking straight at him, "Hugh, there's still a half-dozen men out on the prairies there. Along the Platte somewhere, waitin' beside a big cache of beaver plew. All the gen'ral's wealth. And the gen'ral's rounded up a couple dozen ponies for me and I'm goin' out to get them. How about helpin' me, Hugh?"

Hugh still said nothing. And still he held tight onto Old Bullthrower as if he had to wrestle it down.

Fitz continued to look Hugh square in the eye. "You ain't got your mad up against us boys, have you, Hugh?"

Hugh shivered. *Now?* Old Heyoka flopped her fluted tube ears in turn beside him.

Fitz then held out a leather sack to Hugh. "We boys're also givin' you this." The small sack clinked with silver money.

Hugh looked down at it dumbly.

Fitz put it in his hand. "It's the money the major collected for when Jim and I watched over you on the Grand."

Hugh held it a second, then suddenly threw it down on the ground, threw it so violently the dry leather pouch burst open and a few dull tarnished silver coins rolled out across the dusty fort yard.

Fitz jumped back and looked up astonished at Hugh.

Hugh roared, "What do you take me for? You devil! I don't want my own gravedigger's pay, for godsakes! Not a gravedigger anyway who didn't have the guts to finish his job!"

Fitz continued to look astonished. "Why, Hugh, we boys thought you'd be glad to get the money. It'll set you up for a while."

" 'Glad'?" Hugh managed to croak.

"Sure."

" 'Glad'?"

"Well, Hugh, if that's the way you feel about it, I'm sorry. When Jim told me at the rendezvous that you'd come back alive, come back from the dead, we decided then and there you was entitled to that money."

" 'Back from the dead'?"

"Yes. When we left you, Hugh, you were as dead as ... as ..."

Hugh trembled violently from head to foot. He was afraid he was going to faint. "If I was dead, why didn't you finish your job as gravedigger and bury me decent?"

"Because we didn't get the time, Hugh. The red devils was on top of us." Fitz's brows lifted in surprise again. "You didn't expect us to bury you at the risk of our own lives, did you?"

Hugh stared from behind the half-lidded low-centered eyes. He had trouble seeing Fitz.

Fitz said, "Well, if that's what's botherin' you, Hugh, I hope you forgive us. We boys did the best we could."

We boys. O them haunt sons!

"We just couldn't take the time, Hugh. We'd've been dead too if we had."

A huge and terrible sigh gushed up out of Hugh. This was the hardest of all. Ae, bar none it was.

"I'm sorry, Hugh."

"So I've come to it at last. I'm being asked to forgive the devil who left me for dead by that devil himself."

Fitz backed a step. " 'Devil'?"

"Yes, 'devil.' " Hugh looked down at Fitz from his great height. "Fitz, tell me, why did you lie to the major? Tellin' him you saw me dead and buried on the forks of the Grand?"

Fitz looked down a second. "Well, Hugh, I must admit that there I made a mistake. I should have told that straight. Not that it would have made any difference, of course." Fitz looked up again; tried to smile. "But you see, Hugh, by the time Jim and I got to the major, we'd gone over it so often it'd got a little mixed up in our heads. Got set wrong. You know."

"So you did lie to the major then?"

Fitz looked Hugh in the eye. "Yes, Hugh, yes, I did. And not Jim. I was in charge."

"And ye say it wouldn't've made any difference?"

"No. Not a bit."

Hugh gave the leather sack of coin a kick with his moccasined toe. The sack broke open still farther and more dull old coins rolled out and scattered over the fort yard. The watching eyes of the two blue-clad guards over the gate opened white and wide at the sight of the spilling silver.

"I don't want my own gravedigger's money," Hugh said. "I may have been a one-bite cannibal once, but not that! By the bull barley no."

"Have it your own way, Hugh."

"Ha!"

Then Hugh turned and he untied the hitching strap and got aboard Old Heyoka and kicked her in the ribs. "Hep-a, let's make meat, ol' skate." The old mule was walking again before she opened a dull purple eye. Her tail switched and her big fluted tube ears flopped in rhythm with her slow stilting legs.

As the mule carried him out through the gate, Hugh called out over his shoulder, "Fitz, the next time you see Jim, tell the boy I'm givin' him back his life too. He had it on loan to me, but now he can have it and do with it as he wants—turn tramp or turn king."

And Hugh added to himself in a low mutter, as he cradled Old Bullthrower in an arm, "Turned tame, this child has. Passed through such a passel of things he don't rightly recollect wrong from right no more."

We boys.
O them haunt companyeros.